Praise for

TUMB

"Tackling both tim   and the concept of authorial intent in fresh ways, this romance debut is a joy and its author is worth watching."   —*Publishers Weekly*

"Ingenious! This heartwarming, laugh-filled ride through time has everything a great novel needs. Cready adds even more spice with a dash of mystery and plenty of adventure. Don't miss this story and be sure to keep your eye on this talented new author. Brilliant."

—Romance Junkies

"Keeps its promise of a wild ride into the past and zips through the present at warp speed. Time-travel enthusiasts will have a field day."   —*Winter Haven News* (FL)

SEDUCING MR. DARCY

Winner of the 2009 RITA® Award for
Best Paranormal Romance

"Sexy fun."   —*BookPage*

"Hot, adorable, and irresistible. Rip its sexy white shirt off and have your way with it."   —DarcyWars

"If I had to choose a passenger pigeon search team, Flip Allison is the first person I'd call."

—Tim Gallagher, author of *The Grail Bird*

These titles are also available as eBooks.

ALSO BY GWYN CREADY

Tumbling Through Time
Seducing Mr. Darcy

FLIRTING
with
FOREVER

GWYN CREADY

POCKET BOOKS
New York London Toronto Sydney

Pocket Books
A Division of Simon & Schuster, Inc.
1230 Avenue of the Americas
New York, NY 10020

This book is a work of fiction. Names, characters, places, and incidents either are products of the author's imagination or are used fictitiously. Any resemblance to actual events or locales or persons, living or dead, is entirely coincidental.

First Pocket Books paperback edition April 2010

POCKET and colophon are registered trademarks of Simon & Schuster, Inc.

For information about special discounts for bulk purchases, please contact Simon & Schuster Special Sales at 1-866-506-1949 or business@simonandschuster.com.

The Simon & Schuster Speakers Bureau can bring authors to your live event. For more information or to book an event contact the Simon & Schuster Speakers Bureau at 1-866-248-3049 or visit our website at www.simonspeakers.com.

Cover design by Lisa Litwack
Cover illustration by Gene Mollica
Designed by Jill Putorti

Manufactured in the United States of America

10 9 8 7 6 5 4 3 2 1

ISBN 978-1-4391-0724-9
ISBN 978-1-4391-7124-0 (ebook)

*For Karen Flo, Josh Russell
and Linda Mullens,
and all the people who miss them.*

ACKNOWLEDGMENTS

A big thank-you goes to Manuel Erviti, who as always was willing to break every rule to get me the information I needed. The 1932 article entitled "Lely's Love Story" by Viscount Lee of Fareham that Cam receives from *The Burlington Magazine* really exists and was, in fact, what inspired me to write this book. *The Burlington Magazine* and its editor Richard Shone were especially gracious in letting me use excerpts from the article. I altered the details of Peter's love story only modestly. I'd like to thank Christine Lorenz for her insight into the world of art history and art historians. Thanks goes to my cousin Lynne Crofford as well, who, in an attempt to help me appreciate the historical context of my name when I was a girl— my full name is Nelle Gwyn Cready—gave me the article about Nell Gwyn that first excited my curiosity about the Restoration period.

I really appreciate the exceptional guidance my editor Megan McKeever gave me after reading the first draft. You have her to thank for the book's far more straightforward story arc. All the people at Pocket have been great and do their jobs so professionally. Thanks to Lisa Litwack, Gene Mollica, and Shirley and Victor Forster for this book's gorgeous design. I stand in awe, as always, of Judy Steer, the world's best copy editor. A special shout-out goes to my friend Wileen Dragovan, who has always been willing to share her love for, and deep understanding of, painting with me. And, of course, I have to thank Tracy Chevalier for her wonderful book, which made me ask, "What in God's name would Vermeer think?"

I have friends who have gone out of their way in the last year to cheer me on. Among them are Katie Kemper, Scott DeLaney, Joe Gitchell, Betsy Tyson, Ted Kyle, Mark Prus, Jeremy Diamond, Mike Brown, Dawn Kosanovich, Mary Irwin Scott, Marie Guerra, Valli Ellis, Teri Coyne, Donna Neiport, Mary Parish, Bev Crofford, Jean Hilpert, Gudrun Wells, Stuart Ferguson, Nick Cole, Doris Heroff, Lloyd Heroff, and Sheila Washington. Diane Pyle is among them, too, and she also gets credit for the fabulous line, "Her backstory is so bogus." The line in Latin engraved in Peter's ring, on the other hand, came to this book with the most appreciated assistance of Dr. Judith Hulick, whose *joie de vivre* is truly contagious.

Thanks to Kate Zingarella, Mark Zingarelli and Mary Nell Cumming, who, each in their own way, inspired me to change my life. Thanks as well to J.T. Smith, who made a difficult time fun. For filmmaking magic, I tip my hat to Karl O'Janpa, Drew Nicholaus and Glen Richards. I'd like to thank three great writers—Todd DePastino, Mitchell James Kaplan, and Vince Rause—for many hours of great coffee and conversation. Thanks goes as well to writer Elaine Knighton, who, among her many lessons, taught me the importance of making space in my life for good things.

I can recommend *Painted Ladies: The Women at the Court of Charles II* (Catherine MacLeod and Julia Marciari Alexander, editors; National Portrait Gallery, London, in association with the Yale Center for British Art, New Haven), and *Sir Peter Lely* (Oliver Millar, National Portrait Gallery, London) for a more in-depth understanding of the life, times, and breathtaking work of my hero. I also found *How to Paint Your Own Vermeer* (Jonathan Janson, Lulu Press), very helpful for this story. Pierre Bonnard and Alex Katz continue to inspire, but, like Peter, I would choose Katz and his Ada. You will find the Carnegie Museum much as I described it, though the administrative wing as it appears in the book is purely a product of my imagination.

Claudia Cross is an outstanding guide and companion on this journey. I hope it continues for a long time. Wyatt, I love you, and thanks for telling me about the woman next to you on the Metro. Love as well to Cameron, who charms me daily with her feisty and uncompromising view of the world. It's as if I'm looking in a mirror sometimes. Finally, Lester Pyle is my partner in crime, and every day is made better by him being in it.

I

COVENT GARDEN, LONDON, 1673

Peter pressed an exquisitely cobbled shoe against the side of the desk drawer and rubbed his aching temples. Despite all the appointments of success—the fine clothes, the freedom to paint when and what he chose, the admiration of a highly appreciative king, row upon row of apprentices at his command, a full waiting room and an even fuller account with his bankers—he felt nothing but despair. Even the fat emerald ring, once such a prize, was a torture, for it reminded him of Ursula and how he had treated her. It had been heartbreaking to live through that part of his life the first time. And now to be asked to live through it again was a sorrow so exquisite he could barely speak.

"Peter," Mertons said, "I hope you know how much the Guild appreciates this."

Peter grunted. The Executive Guild managed the souls passing through the Afterlife, specifically those within the artists' section, and Mertons was the time-jump accountant who had been assigned to this case. Time-jump Accountant was his official title, but Peter knew the unofficial reason the Guild had sent him was to ensure the moody, unreliable painter they'd enlisted managed the mission properly and stayed within the prescribed rules, so perhaps *nursemaid* would be more appropriate.

"It wasn't as if I had a choice." Peter slitted his eyes and let the dying November sun warm his face. The evenings were the hardest. During the day he could lose himself in painting, but at night . . . At night, all he had was wine and his memories. How could he have once held success in such esteem?

Mertons shrugged. "You will get what you want, Peter—a new life as an artist." The Guild had the power to choose the new life into which a member of its constituency—in this case, painters—would arrive, bundled in his or her new mother's arms, with only an obscure hint of the sadness or joy of their former life to tint their memories.

And while Peter desperately wanted a new life as an artist—he couldn't imagine himself, or at least his soul, spending the next sixty years as a barber or dairyman— what he really wanted was a chance to redeem himself, which he knew he would never find. He had finally agreed to slip back into the pinched, desiccated skin he had sloughed off at his death two years earlier for one reason only—to try to return Ursula's good name to her, an intention he had purposefully not shared with Mertons, who had been assigned by the Guild to accompany him and who monitored the attacks on his precious time-travel constraints with the ferocity of a mother lion.

"Tell me again what we know." Peter had heard the story several times since their arrival a week ago. Nonetheless, Mertons liked to tell it, and it would give Peter time to prepare for acting out his plan. He glanced at the clock and then at the small storage room off the office. Just before five. Good.

Mertons sighed and looked down at his clipboard. "To be honest, we know very little. The writer's name is Campbell Stratford—a Scot," he added as if that provided a significant detail to the understanding of the event. "The book will be an embarrassment to the Guild—"

"An embarrassment to Van Dyck, you mean." Peter had immense respect for the work of the man he had succeeded as royal portraitist, Van Dyck to the court of Charles I and he to that of Charles II, but it irked him that the Guild would jump through hoops to help certain of its dead members but not others.

"An embarrassment to one of our members is an embarrassment to the Guild, Peter. We do not want Van Dyck's ill-considered contretemps with a few women outside his marriage to overshadow a career that should be judged strictly on its professional merits—merits, I might add, that are both numerous and laudatory."

A *few* women? Peter, who had known Van Dyck well, rolled his eyes. "I expect the Guild doesn't particularly like the idea of someone on Earth running around with access to a time tube, either."

The muscles in Mertons's jaw contracted. The Guild, like every organization that managed souls in the Afterlife, had a stake in ensuring the tubes were tightly controlled. Representatives of the Guild, or, like Peter, those chosen to serve their needs, were the only people allowed to travel the tubes as conscious adults, and then only under very special circumstances. That this Stratford fellow would find a way to breach the tube terrified the Guild, who claimed that alteration of the fabric of time could be as dangerous as an asteroid hit. No one on Earth had done it in decades. Peter didn't doubt there was some level of danger, though he suspected the Guild's concern was just as much about retaining power as averting chaos.

"No, Peter, the Guild does not care for it, and neither should you. The results would be unimaginable."

Peter made an ambiguous noise. A few more minutes, and then all he'd need was a brief distraction. "Tell me, how did you come to know the writer would be traveling here?" This was the one part of the story Mertons had not shared with him, and the calculations showed in the man's eyes. Fortunately, Peter thought, there's nothing like a time-jump accountant for long-winded self-aggrandizement, especially when it comes to the intricacies of time travel.

"I probably shouldn't be telling you this—"

Peter gave him a conspiratorial nod.

"—but it was me. Dawson, the associate in External Affairs, was reviewing the daily log and saw Stratford's book had spiked a seven-point-three on incongruity. Normally you'd ignore something like that unless it happened again, but when Dawson brought it to me, there was just something odd about it. Over a seven on an art biography? An art biography by an unknown author? I got permission to check it against the Alexandrian tables, the safest way for someone in the present to examine future occurrences, and the book—that is to say, the book that Stratford will write if we don't stop him—was filled with details knowable only to someone who'd been back in time."

"Perhaps he guessed. Some writers are very good at that, I hear."

"Perhaps he *guessed* Van Dyck liked his eggs poached in cream and sprinkled with nutmeg? Perhaps he *guessed* Van Dyck entertained his closest friends with a portrait of Lord Harwich painted with horns and a snout?" Mertons lowered his voice to a whisper. "Perhaps he *guessed* Van Dyck needed a brisk paddle to ensure the structural integrity of his 'monument to Cupid'?"

"Oh dear."

"And it's worse than that."

"I'd rather not hear."

"Stratford gave himself carte blanche to fill the rest of the book with whatever lies he wanted. He calls it a 'fictography.' Do you see? A fictional biography. An abomination, if you ask me. Why can't writers stick to the truth?" Mertons returned his gaze to his ever-present clipboard. As tall as a boat pole and nearly as thin, with a crown as hairless as a baby's, he looked about as much like an apprentice painter in 1673 as he did a centurion at the Battle of Thermopylae. Nonetheless that was the cover the Guild had instructed Peter to provide him.

"And why does Stratford come to me?"

Mertons shuffled his feet. "We don't know."

"Don't know?" Peter cultivated surprise. This was his favorite part of the story since the answer could not be found on the clipboard or anywhere else.

"No. Perhaps he's broken the security algorithm. Perhaps he's found a tube we're not aware of. All we know is this biography—pardon me, fictography—will change the way thousands of people feel about Van Dyck. So our job is to stop Stratford from writing that book. The book is nothing but lies."

"*Nothing* but lies? You mean Van Dyck *didn't* pass around a portrait of Lord Harwich?" Peter had seen it himself once. He declined to call to mind the other, more picturesque details of his colleague's personal life.

Mertons flushed. "There's a difference between telling a story and appealing to the prurient interest of readers. Stratford takes the story, embellishes it, and with *The Girl with a Coral Earring* makes the entire seventeenth-century art world seem like some sort of giant sultan's tent in which artists run, satyrlike, over pillowed beds, chasing willing and unwilling women to their reputational doom."

Peter considered the artists he had known, including himself before the settling influence of Ursula, and found the description to be more accurate than not.

"I see you are amused." Mertons crossed his arms. "I wonder if you would feel the same if the subject of the biography was you."

Peter stiffened. He hated to admit it, but Mertons was right. Seeing his own life splashed across the pages, stripped bare for the amusement of a reading public who would not care what parts were true, or regretted, so long as the salacious bits of intrigue kept them turning pages, would be more than he could bear. There was a special place in hell for a writer like Stratford, who picked the bones of the dead to further his own career, and Peter supposed he should be glad he'd have a hand in bringing the blackguard down. But the thought brought him little joy, trapped as he was in one of the most unhappy times of his former life. He wished another artist in the After-life had been given the unusual opportunity. He glanced again at the clock. "And here, in this studio, in this par-ticular time, is the only—what do you call it?—point of intersection?"

"No, there are a number of intersections in Van Dyck's life as well, but the Guild is just about to place him in his new life, and, as you know, we cannot retrieve him once that has been done. You, being between lives, are available. Though perhaps when you said 'in this particular time' you were referring to this time in your own life?" Mertons unclipped the mass of paper in his hand and fanned it. "In that case, the answer is no as well. There were two intersections in your own life, each approximately equal in likelihood, but the other, you may recall—"

Peter remembered and held up a hand to stop him. "I recall. Thank you."

The other likely intersection point had been eight years earlier, when Peter and Ursula had been happy. While Peter hadn't told Mertons or the Guild the reason why, he had flatly refused even to consider returning to such a time. To live through that again burdened with the knowledge of what was to come would destroy him. He'd rather feel the lash of guilt and sorrow in this, the after-math of his vanity, than to see it coming like a runaway carriage, about to crush him. He gazed at the emerald on his finger as one would a malignant tumor.

Mertons was observing him closely. "Peter, is there something I should know?"

But Peter hadn't told anyone in the Afterlife about his despair, and he wasn't about to start. "Only that it's been a week, and I told you I would give you two, no more."

Mertons sighed and examined another sheet of paper. "I've reconfirmed the coordinates. There may have been a little trouble with our original calculation, but I can assure you the writer is within striking distance."

Peter had no interest in Mertons's coordinates or any of the dozens of other numbers the man routinely reviewed. "Well, it must end soon. I can't even take a piss without your approval."

"My dear Peter, it is not that I wish to constrain your freedom. As I have explained, it is that the Guild has given us a range of deviation of only plus or minus three point oh six two four seven. That is an average for the entire trip, which means the overages we anticipate with the writer's arrival must be balanced with something approaching zero deviation as we wait now."

"Hang on. Did you say three point oh six two four seven?" Peter scratched at a loose sheet with his quill in a fair imitation of a time-jump accountant. "No wonder this isn't working. You know I can't work at less than three point oh six two four nine two two."

"Jest if you will," Mertons said icily, "but the limits exist for a reason. Jumps are a risk. We must strive to ensure your days are lived exactly as they were the first time through. Unscrupulous or unthinking trippers could reorder time. We're lucky a novice like you was allowed to attempt it."

"I count my blessings hourly."

"Your intercourse with the rogue will cost us at least

five points of deviation, and that's right off the top. Which means the rest of our time here must be kept below two point six." He scribbled on his paper. "Two point seven at the most. How revealing do you intend the intercourse to be?"

Peter considered both the question and Mertons's susceptibility to a double entendre, but abandoned his ambitions and said only, "I shall endeavor to bring it in under five."

"Excellent."

Peter turned his attention to a stack of mezzotints and reached for the pot of ink and his chop.

Mertons caught his sleeve. "What are you doing?"

"Placing my chop—my mark—upon them," Peter said. "They're for the king. Gifts for the envoy from Sicily."

Mertons held tight. "Were these done in your original life?"

"Aye," Peter growled. "I have not forgotten the proscription against new marks."

Mertons pulled a sheet of paper from the sheath and looked at it. " 'Eleventh of November,' " he read. " 'Mezzotints of Charles II: Eight.' " He scanned the stack of mounted prints, counting, then relaxed. "Leaving your mark in this place—a child, a bride, your name on a painting, anything that was not marked before—will bind you here forever."

"Aye. I remember." Peter shook his arm free. There was no place he'd less like to be bound.

"Your best bet is to stay as close to me as possible. That's why I'm here, Peter. To be your guide."

"As Virgil through the circles of hell."

"And you are certain you recall what you are to do when you finally meet him? Shall I review that as well?"

"No," he said with exquisite politeness, "thank you." He stretched his long legs. Now was the time. "How is my patronage looking, Mertons?"

Peter hadn't been exactly eager to deal with his customers since returning, and the surprise showed on Mertons's face. With a tilt of his head, the thin man peered into the long hallway.

"You have a considerable line out there."

"Excellent," said Peter, who, in fact, couldn't have cared less. "But . . ."

"But what?"

"I admit I am concerned, most concerned, about the appropriateness of each patron as far as our limits are concerned. Might you be willing to size them up, so to speak, from a jump risk point of view?"

Mertons's forehead creased, and he shuffled through the papers before finding one in particular. "I assume they're the same people you saw when you lived this day in your life before."

"Quite likely, aye." Peter carried the prints to the storage room. "But the point is one can't be sure. We assume the writer will be disguised, but what if there is more than a single man with access to the unsecured time tube? What if there is a *conspiracy* to unravel the time fabric?"

Mertons paled. "You're right. There's a Robert de Manville on this list here whose name is giving me pause."

"Robert de Manville." Peter frowned. "I don't remember him. Seems a very likely candidate, Mertons."

Mertons sighed. "I explained you wouldn't remember

everyone. It is just as if you were seventy, and returned to the neighborhood in which you lived until you were breeked. Some faces you will remember. Some you will not. It is not a reliable means by which to judge. You must exercise caution and foresight at all times—*all* times, Peter. Give me a moment. I shall examine the group versus the appointments you had for the day from our records and offer you my thinking."

"Take all the time you need."

And Mertons, feeling more than his usual sense of trepidation, did. Though Robert de Manville, upon rigorous cross-examination, proved unremarkable and the woman with the crimson frock and pockmarks gave him no pause, the man with the hooded eyes beside her—her husband, or at least the man who *purported* to be—alarmed Mertons almost enough to announce Mr. Lely was accepting no more clients for the day. But he took down a thorough description of the man, so thorough, in fact, the elaborate chime of Peter's Ottoman clock entered his consciousness as only a distant, barely noticed melody.

When he felt he'd observed enough to make a judgment on the security of the mission, he stepped back into the office and said, "I would like to offer a caution on—Peter?"

The desk was empty, and the door to the storage room was ajar.

"Er, I say, Peter," he called, raising his voice a degree, "I would like to offer a stiff note of caution on a man named John Howell and his wife. I'm not certain, of course, but you must not take risks."

Peter did not reply. Mertons frowned and started toward the room. "Remember, this writer has enough heartless calculation to fool his readers, destroy the reputation of a gifted man and thus far elude the Guild. I would call that more than a temporary irritant, Peter. I would call that"—Mertons entered to find nothing but curtains fluttering at an open window, and his warning sputtered to a close—"a cold-blooded machine."

2

ADMINISTRATIVE OFFICES OF THE CARNEGIE MUSEUM
OF ART, PITTSBURGH, PRESENT DAY

There are certain things that drive a woman to immediate action, Campbell Stratford thought as she heard the *pop*. A flesh-cutting panty hose run is one of them.

"Oh. My. *God!*" She shoved the manuscript pages aside, knocking over an orange Crush with one hand and a three-inch stack of security audit reports with the other. "How did I ever get a grown-up job?"

"Since when is curating a grown-up job?" Jeanne, her assistant and longtime friend, grabbed a nearby napkin.

Campbell found the scissors and flung her leg on the desk. A run the size of the Grand Canyon with the approximate pain-delivery power of an electrified garrote had laddered between her legs and, like Sherman's army, was about to march down her thigh.

"Avert your eyes!" She thrust the blade under the taut nylon lashes and jerked. The pain stopped, but the laddering shot to her knee. "Wite-Out!"

Jeanne hooked the bottle out of her desk organizer with the efficiency of a surgical nurse and lobbed it across the room. "Cam, hurry," she said, glancing down the hall, "Packard and Ball are on their way to the stairs."

"Crap. Since when is noon 'early afternoon'?" Woodson Ball was the Mount Everest of potential donors, and according to his email to her, he shouldn't have been here until at least one. Cam had planned to use her lunch hour to gobble a hot dog and scour reference books for the one detail about Anthony Van Dyck that would make her long-overdue manuscript spark to life. Spark sourcing at noon. Mountain climbing at one. *Why can't we stick to the schedule, folks? I got a promotion I'm after here.*

She whipped the top off the Wite-Out and pulled the brush free, sending a fine spray of white across the year-end pledge report and most of the front of her pencil skirt. Moaning, she applied the ooze to the hole now eating past her knee, then leaned in and blew for all she was worth. "You haven't seen Anastasia, have you?"

"I thought she traveled in a cloud of black smoke. That's quite an image, by the way. It could definitely get you the spotlight on officesluts-dot-com."

"Does it pay anything?" Cam wondered if she'd have time to eat the hot dog as she was racing down to the first floor.

"Hey, it covers the rent."

Now Cam had a gummy clot of white at the end of a long, pale rectangle of exposed flesh. Actually what she had was a gummy clot of white, an unfinished manuscript, a big donor who seemed to be working on Greenland time, a cutthroat rival with a pick ax and zip line where you'd expect her heart to be and a desk that smelled like the game room of a Chuck E. Cheese's.

No time now. She jumped to her feet and turned. "Does anything show?"

Jeanne frowned. "Depends what you mean by 'anything.' Officesluts would take a pass, but the folks at Hillbilly Hose are gonna love you."

Cam looked down. Panic was seeping in. The hole in her panty hose was enormous. She looked like her thigh had been attacked by a meat grinder. What could she do? She looked around the room for potential fixes. A scarf? Too weird. A Sharpie? Too black. Her yoga pants? Too weird and too black. "Jeeeaaaaaannnnnne!" she wailed. "Help!"

Jeanne sprang into action. She pulled a spray can out of her purse and pulled off the cap. Cam's hands flew up instinctively to cover her eyes. "Mace!"

"Not Mace," Jeanne said. "I used it before my date last night. He liked it."

Cam spread her fingers.

"It's foundation," Jeanne said. "Spray-on."

"It says 'Spray-On Tan.' "

"Half the price." Jeanne put the can in Cam's hand. "Here."

Cam gazed down uncertainly. That run ran really high. "Er . . ."

"Just point and shoot. Like a camera."

"I know you're going to find this hard to believe, but I don't actually point a lot of cameras down there." She lifted her leg tentatively and gave the canister a squeeze. "There. How's that?"

"Great. So long as you're tanning your desk."

Cam looked. The spray had made a happy sunflower shape on the wood. "Oh, man."

"Gimme, gimme, gimme." Jeanne took the can and bent. "I'm expecting to see this reflected in my performance review, by the way."

"Ooh! Felt that one."

"C'mon, you. That's right, that's right. Oh yeah. Beautiful."

"Er," someone said. "Am I interrupting?"

It was Jacket, Cam's ex-fiancé, in dark jeans and a worn leather jacket, looking as sexy as someone could whom she'd kicked out of her bed six months ago. Sexier, actually, which was not a good sign.

Cam closed her leg, then immediately flung it open. "Still wet."

"I'll bet." He slouched against the door and smiled.

Jeanne gave Cam a private eye roll. "Steady, girl," she said under her breath.

"Jeanne was helping me with a run in my panty hose."

"*Mm.*"

God, what was it about that gritty London growl? Even an *mm* sounded like the whirr of some fantastic sex toy. Cam had to be careful. This was how she'd gotten in trouble in the first place.

"I came by to pick up the spare keys."

Jeanne whipped her gaze in Cam's direction. Jeanne was definitely not a Jacket fan.

"Er, well, it is still half your condo after all," Cam said, more for Jeanne's benefit than for his. "You're finalizing your stuff for the exhibit. Offering you the guest room seems like the least I could do, right?"

"Still . . ." He gave her a smoldering look.

"Yes," Jeanne agreed with a look for Cam that far outscorched Jacket's. *"Still."*

"I, uh, gotta run. The spare keys should be in my purse. Jeanne can give you hers if you can't find them."

Jeanne gave him a bland look. "She means for her apartment, by the way."

"Hang on." Jacket touched Cam's arm.

She felt a twinge of the old familiar foolishness as well as a tinge of the old familiar despair.

"Can you stay for a minute?" he said.

"Um . . ." She tried to avoid Jeanne's eyes. "Yeah, sure. A minute."

Jeanne found the keys and dropped them into Jacket's hand. "Careful," she said. "One of them unlocks when it shouldn't." She gave Cam a look and marched out.

Cam immediately wished she'd worn a different outfit. Nothing screamed *needy* like navy gabardine and Wite-Out. "What's up?"

"I meant what I said." He pocketed the keys. "That was really nice."

She could smell the faint scent of his skin. She could also smell the Kleenex into which she'd wept half her body weight last June.

"I brought something for you. I'd call it a peace offering, but it's yours, so it's not, really, but still, I'd like it if you thought of it that way."

He opened his palm. In it was the ring she'd designed, the ring that had been their engagement ring. Blue-black enamel; a flat, round pearl like the moon and a spattering of diamonds across the wide band like the night sky.

She held up a hand. The last time she'd seen the ring was when she'd cracked his tooth with it that fateful afternoon. Those sorts of memories she could do without. "No thanks."

"Please," he said. "You loved the ring. I feel bad enough about what happened. Take it back. Enjoy it. Consider it entirely desanctified."

She *had* loved that ring. And if she hadn't found him in bed with the artist who'd designed it, she would have never let it go.

"I had the guy who repaired it add an extra diamond." He turned the band to show her.

"Repaired it?"

"Tooth mark," he explained.

"Oh, right. Sorry about that."

"Yeah, well . . ." His eyes went to his boots, then back to her. "I deserved it."

"That's for sure."

He laughed and lifted a finger. The ring dangled from a sparkling chain, the way she'd always worn it. *Guess he'd had that repaired, too.*

"May I?" he said.

Cam considered, then nodded. He came behind her and she lifted her hair. Suddenly the room felt much smaller. He brought the chain around to the front, then clasped it behind her.

"Thanks."

He made a low rumble, a cross between a laugh and a sigh.

"I gotta run," she said. True in so many ways.

"What's up?"

"Woodson Ball." Jacket knew him as well as she did. Ball collected a lot of modern art, and Jacket's famous Lucite, fruit and everyday object assemblages had been very collectible once.

"Buying or selling?"

"Giving, I hope. A fantastic Van Dyck. Two-point-one million, at least. That is, if I can reel it in. And in time for the appointment of the new executive director."

Jacket lifted a brow. "Packard's out?"

Lamont Packard had announced he'd be retiring in six months. The board had just begun the process of interviewing candidates. Both she and Anastasia were being considered. Which is why she needed to sell her manuscript and bring in the biggest gift to the museum this year.

"Yep. Retiring."

He looked at her and smiled. He wasn't tall, but he had the bearing of a double-O spy. Taut, chiseled, ready to act. And, of course, as an artist, that came with an ego the size of the Louvre.

"You'll get it," he said.

"You think?"

"You'd have my vote."

Whoa! Who knew the room could get so small? He was about one tablespoon of nitroglycerin away from blowing the top off a Pandora's box that had been nailed shut and dipped in steel six months ago. She touched the chain, flustered. "Okay, well, good luck with the condo—"

"Cam?"

"Yeah?"

"Do you think, I mean, would it ever be possible for us to try things again?"

Boom! A million feelings exploded in her head and heart. Sorrow, anger, lust, forgiveness, fear—and hope.

Anger, her ego said firmly.

Hope, her heart replied.

"Jacket . . ." Her face burned. "I-I don't know."

"I know." He touched her wrist. A crack of lightning shot straight to her belly. The last thing she wanted was her belly weighing in on this. Her belly was a body part of very few words.

Lust.

Lust.

Lust.

Lust.

Cam touched his waist, that hard, hard waist, and he pulled her into a kiss.

Such a bad idea. Such a good bad idea.

Reluctantly she extricated her mouth. She felt like she'd been sucking lust-flavored Pop Rocks.

"I was thinking you might want to take a short leave of absence."

"A short leave?"

"Or a longer one." He grinned. "Maybe come to London with me for a while."

London. She loved London. "I couldn't."

"Anytime. Now. After the gala. To celebrate your new directorship. They let you take a holiday sometimes, don't they?"

He could be very charming when he put his mind to it. Just ask the explosions in her mouth. "I, uh . . ."

"Cam, I— Oh God, sorry."

It was Jeanne, and her voice snapped Cam's ego into action. She broke away and wiped her mouth, embarrassed. "What's up?"

"Anastasia. On the stairs. In a puff of vampire-colored smoke."

3

Peter knew why he'd taken the long way to Maiden Lane. Maiden Lane was where he'd find the king, but the small patch of green behind St. Paul's—Old Pauly, as the residents of Covent Garden referred to it—was where he'd find Ursula.

He crossed the piazza tentatively, ignoring the carriages that passed on either side of him. He made his way past the sanctuary he would never enter again and down the path that ran the length of the church's north wall. When he saw her, his throat began to tighten. He scanned the space, but it was late afternoon, and the only witnesses to his shame would be the wrens, foraging among the tree roots. He dropped to a knee.

"I failed you, my love. 'Tis the worst thing a man can do, and I shall live with the pain always."

If he wanted absolution, there was none. Only the dim reflection of light on this headstone and the one beyond it.

Peter hung his head and let the tears fall down his cheeks.

4

Cam flew down the improbably long treads of the Carnegie's staircase with Jeanne on her heels.

"You don't think she's there already?" Cam said. "That painting's nearly mine, and I don't want her ruining it or, worse, somehow getting credit."

"When you're a successful author, will we be done with all this?"

"Oh, sure. 'Cause you know how many people buy art biographies. I could have them over for cocktails and still manage to be the worst-dressed person in the room."

"Especially with Wite-Out on your hose. So, do you think he's going to say it again?"

"What?"

"You know."

Cam shot her a pointed look. "Mr. Ball is from a very old, not to mention very rich, Gainesville family. Just because some of his words are, well, a little hard to understand doesn't mean he's not sharp as a tack."

"I grew up in Mobile, Alabama. You got any trouble

understanding me? Do I go around telling people I'm a fornicator?"

"It's not *fornicator*. It's *Florida Gator*."

"Oh, I know what it is. It still makes me laugh to hear it."

Cam ignored this. She hit the cavernous entry hall and looked left and right. Ball had arrived in Lamont Packard's office five minutes ago and by now they could be anywhere. They weren't in the little café dominated by Warhol's fluorescent portrait of Andrew Carnegie— "Care for some worker uprising with your Chicken Basil Farfalle?"—nor lounging by the reflecting pool outside.

She turned. Lamont Packard, her boss and the soon-to-be ex-executive director, was emerging from the interior courtyard a step or two in front of Ball, who had Anastasia hot-glued to his arm.

Drat. She had to think fast.

"Remember the Picasso strategy?"

Jeanne gave her a questioning look. "Yes, but I'm not sure how your favorite 'Get me outta this blind date' strategy is going to work here."

"Well, this time it's a Rembrandt strategy, and you need to call Tim Lockport—anonymously."

After a beat, Jeanne's face lit. "You're brilliant—and scary."

"Family survival tactic. Lie or die."

Jeanne angled off toward a museum phone, and Cam headed toward her quarry.

They were an odd threesome, she thought, hurrying toward them: Old School Packard with his investment banker suit; Ball in his linen trousers and orange-

and-blue–striped golf shirt; and, of course, Anastasia, towering over everyone as usual with her willowy, mock-Eurotrash body, purple Christian Louboutin booties, architectural "Oh this? I knit couture in my spare time" dress and a stainless-steel cuff bracelet so thick it looked like it had come off the brakes of a German Wehrmacht tank. Cam, despite Rubenesque curves, tumbling masses of red curls and a penchant for tight skirts and zebra-striped pumps, felt she gave the appearance of being Frodo's long-lost country cousin when standing next to the dreaded Anastasia.

"There you are," Packard said.

Lamont Packard always wore the fund-raiser's flush of larceny, but today his palms were rubbing so hard they ought to have been throwing sparks. Of course, being six months from retirement couldn't have hurt, either. Woodson Ball, who should have looked like he'd just stumbled out of a gang pickpocketing on an Eastern European subway, managed to project warmth and contented largesse.

Anastasia's gaze ran rapidly down Cam's leg. "Afternoon, Cam. Did you have an accident?"

"No." She ground her teeth. "So glad to see you, Mr. Ball." Then, in a move she'd learned from Thomas the Tank Engine, Cam did a one eighty just as the walking threesome reached her, neatly uncoupling Anastasia from Ball's arm. "How was Florida? Did you and Mrs. Ball have a good trip back?"

Ball finished the story of the flight delays just as Jeanne arrived.

"You may remember my assistant, Jeanne Turner. Jeanne, this is Mr. Ball."

"Ha'd'yadew." Ball bowed.

As Cam looked down to avoid Jeanne's eyes, she caught sight of her pumps. In her effort to manage the hose situation, she must have inadvertently mashed her shoe into the hot dog because most of the zebra stripes on the left toe were covered in mustard.

"Jeanne has a few papers for you to sign," Cam said, tucking one foot behind the other. "Nothing major. Just permission to examine the painting, et cetera." She felt Anastasia's critical gaze drop even farther and she began to flush.

Anastasia coughed. "Good Lord, Cam, is that—"

"Mustard is very hot this year."

"Only in *Vogue,* dear."

Cam wished the soaring George Segal sculpture of a tightrope walker, which had once balanced high above the heads of Carnegie patrons, would choose this moment to return to its former haunt and drop on Anastasia's head.

"That's fine," Ball said. "Whatever you need me t'do. Just take good care of my countess." He winked.

The vaunted painting was a gorgeous three-quarter-length portrait of Theresa, Countess of Morefield, that had once been owned by Catherine the Great.

"You know, we already have a fantastic spot picked out for the painting," Packard said. Cam could almost see the saliva running down his chin.

"It ain't yours yet, Lamont." Ball laughed, and Packard looked like someone had just peed on his Gucci loafers. "Not until I hand it over at the gala."

Ball had taken his grandfather's struggling headache

powders business and turned it into the bestselling college study tool simply by adding enough caffeine to make a hippo run a marathon, then sold it to a Big Pharma company for six times its annual earnings. He divided his time between a villa in Tuscany, an antebellum estate on a river outside Gainesville and a century-old former industrial's mansion not far from the Carnegie. Ball had converted the mansion's sixty-foot-long carriage house into a well-fortified, temperature-controlled warehouse for his beloved art collection.

Cam and Ball had known each other for years. She'd put him on the trail of a number of fine paintings and other works for sale in the art world, including Jacket's. Ball's tastes were wide-ranging and constantly changing, and his pockets as deep as the steam tunnels under the museum. He was returning the favor by letting her get credit for the donation of the Van Dyck, a piece in which he had lost interest.

"Sure was good to get back up north," Ball said. "It's been hot as Hades down in Flow-da."

"In Flow-da," Jeanne repeated.

"But so, so beautiful." Anastasia nodded her violently bobbed head. "I remember the orange blossoms—oh God, the orange blossoms." She closed her eyes and clasped her breast as if she were having a small religious epiphany. "I used to live and die for orange blossom time when I lived in Florida."

Cam rolled her eyes.

"Ah didn't know you were a Flowidyan." Ball beamed.

"Yes," Packard said, "Anastasia's been almost everywhere. We were very lucky to steal her from the Getty."

Cam remembered the day clearly, and *lucky* was not the word she would have chosen.

"Did you know," Packard went on, "Anastasia is the author of the definitive critical book on Caravaggio, and—do you want to tell Mr. Ball the news?"

Oh boy.

Anastasia took a deep breath. "You probably don't know this, but I've always been absolutely *enraptured* by El Greco."

Another epiphany, larger than the first. Soon she would be on her knees, recounting secrets from the Virgin Mary, in the grottolike overhang of the fountain outside.

"Well," Anastasia went on. "I've just signed the contract with Harvard Press today for a biography."

Cam felt like she'd just taken a fount of holy water to the gut.

Ball nodded. "Now that's a purdy milestone."

Yes, it was. And in the cutthroat world of art curating, that was the winning hand. A biography would beat the 2.1 million-dollar Van Dyck in the game of publish-or-perish museum life, which is why Cam needed a biography, too.

Aaaarrrrrggghhh.

The truth of the matter was Cam had been dawdling. There were reasons for it. One, she had to admit, was that she was naturally lazy. But there was another. In the last month she and Jacket had begun to email each other. At the start, it had just been an abashed appeal to Cam for her expertise on a certain painting, but it had grown to something more. If she had any hope of being chosen to be the next director next year by the board, however, she had better get her butt in gear and get that book revised. With a manuscript updated to include, as the potential publisher had said, "a bit more excitement," she could announce her own contract. And with a book contract, she was back in the game, directorship-wise.

"Of course," Anastasia added, "the promotional details are still a bit fuzzy at this point. I don't know what Harvard's thinking of from a book tour or personal appearance point of view."

"A book tour?" Ball said. "That's amazing."

Anastasia backpedaled. "Well, perhaps a conference or two."

Yes, the Association of Art Museum Curators Mid-Atlantic Regional Meeting is really the place to make an impact—that is, if they can get out of their J. K. Rowling contract first. Cam coughed to hide a smile, and if looks were lasers, Anastasia would have reduced her to a pile of mustard-stained ashes.

Packard put one hand on each woman's shoulder. "Anastasia's doing a top-notch job on European art. Cam's doing a top-notch job on modern. Imagine one set of parents producing two such talented daughters. I like to think of them as the Serena and Venus Williams of the museum circuit."

Cam was grateful he'd moved on from the Andrews Sisters metaphor he usually employed.

Anastasia clasped Ball's hand as if the holy power of the art world was running down his arm. "I'd like to show you some architectural renderings you may be interested in. We're building a new wing. A new, as yet unnamed wing. If you have a moment, I think I—"

Tim Lockport, the museum's facilities manager, burst into view. "Pardon me, Mr. Packard," he said, breathing hard. "I think we may have a problem."

Packard frowned. "What?"

"Someone reported seeing a patron draw on a print upstairs."

"Oh God. Which one?"

"Rembrandt. The one in the north hallway."

"Rembrandt. That's your area, Anastasia. You'd better go with Tim."

Anastasia gave Lockport a look usually reserved for the phone receiver when talking to Bangalore help desk associates and released Ball's hand. "Will do."

Cam whistled as Anastasia clattered off. "Tough break."

Jeanne, dynamo of efficiency, lodged herself in front of the suddenly unoccupied Ball with pen, permission form and clipboard.

"My gosh," she said as Ball opened his glasses, "those are some bright stripes on your shirt. Do the colors stand for something?"

"They shore do. I'm a Flow-da Gatah."

"A Flow-da Gatah?" She flashed Cam a wicked smile. "Really? And your parents? I suppose they were Flow-da Gatahs, too?"

He signed in one quick motion. "You bet. Big ones."

"Of course, I'm from Alabama, so I'm a Crimson Tide fan myself, but I've heard practically everyone in Gainesville is a shameless public—"

"Thank you, Jeanne." Cam extracted the clipboard from Ball's hand and returned it to her assistant with a gentle shove. "I know you have to go. Mr. Ball, I'd be happy to show you the plans for the addition. There's a gallery entrance hall that will quite literally blow your socks off. And if you've got time, I'd love to talk with you more after lunch."

Ball nodded. "I'll take you up on the plans, but I'm going to have to pass on lunch. Anastasia's invited my wife and me to a gallery opening tonight, and the three of us are meeting at Lucca for an early dinner. Peggy's all excited because Anastasia promised to show her some fancy knitting stitch. So many talents. I don't know how you ladies do it."

It must be an afternoon for epiphanies. Cam had a blistering vision of Serena taking a tennis racquet and knocking Venus right out of her Nikes.

5

With Ball's thoughts on the new wing fresh in her head, Cam wheeled into the workspace she shared with Jeanne, closed the door and fell into a Melanie Wilkes swoon against the medieval coat of armor. " 'Oh God, the orange blossoms. I used to live and die for orange blossom time.' " She growled. "Her backstory is so bogus. You know how long she was in Florida? Three weeks. Three weeks! She was there for a summer course in environmental studies until she'd added that to the long list of majors she couldn't hack. After that it was either art history or clown college."

"I'll refrain from the obvious comment," Jeanne said.

"Thank you. Did I happen to mention her real name is Stacy?"

"Thirty or forty times."

"*Eeeeerrrrgggg!* And now she's stepping on my donor territory. What sort of a person does that?"

"I dunno. The same sort of person who would force someone to claim a guy drew on a Rembrandt when he didn't?"

"Beside the point." Cam started to finger her eyelashes, a reaction to stress she'd been unable to shake since childhood. She knew it made her about as attractive as a junkie six hours past hit time. "Do you think that Van Dyck painting is going to be enough? I mean, the donation's practically in the bag. Do you think that will be enough to convince the board I'm the right person for the directorship?"

"I know they'll be bowled over by your granitelike self-confidence."

"Oh God, I've got to get that book sold."

"Thatta girl. Where do we stand on that rewrite?"

" 'There once was a man named Van Dyck.' "

"Oh boy. I'd say too many late nights IM-ing Britain's favorite bad-boy artist, Mr. Lucite and Blueberries. I'm assuming that kiss was a thank-you for the help on a painting you gave him."

Cam tucked the chain that held the ring farther inside her blouse. The last thing she needed was Jeanne thinking that she was stupid enough to consider Jacket's offer to reconcile. Especially now that she was considering it.

"It was nothing. And as far as the book is concerned, it's done from a fact standpoint, but I don't know. This editor wants me to sex things up a bit."

"Sex and artists?" Jeanne shrugged theatrically. "Well, if you think you can find a connection . . ."

And it did not in any way mean she was falling for the guy again, despite that gravelly Brixton baritone that still made her toes curl, and that kiss . . .

"Cam?"

"Huh? Oh, right. I mean, no. Not too many late

nights." Jeanne was shooting a "Don't tell me you were a fool and fell for his load of crap again" look in her direction.

Most important, however, kissing Jacket did not mean she was going to sleep with him. Oh, no, no, no, no, no. Hence the "I'm not as easy as you apparently think I am" look she was firing right back at Jeanne. It was the kind of light saber clashing that could only come from two friends long accustomed to each other's foibles, and Cam, with the moral high ground of having not actually yet been a fool, clearly held the upper hand. Oh yeah, Jeanne was getting the message—she most certainly was getting the message.

"That mustard in your eye?" Jeanne asked.

"Gah!" Cam stomped to her desk. "And stop calling him 'Mr. Lucite and Blueberries.' He does 'reapings.'"

"Oh, is that what they're called?"

Jacket had wowed the art world ten years ago with his portraits that started on the upper corner of a canvas as a traditional oil painting then grew into pieces of fruit and other everyday items encased in small cubes of plastic, bound together, extending outward toward the viewer and sometimes reaching the floor. Cam hadn't loved it then, though she understood his vision. What she had loved was his motorcycle boots, tight jeans and damn-the-world attitude—especially when he'd led her into the ladies' lounge of the Fulham art gallery where they'd just met for a "Fourth of July meets the 'Hallelujah' Chorus" encounter in an empty stall.

His recent work had become almost a parody of itself, though, with the painting and canvas chucked entirely and the rest reduced to stacks or sometimes just single cubes of plastic. In truth, "Mr. Lucite and Blueberries" wasn't that far from the truth.

Cam grabbed her mug and went to the coffeemaker, dejected. Then she remembered it had shorted out yesterday, right in the middle of the Caffè Verona. The sides had melted into a depressing shade of toasted marshmallow brown and that corner of the room still smelled like burnt socks. Why did it always rain on the unloved?

"So he'll be bunking with you?"

Cam looked to see if Jeanne had served this up with a hefty side of judgment. She hadn't.

"It's only a month or so, just until the exhibit opens. He's trying to finish one more piece for it."

"I know what piece he's trying to finish."

"And don't forget the loft is half his."

"Just make sure he stays on his side of the line. Oh God!" Jeanne's roving mouse had stopped.

"What?"

"An email from the board. 'In anticipation of Lamont Packard's revised retirement date—' "

"*Revised* retirement date?"

" '—the board has made the decision to end the search for executive director early. The deadline for applications is now November twenty-sixth, interviews will follow immediately, and the new director will be chosen by the board at a special session to be held December fifteenth, the day after the gala opening of the new exhibit.' "

Cam's heart sank as she looked at her calendar. It was November fifth. She had exactly three weeks to sell her book. A number of panic-filled visions rocketed through her brain—sleepless nights as she stuck in new chapters, standing in front of a table of twenty stone-faced rich people with the power to make or break her and waiting by her desk for the phone to ring with the decision—but the worst, the most horrible vision that passed through her mind, was that of reporting to her older sister.

Then a sound made both of them stop, a sound that could only be made by a pair of Christian Louboutin booties being driven down the hall like Herefords to the slaughter. Only the Herefords weren't the ones about to get a bullet between the eyes. Cam dove under her desk just as the door flung open.

"You meddling, manipulative *bitch*! If you think you can have me dragged out of— Where is she? Where's Cam?"

She could see Anastasia's seething form reflected on the armor breastplate—a funhouse mirror in a medieval house of horrors. Jeanne straightened papers on her desk with the cool of an ice cube. You could sure tell she didn't have a narcissistic older sister with a Darth Vader temper. You could also tell she was trying not to look at Cam.

Jeanne said, "She's under . . . a deadline."

"What the hell's that supposed to mean?"

"Her book's almost done, you know. Finishing touches. Her editor's talking the *New York Times* bestseller list. First print run: a hundred thousand."

Bless that woman!

Anastasia's eyes narrowed to battleship gun ports. "Well, take a message for me. Tell her she's to call me the instant she sets foot in here, that if she thinks I wasn't going to talk to Tim Lockport and figure out what the hell happened, she's got another thing coming. And you can also tell her if they printed a million copies of her stupid book, it still wouldn't get her one step closer to the executive directorship because that spot belongs to the woman who has demonstrated time after time that she can grow a complex collection, manage the fund-raising needs of an organization, demonstrate academic excellence and eat without getting condiments on her shoes. Did you get all that?"

Jeanne read back from the message pad. " 'Cam, call your older sister.' "

Small tendrils of smoke curled out of Anastasia's ears, or maybe it was just the coffeemaker. She picked up Jeanne's bowl of pink paper clips and reared back.

"Oh, for God's sake, Stacy." Cam crawled out of the kneehole and dusted herself off. "Get over yourself."

"You heard all that?"

"Squirrel Hill heard all that."

"You have a lot of nerve."

Cam mimed an introduction. "Pot. Kettle. Kettle. Pot. By the way, Ball loved the new wing."

Anastasia drew herself up into full Hydra horror. "You don't own Ball!"

"Well, it's not like I need the warning. You slept with my first boyfriend. You slept with my second boyfriend and told me he was gay. You stole my major in college, and now you're working at my museum. I'd offer you an apology, but I'm pretty sure you're going to take it whether I give it to you or not."

"Oh, for God's sake, Campbell. Man up."

"Yes, clearly I ought to keep a pretty deep inventory."

Anastasia gave a howl of frustration, reared back again and threw the bowl, but not before half a dozen paper clips tumbled down her arm and attached to her bracelet. The bowl smashed into a dozen pieces, and Anastasia shook her arm like two attack dogs were hanging there. When the pink wire didn't release, she stormed out.

"Wow," Jeanne said. "It must have been a red-letter day for you when Anastasia left the house to start kindergarten."

"Why does she have to be so mean? You know, I remember it killing me when she ignored me in high school. Who'd have thought I'd look back on those days so fondly?"

She plopped in her chair and returned to the computer. There, on her monitor, the manuscript she'd been kicking around for two months looked out at her. Sex it up, eh? She supposed there were a few ways to do that. She could add sex. Lord knows there was enough of that in the art world even then, and she knew Van Dyck had had a long affair with a woman named Margaret Lemon. She could add a competitive rivalry, going for the Shaquille O'Neal/ Kobe Bryant sort of thing. Even better, though, would be a competitive rivalry over a woman.

Hmmmm.

Cam scanned her memory banks. Surely there had been some woman somewhere who'd been shared by Van Dyck and another artist. Unfortunately most of Cam's research had been about the man and his work. Sure, there had been the various bits of information about his life, but Cam had used that to flesh out the story of his painting. The sources she'd found had been somewhat dry regurgitations of where he studied and how he progressed to being the chosen painter of Charles I. If she was going to sex this puppy up, she needed something else. She was just starting to clear a path to her keyboard when her cell phone rang. She dug it out of her purse and checked the display. It was Joe. She hit the answer button. "How's my favorite sibling?"

"Gee, I'd feel more flattered if I didn't know my only competition was Stacy."

"That's Anastasia to you, pal."

"You guys still going strong?"

"You know I can't get enough. What are you up to?" she asked lightly.

Joe had lost his wife and son in a car accident ten months earlier. It would be a long time before she'd feel him living inside their conversations again.

"You know. Same old. I just wanted to tell you I'm making my reservations for Christmas—"

"Oh, you're coming up!" she cried happily, and instantly regretted it. The accident had happened shortly after the holidays.

"Yeah, I want to do it. I-I can't promise you a lot of Christmas spirit—"

"God, if you can just promise to sit between me and Stacy at dinner, that'll be holiday enough."

He laughed. "I'm looking forward to it."

"Me too."

"Gotta run."

"Yeah." His conversations were often cut short by unexpected short waves of tears, and Cam had grown used to allowing it to pass without comment. "Love you. 'Bye."

She clicked the phone and cursed the Fates for punishing such a great guy.

"Is he okay?" Jeanne asked.

Cam shrugged. "The same. It'll be a while, I guess."

She dropped her phone back in her clutch and checked to see if she still had that half a Mounds bar left over from breakfast yesterday. Nope. Oh boy. Not a good sign. No wonder those Spanx were getting tighter. With a sigh, she dropped the bag on her desk.

She pushed the folders off her keyboard, where she found her smashed hot dog. Sighing, she tossed it in the wastebasket. Then she pushed aside her tubes of paint and the little, half-finished still life of the stapler and pencil cup she'd work on when she wanted to be reminded that she'd once wanted to be a painter and called up Amazon.

She hated to resort to mass-market research, but if she found something that offered a meaty tidbit, she could count on having the book in her hand by tomorrow. If she ordered it from the library, it might take weeks.

She typed "Anthony Van Dyck" into the search box and got two hundred forty-one results. Sighing, she began to page through. Most she'd seen before and either passed on or read. On the eighth page something caught her eye.

Inside the Artist's Studio: A Glimpse into the Personal Lives of the Greatest European Painters of the Sixteenth and Seventeenth Centuries. Well, that certainly had an interesting ring to it. Cam clicked to open it and read the description. There was no review from *Publishers Weekly,* which surprised her, since they were usually all over that stuff, but the first reader review—the only reader review—was eye-opening.

"Everything I wanted to know about my favorites. Reads like Jansen's *History of Art* meets *Sex and the City*. Felt like I was there. Hot, hot, hot." From a "Madame K" in Sofia, Bulgaria.

Well, well, well. This will definitely be worth the overnight delivery charge.

Cam clicked on the "Add to Shopping Cart" button. Her computer made a loud, angry buzz, like she'd given the wrong answer in *Jeopardy!* The screen didn't change. The book wasn't added to her cart.

Hm.

She tried again and got the same angry buzz. On the third try, Jeanne looked up.

"Something I can help you with there?"

"No." Cam tried two more times with no change in outcome. She tried exiting the screen and returning. No luck. She tried another book site, but they didn't have it listed. She went to the website of her local library and couldn't find it there, either. She even tried the biggest used-book site she knew. No go.

Crap!

This book seemed like the answer to her prayers. She tapped her fingers. Well, there was a "LOOK INSIDE!" feature. With a little luck and a hell of a lot of patience, she might be able to find what she needed.

Cam ran her mouse over the cover of the book and the image of the book changed.

Now, that's a little weird.

What had been a bland detail of a Rembrandt painting became a full portrait of a red-haired woman in a gorgeous olive satin frock. Cam looked closer. If she didn't know better she'd almost have to say the woman looked like, well, her.

"Wow."

"What?" Jeanne asked.

"Nothing."

Cam didn't recognize the painting, which didn't surprise her, though she certainly recognized the artist. It was a Peter Lely, a minor painter of the late-seventeenth century—interestingly the successor to Van Dyck as royal portraitist—whom the professors in grad school had only touched on.

She had to admit, though, the painting—what she could see of it—was exquisite. Like Van Dyck, Lely had had a way of rendering fabric that made it practically jump off the canvas. But there was something else about Lely that stuck in her head. What was it? Something that made him a bit out of the ordinary in the art world.

She went to the bookcase and scanned the volumes of art books, looking for the exhibit catalog. And there it was. It had been in the office when she moved in. *Painted Ladies: Women at the Court of Charles II.* She pulled the book off the shelf and instantly gasped.

On the cover was a portrait by Lely. She recognized it now, had seen the original at the Yale Center for British Art a few years back. The young woman, a courtier of some sort, face framed in light auburn ringlets, gazed at Lely with a look of relaxed and bemused understanding, as if she had shared her innermost secrets with him and knew they would be safe. Her frock, if one could call it that, was rendered in a stunning pumpkin silk that draped in gleaming folds so realistic Cam could almost hear the rustle. In the woman's left hand was a pale peony, open and tinged with pink. She held it toward the viewer. But the most eye-catching part of the portrait was the porcelain white breast, curving upward to a firm rose nipple that sat unashamedly above the neckline of the silk.

Cam put a hand to her cheek. "Wow."

"You've been using that word a lot," Jeanne observed.

Taken as a whole, the portrait packed a hell of a punch. A woman of the court, whose hair, makeup and clothes suggested a position of wealth and importance, yet who gazed upon her portraitist with unveiled sensuality, and who, more important, let her portraitist gaze upon her in dishabille. Even in the licentious court of Charles II, this would have excited the attention of viewers—heck, Cam's own belly was tingling. And yet the portrait was not pornographic or leering in any way. It was a masterfully executed study of classic beauty: the proportions of the woman's face, the gleam of her skin, the delicacy of the blossom, the living, moving silk. But it was something beyond mere craft that provoked Cam's admiration. It was the trust the artist had built with his subject and the obvious appreciation with which he had portrayed the woman's assurance.

Cam found herself wondering with some intensity what sort of man was capable of seeing a woman like that.

"Look at this," she said, turning the book toward Jeanne.

Jeanne's head tilted slowly. "Wow."

"I told you. It's by Peter Lely."

"Was he her lover?"

"I don't know. Maybe. Probably. Look at the way she looks at him. I mean, jeez. It's like they just . . ."

Cam nodded. "Uh-huh."

"Her eyes, that smile."

"And let's not forget that breast. Amazing, isn't it?"

"But what sort of woman . . ."

"Peels the papaya? Yeah, I don't know. A damned at-ease one, I guess." Cam opened the book and began to page through it. "Holy moly. There's more."

Jeanne squeezed in next to her. Lely's women didn't all have a breast on display, though a decent—indecent?—proportion of them did. But every one of them beheld their portraitist with the same worldly, self-assured, half-lidded gaze.

"Did he do *all* of them?"

"Probably," Cam said. Painters generally considered themselves the absolute center not only of their own universe, but everyone else's as well. She had to admit, though, this was a little like thinking-women's porn—being adored from across the room by a man, master at his art, who saw you, fat or thin, beautiful or plain, as the most stunning, empowered, attractive woman on Earth.

"He's Jake Ryan," Cam said.

"Pardon?"

"Jake Ryan, the hero of *Sixteen Candles*. The man who falls for Samantha Baker even though she isn't cheerleader beautiful. Lely is the man who loves the woman posing for him for what's on the inside."

Jeanne flipped a page and found a woman with both breasts on display. "That's what's on the inside?"

"But look at her. Look at the way he sees her. And look at the way she looks at him in return." Cam felt her breath quicken. Her eyes met Jeanne's.

Jeanne said, "I'm gettin' a little—"

"Yeah, me too."

But that had always been Cam's problem with artists. That is, until she found Jacket not deep in his latest reaping, as he'd told her that night on the phone, but deep in Cam's jewelry designer. That's when Cam decided she wasn't ever going to be painter-stupid again. If men in bars had beer goggles, women who fell for artists looked at the world through a magnifying ass, a special lens you could only buy in New York or West End galleries that made egomaniacs look like geniuses.

For a moment, neither woman said anything, then Jeanne pulled her eyes away from the book and regarded Cam closely. "So what's it like posing for a portrait?"

Cam flushed. "How the heck would I know?"

"Oh, I don't know. Maybe because you lived with a guy who paints portraits for four years? I mean, even with your boobs laid out like oranges in Lucite cages, it's got to be kinda flattering."

Cam felt the pins of embarrassment prickle her face. Jacket's pieces had always been done without a model. He claimed they were amalgams of many women he'd known, and he did them from memory. Thus, she had ended four roller-coaster years of happiness, hot sex and knock-down, drag-out fights with not so much as a sketch on a napkin to show that she had inspired anything in his work.

"No," she said. "Jacket doesn't use models. His work

isn't about people in particular. It's about both the objectification of subjects in art and the rising of the human spirit against it." She'd repeated this phrase so often in her life, she felt like she had it tattooed on her forehead.

"Really?"

"Yes."

Cam returned with the book to her desk. She flipped by two more pages, but the self-portrait that dominated the third made her stop. Where Rembrandt's self-portraits projected impishness and Van Dyck's a quiet self-confidence, Lely had chosen to portray himself as both knowing and seeking, as if his life's experiences had left him slightly adrift. His hair, luxurious and auburn, framed his face in loose curls that reached to his shoulders. A strong nose led to a pliant mouth with full lips that looked capable of both an easy smile and something more complicated. The gentlest curve of cheek hung by the corners of his mouth, a signal of middle age in an artist unafraid of such trivialities. The shadow of a late-day beard burnished his cheeks and chin, but it was his eyes that struck her most.

Cam eased her glasses out of her purse and slipped them on. She didn't like to wear them and only needed a little magnification, but for this she would endure the potential embarrassment.

Lely's eyes were dark and liquid—Sierra Nevada Porter on a warm summer's night. And the single dot of cream in the irises—a painter's trick, she knew, but in Lely's capable hand a trick for which she willingly suspended disbelief—signaled such a potent mix of pain and joy it made her heart cramp.

She exhaled, unaware she'd been holding her breath. "Wow."

"Wow *again*?"

"It's Lely." Cam's gaze returned involuntarily to the self-portrait. "He was, uh . . . uh . . . uh . . ." Those eyes seemed to be looking right at her.

"Such a well-nuanced argument. I don't understand why you're not on the lecture circuit."

Cam ran her finger across the portrait's glossy surface, recalling her grad school reading. "He was German, I think. No. No. Born in Germany to Dutch parents. That's it."

"Who? Van Dyck?"

"No, Lely. And he moved to England young, I think. Like twenty-one or twenty-two. After being admitted to the Guild of Saint Luke, the trade association for painters in Holland."

"Have we changed the subject of the book? Because I'd sure hate to lose that first sentence. It's a killer." Jeanne picked up the Lely exhibition catalog and returned to her desk with it.

With an effort, Cam returned her gaze to the screen. *Sex and Van Dyck,* she reminded herself. *You're here for sex and rivalry,* and ran the mouse past the picture on the screen, to where the large "LOOK INSIDE!" was perched, and when she did, a menu popped up. " 'Front Cover,' 'Back Cover,' 'Table of Contents' or 'Surprise Me!'?"

The choice was obvious. She let the cursor hover over the words and pursed her lips, saying a quiet prayer that the click she was about to make would deliver her directly into Van Dyck's bedchamber, with a tale of sex, lies and oil paint that could be knitted directly into her biography. *Oh God, please surprise me.*

As she brought her finger down, Cam's gaze slipped to the cover of the Lely catalog in Jeanne's hand, wondering once again what sort of man it took to earn such a bemused, smoky look from an obviously entranced subject.

Click.

A noise like a giant vacuum cleaner filled the room, so loud Cam clapped her hands over her ears, and wind blew everything off her desk, flinging her purse like a rugby ball into her lap and her chair into the radiator behind her. It was like the blast of a jet plane, only Jeanne, who looked at her, horrified, didn't seem to be affected by it at all. Cam was on the verge of dropping to the floor for protection when the wind stopped, the room went black and the edges of her laptop stretched out like arms to envelop her.

6

Boom.

Cam exploded into the doorway of a high-ceiled, rococo-trimmed room filled wall to wall with naked women—a good thing, she thought with a part of her brain that apparently processed input even in the face of chaotic upheaval, since she, too, was naked. She flung her arms around herself and gasped for air.

A thousand questions flew through her head. Where am I? Who are these women? Where's my laptop? Am I dead? She felt confused, slightly nauseous and hugely exposed.

"My apologies," she said as the women's heads swiveled. "I, ah, tripped."

Several had been playing cards on a heap of cushions, two were admiring a horned hat, one was leaning on a carved club, another was dangling a loop of yarn over the batting paws of a kitten and one, holding a shield and wearing an armor helmet with an enormous plume on top, was swinging a wooden broadsword, chanting "I am

Athena. I am Athena." Not one seemed even moderately concerned by her own state of undress or the arrival of an equally undressed companion.

The women were long-limbed and shapely, and Cam scrambled to determine which prospect of her body would be the least revealing to share with the room, deciding at last on a foot-forward beauty pageant stance, with her arms taking the place of both an underwire bra and Spanx and her ass tucked beside the doorframe. The woman with the kitten said, "Oh, look, Kate, 'tis the new girl."

Kate tucked the club under her arm and ran over with an amiable smile. She wore cuffs of maple and oak leaves around each ankle.

"Oh, thank the Lord," Kate cried, "a tall one! At least we are matched." Kate drew a hand along an invisible line between the top of Cam's head and her own. She extended the club, which, after a spit-second deliberation, Cam accepted with her Spanx hand, and picked up another. "Supporters make a very poor showing if they are not matched, I think." Kate laid the club across her shoulders like a Highlander ready to do battle and took on what Cam assumed to be a supporter's proper sneer. "We are the wild men on the Danish coat of arms, do you see? The lord-general of the Danish army is coming. Peter said it would amuse him. Are you cold?" she added, looking with curiosity at Cam's still-rigid arm.

One of the card players said, "I'd be more interested in amusing Peter," and they laughed.

Cam heard the sound of a far-off door opening.

"You had better get your headdress on and be quick about it. He doesn't like it when we're late."

Kate held out a large furred and antlered headdress, which made Cam think of Fred Flintstone's Loyal Order of Water Buffalo or the natives who hunted the castaways on *Gilligan's Island.* Reluctantly Cam freed the bra hand to accept it.

"Put it on."

Cam did. The front hung past her nose, like a centurion's helmet with two eyeholes. Great. Now the only thing she had covered was the one part of her she didn't care if people saw.

"Oooh, this is a fine bit of enamel work." Kate touched the ring at Cam's breastbone with awe on her face. "Was it a present from Peter?"

"I, er—" There was more going on than she could process. But before Cam had a chance to answer, the sound of men's voices rose beyond the doorway and terror leapt up in her now uncovered chest.

"Peter's here!" Kate chirped. The women bounded toward Peter, and Cam flew in the other direction, toward the open door of a large darkened closet, slipping between a ladder and some stacked buckets. It wasn't till she was safely in the dark, however, that she noticed the painter's drop cloth folded on the floor on the opposite side of the doorframe.

Thank God. Whatever was coming next in this nightmare could only be made better with a cloth around her.

She stretched out a toe, but the doorway was large and she couldn't quite reach the edge without bringing her body back into view of the room.

Should she dare it? It was the old "bird in the hand versus two in the bush" question. On the bird side, she might be naked but she was out of sight. Given the bush in question, however, she decided that trying again was the only option.

She hugged the wall next to the door, and did a squat with one leg while extending the foot of the other. Jeez, how wide did a closet door need to be? No luck. Sighing, she decided to hold the headdress at her side and use it like a shield. With that blocking her body from the view of the room, she'd just hop over, grab the cloth and hop back. Surely the forest of gorgeous naked women would keep the eyes of whoever this Peter was off a single, mortified tree for the two seconds it would take her to snag some covering.

Cam lowered the headdress, shot across the doorway and bent. Just as her fingers grasped the cloth, the closet filled with light. Only it wasn't a closet, it was a hallway, and two men now had a bird's-eye view of her ass.

"—better if we tried a more private entry— *Oh!*"

Cam jerked the headdress over her face and unbent. She could see the looks of surprise on the faces of the tall, handsome man in centuries-old clothing and a companion behind him. It took one of her hands to hold the headdress upright, which left only one to serve as a wholly inadequate bikini bottom. Unlike those of his companion, the eyes of the tall man stayed on her face. He was exceedingly handsome. If this were the Peter they were waiting for, she could see why they were excited.

"I beg your pardon, er . . ." He attempted to see into the eyeholes. "Er, well, I beg your pardon. We were just heading for the salon. Would you let the other models know not to disturb us?"

"Yes," she squeaked.

With an abbreviated bow, the man passed by, clearing his throat sharply to snap his colleague out of his open-mouthed reverie. He opened a door at the other end of the narrow stretch and the two disappeared.

Cam blinked. Where in the name of God was she? Naked women and costumed men—Cam could only imagine an adult version of a Shakespeare or Christopher Marlowe play. But how had she gotten here? And where were her clothes?

She peered around the door back into the room. The women, having given up on Peter's arrival, had begun to disperse. They spoke with English accents, and so did the tall man—Peter, she had to conclude—though his accent had an odd, guttural tone to it.

She needed to find out where she was, and in order to do that she needed clothes. She grabbed the drop cloth and was just wrapping it around herself when Kate wandered up.

"Is this reticule yours?"

The object dangling from her hand was Cam's small fringed clutch.

"Er, yes. Where did you find it?"

"In the doorway. It, er, seems to be growling."

Kate held the clutch to her ear. Cam could hear the sound of her phone vibrating.

"It's my phone."

The woman stared at her blankly.

"My phone." Cam held an imaginary phone to her ear.

Kate shook her head.

Cam had a sinking feeling. "Are you an actress?" The tremble in her voice surprised her.

"Oh my, no." Kate smiled. "Just a model."

"Is this a backstage?"

Kate shook her head. She was beginning to look as spooked as Cam felt. The phone stopped vibrating.

Kate said, "Do you have a puppy in there?"

Cam nodded slowly. "Yes." The sinking feeling was sinking lower.

"Named 'Fone'?"

"Y-Yes."

"He must be very small."

"Yes." A vague dizziness was overtaking her. "Can you tell me where we are?"

"Do you mean where in London?"

London! Cam clutched the wall for support. "Sure."

"Covent Garden, specifically, Peter Lely's house in Covent Garden."

Oh my God! *Peter.* The man was Peter Lely! How could she have missed it. He looked exactly like his self-portrait—dark, wavy hair, warm brown eyes and rugged profile.

"Either is fine." Cam needed to sit. Lely's house. In Covent Garden. A moment ago she'd been at her desk with mustard on her shoe in Pittsburgh. She looked at her foot. No mustard. Not even a shoe. Holy crap. She was in another time with a Restoration-era painter! It was almost too much to integrate. "I-I . . . Can I have a seat?"

Kate ushered her to a chair. "Quick, ladies. She's ill."

The women circled her. One offered a glass of water. Cam gulped it.

Kate removed Cam's headdress and petted her forehead. "You're not warm. Did you get a bad eel? The cook here is wonderful, but you never know with eel."

Bad eel? Maybe a bad hot dog. Cam shook her head, which was already shaking.

"Are you with child?"

Cam choked. "No—heavens, no."

Kate turned to her friends. "I think we should call Peter."

"No!" For some reason, the thought of facing Peter Lely terrified Cam. There was something about coming face-to-face with someone from her university art history book that scared her. "I-I'll be fine. I just . . . need a dress."

Another woman clapped excitedly. "A dress! Is Peter doing you in a dress?"

Whatever reply Cam was forming stuck in her throat like a wine bottle cork. "Doing me?" Then it struck her. Painting. The woman meant painting! "Yes."

"Are you standing in for Nell? If so, you won't need a dress."

Cam was definitely not standing in for Nell, then. "No. I'm on my own. And in a dress. Definitely."

"And how did Peter say to look? Like a goddess? A shepherdess? A lady? A whore?"

"Er, not that last. A lady, I think."

Kate turned to the woman with the kitten. "Mary, find something in the trunk. Several new ones came in last week. Something dark, I think, to set off that hair."

Cam's hair, her one source of physical vanity, was long, curly and bright copper.

"Peter keeps dresses on hand?" she asked.

"You never know how he'll want us to look. And many ladies prefer a new gown when they pose. It's one of the reasons they come here. Peter encourages women to become something new when they sit for him. He calls it 'putting on a second skin.'"

Cam remembered Peter's particular penchant for skin. She hoped the gowns had bodices. Her mind searched for possible explanations for her appearance. She remembered having dreams where she became aware she was dreaming, but she also recalled that that realization usually made her wake up. This felt nothing like a dream, nor was her obvious awareness of the incongruity having any impact on her state of wakefulness.

The phone booped. The sound of a text. She made a show of peeking inside her bag, as if to root for rouge or cheek lard or whatever they called it here.

"Is the puppy asleep?"

Cam halted for an instant, then found the phone and made a show of patting it gently while still keeping it out of sight. "Good little boy," she said in a baby voice. "Yep," she added to Kate, "sleeping." The text was from Jeanne. "WHERE DID U GO?!!!!" Cam flung her hand back like she'd been burned.

Kate's brows knitted.

"He nips."

"Typical man."

Jeanne didn't know where she was. A bad sign. A very bad sign. Cam felt terror beginning to tighten around her chest. She needed to move, to act, to do something. She jumped to her feet. "I'm going for a walk."

"Outside?" Kate eyed the drop cloth.

"Bathroom—er, privy?"

Kate pointed to the closet/hallway Cam had just left. "To the right. Down the hall. Left at the statue of Mercury. First door on the right. Ring the bell when you finish."

Cam fled, jogging through the maze of hallways and past Mercury, who not only towered over a curved staircase leading to a downstairs entry hall but was unquestionably a Bernini, which nearly caused her to fall down the steps.

A Bernini. Jeez. Lely was wealthy. There was no doubt of that. She whipped out her phone and hustled into the first door on the right. Then she froze. She wasn't in a privy. She was in a small alcove adjoining a much larger room in which two men's voices could be heard. One was Lely's.

"Sir David," Lely said with impatience, "'tis not a matter of an unfinished portrait. 'Tis a matter of a woman seated in my waiting room who desires to be painted."

Lely spoke in a courtly bass, and Cam decided the undercurrent she'd heard there was Teutonic—a preciseness that gave his words quiet resonance.

She flattened herself against the wall and immediately regretted the movement, which she saw reflected on wall-to-wall mirrors across the room. But the mirrors also gave her a view of the men's backs. The men didn't move, however, except for Sir David, who shifted under Lely's obvious displeasure like a child reprimanded by a teacher. She tightened the canvas she had wrapped around her and slowed her breathing.

Lely's clothes were as finely cut as his companion's,

Cam noted with interest, with white silk stockings, low velvet shoes and a gleaming expanse of charcoal breeches adorned with crimson ribbon that showed beneath his long frockcoat. As confused and frightened as she was, Cam couldn't help but feel a small thrill at seeing a painter like Lely in the flesh. Too often when studying long-dead painters students were left feeling a distance that didn't occur with more contemporary artists. Yet here he was—a handsome, living, breathing and obviously irritated man.

Beyond the double doors, she could also hear the sounds of industry—voices engaged in conversation, the random movement of feet, the squeak of a chair on wooden floor, the sounds of cloth being torn. Lely's studio was a hive of activity, and this room was the quiet eye of a well-oiled and hardworking storm. All of it, she thought distractedly, her authorial mind turning even as her practical mind was struggling to keep afloat, would paint an exceptional scene in a book.

"My relationship with Miss Quinn is at an end," Sir David said, "a fact of which Miss Quinn has been informed. This appointment should have been canceled weeks ago—"

"But wasn't."

Sir David shifted. "Aye, I apologize for that. My secretary has been ill and—"

An older man—a servant—with pale eyes, a shock of white hair and a well-worn smock, opened the hallway door and looked in. Cam held her breath. The man bowed to Sir David but spoke directly to Peter. "Miss Quinn has been moved to the Red Room, sir."

"Thank you, Stephen."

The servant bowed and exited.

Sir David cleared his throat. "I mean to do my duty. Tell her to go to this address." He handed Peter a card. "She knows it. It is a place where I conduct my business affairs. Desire her to come in a quarter of an hour. My secretary will explain the situation. You need not be further discommoded."

Peter placed the card on a nearby table with a snap that made Cam straighten. "The portrait, then, is canceled?"

"Yes," Sir David said with a rush of relief. He turned as if an exit were imminent, but Peter readjusted his stance, facing the nobleman head-on, which made his companion shrink.

"As I am sure you understand," Lely said carefully, "I do not charge by the hour. I charge by the commission."

Cam rolled her eyes. Shelter, food, water, air, adoration. Only one thing ranked higher in an artist's pyramid of needs and that was cold, hard cash.

Sir David straightened his cuff. "Naturally I have no objection to paying you. My wife's portrait was eighteen six. I shall offer you half that for Miss Quinn?"

Lely's lip rose perceptibly, and for an instant Cam wondered if he intended to bloody the man's nose.

"Keep your money, sir," he said with manufactured bonhomie. "I shouldn't be able to live with myself were I to treat a treasured acquaintance so abominably."

Sir David blinked, wondering with understandable justification if he had just been insulted.

Lely returned the small card as if he were removing

offal. "You may settle the details of this arrangement with Stephen." With a bow, he withdrew, followed, after an audible *harrumph* by Sir David.

Cam peeked down the hall and, over Sir David's head, spotted Lely disappearing into another doorway guarded by a well-fortified desk. Like painters in her time, painters in the seventeenth and eighteenth centuries often had a secretary or assistant to negotiate arrangements for a commission, freeing the painter to concentrate on his work. That desk reminded Cam a patron would have to be very rich or very determined to score face-to-face time with that god among men, the artist. She found herself making a mental note to include this in the Van Dyck bio.

She lifted her phone, got into Favorites and pressed the button for Jeanne. She held the phone to her ear, waiting for the silence to turn to a ring. One beat. Two beats. Three beats. Exasperated, she pulled the phone down to look at it and saw "Call Failed." She checked. No bars. No signal. No tether at all to the place she'd left. A chill went through her.

Then she remembered Jeanne's text. *Wait a second . . .*

She typed out a quick "U THERE?" and hit SEND. The green sending bar didn't budge. No service meant no service for texts, either. But how could that be? She'd gotten the text from Jeanne, after all. There must be a signal there. She held up the phone like the man in the Verizon ads and began to retrace her steps. What she saw when she turned, however, made her stop.

There, in front of her, was a wardrobe stuffed with gorgeous gowns spilling their skirts like satin waterfalls to the floor.

This must be the cache. And a cache it was. There was a pale pink with ermine trim, a crimson with jet beads, a Kelly green with lemon yellow panels in the skirt and a dozen others. Cam reached for the plainest she could find in case someone here would recognize it—a gray moiré silk that slipped like water through her hands. It also had the benefit of a looser bodice that tightened with laces as each side and sturdy shoulders, critical for someone whose bra usually prayed for mercy.

It wasn't till she removed it from its hanger that she saw the exquisite embroidered lining upon which peacock feathers in brightest cobalt, purple and green thread appeared to float on air. What sort of a man furnished a woman a dress like this? The sort of man who liked to share the private knowledge of what was hidden beyond view with his sitter.

The dress fit her perfectly. In fact, it took her breath away. The silk cupped her breasts like a lover's hands, and when she tightened the thick, luxurious fabric with the laces, she felt an amazing transformation. She might not feel confident, but damn if she didn't look it. If she could just get back to the model room, perhaps she could reach Jeanne, and then what would happen she didn't know, but making that connection to the place she belonged seemed an absolutely essential first step in keeping herself from sinking into sheer, asphyxiating terror.

She pelted down the hall, past Mercury and through a group of several surprised young men in smocks who had to be apprentices, and found herself once again in the hallway with the buckets. She grabbed the first doorknob and ran in, phone held high.

But she had chosen the wrong door. Here was Lely's empty studio, laid out before her like a treasure—workbench, paints, stacked canvases and an easel.

She found herself exhaling slowly. For a lover of art, this was heaven! A Restoration master's studio! She tiptoed forward, almost afraid it would disappear if she approached. She wanted to see the tints, the fabric, the workmanship on the canvases. She wanted to smell the turpentine. She wanted to feel the texture of the brushes. But most of all, she realized, she wanted to see Lely paint. He wasn't Van Dyck, but there were only thirty years separating them at their peaks. Techniques wouldn't have changed much. And, in any case, he would have stories of Van Dyck. They'd been alive at the same time for a number of years, and she'd never met an artist who didn't enjoy dishing about a rival.

She leaned forward and sniffed, letting the rich, distinctive scents of a painter's craft fill her head. This was a part of Jacket she loved. There were certainly parts she didn't love—parts that had hurt her deeply—but this, the gritty world of artistic creation, was definitely in the plus column.

She didn't know how she'd gotten to this strange world, and she was desperate to get back, but the researcher in her couldn't help but hope she'd have a chance to see the painter in action. She ran a hand over the silky brushes, fat and thin, that extended from a pot on the workbench. The researcher might hope, but the aesthete—that being who, like her sister, had been nurtured by her art historian father to find the divine in every artistic endeavor—knew with absolute certainty she would never pass up the chance to see the act of creation in process.

A noise made her turn, but it was just another apprentice, trotting hurriedly by the door. Reluctantly she exited and took her bearings. When she spotted more buckets and a ladder, she hurried farther down the hall, only this door was closed.

She reached for the knob, but just as her hand gripped the cool, polished brass a voice behind her made her jump.

"*Madam*. These rooms are off-limits. May I show you the way to the waiting room?"

Cam wondered how hard it would be to pretend she didn't speak English. Her college roommate, Natalie, had been Puerto Rican, and Cam had picked up a few key phrases. "*Qué?*" She jerked the knob but her effort went unrewarded. The door was locked.

"Madam, please!"

She turned. A tall, extraordinarily reedy bald man with an armful of papers gazed at her sternly. She slipped the phone unobtrusively into her bag. "*Qué?*"

"Kay?" he repeated blankly and looked at a paper in his hand.

"*Qué. Qué?* *Oh, the hell with it.* "My name is Kay, er, Katie Holmes." She dipped a curtsy. Her English accent ranked somewhere above Madonna's but below Renée Zellweger's. The man frowned and began a slow, careful review. Realizing with a horrified start she had no shoes, she thrust her shoulders back, and the man's eyes screeched to a halt at her neckline. Different ages, different clothes, same hormonal magic.

His face relaxed into a slightly less concerned smile. "I presume you wish to see Mr. Lely, aye?"

"Ye— Er, aye."

"About a painting?"

"Aye."

"That is possible, of course, only with an appointment." He scanned the paper in his hand. "I don't see a Katie Holmes here. You do have an appointment, I presume?"

Cam shifted. Run or lie? Running would likely get her removed from the premises. She fingered the phone in her pocket. She had to stay, one way or another. "I, well . . . It's complicated."

7

Peter brushed by the desk usually occupied by his clerk, Stephen, and let his office door shut behind him. After a quick look to ensure it had closed, he went to the storage room and lowered the window to its original position. He damned his luck at running into that blackguard, Sir David. Even entering by way of the servants' door had forced him to take a hell of a chance of running into Mertons.

Charles's entourage had been at his club in Maiden Lane, but not Charles himself, and it had taken Peter more than three-quarters of an hour to track down the king in the Berkeley Square dressing room of the Honorable Genevieve Longchamps, though how much longer that title would apply given the king's obvious intentions he could only guess.

He slipped a hand in his waistcoat and touched the letter, more valuable than gold. He believed the king would keep his word and sign it. He had to believe it. Charles had his faults, to be sure, but for the most part he was a man of honor in business, and he had always treated

Peter relatively fairly—as fairly as a monarch could treat anyone—though he had certainly extracted his pound of flesh in the years since their first meeting thirty years ago, Charles the wide-eyed, ten-year-old son of the king and Peter the scrape-farthing Dutchman with the striking palette of colors.

Six years hence, Peter knew, Charles would bestow a knighthood on him. Charles would say it was for a lifetime of contribution to English art, though Peter knew it had been as much to lift his friend's spirits. But the gesture would fail, and Peter would be dead within the year, collapsing at his easel and finally earning the peace for which he had so longed. Or so he had thought until he found death, at least the part of death spent in the Afterlife, had not erased any of his memories.

How long would Ursula's death haunt him?

A double tap at the farther door roused him from his thoughts. Stephen. Peter felt disloyal for returning here, like a spy, into the lives of his friends and the people who worked for him, with no admission of his prescient knowledge of his future as well as theirs. Mertons, however, had insisted Peter tell no one, and so no one had been told.

"Come," Peter said.

Stephen, as upright as a bishop, but with the broad, good-natured face of a tavern owner, ducked in and began to gather the stray dishes from breakfast.

"Miss Quinn?" Peter asked as he took his seat.

"Attended to."

"Good. And Sir David?"

"Gone."

"Which reminds me." He caught Stephen's eye and let

the corner of his mouth rise. "The king has taken a new fancy."

A look of horror came over Stephen's face. "We cannot begin the painting over. Not again. First Nell, then Barbara Villiers, then Nell again, and now someone else? The paint on the face has been scraped down so many times the canvas is getting to look like my gran's lacework underneath."

"I think we are safe with Nell for now," Peter said. "We should endeavor to finish it this week, however. With that delivered the king's only choice will be a new commission." So long as the king maintains his royal prerogative with the women of the court, Peter thought, I shall always have work. "How are the mezzotints today?"

"Good, good. Except for Collins with the broken finger, we've been producing at a prodigious rate. Nothing to worry about there."

Peter felt the pause. "But?"

"Might I observe the new apprentice, the tall one with no hair, is not going to make much of an artist."

He meant Mertons. Peter snorted. "He is my cousin. From my mother's first marriage. I'm afraid it was this or transportation to the New World."

"Ah. Well, perhaps a stint stretching canvas would be more to his liking."

"Excellent notion."

Stephen started out but paused at the door. "Peter," he said, taking a deep breath, "I have taken the liberty of placing one or two very handsome widows on your diary this week, and I thought perhaps—"

"No," Peter said with a choking rush of sorrow. "It has been but a year."

"Nearly two, Peter. Nearly two. And one of the widows has twice been kind enough to—"

"Enough," Peter said. It had been two years in Stephen's memory, but for Peter, who had already endured the rest of his life here and more beyond, it had been eight. Eight long years, and even now his heart felt as lifeless and ill-prepared for the intimacy of another person as a stone.

"You mope," Stephen said. "You brood. You bury yourself in your work. Ursula would not have wanted this. There. I've said her name. I'm tired of tiptoeing around as if she never existed. We all are. Peter," he said more softly, "she was my friend, too. I know she would not have wanted this. You know what she would have said. She would have damned you for your foolishness."

Peter smiled in spite of himself. "Aye, I can hear her now."

Stephen's eyes twinkled. "A fair temper, that one. I could tell the day I first laid eyes on her, the first day she came in to model."

"'Twas the coloring. The red hair."

"The coloring, the eyes, the way she refused to lower her shoulder."

An obscure sentimental joy came into Peter as he considered the scene, as clear in his head as if the years gone by were no more than a snap of his fingers. "God help us, she was a terrible model—stubborn, short-tempered, easily bored."

"But so, so beautiful on canvas."

"Indeed." Peter's eyes started to smart, and he turned away.

Stephen sighed. "I have said enough. More than enough, I expect."

Far more. Peter felt the familiar wave of grief.

"I have finished tomorrow's schedule," Stephen said, deftly changing the subject. "Might I observe your trade is as strong as ever?"

Peter grunted. At this point in his career, his schedule had always been full, not that the schedule had mattered to him. He had always taken the commissions he desired, worked until he was done, and let Stephen handle the patrons whose appointments had been delayed or canceled. All that mattered to him now was appeasing the king until he signed the document that would issue an edict of marriage for a long-dead woman and the man who had loved her.

Stephen, evidently sensing his master's wish to be alone, made his exit bow. Peter held up a hand.

"I know your intentions are good, my friend," he said. "But I . . . I cannot. Not yet. Do not ask it." He cursed Mertons and the Guild for the torture he must relive.

Stephen bowed again, added a long-empty wineglass to the collection of dishes in his hand and went out.

8

Cam fidgeted on the hard bench. She'd been marched to the waiting room by Mertons, who was now describing the process patrons must follow to secure a place on Lely's schedule. She was waiting for a pause into which she could reasonably insert a request to use the privy, cover for another try at the models' room, when the door behind the secretary's desk opened. It wasn't Lely, but the man in the smock who had reported on Miss Quinn's disposition earlier. The man looked at her and nearly fumbled the stack of dishware he was carrying.

"Mary, Mother of God," he uttered.

"Stephen, any word on Peter?" the reedy man said, breaking off midsentence. "I even checked the place you suggested. No sign."

Stephen pointed wordlessly at the doorway behind him, though his gaze never left her face. He looked as if he'd seen a ghost. Actually he looked as if he'd seen a ghost standing between Amelia Earhart and Jimmy Hoffa, holding the lead to a unicorn.

Stephen's colleague rushed toward Lely's door, clapped the list under Stephen's arm as he passed and disappeared into the office.

"I think," Stephen said firmly to Cam, "you must leave."

9

"But I haven't seen Mr. Lely yet," Peter heard a voice in the waiting room declare.

Despite the explosion of Mertons into his office like a misfired mortar, he smiled. The woman had an odd, eager lilt to her words that reminded him of his country-men when they first grew conversant in English. He knew only too well what it was like to be a stranger in a new place. He wondered if perhaps she was Dutch or had a Dutch parent.

"Where have you been?" Mertons's gaze went straight to the now closed storage room door.

Peter kept his eyes from following Mertons's. "I do apologize. I was napping."

"What is your name?" Poor Stephen was checking the woman against the list, and Peter found himself listening for the reply, partly because he thought it might give him a further clue to her origin, and partly because he had always favored contraltos.

"It's there," she said. *"On the list."*

"Peter?"

"Pardon?" Mertons had said something, though Peter had not the faintest idea what.

"I said I checked your room. You were not napping there. I checked everywhere."

"On this list?" Stephen said, surprised. *"I made most of it myself. Where is your name?"*

"I was in the wardrobe," Peter replied impatiently. He wished Mertons would stop talking so he could hear.

"The *wardrobe?*"

"Oh, dear," the woman said. *"I can barely read your writing."*

"Lady Humphries," Stephen began, evidently reading off the patrons on the list, and with a spark of delight, Peter realized she was shopping for a name. *"Miss Mary Tallyrand, daughter of Lord Tallyrand. Henrietta, wife of Mr. George Palmer. A widow, Mrs. Eu-jeanne Eu-jen Eugenie Post—"*

"Mrs. Eugenie Kay Post. That," she said firmly, *"is I."*

"The wardrobe, Peter? Really?"

Peter stood, unable to stifle his curiosity. "It is dark, it is cool, and at least until now," he said, drifting toward the door, "no one has thought to look for me there." He thought if he took a spot three-quarters of the way across the room and tilted his head just far enough . . .

Mertons blew out a long exhale. "I-I know you don't enjoy being here, Peter, but we've talked about this. You must realize your absence could have been disastrous. If the writer had arrived while you—"

"Bugger the writer, Mertons. Mrs. Eugenie Kay Post has arrived, and I intend to enjoy this little performance—"

Then Peter saw her, and a searing pain cut his heart. Sorrow, betrayal, fear and, above all, a burning anger flared like a gunpowder charge, sucking the air from his lungs. She was beautiful, with ringlets of sun-polished copper, eyes as crystal blue as the Zuider Zee, the proud shoulders of a sultan and a fine, high bosom. And beautiful she should be, for she was almost the dead spit of Ursula. He knew she must have been picked by Stephen like an apple in Eden to tempt him.

Well, damn Stephen and his detestable machinations. Damn his handsome widows. He wondered if she were a widow at all. He wouldn't put it past his meddling friend to have hired an agreeable whore so long as she had the right face and hair.

Peter retreated a step but it was too late. The woman spotted him and smiled tentatively.

His head started to buzz. He felt manipulated, his fastidiousness made to look ridiculous. He would be forced to talk to this woman as Stephen looked on. Peter's cheeks flushed, and a sweat broke out on his lip. He wished to run, or to shout—something, anything to master this upsetting tumult of emotion.

Stephen looked as if he would prefer to be hanged, and if Peter had had easy access to a rope he would have accommodated him without a second thought.

"Peter," Stephen said stiffly, "may I introduce Mrs. Eugenie Kay Post. Mrs. Post, this is Peter Lely, court painter to His Majesty, King Charles. I was just explaining to Mrs. Post that you are—"

"I need only a moment of your time, Mr. Lely," the woman said, interrupting. She extended an arm the color of glazed bisque. "I wish to discuss a commission for a landscape. My time in London is limited."

"I imagined as much," Peter said coolly, but his words emerged through a mouth so dry they lost their resonance, heightening his embarrassment. He kissed her hand quickly, then released it as his own started to quake. He hated that she had this effect on him. To have felt so little in the way of attraction for so long and then to feel this . . . It was too much. "My clerk has failed in his duty. Desire him to explain the complexities of my diary. I am a very busy man. I suggest you take your custom elsewhere. Good day."

10

And this, Cam thought, is why we need men like Jake Ryan. She felt like she'd been slapped. She'd been sized up—that rake of eyes over her body had been undeniable—and dismissed. She'd known men like this before—hell, she'd *had* men like this before. They were generally self-involved windbags who felt the size of their wallet, talent, Mercedes or dick made up for a lack of soul.

She watched him stride down the hall, shoulders back, head high, emperor of all he surveyed. *Grrrr.* She'd had enough of that in her life. Had had it up to here. First her father, then her sister, then Jacket. Someday, someone would get a piece of her mind. But at least her dismissal meant that longed-for opportunity had arrived.

"Privy," she barked to a startled Stephen and slipped away.

She turned the corner, heading straight for the models' room. *Take my custom elsewhere, huh?* She'd like to tell him what he could do with his freakin' custom. She flew past Mercury, past the stairway, past the studio.

She screeched to a halt. Peter was in there, rifling a drawer in the bench, his back imperiously straight. She looked at the models' door, locked but surely penetrable, then back at the studio.

The hell with it. This guy needed his ass kicked.

Mrs. Post burst into his studio like a savage, shoving the door aside with a bang, but Peter, who heard her in the hall, ignored the theatrics. He gave her a cool glance, damning his heart for its inexplicable rise, and returned to the mixture of cobalt and oil.

"I have come for a commission," she said.

"My diary is full."

"Is this how all of your patrons are treated? I had heard you were rude. I didn't realize you were also a fool."

Peter stiffened. Only one other person in his adult life had ever dared speak to him in such a manner. He thought of Ursula with a viper's tongue when she so chose and an angel's mouth. How he had liked to put that mouth to use when their arguments had ended. He looked at his companion's full, wide lips and found himself unexpectedly wondering if she'd resemble Ursula in that way as well.

"I apologize if I have offended you." He bowed briskly and reached for the bowl.

She didn't move.

"Is there something more, Mrs. Post?"

"Aye. You're a total shit."

Peter jerked upright, unable to believe his ears, and Stephen, who had just reached the doorway, stopped dead in his tracks.

"Madam—" Stephen began.

"Leave us." Peter held up a hand and turned the full power of his gaze on the woman. He was a large man, and his glare made the blue fire in her eyes rise, just as it had in Ursula. A charge ran down his back. Stephen wheeled in a half circle and disappeared.

Peter clasped his hands behind his back and surveyed his companion. However despicable Peter found the effort, Stephen had executed his job well. She had the shapely hips and earthy, round breasts of Ursula as well as the damn-you-to-hell face when she was crossed. His only question now was, was this interloper a woman freely interested in him or had Stephen purchased her interest in the back lanes of Covent Garden? He was surprised and a bit ashamed to find himself pruriently eager to know the answer.

"What is your name?"

"Mrs. Eugenie Post."

"Your *real* name."

She seemed to falter. Had she thought him blind to the game?

"None of your goddamned business."

He exhaled. There was something irritatingly entrancing about a woman who refused to bend.

"But you *are* a widow?"

"I am."

Then not a whore? He narrowed his eyes. The dress was beautiful—especially with her coloring—but dresses could be bought. There was a regality to her posture, however, that could not be pretense. She was an intelligent, well-bred woman.

"Did you speak in such a manner to your husband?"

She picked a speck of lint from her sleeve. "When he deserved it."

He had circled behind her now, and the woman turned to hold his gaze.

"I should speak to any man or gentleman so," she added with a significant look, "should he deserve it."

He dropped his gaze, abashed. He *had* been inexcusably rude in the waiting room.

"I beg your pardon. I was unnecessarily abrupt."

She pursed her lips. His defenses were crumbling.

"You understand I am in no mood to be played upon," he said.

"I have no intention of playing, I assure you."

He gave her a sidelong glance. "Whence are your people?"

She blinked. "My people? I am German and Welsh. Is that what you mean?"

He'd been right. The accent, the eyes, the skin. "German, is it? Where?"

"North. Bremen, I believe."

He nodded. He knew Bremen.

"It is not," he said after a long pause, "that you do not tempt me. If I am honest, you do. But I am simply not capable of such a thing now."

"Of a commission?" She looked at him, confused.

"I treated you like a scrub, and for that I apologize, but I cannot . . ." Oh, why had Stephen chosen such a moment to push this?

"Cannot? Cannot what?"

As he searched for words, he discovered he was not

as certain about what he could and couldn't do as he'd thought. "I-I—"

His answer was cut short by the sound of a large group of people trooping up the stairs. "The royal entourage!" someone wailed.

Stephen reappeared in the doorway. "The Duchess of Portsmouth is with him."

"Bloody Christ!" Peter paled. If the king were to be embarrassed in front of his lover, he would be furious, and the last thing Peter needed now was a furious king. "What about Nell?"

"Locked away."

"And the painting?"

"I will send someone to remove it."

"Hurry!"

"Peter . . . ?" Stephen tossed a worried expression in Mrs. Post's direction.

"Aye, I know."

"What?" she demanded.

"Put Charles and the duchess in the Gold Room," he said to Stephen. "I will attend shortly."

Stephen disappeared, and Peter shut the door and leaned against it. "I must insist you stay here. Do not exit this room."

"What? No. I should like to meet the king—I mean, if it's possible. I should like to very much, in fact."

"I cannot allow it."

"You have redeemed yourself, Mr. Lely, but you are not my keeper. I refuse to be held against my will."

She started for the door, and he angled his bulk in front of her. The blue flames returned to her eyes, and while Peter wished for time to find out what else might fan them, time was a luxury he didn't have.

"The king has more power than you can imagine," he said flatly, "and a disturbing predilection for redheads. I see you smile, milady, but I assure you, 'tis not a matter for lightheartedness. I have seen women seized who have been foolish enough to catch his eye and then reject his invitation. Your liberty would be restored in a matter of hours, but I do not think you'd care for your state when he is done. He is a king, and I make no apologies, but if you wish my protection, you must stay here."

II

"If you wish my protection . . ." Despite a growing fear about her presence here, Cam thought there was something wildly romantic about the phrase, especially accompanied by the earnestness in those warm brandy eyes. She leaned against the door, tingling as Peter locked it, and it was with a small smile she pulled the phone from her clutch and checked the display for a signal.

Nothing.

Of course, she reminded herself as she journeyed closer to the wall most likely to be adjacent to the models' room, tingling had rarely been a harbinger of good decision making. Jacket hadn't offered her protection before he'd dragged her to the ladies' room that night—in fact, she'd barely gotten him to *use* protection, if she remembered correctly—but he had whispered to her that the seriously sexy real-estate developer eliciting her opinions of postmodern art and buying her fifteen-dollar martinis that evening was rumored to have started the most virulent strain of genital herpes this side of the

Atlantic, which, when you think about it, was about as close to protection as one was likely to get in the modern art world.

She remembered with a smile how the brandy in Peter's eyes had stirred at her acquiescence.

"Thank you," he'd said gruffly. "I will repay your trust."

And as much as she'd like to meet the king who had not only known Van Dyck but actually posed for him, she was willing—for a bit, at least—to put her faith in Lely.

"Ah, Peter," she said. "You are a curious man."

"Curious?" said a voice behind her. "Upon my word, if you two aren't fucking by Friday, I'll be a baboon's berth mate."

Cam spun around and nearly dropped the phone. A slim woman in a robin's-egg blue dressing gown emerged from a neighboring room. She held a shepherd's hook in one hand.

"Then I hope you've got a double hammock," Cam said, slipping the phone back into her bag. "I am not one to be mastered by impulses." She checked to see if her pants were on fire.

The woman eyed her as long as she politely could, then added, "I'm Nell, by the way." She set the hook against the wall.

"I'm Campbell Stratford. Er, Eugenie Stratford. Eugenie Campbell Stratford Post."

"That's a mouthful."

"Call me Cam."

"Very nice to make your acquaintance, Cam." She took Cam's hand and smiled, sprouting dimples.

She had bright pink polish on her fingernails and a personality that filled the room.

"Aren't you supposed to be locked away?" Cam asked.

"Aye. 'Tis standard procedure when Squintabella arrives. But I suspect poor Stephen thought I was in the dining room and locked that. I finished my eel pie there a quarter hour ago."

"Squintabella?"

"The Duchess of Portsmouth. Bit of a cockeye, you know. I believe there may be hunchback blood in the family."

Cam heard the patter of running feet and furiously whispered orders. She examined Nell's ankles. No wreaths of leaves, but there was that shepherd's crook. . . . "Are you to be a royal supporter as well?"

Nell laughed. "Only if cockstands are the object in question. I am the king's *other* mistress."

Cam felt the smack of surprise. This was Nell Gwyn, the spirited young actress with whom Charles dallied for almost a decade and who was the mother of at least a couple of his illegitimate children. And while Nell's hair was more of an auburn than the copper of Cam's, there were enough streaks of red to explain Charles's attraction. *Nell Gwyn and the king!* The bubble of authorial excitement nearly made her clap.

Cam said, "So no posing as the Danish coat of arms for you, then, eh?"

"No. I am the Madonna." Nell gestured toward the opposite end of the room. There, next to a cushioned chaise, sat a nearly finished painting of Nell, utterly nude, lying on the same chaise, accompanied by a small cherub.

"Madonna," Cam repeated, "the mother of Jesus?"

"Madonna or Venus. I forget which. Charles changes his mind so often."

Apart from the questionable portrayal, the work was stunning. As Cam approached the canvas, the flush of Nell's skin gleamed in warm light, the pillows on which she lay looked as if they would rise like clouds into the sky, and the pale blue dressing gown, the very one she now wore, draped off her shoulders, exposing pale breasts, a curving waist and a long, slender leg bent at the knee. Her head was reclined against the pillows, angled slightly as if she were sharing a sly secret with the viewer, and sensuous waves of red-brown hair trailed across her shoulders and onto the white silk. Cam could almost see the individual strands, feel the lush fabric, smell the perfume on her skin. Cam saw what Peter saw, and for a long moment she wondered what it would be like to be thus observed. She also wondered if Peter was in love with Nell.

"It's beautiful," Cam said truthfully. It was also mildly shocking. It wasn't that artists hadn't been painting women nude during this time. They had from time immemorial. What made it shocking was that women of the court—she could hardly add *upstanding* as she knew Nell had been a prostitute as well as an actress prior to going to bed with the king—did not pose without clothes. It was one thing for a woman of the street or the artist's wife to pose for him. It was quite another for a woman who expected to maintain a place of honor and position to do it. This was the same quality that had made Peter's paintings of the women with a breast exposed so intriguing.

Nell dimpled again. "Peter knows how to make a woman look beautiful."

Cam stepped back to admire the whole.

The only part unfinished was Nell's face. It looked as if he had started over at least once and possibly twice. Her eyes, nose and mouth were no more than ciphers.

A young man wearing a leather apron unlocked the door and slipped in. "Pardon me, m'um—oh, good afternoon, Miss Gwyn," he added, his pocked face lighting up.

"Good afternoon, Moseby."

"Regrets, ladies, but it'll be my hide if I don't get this painting stowed. The duchess is in high dudgeon. She wants to know when Mr. Lely will begin her portrait."

"Advise her not to choose a three-quarter view," Nell said. "The hump may show."

Cam stepped out of Moseby's way as he unfastened the canvas. "I'm getting the impression," Cam said to Nell, "you're not an admirer of the duchess."

"She makes things damned uncomfortable for Peter. She's figured out Charles likes to have portraits painted of his lovers—and for some reason she thinks that because she's Catholic she should be the only one. She's taken to dropping in unannounced to see what she can sniff out—like one of them Frenchy truffle pigs, upon my word. Charles just assumes Peter will keep the royal lovers separated and his affairs discreet, and he has a mighty temper, which is why Peter has to go through this ridiculous Merry Andrew show whenever she shows up."

Cam shuddered. Her family had been divided into the lions and the lambs. Anastasia, who took after their father, practically grew fangs and a stinger when she was mad. Cam, like her brother and mother, approached the world with unwavering calm, and she had had to work hard all her life not to be crushed in the onslaught. She hated the tyranny of temper.

"That doesn't seem exactly fair."

Nell laughed. "Fair doesn't come into it. Charles is like a lava flow. It isn't that he assumes everyone will get out of his way—he just happens to destroy the ones who don't."

"He wouldn't destroy Peter, surely." Cam didn't know much about Lely's later years. Was it possible he'd lost the favor of the king?

"I heard he nearly chucked him once. There was a misunderstanding over one of Peter's whores. The king wanted her. Peter refused. Said he needed her for a painting he was completing that night and suggested one of the other girls might be more in the way of the king's liking. It was a reasonable suggestion, and the king is known for giving his bedmates expensive gifts, so I'm certain any of them would have been happy to take her place. Charles was in one of his Falstaff moods, grinning and playing the host, so he didn't want to be seen losing his temper. He agreed to choose another and laughed as if the whole thing had been a joke, but the footman who was there told me Charles didn't see Peter for a year after that, and half the court stayed away as well out of fear of inviting the king's displeasure."

"Oh dear. Poor Peter."

Nell grabbed a plum from a bowl of fruit, wiped it on her gown and sighed. "I've painted Charles to be a positive Old Nick, I know, but he's a rattlin' good cove when it comes to fun, and I do think you'd like him if you met him, but I guess Peter has other ideas." She gave Cam a curious smile and bit into the purple flesh. "Has anyone happened to mention you're practically the twin of his lover?"

Cam started. "Charles's?"

"Peter's. That is, before old Pauly got his arms around her."

The young man stole a look at Cam, then hoisted the painting free and hurried to the door. "Sorry for the intrusion." As he saluted and bounded into the hall, Nell said, "You'll want to make sure—"

A shrill, murderous scream exploded in the air.

"—she's not in the hall. Oh no! Poor Peter!"

"*That's Nell in that painting!*" a Frenchwoman cried. "*Nell!*"

Then men's voices—Peter's and what Cam assumed to be the king's—joined in with urgent reassurances. The woman on the canvas, Peter explained, was the mistress of a Spanish count. She wasn't Nell. Couldn't possibly be Nell. Why, the hair was all wrong, as anyone could see. Nell's was much darker. But the duchess would have none of it.

"*She's here, and I'll find her. That irritating little beetch!*"

The last words sent a bolt of fury through Cam. Of the dozens of painters in the art book on Amazon, she'd managed to find the only one with the Restoration equivalent of Anastasia as a client. There was only one way to deal with people like that. She grabbed Nell's arm and dragged her toward the storage room. "Hide."

12

As Peter hurried after the duchess, he felt his heart sink. Around him, apprentices were running like rats before a flood, the king was alternately arguing and soothing, Stephen was quietly locking doors as if the horse hadn't already jumped the stile, and even Mertons was rushing about trying to reassure Peter's bewildered patrons, but all Peter could think about was that if Charles lost his temper over this, as he rightfully ought, Peter would never get his paper signed. And that paper must be signed. He owed it Ursula.

"Your Grace, please," Peter implored.

"I will not hear it," the duchess snapped. "You conspire with him."

Peter was a Dutchman, but he loved the English and had long ago acquired the disdain they nursed for their reckless, power-hungry neighbors across the sea.

"Never, Your Grace, never," Peter said. "Why, I should rather consign my soul to the fires of hell than lie to you. You are welcome to look anywhere you please."

She paused. "I am?"

Peter looked at Stephen, who gave him a nearly imperceptible nod. Peter dropped a deep, courtly bow in acquiescence and hoped Stephen was surer about this than he had been about the painting. If Nell was found anywhere in a five-mile radius, the king—and therefore, Peter—would have the devil to pay.

The duchess flung open the first door she found, and a half dozen of his newest apprentices, already keenly aware of the maelstrom engulfing the studio, gripped their brushes, unsure what new terrors might lie ahead.

With an aggrieved huff, the duchess spun around, clipping the closest easel with her skirt and causing the owner to drop his palette. She swept back into the hall and tried another door, only to find a closet filled with pots of painting supplies.

The next door was the dining room, and Peter's heart was in his throat. Nell would certainly be smart enough to hide if she had heard the duchess. But had she heard?

The duchess jiggled the knob and turned with a triumphant "Locked!"

Peter already had the key on his outstretched palm. She grabbed it and jammed it into the lock. An instant later, the door opened onto the empty but exquisite room, decorated in shades of turquoise and brown in the style of the Turks, with lacework brass lamps, minaret centerpieces and tufted, tasseled ottomans in royal blue instead of the usual chairs. It had been the only room of his home accessible through the studio, laid out by the architect to extend like an arm from the town house next door, where he and Ursula had lived, in order to facilitate the dinners he'd been expected to provide his patrons. Its contents, from the rubbed teak table inlaid with bits of mirror and lapis to the solid silver, hand-chased drawer pulls, had been chosen by her. Peter had shuttered the town house after her death, and though Stephen had insisted in keeping this room tidy and inhabited, Peter himself never entered it and even now felt the deadening stab of sorrow that overtook him whenever he saw such a reminder.

But his heart lifted as the duchess gasped. Even she appreciated the sheer delight of Ursula's decoration. Stephen's furtive glance toward the sideboard, however, the only possible place for Nell to hide, and his resultant look of concern worried Peter.

"Where is she?" he whispered fiercely.

"I don't know! Oh, Lord, I don't know."

Charles, who had witnessed this exchange, gave Peter a warning glance. Peter in turn gave Stephen a glare which suggested Nell had better be found and rehidden if Stephen were to have the slightest hope of keeping his position. Stephen hurried off.

"Here," the duchess demanded. "Open this one."

It was the door to his studio.

"Let me ensure there is no sharp glass or metal lying about. This is a room used for—"

"Open it! Open it now!"

Peter bent reluctantly and opened the door.

The duchess barged by him. "There she is!"

Peter's heart dropped into his shoe.

"My dear, I can explain— Oh!" the king exclaimed. "Oh dear."

Peter drew up behind the duchess and looked past her heavily powdered wig. There, on the chaise, laid out like Venus herself, was Peter's visitor, Mrs. Post, or whatever her true name was, reading a broadsheet. Unlike Nell, however, this Venus had her robin's-egg blue dressing gown knotted demurely at the waist, though the fabric yawned enough to give everyone in the room a glorious view of a pink calf, a flawless knee and the most remarkable sliver of thigh.

He didn't know how or why she'd done it, but wanted to fall on his knees and thank her for the deception.

The woman lowered her broadsheet, gazing at the spectacle before her. She'd undone her hair, Peter noted with a tickle in his belly, letting it trail over her shoulders exactly as Nell's hair was in the portrait, even though her hair was not quite a match. For an instant, Peter imagined the weight of that liquid fire in his hands and wondered what it would be like to pull the hairpins free himself. . . .

"Good afternoon," the king said warmly, and Peter woke from his daydream. "This must be the Spanish countess Peter mentioned," the king added to the duchess.

The *Spanish* countess? Good Lord, thought Peter, who had forgotten this important detail, I'm ruined. "Er, I beg your pardon. Your Majesty, may I introduce . . ." He gave his savior a panicked look.

"I am Countess de Iñigo Montoya," she said in an eager but far-from-convincing accent, "widow of Antonio Banderas."

Peter held his breath.

"An honor." Charles's eyes trailed slowly over Mrs. Post's leg.

Peter inserted himself between the two, being struck most forcefully by the reason he did not wish Charles and his guest to meet. "Countess, may I introduce His Royal Majesty, Charles, the King of England, Scotland and Ireland, as well as Louise, Duchess of Portsmouth."

Mrs. Post rose, a breathtaking column of blue, and dropped a handsome curtsy.

All eyes turned to the duchess. Her reaction would spell success or doom. Lord knew, every person in the room was pulling for the countess's affirmation. Peter hadn't felt such religious fervor since the night Charles bet the entire phalanx of Princess Elizabeth of Bohemia's ladies-in-waiting that they wouldn't run naked through the maze at Hampton Court.

The duchess's odd cockeye worked the room like a beacon on a stormy night. "But . . ."

Stephen reappeared from nowhere and set Nell's portrait on the easel with the charm of a mountebank. Despite what was to Peter an obvious difference in their frames—the painted Nell had the slimness of an adolescent while Mrs. Post's body suggested a more nuanced and, to Peter, far more interesting maturity—the dressing gown hid much and hair color provided the only visible distinction. Both heads could reasonably be described as red, though Mrs. Post's was slightly lighter, with eye-catching streaks of pumpkin, amber and even a sunny marigold.

Without conscious intent, Peter's mind began to calculate the mix of pigments such a heady confection would require. Red madder and yellow ocher were the obvious choices, but white lead, raw umber and even verdigris would have their place. His hands began to tingle at the prospect—that is, were he to have further prospects of any sort, for if the duchess didn't swallow the tale, Peter would be sketching Whitehall Palace for coppers in the street.

The duchess thrust out a trembling lip. She was not so dull as to be entirely swayed by this ruse. Nonetheless she could hardly accuse Peter or the king of setting up such a verisimilitude with no more than a moment's notice, especially when that moment had been spent entirely under her observation.

Peter said a prayer to Saint Luke, the patron saint of painters.

The duchess's eyes narrowed, and she threw a shoulder back in challenge. "*Vamos a ver si entiende esto, coño,*" she said to Mrs. Post.

Peter gasped, as did the king. Peter's Spanish was poor, to say the least, but there was no mistaking the wallop of the last word. He'd heard Carlo, a bargeman on the river, call a sailor that once, and Carlo had taken a pole across the cheek in answer to it.

His gaze cut to Mrs. Post. How does one signal to another that the other has just been called the worst name a woman could be called? He cleared his throat and raised his eyes meaningfully, but he might as well have been waving English signal flags at a Chinese prow. There was no mum show equivalent for the insult that had just been hurled, and if there were, no gentleman would employ it.

Mrs. Post chewed her lip as she attempted to decipher this sentence. Spots of red appeared on her cheeks. Her eyes darted from one face to another. She twisted the broadsheet in her hands and coughed. It was more than Peter could bear.

He held up a hand. "I am putting an end to this. I must confess—"

The rest died in his throat. Mrs. Post lunged forward and smacked the duchess across the nose with the broadsheet.

The duchess squawked in surprise, and for an instant Peter's heart stopped. No one spoke. No one moved. Peter could hear a dog braying in the street outside. He wondered if he'd be joining the brute there soon.

The king threw back his head and laughed.

"I must confess"—Peter stepped in front of the duchess to block what looked like the start of a second assault from Mrs. Post—"your language surprises me, Your Grace."

The king clapped his hands, filled with the sort of delight he displayed at the Windsor wrestling matches. "You have been routed, my dear. You have made an attempt, and you have been routed. Make peace with the countess. I shall not have a war started over this."

But the duchess's fury was not so easily doused. Her face contracted, and Peter could see another outburst coming.

"Make peace, I said," Charles repeated sharply, all humor gone.

The duchess curtsied meekly, then turned to the king. "Please take me home," she said with a peevish pout. "I have a headache."

13

When the door closed, Cam collapsed on the chaise in relief. A Spanish countess?! Jeez, what next? A Sri Lankan snake charmer? Her Renée Zellweger was bad enough. Anything beyond that obviously required more than her three-DVDs-a-month Netflix account was providing. Thank God for Natalie and her Latin temper. Cam hadn't understood anything else, but that *coño* had been as clear as a bell.

Nell poked her head out of the adjoining room. "All clear?"

"Ugh."

"You smoked 'er!"

"I don't think she was entirely persuaded. Though I suspect the newspaper across the snout will keep her from trying that a second time. At least, it always did with my dog."

Cam could hear the sounds of the royal entourage dispelling into the distance. Sex, betrayal, the capricious powers of a king. It was a tale that would fit with ease into any book, and she wondered if she could reasonably refashion it for hers on Van Dyck.

The door cracked. Peter stuck his head in, looked from Cam to Nell, who was doing little twirls in Cam's gown, gave Cam a hurried but grateful smile and closed the door again.

Cam eyed her bag, tucked carefully under the chaise. There was no way she was going to be checking the phone with company around.

"You are not the first to pursue him, you know." Nell grabbed a handful of the gray silk, admiring the drape.

"I am not pursuing him."

"Many before Ursula and many after."

Typical artist, Cam thought, though with a pang. He probably keeps a little black quarto somewhere.

"But none so much like Ursula," Nell said. "Your hair is just like hers. Has Peter unpinned it?"

"I beg your pardon?"

"If you haven't posed for Peter, I recommend it heartily." She dimpled. "There's something about the way he looks at you when you're lying there, swimming in silk. There's simply no word for it."

"Ogling?"

"What? Oh no. Not Peter. Peter would no more be moved by a pip than a sailor by water. He's like a medico, he is. No, it's what you see when he's looking at your face. You just feel so . . . so . . ."

Panty free? she thought fliply, but wondered if the real answer was scared.

"Exalted."

"Exalted, eh?" Cam worked the image around in her

head like a piece of mental bubble gum, but when it came to painters she had seen too many women abandon their common sense and then their clothes to find this pronouncement credible. Bewitched, perhaps. Exalted? Unlikely. "I don't suppose you ever posed for Van Dyck . . . ?"

"Davey Van Dyck, the theater manager at the Drury Lane?"

"Never mind." This was getting her nowhere. She'd irritated a minor painter, crossed wits with Nell Gwyn, pandered her dignity in order to mollify a king one mustache twirl shy of a Central Casting lech and smacked a duchess. Unless she was planning to write the Restoration version of *Fawlty Towers,* she'd done nothing that would take her closer to sexing up the Van Dyck biography.

Cam sighed and stood. "I guess we ought to exchange gowns."

"Are you sure?" Nell gave her a mischievous smile. "'Twill be far easier for Peter to get you out of that one."

14

Peter waited until the king's carriage disappeared into Bow Street, then turned and took the stairs two at a time, those stray ringlets of cinnamon and marigold playing a prominent role in his thoughts. He didn't give a farthing about what he had scheduled or what Mertons would say. All he wanted was to return to that spirited flame-haired visitor who had saved his skin and find out more.

Mertons stood, Cossack–like, at the top of the landing. "Peter—"

"I am officially done for the day," Peter said as he brushed by. "Tell Stephen to cancel the Danish general. If the author arrives, my compliments, and he—and you—may cordially hang fire until the morn— Oh, Stephen, there you are. Do you hear?"

Stephen, who was deeply relieved to be keeping his position and had twisted poor Moseby's ear until tears ran down the lad's face, said, "Aye, sir. What about Nell's sitting?"

"Move the appointment to Friday," he called. "I shall finish the painting then."

"'Tis an interesting thing," Stephen said, watching Peter's disappearing form, "the impact of color."

Mertons frowned. "Pardon?"

"Hair. Some men favor moonbeams and corn silk. Mincemeat on the table and pudding between the ears, that's their thought, though for my own part I haven't found them to be cooks of any great sort. I myself prefer a brown-haired lass. They may not be the beauty of the room, but one can have a reasonable conversation with them. Ten years can seem ten lifetimes without that. But men like your cousin . . ." He shook his head and allowed himself a contented smile. "They can only spark to fire."

Mertons blinked. "My cousin?"

15

Nell squealed behind the changing screen. "Oh, my Lord! Look at the peacock feathers in this lining! It's stunning!"

Cam was swinging the phone wildly in the air. If she could get three bars in the Carnegie's lead-lined basement, why couldn't she raise at least one bar in the seventeenth century? She was practically pressed to a window, after all. "I agree. They did a beautiful job."

"Where do you go?"

Oops.

"You wouldn't know it. It's . . . it's . . . in Bremen."

"I never thought the Germans would come up with peacock feathers and silk. They're more in the burlap-and-ironed-creases line, if you know what I mean."

A knock sounded at the door.

"Come," Nell called without checking, and Cam yanked her dressing gown closed.

Peter stepped in, more diffident than he'd been earlier, and bowed. Cam thought she saw a flush on his cheeks.

There really was something quite charming about him—when he wasn't being an ass.

Nell peeked over the screen. "Has the dragon departed?"

Peter smiled. "With Saint George at her side. Nell, about today's sitting—"

She popped from behind the screen still wearing Cam's dress. "Peter, no more today. I'm tired of posing. Lend me one of your men. I want to have this dress sketched out for my dressmaker."

"Well, I suppose we can manage something for you. Ask Stephen to pass the word for Francis. He has a crack hand at that sort of thing." He fiddled absently with a large green-stoned ring on his finger.

"Um . . ." Cam drew the dressing gown more tightly around her.

"You don't mind, do you, Mrs. Post?" Nell said. "I know you mentioned something about posing earlier. Perhaps you can take my session." She gave Cam a wink and sashayed out.

"Posing? You are interested in posing yourself?" Peter's brows rose. "I understood you to want a consultation on a landscape."

Now it was Cam's turn for flushing. "I-I—" She hadn't really thought much about it when she'd said it, and she certainly hadn't thought she'd be here long enough for it to matter. What she wanted was a chance to return to the models' room.

"Did I? No, 'twas a portrait of me I wished to discuss. I was imagining myself as Athena."

At this his eyebrows nearly jumped off his head, though he quickly concealed his surprise. "Indeed?"

She had no intention of posing as Athena or anyone else, but the look on his face was enough to remind her why she'd never brought up the subject of posing to Jacket. She didn't fit the mold of a classical beauty, and the inspiration she could provide from a creative stand-point was limited.

"Aye," she said coolly. "I believe I saw a shield and sword in the adjoining room. Might we conduct our conference there as I try them out?"

"If you wish."

She snatched her bag from under the chaise, and he led her wordlessly into the hall.

The models' room was abandoned now, undoubtedly cleared during the duchess incident. When they entered, Peter paused. "Before we go on, I should like to thank you for your help. It was a daring action. Very spirited. I am most grateful. Though," he added with a small smile, "smacking the duchess was perhaps a touch more spirited than I could have wished."

"She called me a—"

"Countess. I remember she was quite definitive.'"

"That wasn't the word she used."

"Aye, well, we're lucky the king has an appreciation for the absurd."

"Oh, he's a regular Mark Twain."

"Who?"

"Er, my sister Shania's son. A right comic lad, that one."

His gaze flicked briefly to her now bare shoulder. Even with careful monitoring, the luxurious weight of the dressing gown's fabric was making it hard to stay covered.

"I apologize," he said. "You were kind to allow Nell to borrow your dress, but you do not have to spend the wait in a dressing gown. I'm sure you must be cold. May I offer you . . ." He looked around the room. In addition to the shield, spear and clubs, there were a set of angel wings, a large stuffed boar, a harp, a drum, a ship's wheel, a cradle, several large swans made of wool and an armor chest plate that had holes for breasts cut out of it. ". . . my frock coat?" He slipped off the jacket and held it open to her.

She gazed at the coat, glossy and green, and then at the finely cut shoulders and arms now outlined under his bleached linen shirt, and in a small voice said, "Thank you."

Peter was not quite barrel-chested, though he was broader than most, and when he slipped the well-tailored wool over her shoulders she felt like a small animal hibernating in a cave. She could smell the barest hint of vanilla, as if he'd scrubbed paint off his hands with scented soap. She looked at his nails. Fingernails were the windows into a man's soul, and so often the windows were something you had to run by with your eyes averted, but Peter's were clean, pink, and well tended.

He reached for a cuff, unbuttoned it and began to roll up his sleeve. "Would you like to sit?" He paced to a stool, grabbing a pencil and a large tablet on the way, and took a seat.

This left Cam with the only other seat in the room, an armchair on a pallet. She slipped into the seat, placed her bag on her lap and gazed down at him. If she moved slowly, she might be able to withdraw the phone unnoticed and at least check the bars.

He opened the tablet, found a clean page and pressed the binding flat. His forearms, now uncovered, were muscular and long, swept with russet hairs that caught the last rays of sun, and his hand moved over the page with a practiced ease.

"I do not see you as Athena." His eyes stayed on the easy line running from his pencil.

"Don't you?"

"No. I shall paint you that way if you wish, of course, pray do not misunderstand. But . . ." The line stretched long then reversed itself and returned.

"But?"

"But you are familiar with the phrase 'to paint the lily'?"

She knew "gild the lily," but not "paint." "No."

"The lily is on my heraldic arms, so it is a phrase dear to me." His pencil work changed to shorter, faster strokes. " 'To gild refined gold,' " he began, " 'to paint the lily,/To throw a perfume on the violet,/To smooth the ice, or add another hue/Unto the rainbow, or with taper-light,/To seek the beauteous eye of heaven to garnish,/is wasteful, and ridiculous excess.' Shakespeare," he added, smiling. "*King John.* I should prefer to paint you without artifice. As unadorned as possible."

Oh.

Her throat dried, and for a moment the scratching of the pencil on paper was the room's only sound.

"I, ah, thought this was to be an interview." She tilted her head toward his tablet.

He laughed. " 'Tis an artist's interview. I draw. You talk."

"And then you will decide if you can paint me?"

"Have no fear on that account, milady."

He turned the tablet and began at another corner.

"I am sorry about your husband," he said. "Were you long married?"

She thought of her time with Jacket. "Four years."

"It must have been heartbreaking." He stole a quick glance at her. "Four years is not a long time."

She felt a pang of guilt, thinking of her brother's loss of his wife and son. "I— Yes." She scoured her brain for a route into the conversation she wished to have. "I have heard a good many things about your work, and, of course, I have admired it myself."

"Have you?" His fingers worked the page, making long strokes and more detailed ones, thick lines and thin. Jacket never worked from a sketch. Wherever his reapings came from, it wasn't a sketch pad, and Cam hadn't seen an artist work like this in some time. It reminded her of her own drawing classes in college. It struck her as oddly interesting that the process hadn't changed much in three hundred years.

The drawing had become an angular thing, with many lines in parallel. Cam leaned forward. "Ah, that's not my face."

He laughed again, a rich, throaty laugh that emanated from deep in his chest. Still, he didn't look up. "No. It is your hand, milady."

She felt an unexpected sense of discomfort. She thought he'd been sketching her as a whole, though, in fact, he hadn't looked at her more than once or twice since they'd sat down. It seemed more intrusive, somehow, for him to focus on a single part of her body. The thought was irrational, she knew, but that didn't stop the rush of heat across her cheeks.

"Your fingers are slim and strong," he said, defining a nail with a few quick curves, "yet without any of the coldness or implacability that can detract in such matters. There is a determined grace here which I find interesting."

Immediately her fingers laced together in a nervous grip.

He caught the movement and bowed his head. "I beg your pardon. My attention has made you uncomfortable. The cardinal sin of portraitists. May I have your leave to sketch the drape of the dressing gown? 'Tis less intrusive, and the contrast of the dark against the light is really quite remarkable from this angle."

Cam relaxed as he turned the page. "Aye." The three tall windows in the room showed the purple-blue of the sky to the east and the orange-red in the west, reminding her of the view from her loft at twilight, the south hills of Pittsburgh laid out like some sort of Tuscan landscape, with the towering squared spires of the Presbyterian church and the neighboring conical tower of the Catholic one sitting like a pair of medieval fortresses on the highest ridge of town. In the winter the structures were lit with spotlights and reigned triumphantly over the coming darkness.

It had been a December night four years ago when Jacket found her watching the same scene from the top of Mt. Lebanon's open-air parking garage and had swept her into his arms, offered to move to the States and asked her to marry him. A month later he'd bought them the loft space, high atop the building across the street from the garage, having convinced the building's owner to scrap plans for a floor of offices. As Jacket said when he handed her the keys, "I want to give you the night sky."

It seemed like such a long time ago. But when he'd given back the ring, she'd felt some of the same sort of magic again. Her heart twinged. Would see ever see him again? She knew where she was, but not how she'd gotten here or if she'd ever get back. She couldn't even get a look at her phone for fear of Lely seeing it. While she couldn't help but admit she was enjoying his company, she wished she could get just a moment or two alone in this room.

The phone buzzed to flag a new text. Oh God, she had service! But then she saw Peter's eyes.

"Um." She jerked the chair forward. "Sorry. Readjusting."

He returned to his tablet.

Whew! She slowly moved her hand to her purse. His gaze lifted, and she stopped. If she could only get him to leave.

"Mr. Lely, might I have a glass of water. I find I am quite parched."

"Certainly." He went to the door, and she reached for her phone. But then he tugged a brocade pull beside the door, and in the distance she heard the faint ring of a bell.

Crap! How hard was this going to be?

"Someone will be here in a moment." He lowered himself once again to the stool.

"Thank you." She sighed and inclined slightly. "'Tis not the best light for sketching."

He paused. "You are versed in an artist's needs?"

She nearly laughed. An artist's needs. Did she have the energy to do that again with Jacket? "A bit."

"Do you draw or paint?"

Cam started. He meant her. It wasn't uncommon for a woman in Lely's time to have been tutored by a governess in sketching and even watercolor—Dürer had popularized the latter as a medium in Western Europe in the early sixteenth century—but from the time Cam had abandoned hopes of becoming a painter herself any direct question about her own artistic abilities made her self-conscious.

The door opened before she could answer. It was Moseby, who started visibly at the sight of Cam. The look of horror that followed suggested the rules about when the master may and may not be interrupted were well known and strictly enforced. Poor Moseby. It just wasn't his day.

"I do beg your pardon, sir, most humbly I do. I thought you had rung," he said, and attempted to slip back into the hall.

"I had, Tom. Come in."

Moseby reentered, cap in hand, looking as if he'd rather be carved into pieces and served en brochette. "Sir?"

Cam thrust her hand in her bag and jerked the phone into view. "WHAT THE HELL JUST HAPPENED?" the text read. Poor Jeanne. She looked at the signal. One bar.

"We should like some water and wine," Lely said, "as well as cheese and fruit."

Cam tilted the phone, and the bar disappeared.

"Immediately, sir." Tom shifted from foot to foot. "I am most grievous sorry about the painting of Miss Gwyn, sir. Most grievous. You were quite the canny one, miss," he added enthusiastically in Cam's direction. "A right bit of sleight of hand, what with donning that gown in a whore's trice. It was downright—"

Lely cleared his throat significantly, which almost made Cam drop her bag, but the noise had been aimed at Tom, who paled and retreated, though he only made it two steps before reversing himself and returning.

"Tom, this is more time than I wished to spend with you this afternoon," Lely said, returning to his sketchbook.

The young man relaxed, and even managed a lopsided smile, the master's teasing tantamount to forgiveness. He said, "The cheese and fruit, sir, is that to be your supper?" Then, apparently deciding there was a better path into the matter at hand, tried this instead: "Sir, Miss Kate sends her compliments. If she is not to be a Danish supporter, she wishes to eat, and would you be wantin' to join her at the Orb and Scepter for joint of suckling pig? No charge for her time." He blew out a long breath, grateful to have completed his mission.

It seemed to be Peter's turn to long for the skewer. His cheeks turned ruddy, and Cam didn't know if he regretted the revelation of his model's status as a prostitute or the fact that, despite having taken advantage of her marginalized position by employing her for his patrons' pleasure, he was still ungenerous enough to require a free ride when her own meter was running. Cam hoped it wasn't the former. It would have been hard to imagine a woman willing to pose entirely nude coming from any other profession in Peter's time. And as for the latter, well, Cam had hardly met an artist who didn't feel as if every pleasure in the world was owed him. Why should Peter be different— other than the fact, of course, that she'd begun to think he might be?

Peter dropped his pencil and had to bend to retrieve it. "My compliments and regrets to Miss Kate," he said stiffly. "I am otherwise engaged."

Moseby nodded happily, this message being far easier than the first. "Otherwise engaged." He bowed. "I will inform her immediately."

Peter reached for the pencil blindly. He had no wish to meet his companion's eyes. There had been a time before Ursula when neither his supper table nor his bed had lacked for companions—lithe, accommodating beauties from all reaches of the court who had sought his company with eagerness. But he had never been a whore-monger, and he employed the women to keep them off the street. If you had two eyes, two arms, two legs and the semblance of a smile—and often even if you did not—you could find a place in one of Peter's tableaux. His patrons liked to have the beautiful ones around. If you were not beautiful, you cleaned or cooked. But beautiful or no, you did not warm the bed of Peter Lely. Kate knew that even if she chose to pretend she didn't. And all of the women received a decent wage, all the food they could eat and a place to sleep in the studio if a place was wanted.

No, he had no wish to glimpse the look on Mrs. Post's face. What he wished was to lose himself once again in the sketch and their easy conversation. Forgetting himself, even for a moment, had been nectar indeed.

"I do not mean to displace Miss Kate," she said. "If you have an engagement, you need not cancel it. We will not be long."

He gripped the pencil and continued to fill in the shadow. The lily of the valley scent that seemed to blossom off her skin was torture. "Kate is in my employ. She will understand."

"As you wish."

"Tell me," he said, capturing the puddled line of hem, "what size portrait you seek?"

He felt rather than saw her shift.

"I don't know. The usual, I suppose."

"We have full-length, three-quarters and half, depending on your needs. Is that his ring?"

She touched a chain at her throat, then followed the line of his gaze to her hand.

"Oh, this? No." She held out the aquamarine in filigree. "This was my mother's. She got it from her mother-in-law after my father proposed. Then she gave it to my brother's wife when he proposed."

He looked up, curious. "And then your brother's wife gave it to you?"

"No, she passed away, actually." Her face clouded, and he regretted the question. "My brother wanted me to have it. I think he felt it would keep a piece of her alive for him."

Aye, Peter thought, to send both a bolt of joy and

sorrow through him each time it came into view. How tiringly predictable the despairing are. He touched his emerald and wondered what sort of bittersweet treasures Mrs. Post kept of her dead husband.

"You have seen a world of unhappiness," he said. "A husband, a sister . . . 'Tis a comfort, I suppose, you have a brother with whom to share—"

She held up a hand, wrenching discomfort on her face. "I have a confession to make."

"Oh?"

"I am not a widow. I have misled you."

Peter, who had anticipated the revelation of her real name, felt his stomach lurch. "I see. You are married."

A beat. "No."

But this was not the "no" of a maiden. He steadied the pencil and waited. *You fool.*

"There is a man—"

Peter's heart clenched.

"—though we are not married."

"You are lovers?" The words were as natural as if he were asking about the tides or the upholstery on a carriage. He finished the drape of the gown and flipped the page in the book. He would not deny himself at least a small sketch of that hair, even if it were the only way he might possess it.

"Yes," she said with a hard, crimson flush. "Well, no, not now. We were once. We were engaged to be married, though it ended badly, and I left him. That was in June. He has asked me to reconsider."

The blood howled in Peter's ears, though he noted instantly she did not say she'd accepted. He brought the pencil in an untamed curve across the page, followed by another, and another. "Tidings of joy to you, then," he said, trying to keep the question from his voice.

"Aye."

The look on her face did not match the pronouncement.

"When is the happy day?" he asked.

"What? Oh, I don't know. His offer was very recent."

Which is why, Peter thought, she came to me. The portrait would be her answer.

In the face of this burning disappointment, he had two choices. He could tell her his diary was full, thus ensuring this foolish misadventure of his would be stopped before it began. Or he could paint her and accept their time together for what it would be: a stupidly painful crush played out in a series of sittings in which Peter would lose himself in her image if not the woman herself while the flames of intimacy licked painfully at his heart.

It had been a long time since he'd felt anything in that stony organ except despair, so it was with some surprise he found himself willing to trade one punishment for the other.

His shoulders relaxed. The terms, as it were, had been negotiated. He would burn and twist, like a pig on a spit, but he would possess her metaphorically. And no woman who had ever been possessed by Peter Lely left without the stamp of him on her somewhere.

"Come," he said, jumping to his feet and offering his hand. "Let me take you to the portrait studio."

"But why not stay here?"

"The studio has better light."

"But . . ."

"Come. The room is just upstairs."

"Over this one, you mean? Directly over this one? At the top of the house?" She clutched her bag possessively.

He looked at her, confused. "Aye."

She put her hand in his. "I should like to see it."

16

Cam gazed around the small space in surprise, her hand still warm from his touch. He had led her up a short flight that reversed at a landing, to a long but narrow room. The space was lit by a row of windows angled above them, following the line of the slanted roof overhead. Four bars, here we come, she thought. Through the diamond-paned glass, the orange-red rays of the sun spread like the layers of a tequila sunrise. Across the room, a set of double doors led to a narrow balcony. An easel stood against the south wall, next to shelves of brushes and jars. In the center of the room a double-sided fireplace, beside which Peter now crouched, rose from the floor to the roof. An upholstered chaise sat across from the easel.

"This studio is for my evening work," he said. "We have light full west."

The room's sensibility differed immensely from that of the lower rooms of the house, partly because of the smaller scale of the elements—a lantern instead of sconces and chandeliers, shelves instead of a workbench—and partly,

Cam realized when she turned, because of a low, wide settee that stretched out in the darkened space on the other
side of the fireplace.

Covered in etched dark velvet, the settee's cushion was
perfectly flat and long enough to seat four with ease. Several plush throws lay folded near one arm, and a dozen or
more cushions in various silks and Far Eastern prints cam-
ouflaged the settee's odd depth and high-backed frame.

It wasn't until she spotted the decanter of pale yellow
wine and glasses on a low table to the side that, with an
unexpected pulse in her belly, she saw that it wasn't just a
settee, it was a seducing couch.

His evening work, eh?

She turned and crossed her arms. "My fiancé says he
despises an evening light."

As she had hoped, Lely flinched at the word *fiancé.*
Nonetheless, he continued his arrangement of dry grass
and kindling beneath the grate.

"Why is that?" he said.

"He says it makes every brushstroke lie."

Peter stopped and turned, and Cam instantly realized
her error.

"Your fiancé is a painter?"

"He is . . ." The wheels of her mind spun but nothing
came. ". . . a painter, aye."

"Would he not prefer to paint you himself?"

Cam felt the familiar rush of embarrassment. "No.
This is meant to be a surprise."

He returned his gaze to the kindling. "What is his
name?"

"Oh, you wouldn't know him."

"I know almost all of them."

"Jacob," she said. "Jacob Ryan."

"Ah," he said, brushing his hands on his breeks and standing. "You are right. I do not know him. Irish, is he?"

"His father, yes. His mother is from London."

"And his work?"

"Portraits, mostly." She thought of the fruit in Lucite. "Some, er, still lifes." Still lifes were what she had once painted. She waited for Peter's dismissal of the genre. Portraitists were notoriously snobby when it came to still lifes. Of course, in the 1600s, "historical" paintings— scenes from the Bible, mythology or history—were considered the highest form of painting, so Lely's work was already a step down from the highest rung of the ladder. She wondered on what rung of the ladder Restoration-era painters would put the sort of postconceptual art Jacket did. Probably a ladder in a different universe.

Lely made no comment, just picked up the lantern he'd brought from below, and used a stiff piece of paper to move the flame to the kindling. The room filled with a golden glow just as footsteps sounded on the stairs.

"Who goes?" Lely demanded.

"Tom, sir." The lad popped into view with a tray of food in one hand and a decanter of ruby red liquid in the other. "I have given your message to Miss—"

"Thank you, Tom. Put the tray there. Instruct Stephen to prepare my standard palette, with the exception of carmine and ochre. Four brushes. Not the boar's bristle." Tom nodded and placed the tray as directed.

Like an architect envisioning a cathedral, Peter appraised her form. "A quarter-size, I should think," he said, more to himself than anyone else, as he flipped through bare canvases leaning against the wall. He untied his neckcloth and tossed it on a table. "May I assume we have abandoned the notion of Athena, Mrs. Post?"

She wasn't even sure she wanted a portrait, but the room appeared to be fitted for only one other potential occupation. "Aye."

"Have the apprentices finished for the evening?" Lely asked Tom, who paused at the top of the stairs.

"Aye, sir."

"And Miss Gwyn?"

"Gone."

Cam wondered if the dress had gone with her.

"Thank you, Tom. No interruptions. Let Stephen know. Handsomely, now."

Cam gazed longingly at the cheese, olives, grapes and rolls. She hadn't actually eaten that hot dog.

Unbuttoning his waistcoat, Lely caught her look and smiled. "The cheese is from Gloucester. The rolls from my cook. She has a delicate hand. Eat. You cannot after I begin," he said and disappeared into the area with the seducing couch.

Cam dropped reluctantly on the chaise, still clutching her purse, and cut a slice of cheese. She gazed at the knife, steel with a narwhal and mermaid entwined in the carved wooden handle. It was a fine detail, and she was determined to add it to her manuscript when—if—she returned. Distracted, she chewed without thinking, but the cheese's smooth, buttery flavor was hard to ignore. She wondered if she could hide the removal of the phone in another movement, like the filling of her glass.

She adjusted her body so that her back was between the purse and Lely, and popped the flap open. She turned to check on him. He was out of sight. She'd ease the phone out, walk to the window and she'd be golden. She turned back, slid her hand forward—

Lely lifted the bag from her knee.

Oh.

"Try this," he said, the purse and the decanter of white wine in one hand, a glass outstretched in the other.

"Um . . ." She took the glass. It was filled with the same white wine as the decanter. "You do not care for the red?"

"Not for our work." He placed the bag on a table by the easel.

Out of ideas, she tossed back a gulp. The wine was cool and velvety. Unlike a Pinot or Chardonnay or, in fact, any other white she'd ever had, this wine boasted the intensity of a brandy or sherry. Prickles of warmth stung her cheeks. *Yowzah!* It was heavenly. The Macallan of whites. She took another sip and suddenly the wool of Lely's coat began to feel warm. She flipped it off her shoulders and caught him observing her.

He looked away but not before another round of warmth rose up her neck. She liked the way he looked at her. It was neither intrusive nor surgical. It was warm and admiring.

"Won't you pour one for yourself?"

"I don't drink while I work."

Cam wished she had something on which to take notes. Lely was emptying powders and liquids from different jars into tiny ceramic bowls. She thought it might be alcohol, but when the scent reached her nose, she knew it was turpentine. The techniques of Lely's time were the subject of a certain amount of conjecture by art historians. She watched his preparations with interest. She watched his face with more interest.

"That's quite a selection," she observed, gesturing toward the shelves stacked with supplies.

He shrugged. "Tools of the trade."

"I thought you asked for Stephen to prepare your palette."

"There are a few colors I'd prefer to do myself."

The fire began to do its job, and he loosened a button under the hollow of his throat. The linen fell open and a narrow swath of chestnut hairs came into view. Cam took another long sip and watched them sparkle in the firelight.

"This is really strong wine."

"Rhenish," he said without lifting his eyes from his work. "Finish it and pour yourself another."

Ah, so that's how it worked, was it? The wine loosened the tongue, then the inhibitions, then the dress. She thought of the woman with the peony and that pale, unfettered breast. Had that been the gleam of Rhenish in her eye? Is that what that finishing touches of white in the iris had captured? And what had come after the finishing touches? Or in an artist's garret like this, were the finishing touches something quite removed from the canvas? Cam turned her gaze to that low, cushioned settee and drained the glass.

She had been seduced a handful of times—not that she intended to allow Lely to seduce her, of course—but she didn't think she had ever been so acutely aware of the machinations of seduction in a man who had not touched her and who, in fact, had barely spoken to her. It was unusual and intriguing.

He finished his table work and gave her a long, considering look.

"The blue," he said. "It will not suit."

She almost laughed. If he intended to strip her of the dressing gown, it would take more than a simple declaratory sentence.

"I don't know what you mean." She refilled her glass and stretched out on the chaise. "It's stunning."

"It brings out your eyes," he said, raising the tray of the easel a few inches, "which *are* stunning. But in this portrait your hair will predominate. We need a paprika or an olive. If you do not mind, find something pleasing in the wardrobe. There's a mirror. Make certain it puts flames to your curls."

Cam was flattered he had chosen to pay homage to her hair. She knew exactly the colors that set off the lustrous red-blond best, and she made her way to the choices.

"Mr. Lely? Are you there?"

A thin, quavering voice rose on the stairs. A woman. Not Miss Kate.

Lely's eyes narrowed. Rubbing his hands on a clean rag, he stepped to the top. "Aye?" Immediately he clapped a hand to his forehead. "Dear heavens. My poor Miss Quinn. Has someone not attended to you?" He hurried down the stairs to the small landing.

Miss Quinn of Sir David and the canceled portrait. Oh dear, Cam thought, this is going to be awkward. Had Miss Quinn not been sent to Sir David's place of business for the brush-off from his secretary?

Cam had been the recipient of more than one unde-servedly harsh brush-off in her time—what woman of thirty-four hadn't?—and while none had been quite so lung-chillingly crushing as finding Jacket and the ring de-signer settling their creative differences in her bed, both the breakup phone message left with her admin and the guy who'd arrived at their six-month anniversary dinner with a box of Kleenex for her and a minister to referee the breakup ranked high on a list of experiences she wished never to repeat. Her heart went out to Miss Quinn, but she had to admit it amused her to imagine the squirming Lely would have to do.

"Miss Quinn," she heard him say, "I am most sorry. Did Stephen—my clerk—not explain to you about the portrait?"

Stephen, Cam thought, had only been instructed to provide her with the address.

"No," Miss Quinn said. "I have been waiting since you moved me."

"Come. Step up to the landing, where we shall be a little more private."

"Why?" Her voice quavered. "What have you to tell me?"

He cleared his throat and said in a tone Cam had to strain to hear, "I understand you and Sir David have ended your acquaintance?"

"Aye."

Cam heard the hitch in the woman's voice. Lely would soon have tears on his hands.

"And the painting was to be a final gift to you of some sort?"

"Aye. I am not a bitter woman, Mr. Lely, but I would like to leave this friendship with something."

"I see. Well, I'm afraid I must inform you of a change in plans."

Oh, Peter, don't . . .

"Sir David made it clear to me today—"

Cam wanted to yell "Fire!" or "Man overboard!" or "Justin Timberlake!" or something—anything—so that Peter would not finish the sentence.

"—that he cannot part with such a value, that he wants you to pose, and that he begs that you will consider sending it to him when it is complete."

"He did?" The woman's voice filled with joy.

Cam collapsed against the wardrobe, amazed. *Jake Ryan lives.*

"He did," Peter said, "though he did not want to impose by asking you himself."

"Oh. No, I understand. His wife—" The woman caught herself. "His circumstances make it difficult."

"Ah."

"But how can he . . . ? Mr. Lely, where would he put it?"

"You ask an important question. Have you heard of a private gallery?"

"No."

"Sometimes it is no more than a secret panel upon which a painting sits behind a false front. Sometimes it is an entirely hidden room. The king himself has one."

"He does?"

"Aye, to mark the friendships whose remembrance would bring the queen pain."

"And Sir David has such a thing?"

"If he is the recipient of such great joy, he said, he would build one. Now, make arrangements with Stephen downstairs. I apologize for abandoning you. The events of this afternoon seem to have gotten away from us. You will return tomorrow, though, aye? It will take five or six sittings."

"Five sittings?"

Miss Quinn's words were filled with concern, and Cam heard the sound of a purse snapping open.

"I suppose I can secure a room for the week at my laundress's house," she said uncertainly.

"Oh, Miss Quinn! How can you forgive me? I have forgotten the most important part of the message. Sir David left an envelope for you, a token of his affection. I cannot be certain, and you will pardon my coarseness, but he gave me to believe it contained money."

"Money?" Miss Quinn was crying now.

"Aye, and no little amount. Desire Stephen to fetch it for you. Tell him that if he does not remember where we put it, he is to come to me and I will remind him. Do you have that? If he does not remember, he is to come to me."

"I have it. Thank you, Mr. Lely."

"It is nothing, nothing at all. I am glad of it. I would hate to see a friendship end on an unhappy note."

He started up the stairs, and Cam flung herself at the wardrobe, trying to digest the discovery of such surprising generosity in a man she had taken for an egocentric painter. She stole a glance at his profile as he rounded the top of the stairs, and wondered what other of her assumptions might be incorrect.

"Who was it?" she asked casually.

"What? Oh. The cook. Something about tomorrow's menu and a leg of lamb. I told her I cannot concern myself in such matters. I do wonder sometimes at the wont of initiative in the servant ranks. Did you find a gown?"

Cam had not found anything. With reluctance, she pulled her eyes away from Peter, opened the wardrobe door and gasped. Another treasure trove of dresses. This man liked to dress women. Which, of course, probably meant the corollary was true as well.

A dozen gowns hung here, each of thick, raw silk and each in a color more brilliant than the last—ruby, emerald, sapphire, aquamarine, topaz, amethyst. But Cam had no eyes for jewel tones. She pulled out a burnished olive green that picked up the gold of her skin and the cinnamon-blonde streaks in her hair.

"There are undergowns there as well," he said.

In the drawers below, laid out like the petals of a pressed ivory rose, were linen and muslin shifts, as intricately detailed as wedding gowns, with falls of ruffles and lace and beading.

"Choose something ethereal," he said. "I like the Flemish lace. 'Tis the one with the lilies."

She dug until she found it. A beautiful pattern of interlocked flowers ran around the skirt and throughout the lace at the sleeves.

She stole a look at Peter, who was busy laying different colors of velvet on the chaise, pulled the undergrown out and let it drop.

Ethereal, eh?

The fabric was as thin as gossamer, and the front of

the undergown lacked any means of closure. There were no hooks, no ribbons, no fasteners, only a narrow V that yawned almost to the waist, like a floor-length dress shirt with all the buttons removed.

Nonetheless, Cam found herself longing to put it on, to feel the cool weave glide across her skin and hear the glissando of muslin under silk.

She heard a knock at the stairs and then Peter's deep "Aye?"

Stephen announced himself, and Peter beckoned him to the landing.

"I am to see you about the matter of an envelope?" Stephen said, perplexed. "Apparently I have forgotten where we put it."

Cam grinned.

He added, "It pertains to Miss—"

"I know to whom it pertains," Peter said gruffly. "Take twenty crowns out of petty cash, place them in a pouch and see that they are delivered."

Stephen, who clearly didn't need a brick heaved at him to take a hint, said, "To the person in question?"

"Aye."

"Five sittings *and* twenty guineas?"

The look Peter gave him must have ended the discussion for Cam heard only the quietly muttered "We'll all be in a sponging house by Whitsuntide" as Stephen returned to the floor below.

She turned her mind to the matter of changing.

The fireplace rose to the ceiling in the center of the space, and since it stood between her and Peter, it screened her from both the stairs and his side of the room. The fire was open on both sides, but the opening rose to no more than knee height. Nonetheless, it was mildly unnerving to imagine herself naked, as she'd certainly be, if only for a moment, standing in the middle of Peter's studio.

Peter appeared to have no sense of the upheaval, for he remained busy with the adjustment of the chaise. She took a deep breath, snuggled as close to the hearth as the heat of the fire would allow and let the robin's-egg blue gown drop.

Peter had heard her gasp as she opened the wardrobe. It pleased him immensely that she was so delighted. The dressing gowns, prepared for him by a seamstress near Lincoln's Inn Fields, were entrancing to women. He'd rarely had a sitter who did not marvel over the workmanship.

He wondered if she'd choose the lily-embroidered one as he'd recommended. For a moment he was taken back to that house, his father's house in Soest, with the heraldic lily over the door. It was the name Peter had chosen when he cast his lot with the English. How he had missed his parents when he'd come here. It seemed his whole life, except for one short period, had been about missing one person or another.

Another knock sounded. "Sir?"

Dammit. "What is it, Tom?"

"The palette, sir. As you requested. May I come up?"

"Leave it on the landing. I'll fetch it in a moment."

Peter could see the pale blue of her gown through the lens of fire. Then he saw it fall. Her calves were slender, and each movement stirred a part of his mind that he had thought was unstirrable.

You old fool. He had painted many women, possessed even more. The notion of the calf of a woman he hardly knew sparking his desire was beyond imagining. Her shadow stretched across the wall like some Stygian shade. He could see the easy fall of her breasts as she lifted the gown over her head. He would have given many ducats to see the muslin slide down those shoulders. He could imagine the rosy nipples catching the thin fabric and the inviting triangle of curls below.

He put a hand on the railing and caught his breath. *Idiot.* She was a client, and what's more, she was newly engaged. Nonetheless, he hurried down to the palette, scooped it up and returned, two steps at a time, in order to not miss her as she emerged from the shadows.

She came out like a new queen—regal, uncertain, rising to the weight of the occasion. The color of the gown made her hair spangle and flash as if she wore a crown of candles, and his heart soared to see the glimpses of lilies. They crept around her neck and followed that long, glorious line southward into the valley between her breasts. He wondered if her skin gave off the same lily-of-the-valley scent as her hair had when he'd been sketching her.

He loved the look of women in dishabille, as they called it, certainly loved the look of this woman in it. It was fresh, natural and bewitchingly erotic without a whisper of impropriety.

"Are you ready?" he said.

Her fingers worked the edge of a sleeve nervously. "I feel like a bride on her wedding night."

"Oh dear. Whatever minor confidence I'd had in approaching this painting has now officially taken its leave."

They both laughed.

Despite an education that included seven long years under the fastidious eye of the monks at Saint Étienne, Stephen felt his mouth, still in possession of that last morsel of ham and bread, fall open.

Peter's cousin, who had long since pushed his plate away and awaited a piece of the cook's fine gooseberry pie, cocked his head. "Was that *laughter*?"

Stephen swallowed and let out a satisfied smile. "We must let the cook know to keep the kitchen fire lit. I do believe it's going to be a long evening."

17

Without a way to get to her phone, Cam was stuck. No alternate next move presented itself. She could run, but to what end? She had arrived after an earthshaking mouse click, and now she felt like a mouse caught in a trap, in a painter's studio that had closed for business three hundred years before she was born. There were no rules for the situation in which she found herself. At some point, Lely would either return her purse or leave the room. Until then she would soak up some color. After all, it wasn't every day a historical biographer landed in the same century as her subject, and with a man who succeeded him as royal portraitist and presumably knew him.

"It must be a very grand honor to be the king's portraitist."

Lely made an indeterminate noise. "Words do not do it justice."

He had decided on velvet the color of chestnuts for draping the chaise, and it was the edges of this material

Cam now gripped. Despite all her years in the art world, she was unprepared to be the focus of a master's efforts.

"Um, how would you like me?"

He gave her a brief smile. "Given your comment on the wedding night, I'm unsure how to answer. To what are you used? How does your fiancé pose you?"

"My fiancé does not pose me."

He laid down his mixing knife and gave her a careful look. "Do you mean to say you have not posed? Ever?"

She flushed. "No."

"Then I suppose it truly shall be like a wedding night."

The warmth rose to her ears and scalp. She reached for the glass of Rhenish, which had been refilled in her absence.

"Have your last," he said. "I should like to have you lying down."

With a sharp inhale, she set the glass on the table and reclined on the chaise, finding a place among the pillows tucked against the rise at the back. The curtain of olive silk rolled in a graceful wave across her legs. She lifted a heel under her hips to anchor her against the velvet. The other foot peeked from the fabric. Several pillows buoyed her back. A small one supported her neck. It was wondrously comfortable. And then, of course, the way that he looked at her was making her feel pretty at home as well.

"You will have to do without the head pillow when I block in your face. After that, when I begin your body, you may have it again."

"All right."

"It may hurt a bit at the beginning, but after that, I promise, you may relax and enjoy."

"The metaphor is growing uncomfortably warm."

Peter let out a small, deep laugh. "The chain is lovely."

She touched it, flustered. No matter what Jacket had said when he'd placed it around her neck, it represented an offer on his part, an offer about which she was strongly conflicted. She wished Peter had not seen it. Though she couldn't quite express why, she wished it had gone unnoticed.

"Is there a pendant with it?" he asked. "It might make an interesting point of focus. And if it is a gift from him, it will please him to—"

"No," she said. "'Tis mine. I'm glad you reminded me, though. I was going to take it off." She twisted her body until she'd blocked his view, unclasped the chain and slipped it and the ring into the pocket of the dressing gown.

He gave her a warm smile and picked up his palette. "Now loosen your gown, if you please."

If I please? She reached for her belt, wondering what other commands he thought she would follow without question that evening. She loosened the tie with one hand and let it drop. Immediately the silk resettled, falling in an unrestrained heap that ran from her shoulder to her hip. The fabric gaped, exposing an easy swath of white muslin, which, in turn, followed the curve of her breast. She could feel the air on her sternum. She wondered if he could see the beating of her heart.

"How do you want me to look?" she asked.

"I do not want you to look. I want you to think."

"Think?"

"Aye. The portrait is for him, aye?"

"Aye."

"You are to imagine him. When he looks at this painting he will possess you. Each time he sets eyes on it, he will know he, among all men, has triumphed to take your hand. This is his Troy. Do you understand?"

"Aye." Her voice was barely a whisper. What she wanted to think about was Peter, not Jacket.

"You are to show him what it is to be possessed."

A tall assignment. She thought of Jacket on that long-ago night in the ladies' lounge. He *had* possessed her. No question. He had filled her senses and loosened her tongue and made her mistress of some very surprising behavior.

She watched Peter mix his paints and wondered if he had possessed Ursula in such a manner. Had Ursula broken his heart? Or had their relationship been at an end when she'd fallen into the arms of the man Nell mentioned. What had she said his name was? Old Pauly?

The color on his brush was dark. He would have to do the underpainting first, the base from which the bright of her hair, face and gown would rise. The easel blocked much of his body, but she could see his face, which took on a quiet intensity as he calculated the ratios of his arrangement. Part of her was noting the workings of a seventeenth-century master, but the other part of her, fueled by the potency of the wine and Peter's noble gesture with Miss Quinn, was heading in an entirely different direction.

She watched the movement of his thigh, the nearly imperceptible flexing of muscle as he worked, and the fine, muscled calf below. Nell had said Cam resembled Ursula. There were certain sorts of men who were besotted with red hair, just as there were certain sorts of women besotted with artists. She wondered if Peter was imagining Ursula laid out here. She wondered if Peter had painted Ursula nude, and if he had, if it had evolved to fevered lovemaking, right here on this chaise?

The picture of Peter crouched over her, his powerful hips, stripped of their proprietous wool breeks, moving to hastening beat, danced in her mind. She was liking this mixture of strong wine, a man who knew how to make a woman feel like she was the only person on Earth and a very active imagination.

"I am about to begin," he said in a low voice.

Yes.

The first scratch of brush on canvas sent an electric shock through her. It was as if he had drawn the brush down her flesh. A delicious tingle slithered through every nerve, and a welcome warmth bloomed under her gown where her heel was tucked between her legs. She took another long sip.

"You are perfect," he said. "'Tis exactly what I want."

Exactly what he wanted. She closed her eyes and smiled. There was something powerfully seductive in that phrase. The image returned readily—Peter, with his hand on her face, guiding her hungry mouth to his. When his hand in the vision ventured lower, her own nipples tightened. Cam wondered if Peter could see the change through the thin muslin. She found herself reveling in the notion and grinned. Lost in time? Why not make the best of it? She settled her weight more firmly upon that heel.

The brushstrokes continued. Peter worked briskly, and every scrape translated to the rustle of silk as flesh met flesh. In her mind, he took her hips and held them hard as he plumbed her depths.

A wild heat rose between her legs, and Cam found herself responding as easily to the image in her head as she might to the real thing.

Good God, where are you going with this, girl?

It had been six months since she and Jacket had made love, and during that time she'd had no desire to go to bed with anyone. The part of her that responded blindly to the call of lust had been muted that day after she'd opened their bedroom door. Yet here she was constructing an interlude as erotic as those in the novels she'd read.

There was a strange freedom to being cast into another time that she'd never felt before. It was as if she were in a dream of her own making, with no one to justify her actions to but herself. This, she decided, could be a very dangerous thing.

She turned, and a nipple brushed the carved wood of the arm, sending a magnificent plume of heat through her. But the wood was Peter's finger, and she longed for his touch. She moved gently, no more than the motion of inhaling and exhaling, and let him rub the tender flesh. He taunted her. She could feel his throb, let her fingers ride the satiny flesh. He drew up beside her, spoon to spoon, and rolled the nipple slowly, kissing her neck and ear, the barest scent of vanilla reaching her nose as she stretched against him like a cat.

Oh, the Rhenish is definitely working.

She stole a glance at Peter. He was laboring intently now, brushing the paint on with short, expert strokes. She closed her eyes and opened them again, and this time he was looking at her. Her breath caught, and he looked away.

"Is he in your thoughts, Mrs. Post? I do not wish to shock, and you will pardon me for saying this, but as you carry yourself with far too confident a grace to be a maiden, I intend to speak plain. You must be *filled* with him, do you understand?"

His brown eyes deepened in color, and she felt her blood pound in her ears. "Aye, I understand."

"Some women cannot do it. But I see you have no fear."

" 'No fear' might be overstating things." Her heart was thumping so hard she wondered if he could hear it.

"There are certain things I can do to enhance the effect—if such an aid is needed."

Blood roared in her ears. What had he seen? What was he offering? She thought of his mouth on hers, a welcome hand between her thighs. "What?"

"There are tricks. A wash of rose madder on the cheeks, a pinwheel of gold in the eye."

She flushed deeply at her mistake, so deeply that for an instant the world blurred.

He saw her embarrassment, and guessed its source. "To that end, milady, I have but one aid, though it is extremely adaptable."

She closed her eyes, too embarrassed to look at him. "Aye?"

"To be honest, 'tis not my practice to share this with my sitters. It is far more potent, I think, if it happens without their notice, but you are a woman of the world. I assure you, it will work for you if you let it."

"What, sir? What?"

"I can help bring your lover to mind through judicious use of his, er, methods of seduction—only the most proper ones, of course."

"Meaning?"

"Meaning," he said shortly, "I can pour, I can praise, I can command. If I strike the note that brings him to mind, you will respond. Which path shall I follow?"

Jacket had charmed and cajoled, and when he hurt her feelings, he had charmed more. Cam would not waste a thought on that now. But the right words from Peter could turn what she wanted—what she had already begun—from a flame into a fire.

"*I* can pour," she said. "Command me."

For a moment he said nothing, then he nodded and stepped behind the easel. "Remove your gown."

Flames roared through her. She sat up, finished the rest of the wine and poured another. Then she loosened the silk and let it slide off the muslin.

He turned toward the canvas with a wry chuckle. "The muslin as well, please."

Sheer terror flooded every nerve. "I am not comfortable with that."

"You have contrived to put yourself on a painter's chaise in a remote studio. That is the natural outcome."

Her hands shook as she brushed one shoulder off and then the other. The fabric slipped to her waist.

"Madam—"

"No more. Please."

His eyes did a slow review. She felt adrift and more than a little frightened.

"Your breasts are generous. Offer them with generosity."

She pressed her shoulders back, wincing with vulnerability, and felt her nipples lift higher. She tried to master her breathing, but every nerve in her body was firing at once. She, Cam Stratford, who had never sunbathed topless, who had never skinny-dipped, who wouldn't even get in a hot tub alone with Jacket, had taken the plunge. She could feel both the heat of the fire and the cool of the evening on her skin, and she held herself still. It was thrilling to be exposed, and to pretend, even for a quarter hour, that she was always this bold.

"That's right," he said. "Now angle them toward me."

She wished he would take her in his arms. She wanted to feel him command her with his hands, not just his words.

"I do not think," she said with only a small crack in her voice, "this will be a painting for the dining hall."

"A private gallery, I should think. Though I would not put it past any man to let it fall into the sight of his acquaintances. How can they covet what they do not know exists?"

She imagined this painting hanging in Lely's private office, or tipped against the wall of one of his workshops, open to any curious eye, or in his bedroom where he could admire it while the real sitting took place across his lap. She wondered in how many rooms she could bring him pleasure.

"Your man is here. He stands over you. He is drunk, perhaps too drunk. Will he sleep or serve?"

"Serve," she said huskily.

"Offer. And make it clear. He is barely able to stand."

And there was Peter in her head, pulling at his boots, smelling of whiskey. He would need no encouragement. He would lower his breeks, scrabble at his shirttails and thrust his way inside her, making up in blunt determination what he lacked in elegance.

She settled back on the pillows and turned her body seductively toward this unseen lover. The muslin at her waist was slipping, and she lifted the knee nearest Peter to stop it.

The fabric, so thin it undoubtedly offered a fine view of hip and thigh, ruffled slightly in the draft from the windows, but it was all the coverage she had, and she would not let it go. She laid her right arm along the rise of her hip. It was a brazen pose, and she was still quaking, but she liked the glow that had sprung up in Peter's eyes.

He considered her from head to foot. "'Tis a very fine offer," he said at last. "Very fine indeed. Let him take it, shall we, while I begin."

He picked up his palette, and she closed her eyes.

The wine had loosened her scruples. She did not feel so frightened. She liked his eyes upon her and had a sudden overwhelming desire to make him ache. She very much liked his eyes upon her, but without the cover of the muslin she could not return to that gentle, inebriating rub against the arm of the chaise.

Her nipples peaked instantly at the memory, and the brushstrokes stopped. She smiled, though the ache she had hoped to cause him had been visited upon her, sharper even than before. She rubbed her legs together, like an evening cricket, but the pain only magnified. It beat hard, like a heart, hotter with each thump. She brought the heel of the folded leg closer . . . closer.

The throbbing pleasure of contact nearly made her cry out. Now if she could only lift herself against it, against his touch. She arched infinitesimally, and the charge went up her spine. She couldn't let him see this. Or could she?

Again she lifted and again. It was a slow undulation of her hips, that's all. The instinctive movement to some internal music. In her mind, though, her private Peter suckled those nipples, drawing them into an exquisite tightness, while his hand caressed her hip, her thigh and dipped easily into the space between her legs. Slowly, slowly he stroked her, stoking the fire.

Cam slitted her eyes. Peter gazed upon her, his attention undivided. What did he see? The bare-breasted fiancé of an unworthy painter or a woman openly disporting herself before a man she hardly knew. She willed him to see what she saw, to feel the primeval pounding of desire.

Her lids fluttered shut, and the Peter of her dream was there waiting. His hands were in her hair, plucking her pins loose and combing out her curls. He spread them over her breasts, rubbing the strands between his palms and the taut flesh. She turned to meet his lips.

"Beautiful," the painting Peter said, and so did the one lying next to her, just before his tongue met hers. With a shift of her thighs, she let his fullness come between them, prodding her throbbing bud gently. Ignoring her trembling, he brought his hand to join it, a perfect triumvirate—hand, mouth, cock.

At the easel, the painting Peter made a distracted noise. He retreated to the shelves, searching for something. When his back turned, she slid a finger under the muslin, hiding the motion behind her knee. Immediately the glow turned hot. And this was Peter's hand, obliging her, but he was growing rougher—oh, so rough—and his need bigger and bigger.

Her nipples tightened into ridged nubs of iron.

She pressed her legs together as hard as she could, lodging the roving fingers there like a cork. Oh, dare she? Dare she? Peter turned from the shelves, and she closed her eyes. She could feel the rhythmic shake of her breasts, the growing warmth in her hips and belly. Without warning, the blinding pleasure roared through her like a freight train. With prodigious effort, she clung to a semblance of rectitude, holding her legs and arm still and letting the heat that would have been dispelled with wild bucking set her body on fire.

Hhhhhhhhhh, she said in a long, desperate exhale.

With eyes shut tight, she cursed her foolishness. To have allowed him to bear witness to such an act now seemed wanton beyond description. Yet she regretted nothing at all she'd let the dream Peter do. If only she had not confused the dream world with the real.

She waited for the lighthearted aside or the suggestive comment, but none came.

When the rush of her blood quieted, she heard him at last.

He was painting.

*   *   *

Peter held his arm steady. He knew what he'd seen. He'd seen it often enough on the faces in his bed. He had asked her to think of her fiancé, and she had taken him at his word.

He wondered what it would be like to be the man who engendered such a look of desire. He wondered what it would be like to loosen that hair and let it slip through his fingers. He wondered at the fine fire of a woman that had such intoxicating heedlessness in her. But most of all he wondered why any painter, even the most brick-headed picket-post scrub, had not taken the opportunity to paint his lover, even once. Painting one's lover was the most exquisite act of lovemaking. Not just in the carnal sense, though it was that and more, but in the giving of love, the elevation of one's partner above all others.

It had hurt her, he knew, to admit this portrait was her first. He wished he had not made such an assumption, let alone voiced it, but now that he knew, it pleased him deeply that he would be the one to show her this joy.

Peter had painted Ursula many times. His favorite was a painting in which she appears four times, once unclothed and with her back to him as a classical goddess, once in the maternal guise of a Madonna, once as the rich wife of a painter, and finally, with her breasts bared and looking straight at him, as the woman who had turned his bed into an inferno of pleasure and his heart into a willing supplicant.

His eyes returned to the chaise and the woman, eyes closed, who lay there.

She wasn't Ursula. The carmine hair did not make her so, nor did the unfettered tongue, though he would be lying if he did not admit both captured his attention. No, this woman was unto herself. A proud, spirited woman, perhaps from a background like his, who had used her wits to insert herself into his diary, who had not hesitated to save his skin with the king, and who had now allowed him to witness her most private imaginings. It was a most provocative act—most provocative—and even if he could not be the man filling her head, to have witnessed the stripping bare of her desires was an aphrodisiac, in this case a very potent one.

He gazed at the tightly quilted flesh of her nipples, and his brush, once abstracted, stopped entirely. God, he ached with desire, something he had not felt in so long. If he weren't so pained, he would laugh at the comedy of it. Lustful at last, but for a woman who could never be his.

He tried to turn his mind to the painting, even going so far as to consciously draw the sable down the canvas, but he could not.

He wanted to take those wild summer berries in his mouth and hear the noise she'd make, and suckle those glistening fingers to taste the melon there. He wondered if that hair would wrap like silk around his fingers, if he could draw a ringlet across that peaked, pinched flesh.

The last vision flooded his head, and he was overcome. He couldn't stop himself. He would command what he saw for his painting even if he could not command it for his bed.

Her eyes flew open as he drew near. Was she fearful?

Modest? He no longer cared. If her fiancé could provoke so much wanton desire in a woman, he would have no objection to enjoying her exactly as Peter wanted to portray her. He pulled a pin from the mass of curls, and she gasped, which made the ache in his belly redouble. He caught the tendrils as they dropped and fanned them over her skin, cinnamon on porcelain, and where the ringlet caught her nipple, cinnamon on cinnamon. It was all he could do to keep from taking that silk-wrapped flesh and teasing it until she opened her legs to him.

But he held himself in check. Slowly the burn receded, replaced by a tingling in his fingers. Now that he had her exactly as he'd imagined her, he wanted to paint.

He took a deep breath, stepped to the easel and realized that for the first time in years Ursula was miles from his thoughts.

18

Cam watched him work. The sun had set, and she knew there was not enough light to work, yet he continued. She could tell by the way his eyes shone when he peered over the top of the canvas that he liked her. He had watched her, and he had remained at his easel. Apparently he was not given to impulse when the impulse was to serve himself. He was the rarest of men: one she could trust.

Which is not to say that if he had taken her in his arms and carried her off to that seducing couch on the other side of the fire she would have protested. No, she would have welcomed it and enjoyed every moment. But the fact that he had not taken advantage of her in her recent improvidence—when he clearly could have—meant he was willing to respect the fact she was involved with someone else, or as she preferred to think, he would court her until he'd driven the thought of her fiancé out of her head. Either way, it suggested he was an honorable man who put their relationship above his desire. It was surprising and attractive.

His brush worked the canvas, still sending sparks to her fingers and toes. She had to admit she enjoyed posing for him, even now, after the foolish escapade, and as unrealistic as it might be, she found herself imagining an endless series of afternoons, nestled among these pillows as he painted, telling her she was beautiful.

"It's growing cooler," he said. "Are you all right?"

"Aye. Thank you. The wine, you know . . ." She lifted a finger toward the glass.

"Indeed." He smiled. "At some point it might be easier if you told me your name."

She stirred, flustered. "Cam."

"Cam," he repeated, nodding his approval. "As in the *Aeneid*?"

"The *Aeneid*?"

"Cam, well, Camilla, fought the Trojans. Though she was a mortal, Virgil described her as having mythical powers. She was so fast, she could run across the sea without getting her feet wet. It was as if she could be in two places at the same time."

Cam thought of her office and that Amazon screen. She hoped she could get to that phone soon.

"Does he live in England, your fiancé?"

She did not want to think about her would-be fiancé. It seemed intrusive in this interlude she was sharing with Peter, and she shifted guiltily. "If you don't mind, I would prefer not to talk of him. It feels strange. Until we've finished here, you understand?"

He bowed.

"It's only that we have not had an easy time of it," she added.

"Is that so?"

"He has not exactly proven himself to be faithful and true."

He shook his head. "Men change."

"Aye. They can. I think it's better, though—safer—when they are born faithful."

"Safer?" He scoffed with a smile. "Who wants that?"

She watched the way he approached the canvas. It was confident, precise, controlled—very different from the disorganized chaos of Jacket. But it was also guarded. She wondered if Ursula had departed because Peter withheld a part of himself from her. Had he known the breakup was coming or had he been blindsided, just as Cam had been?

"Did you paint Ursula?"

He stilled. "Who mentioned Ursula?"

"Nell. She said I resemble her."

She saw the muscles in his cheek contract. "You do, in truth. The hair and . . ." He made a vague gesture that seemed to encompass most of the features above her shoulders and cleared his throat.

More footsteps on the stairs and Peter yelled, "Dammit, Tom, I said— Oh!" He dropped into a formal bow.

Cam covered herself, but it was too late. The king's eyes, as well as Stephen's, had raked her. Stephen's gaze dropped instantly, ears reddening. The king's lingered considerably longer. Cam jumped to her feet and grabbed the dressing gown before curtsying.

Peter, who looked horrified at the intrusion, said, "Your Majesty. What a great surprise."

"Aye. I see that." Charles nodded at Cam. "Good evening, Countess. 'Tis a pleasure once more. I wanted to thank you for the masquerade earlier. It was most helpful."

Cam resummoned her inner Penélope Cruz. "'Twas nothing."

Charles looked around the room. "Peter, is this your private studio? I have never seen it."

"'Tis the quietest."

"Quiet being an uncommon virtue. I should like to have a word."

Stephen, who looked pained to have been part of this interruption, said, "His Majesty said it was quite urgent."

Cam understood her removal was being requested. "I could—"

"No. Stay," Peter said. "There is a painting I wish to show His Majesty downstairs, in any case. Though it is nearly six, I do believe the light will still do for viewing."

Charles nodded and began down the stairs, followed by Stephen.

Peter gave her a deep bow. "Until I return."

19

Mertons watched Stephen bustle into the larder and begin to gather glasses, with the cook, a full-bosomed Scot with raven hair and sparkling eyes named Morag, directly on his heels. Mertons, who had been rerunning the calculations this last hour, trying to narrow the window of time in which the writer might arrive, found the spare amenities of the Restoration period charming—like camping for time-jump accountants. He clutched his ale with a happy smile.

"How many times can we expect Himself in a day?" Morag said with a huff of outrage. "I barely got my floors swept from the last visit. Does the king have nothing better to do? Not that one, you great gowk!" She waved Stephen away from an intricately carved decanter. "That's for special guests."

"He is the king, madam," Stephen said.

"Your king. We Scots have set our sights a wee bit higher, thank 'e. He may have that one," she said, pointing to a far simpler vessel, "and the second-best brandy."

Mertons dabbed the corner of his mouth with his fist. "Did Peter finish with that last sitter, then?"

"Finish with her?!" The cook's eyes darted worriedly to Stephen's.

"Well, I hope not, though the king could not have arrived at a worse moment. They had clearly, er, come to some sort of understanding."

Mertons's gaze went from Stephen's private smile to the hand Morag now flung over her heart. He had made no calculation for a love affair, though if this was a continuation of something from the past it would be of little consequence. "Is the woman Peter's mistress?"

"Mistress?!" Stephen laughed. "I can barely get your cousin to converse with a woman, much less"—he stopped, evidently remembering Morag—"court her. The man is a monk. Has been, ever since Ursula's death."

Ursula? Who was Ursula?

Stephen lifted the salver and headed toward the hall. "Say a prayer the king's visit is short."

"The cheese has turned," called Morag. "Start him on that."

Mertons tapped a finger. How had the intelligence failed to include any mention of Peter's wife? Such an oversight undermined an operative's performance and added significant risk to the plan. The Executive Guild must have known, had to have known. They had probably been too concerned with stopping the tube hole to worry about an operative issue. The specifics of travelcraft were hardly their long suit. It certainly explained Peter's dourness this past week, and it might also explain his disappearance this afternoon. He might have gone to her grave, for example, or another place important in their relationship—and neither of those were within spec, of that much Mertons was certain. Neither, of course, was a new love affair, though the log did show Peter holding weekly sittings with a number of women, and who knew what went on in those private rooms. It wasn't as if the log was that specific. Nonetheless both the wife and lover were of considerable concern to him, especially if the lover were not from his old life. Romantic intrigue was one of the hardest factors to forecast in time science. It emerged spontaneously, even in the most controlled environments. It could swamp a smoothly running calculation in a matter of seconds, and it left anywhere from a 3 to 19 percent wobble in even the most airtight forecast.

Which only corroborated what he knew from his own experience, since he'd dropped like a ton of time-tube liners when he'd met dearest Joan, and what a trial by fire that had been.

"This woman upstairs," he said to Morag. "Is she a new client?"

"So I'm to understand. I haven't seen her, though Stephen says she's the saint's own image of Ursula."

Mertons had to smile. He himself had a soft spot for a fine ankle, and he understood what it meant to follow type, even against reason. "It would be a good diversion for him, I suppose."

"Oh, aye. A man needs a woman's touch. Though I could have wished her an Englishwoman."

Mertons felt a disconcerting twinge. "Oh?"

"Aye. Stephen says she has the oddest accent."

Oddest accent?

Stephen heaved himself to his feet. It wouldn't hurt to give this new woman a recheck.

Cam grabbed her purse and flew to the stairs.

She didn't know where Peter and the king were heading, but when she heard their footsteps fading in one direction, she padded down the hall in the other. Past the staircase, past Mercury and down into the models' room, which—yes!—Peter had left unlocked.

She closed the door behind her and ran to the windows. She pulled out her magnificent, butler-in-a-pocket iPhone and called up the screen.

"NO SERVICE."

Her heart fell.

"How do you intend to paint her?"

"Pardon?" Peter rolled down his sleeves, still lost in the heady reverie of the sitting. He felt as if he had been transported to the moon and back. With a silent sigh, he brought a hand to his nose and drank deeply of the scent of her hair. A hairpin was tucked safely in his pocket.

"The Spanish countess," Charles said. "Will it be mythological?"

"Mythological" was the king's term for unclothed. The king's question cleared the fog from Peter's head like an icy wind. "'Tis a portrait," Peter said coolly. "For her fiancé."

The king's eyebrow lifted, and Peter saw his gaze travel to the gray silk dress hung carefully from a hook on the wall.

"I know the king's time is valuable," Peter said, "and Stephen says your need is urgent. How may I serve you?"

"'Tis about the paper you asked me to sign today."

"My solicitor assures me it is a mere matter of your official stamp, and the marriage will be entered upon the record."

"And the fact that Ursula is dead and buried is not a deterrent?"

"According to the law, if you make it so, the marriage will be as if it had existed from the first. It is entirely legal, I assure you."

"So with a scratch of the quill I make you a widower without your having ever been a groom."

"Aye."

"Peter, I don't know—"

"Your Majesty was most generous to offer to do this for me. As I have explained, it is a wish I hold most dear."

"It will not bring her back, you know, my friend."

"No . . . but it might let her rest in peace." And me, he might have added.

The king clasped his hands behind his back and gazed out the window into the street below. "Peter, I should very much like to borrow the countess for the evening."

Peter felt ice chill his bowels. "She is not mine for the lending. And there is the matter of the fiancé."

The king smiled. "'Tis a minor matter. And you will explain to her the benefits of befriending the English king. Why, if she actually happens to be Spanish, she'd be looked upon as a national hero."

Peter's vision darkened. "You are kind to offer your friendship, but this woman will decline it, I fear."

"My advisors tell me that this writ you wish me to sign, it is an unusual matter. There is the potential for embarrassment to the crown, the king gratifying the request of a friend."

Peter thought of the endless series of grants and titles Charles made, and his bile rose. Charles had granted his lovers duchies. He had made their sons dukes.

"What I'm saying, Peter, is that I should feel far more accommodating after a relaxing evening with the countess."

"It will not be possible," he said through gritted teeth. "Not with this woman."

The king swiveled, the cunning on his face replaced by joyful surprise. "Peter, my dear fellow! Have you yourself fallen?"

Peter's face grew hot. Charles had seen him in his darkest despair and had used every resource at his command to divert Peter after he'd emerged, lifeless and wan, from his bed after Ursula's death. But despite an offer to make any sort of eligible or even ineligible match, Charles had never been able to convince Peter to bury his sorrow in another woman. "I-I—"

"I should never stand between you and such an opportunity, my friend, even if it means dashing my own hopes on the rocks, and I might fairly add that you are the only man for whom that could be said. Do you intend to claim her?"

The king regarded him closely, an uncomfortable mixture of regard and titillation on his face.

Peter swallowed his disgust at having to reveal so personal a feeling. "Aye."

"Excellent. A fine catch. I have only one request, then."

"What?" Peter had had his fill of the king today.

"I should like a painting of her."

A dark tide swept over Peter. "Your Majesty?"

"Venus, perhaps. Or Athena."

Peter's violent opposition to this suggestion must have been evident on his face.

"I am the king, aye? You acknowledge my supreme authority over you, her and every other soul on this island, do you not?"

Peter gurgled an affirmative.

"I want a painting of her for my collection—my private collection. Once you have bedded her, 'twill be no hard rub to get her to pose. Tell her it is how you should like to remember her. Tell her she will make a sublime Athena with that hair streaming down—and she would, you know, you must admit it."

Peter could make no reply. It took every ounce of fortitude he possessed to keep from launching his fist into the king's nose.

"Do you not see her as Athena?"

"I believe her time in London is quite short. We would not have time."

Charles paced to the window and gazed upon his subjects hurrying through Covent Garden. "The writ makes me uneasy," he said after a pause. "I am not certain I will be able to overcome my objections."

Peter felt a sickening lump in his gut. He saw that headstone in St. Paul's yard. He knew what he owed Ursula. It was the only reason he'd agreed to return to this place. He also knew what he owed Camilla. But he had no choice. Peter forced himself to lower his chin in a poor substitute for submission.

Stephen returned with a salver overflowing with brandy, cheese and cakes, but the king waved it off. Stephen placed it on the table and, after a word from the king, went to alert the footmen of His Majesty's momentary approach. When they were alone, the king, evidently sensing the hint of insubordination in his friend, added as he passed, "Deliver her, Peter. One way or another."

When the king's footsteps receded into the street, Peter picked up the decanter and hurled it against the wall.

"No service?" This had been her only potential lifeline. Her eyes began to sting. She was sunk. She'd only meant to buy a book, and now she was cut off from her friends and loved ones forever. Here, she had one friend and no home. When Peter put his paints away, she would have nowhere to go, nothing to eat, no way to earn money. It had begun as an adventure—and had turned into an exhilarating one—but now she wanted to go home, or at least know she could go home when she wanted.

Something flickered at the corner of her eye.

It was a bar! A bar appeared on the phone! Bless you, AT&T! She thrust the phone higher and the bar disappeared. Didn't matter, she thought. When there's one bar, there's always another. Why, one time she'd scrabbled down three rows and across seven chairs at the local cineplex to find out how Jeanne's text stream ending with ". . . so embarrassed, but my partner, whom I'd never met before, said not to worry, he could come in spades" began, only to find Jeanne had been recruited into an impromptu bridge tournament at her great-aunt's house.

Cam held the phone high. No joy, and no matter how close she got to the windows, the bar would flicker and disappear. She pressed. One of the windows moved. It wasn't just built right into the wall. Up, down, up, down, she looked, then spotted it. A lever to open the last window. She pulled it and the window cracked open. Then it was simply a matter of pushing it a little harder . . .

Ta-da!

She shoved the phone as far outside as she could reach, peering at it through the odd, wavy glass. Still nothing. Then suddenly one bar, then two.

Peter felt rather than saw Stephen behind him, gazing at the burgundy-stained wall, and Peter was in no mood for questions.

"Sir?"

"One more interruption tonight and 'twill be your job." He strode out, leaving Stephen openmouthed.

He had no intention, of course, of providing Camilla in any form to the king. Even the thought of painting her head on one of his model's bodies made him angrier than he thought possible, though if push came to shove he would have to do it.

She was achingly beautiful, of that there was no debate.

And he had seen the fire that ran in those veins. He found himself quite lost in the picture of her, as canty as a jade, lying before him, her breasts shifting with each movement—

He took the stairs two at a time.

She might not be his, but for the next glorious hour it would be as if she were.

She was gone.

"Camilla?"

Silence.

He hurried to the other side of the fireplace. The space was empty.

"Great," Cam said. "My hand has two bars' worth of phone reception, but my mouth is in no-man's-land." She pulled the phone in, and pushed the window again. It probably hadn't been opened since the last time Isaac Newton visited.

It creaked and groaned, but at last gave way, enough way for Cam to thread her shoulder out and, with a little more effort, one of her breasts. "Sorry," she said. "I know I've put you through a lot today."

The window was on the second floor—a tall second floor—and Cam got her first view of the world beyond the studio. Dozens of people in period dress—well, contemporary dress to them, she supposed—filled the street. There were couples laughing, a group of young men shoving and talking, an obviously drunk woman retching on her shoes and four or five dogs fighting over a scrap of food—in short, just like a late-night stroll down Craig Street in Pittsburgh.

She held up her phone and with three proud bars showing dialed Jeanne's cell.

"Holy Christ!" Jeanne screamed. "Where are you?"

"You're kinda not going to believe this."

"You freakin' blew out of here like Dorothy from Kansas. There's orange Crush everywhere."

"Calm down. I'm okay. Well, relatively." Cam thought she heard a noise at the door and looked over her shoulder, but the noise stopped.

"Where are you?" Jeanne repeated.

"Okay, remember how I told you I was looking for a book on Amazon?"

"Omigod! You're starting this story with book shopping on Amazon!"

"Jeanne, I found a book I needed there. I started to search inside. When I clicked 'Surprise Me!'—*poof!* I disappeared."

"But where are you?"

"In the sixteen hundreds."

"In the sixteen hundreds where?"

"In the sixteen hundreds of the sixteen hundreds. Sixteen hundred. One-six-oh-oh. The century. You know, Shakespeare, Galileo, the Great London Fire— Oops." Cam wheeled around to check the candles in the room.

"You're telling me you're in a different century."

"Yes."

"I ain't buying it. You're hiding somewhere. Can you see me on the phone?"

"Jeanne, really. I'm here. It's London, sometime in the reign of Charles the Second."

"Send me a picture."

"I can."

"I know you can. You do it all the time. I even got to share your joy when your Snuggie blanket arrived. Send one."

"What are you, from Missouri? You could just try to believe me."

"Two words: *pic ture.*"

Muttering, Cam clicked on the camera and stretched her arm as far out as she could. "Can you still hear me? I'm taking the picture."

"Goody," came the faint reply.

She angled the camera so the armor chest plate and stuffed boar were directly behind her. The sun had dipped below the horizon, but there was still light in the sky.

Click.

"Did you hear that?" She pulled the camera in and thumbed in Jeanne's email. "It's coming."

Whoosh. The picture went.

"Hang on," Jeanne said, and Cam heard the keyboard clicks. "Got it. Jesus. Are those cutouts for *breasts*?"

Cam turned to look at the armor breastplate. "Yes."

"You're not in the sixteen hundreds. You're at the GLBT Affinity Group's Lascivious Costume Ball."

"Jeanne, it's like nirvana for a researcher," Cam said excitedly. "The studio was filled with nude models when I landed. Peter spends half his time hiding the king's mistresses from one another. Nell Gwyn thinks I have an excellent eye for gowns. And I'm pretty sure I've figured out how the old breast-out-of-dress thing happens."

"Now I know you're lying."

"Jeanne."

"Gimme a break, huh. You're asking me to believe you're hanging around with, like, Marie Antoinette."

"She was a French queen and a hundred years later, but I see your point. Nonetheless how else are you going to explain the orange Crush?"

There was a long pause. "I'll give you a temporary pass. Very temporary."

"Thank you. I feel better knowing someone believes this."

"Peter Lely, huh?"

"Yes, and he's amazing. You'd think he'd be such a narcissist—I mean, you know how painters are—but he's really so sweet, like this closet good guy. And he's cute, with these eyes the color of . . ." She groped the air, searching for the right words. ". . . Kit-Kat bars. And he's got this sort of *Karate Kid/Crouching Tiger, Hidden Dragon* thing going on the way he can just look across the room and make magic happen. And don't even ask about the way he moves when he paints. Oh my God. You can tell by the way he runs the place that he can do absolutely anything."

"Jeez, you must have gotten a ton of stuff on Van Dyck."

Cam clapped her hand over her mouth. She'd totally forgotten Van Dyck.

"No," Jeanne said in disbelief. "You are *not* going to tell me you've been in the sixteen hundreds for an hour and didn't ask anything about Van Dyck."

"I-I—" Cam wracked her memory. Had she heard *anything* on Van Dyck? "He might have had a relative who managed a theater."

"Wow, that's gonna bust the art biography world wide

open. What about dirt? And what are you doing in that getup?"

Cam looked down, confused, then remembered Jeanne had the picture. She clutched the gown tighter.

"Ah . . . there was an accident."

"Mustard?"

"Funny. No. A too-many-mistresses-at-once accident. Nell Gwyn, the one I mentioned? She's one of them—the good one. There was a bit of a kerfuffle with the other one—a real bitch of a duchess. But anyhow, she—Nell, I mean—really admired my dress—long story, but we had to switch."

"I see. Then the olive gown in your picture is Nell's?"

Cam thought of Nell's robin's-egg blue dressing gown upstairs on the floor near the fire. "Well, no. Not exactly."

There was a short pause in which she could feel the wheels turning in Jeanne's head.

"Really?"

Cam yelled, "Wait!" but it was too late. She heard the sound of the phone drop.

Oh, I'm toast.

"Well, well, well," Jeanne said. "Here I am on page twelve of that lovely exhibition book and what do I see? An olive gown with ruffled sleeves. You're posing for him!"

"What? No. Me?"

"You're posing for him, don't lie."

"I-I—"

"Tell me," Jeanne said, "that breast was not exposed."

Cam bit back a smile. "I, uh, can't actually."

Jeanne whooped so loud, Cam had to pull the phone from her ear.

"You didn't!" she screamed.

"I did! I did!"

"Verbal high five! So how did he get you to do it?"

"What?"

"The breast. What was the secret? Magic? Hypnosis? Some sort of Restoration era date-rape drug?"

Cam considered her answer.

"Oh God," Jeanne said. "He didn't actually drug you, did he?"

"Well, no, it wasn't like that."

"What was it like?"

Cam shifted. "Well, he did offer me a glass of wine."

"We're going to have to file charges. I hope you kept the glass."

Cam laughed. "It was pretty strong wine."

"The rogue. And then I suppose he made some sort of offhanded comment like 'So how do you want to pose?' And the next thing you knew you were clawing your gown open. I mean, what's a girl to do?"

"Wow, it's like you were there."

"Cam."

Cam looked at her bare toes, smiling. "I don't know. You'd have to meet him. I just wanted to do it."

"Well, I guess that's better than 'He saved me from genital herpes,' which is how you hooked up with Jacket."

"I didn't 'hook up' with Peter," Cam said, "or Jacket, for that matter. My God, I'm practically a journalist. I was just doing, uh, a little first-person research."

"On Van Dyck."

Cam felt her ears redden. "Ha-ha. So how do we get me back?"

"Maybe you should ask Peter. He clearly knew how to get you front."

"You're hilarious."

"Thank you. Well, it seems pretty straightforward to me."

"Really?"

"Sure. I mean, if you got there with 'Surprise Me!' why wouldn't it work going in the other direction?"

"Omigod, Jeanne, you're amazing! Why didn't I think of that?"

"Mrs. Post?"

Cam jerked back into the room. Mertons was standing at the door with a look of confusion on his face. She swung the phone behind her gown, but had it been too late?

"What are you doing here?" His eyes narrowed. "To whom were you talking?"

"Myself."

"What are you doing in this room?"

Cam could feel Jeanne squawking into her hip. "I was looking for the privy."

"Wedged out the window?"

"Sometimes they're in the oddest places."

Mertons looked at her as if he were trying to tease out a puzzle. All he needed was a magnifying glass and one of those Sherlock Holmes hats with the earflaps. She prepared for a run.

"There you are." Peter appeared in the doorway. "I thought I'd lost you."

"I was looking for the privy."

Peter bit back a smile. "I hope you've satisfied your curiosity here, then."

"Thank you. Yes." *Men.* She gathered her purse and slipped the phone in her pocket in one smooth move. "Would either of you be willing to redirect me?"

Peter coughed. "Certainly."

"Peter," Mertons said. "Might I have a word?"

"Aye. Just one. No."

"But, Peter, there are certain oddities—"

"Mertons, I know we have a shared appointment. But as far as I can tell, the sitter we so anxiously anticipate has not arrived. Am I correct?"

"Well, aye, but—"

Peter took Cam's arm and began to pull her out of the room. "Then I think you might do well to concentrate on your brushwork. I'm afraid Stephen has commented on your lack of practice. Twelve hours a day, my friend. That's what makes a painter. Familial connection can only carry you so far."

Cam frowned. Bald-headed Mertons was related to Peter?

20

As Peter fiddled with the paints, waiting for her return from the privy, he found himself almost nervous. "Good God, man," he muttered, smiling, "you can't even hold a brush."

He heard her footfall on the stair and watched as those beautiful blue eyes found him.

"You're back," he said.

"Indeed."

He couldn't help but remember a time before Ursula, when the measure of a good time had been guiding whatever lady-in-waiting had met his eye that evening to the closest private wall, where he would loosen her gown, hook her leg over his arm and plow her until she cried, dry mouthed, for more. Ursula had taught him the value of soft bedding and long-drawn-out afternoons, but looking into Camilla's eyes now, the thought of those rough walls and incandescent joinings seemed very, very appealing.

Did she see his longing, feel him stripping her with his eyes? He hoped not.

He dropped his gaze. "I do apologize for the king's intrusion."

"'Twas nothing. Really." She darted to the chaise and dropped her bag before returning to his side, a tentative smile on her face. "I take it he requires a lot of attention."

Peter laughed. "Aye, like an underdisciplined child with the army of Hannibal at his command."

"Not a promising combination?"

"No. He is a most demanding patron."

That ringlet still hung loose. His fingers burned as he remembered pulling the pin. She caught him gazing at the tendril and tucked it over her shoulder self-consciously. He wanted her—in every way a man can want a woman. He had been moved at the beginning by her resemblance to Ursula, but now his desire had many sources—her courage, her wit, her wild, untamed spirit. There wasn't a woman in a hundred who would have inserted herself into Nell's spot to save him, and there wasn't a woman in a thousand who would have bared her desires before him the way she had.

He said, "Shall we rest a bit before I begin painting again?"

"Yes. That would be good."

"Perhaps something warm to eat or a—"

"Is this yours?"

She had stopped in front of an unfinished canvas. It was of little Jane, the daughter of Viscount Harrison. The day had been warm, and the girl, no more than ten, had found the long period of enforced stillness difficult. He had said he would allow her to move the rest of her body if she would keep her hand still. She agreed readily, and he placed a peach in it. Jane's image, therefore, was barely started, though the hand and especially the thick impasto of fruit and its green-brown leaf represented a nearly finished passage.

"Aye. I do not normally start on the hand"—he flushed again, thinking of how the movement of Camilla's hand had drawn his eye earlier—"but it helped the girl sit still."

"And me. How do you do this, the shade just under the leaf? My God, it's as if an actual leaf sits there. I can see the sides."

He chuckled. "'Tis nothing. A trick my teacher taught me. Only a bit of incising." When her brows knitted he added, "Come. Let me show you. 'Tis easier than explaining." He reached for the palette and offered it to her. "You said you paint, aye?"

"Oh no. I couldn't."

"Of course you might."

He guided the wood over her thumb, ignoring the flicker of heat, and handed her a brush. "Start with the ochre and a bit of the black." He watched as she mixed the paint, diffidently then with greater assurance.

"That's right," he said, "only a touch. Now, I want you to let go and just guide the brush as if the painting were yours and the leaf a mere impediment to your objective."

"My objective?"

"Aye. You have to keep your objective in mind."

Cam's objective was growing unclear, even to her. What she should be doing is asking him all the Van Dyck questions she could think of, as quickly as possible, then buying a one-way "Surprise Me!" ticket straight back to Pittsburgh, assuming she could ever sneak past Peter's nosy relative. But a part of her just wanted to be with Peter and enjoy the fine night.

She could feel him willing her to try her hand at painting. He had no idea that she'd once fancied herself a painter, nor how long it had been since she'd worked upon a canvas with anything more than halfhearted interest. The small still life on her desk didn't count.

"Where?" she asked. "Where do you want me to paint?"

"There. You shall add a second leaf."

"What? No! Large or small?"

"Your choice. The canvas is yours, milady." He bowed.

She gazed at the stem he had begun and was surprised to see the new leaf form clearly in her head.

"Layer it on like silk," he said, "with just as much texture. This is the underlayer, you see, the part that will be hidden."

She drew the brush along the canvas, letting the bristles flip upward. It left a perfect leaf shape on the blue background.

He cocked his head and, after an instant, nodded his approval. She smiled. She'd been damned good at this once.

"Now," he said, handing her a thicker brush, "the verdigris."

"Shouldn't we let it dry?"

"We should," he said. "But I would not sacrifice this

moment of teaching to the perfection of the viscount's painting. He has an unskilled eye, and if he does not care for the paint cracking on this glorious leaf in twenty years' time, he may rot."

She laughed. The verdigris was thicker than the other colors, like a small blob of Jell-O on the palette. She pushed it left and right, automatically feathering in a daub of yellow.

Peter's brow went up.

She considered an addition of blue.

"I might try the red madder," he said.

She looked at the red, but the resultant gray-brown would deaden her green. She flicked the tip through the blue.

She could feel the corner of his mouth rise. "The student rebels."

"I am no man's thrall," she said, and the look that followed sent a pleasurable shiver down her back.

"Now for the shadow you admired so fervently," he said. "Turn your brush."

Uncertain, she flipped the sable from left to right.

"The other way," he instructed, then gently slid the brush from her hand and returned it with the wooden point down.

"You use the other end?"

He picked up a clean brush from the shelf, as thick and wide as the one she used for her facial powder. "A brush has many uses. A good artist does not limit himself to just one. Take the point and draw it along the left there, flipping the edge of the verdigris up as you go. Go on. Do not hesitate. Exactly! You see, you have not only exposed a trace of the yellow below, but created a tiny hillock of verdigris as well."

The suggestion of contour made the image leap from the canvas. "Amazing!"

"Just a trick. There are dozens and dozens. I could teach you all of them if you had time."

If you had time. The offer warmed her heart, but more than that, it unleashed a longing for artistic connection in her that she'd had no idea existed.

"I wish I did," she said truthfully. "I cannot stay much longer."

"Of course. Tonight of all nights. I don't wonder you have an obligation. But you will return? Tomorrow, aye? Then every Wednesday? Say three o'clock? You would be my last sitter of the day."

"Wednesdays, huh?"

"You smile. Why?"

"I don't know. Wednesdays always seem to be the day for weekly meetings."

"Liaisons, you mean?"

"Yes, actually." She giggled. "Especially the afternoons."

"Is that an aye, then?"

The guileless look of hope on his face sent her back almost to her teen years. She would be courted. First, out of her gown for the painting, then, after many long weeks of laughter and wine, out of the chaise and into his bed. His reward for winning her trust. She wondered what it would be like for a man to seek her heart first, not her body—to be slowly won, not claimed. She was a castle, and Peter was willing to lay patient siege to her.

"Aye," she said softly. "I should like that very much."

"How much time do you have?"

"A bit. Why?"

"I'm glad. I think we have two choices, then—"

A boom sounded in the distant night.

"What's that?" She looked out the windows.

He smiled in surprise. "Do you not know?"

When she shook her head, he took her hand, fetching his coat from a hook on the wall. "Come. This is one of the choices."

Mertons collapsed on a chair in the scullery. The woman was odd. There was no doubt about it. Was it possible she was an ally of Campbell's? The calculations had not shown the presence of a second conspirator. And yet . . .

Morag brushed by. He saw a smidgen of ankle as she stepped onto the hearth to reach a high-hung pot.

"Morag," he said, hoping the movement as she turned might provide another flash, "are you aware of Mrs. Post's origins at all? Was she recommended by another patron? Have you ever seen her in Peter's studio before?"

"First, Mr. Mertons, 'Mrs. Post' is not her name."

"Not her name?"

"No. 'Tis *Miss* Post. Miss Eugenie Campbell Stratford Post. See the note from Miss Gwyn there." She picked it up and read. " 'Attached is a sketch done by Francis Conley at Peter Lely's studio. It is of a dress owned by Miss Eugenie Campbell Stratford Post. I should like it duplicated in a charcoal moiré. Please note the lining.' I am to have it delivered to her tailor on Half Moon Street in the morn—"

Campbell! He snatched it from her hand, horrified.

"Mr. *Mertons*!"

"My apologies." He ran.

At the first turn, he came face-to-face with Stephen and two large apprentices. Stephen carried a salver filled with cheese and broken glass.

"Is he upstairs?" Mertons demanded.

"Peter, do you mean?"

"Aye, of course. I need to speak to him."

"Impossible."

Mertons snorted. "It's urgent. Is he upstairs?"

When Stephen failed to reply, Mertons turned to find out for himself, only to find his egress halted.

"Take your hand from my sleeve, sir," Mertons said sharply.

"The master is not to be disturbed."

The apprentices, approximately the size and tensile strength of marble columns, spread to fill the hall.

"This is a matter of extreme urgency."

"If it don't involve blood, it can wait until morning. In fact, even if it do involve blood, it can wait until morning." And when Mertons attempted to shake the hand loose, Stephen added, "Do not make it involve blood, sir."

The apprentices stepped forward.

"You'll regret this," Mertons said.

"Please usher the master's cousin to his room in the cellar. See that he rests there until morning."

*　　*　　*

Peter's hand was warm and dry, and her own felt like a child's within it. He opened the double doors and led her to a small balcony. The sun was gone, replaced by a blue-gray black, and a field of stars adorned the sky. The balcony stood high above the street, and they had a clear view across the roofs of the city. The vastness of such a vista, as always, sent a pang of awe through her. She loved the way the southern hills of Pittsburgh looked from the windows of her loft—there was something about the way the sky enveloped you when you had the long view that really took your breath away—but this was even more spectacular: squat chimneys, unknown spires, glimpses of cobbled streets abuzz with Londoners and, on a far hill, even a windmill silhouetted black against the sky.

"Oh *my*."

He smiled, slipping his coat back over her shoulders. "I know. I love the feeling of gazing over the city. It's as if one has been transported from one's problems."

"You have problems? Well, the king, I suppose. But I should think there are many rewards to being the royal portraitist as well."

"There are. Look around. The house, the staff, the line of patrons. I am very grateful." But his hand went to his ring, and there was something in his voice that didn't quite ring true.

She was torn. She was tempted to pursue a line of questioning related to this ambivalence, but she knew she had a job here.

"I, uh, know there's a lot of rivalry in the art world. You must have dozens of unpleasant stories of other painters trying to insinuate themselves with the king to take your place. I mean, how did you come into the position yourself?"

He laughed. "I hope, milady, I am not reading an implication of misconduct into your question."

She flushed. "No, of course I did not mean you. Still, the story of how you got your start would be most interesting."

"Well, of course, the position had been Van Dyck's for many years. I was a great admirer of Van Dyck. He has certainly had a profound influence on my work. And you are right about rivalry. I do not think he cared o'ermuch for me, and he would certainly not have considered me an equal, with me being half his age and he being a man of preternaturally large pride."

"So rare to find that in an artist." This was exactly what she needed.

He smiled.

"And . . . ?" she prompted.

"And I suppose I find myself in his shoes now. His age. Past the peak of my career. And yet I find myself far less eager than Van Dyck to cling to what I have."

There it was again. That note of sorrow. She had the next Van Dyck question on the tip of her tongue, and a dozen more after that, but somehow the woman in her was more curious than the writer.

"You have problems? I mean, apart from the king?"

An uncomfortable quiet came over him. She waited, wondering if he'd say more. He lifted his chin, as if to reply, but he must have changed his mind, for all he said was "Come."

He led her to the edge of the balcony, and she took a place along the wide, low balustrade by his side. He splayed his fingers on the marble, elbows straight, abstracted. She held her tongue, waiting for him.

"There," he said.

She turned. In the distance, toward the river, tiny streamers of white fire rained down on the river, illuminating for an instant the decks and yardarms of several tall-masted ships. Muffled cheers from a crowd rose over the night.

"Fireworks!" she cried.

"The usual for Guy Fawkes, I should think."

The Guy Fawkes celebration in England was akin to Halloween, she knew, and had something to do with the defeat of a plot to blow up Parliament, though her knowledge of English history was more than a little hazy, and she had not been aware the holiday had been celebrated as early as the seventeenth century.

"It's still a bit early. Another quarter of an hour will see the start of something more organized. I take it you're meeting someone?"

Meeting someone? Then it dawned on her. He thought she had a date for Guy Fawkes, which is why he had said "tonight of all nights" when she'd mentioned she couldn't stay much longer. "No, I . . . It is something else. But surely you had an engagement?"

He smiled. "No, I am practically chained to the studio."

Still he maintained his rigid grip on the railing. What haunted this man?

"Your ring is quite unusual."

His hands came up as if he'd been burned. He nearly tucked them under his arms, but at last he brought the ringed one forward with evident will. "It is my mark."

"In an emerald?" She could see the *P* and *L* etched backward in the surface.

"Not just an emerald. The Kingfisher of Istanbul."

"Oooooh," she said, impressed, for the only named jewelry she owned was a Joan Rivers bracelet from QVC. "Does it come with a curse?"

"It did for me."

She held her breath.

"I bought it six years ago, after a particularly large commission from the Duke of Silverbridge. Once I saw it in the jeweler's hand, it was the only thing I could think about. It cost a king's ransom, but to me it repre-sented reaching the height of my profession. The woman I loved—Ursula—laughed when I told her I planned to buy it. She thought I was making jest with her. When I told her why I wanted it, she told me that if I depended on the adulation of gemstones, I would never be fulfilled. We quarreled. I bought the emerald, had it engraved and we never spoke of it again. It wasn't until years later that it dawned on me I would have been far happier if I had given her the stone, and watched it blaze away the rest of our days on her finger."

Odd, Cam thought. *He has a ring that brings him pain, but he wears it, and I have a ring I love that I hide.*

"Were you together long?" she said.

"Ten years."

"That is a long time." *And a lot to regret. But the trick*

had to be letting go of the regret. Starting over. That's what Jacket wanted her to do. She'd been so angry for so long. She had to teach herself to cling to what she had, not what she'd lost.

"Why do you wear it?" she asked.

For a long moment he was silent. Another flash of spangling lights brightened the night sky, and a soft wind blew the hair around his shoulders. "I don't want to forget. I don't deserve to forget."

As he gazed at the ring, she watched his face: the pained eyes, the strong, determined mouth. "In my opinion," she said, "one of the hardest tasks for a human is to accept that what comes our way is a journey we need to take," she said. "If we err, we should not add unnecessarily to our burden. Failure is enough. Nor should we try to avoid the good things that come our way serendipitously, even when the reasons for them are unclear."

She thought of that book on Amazon and the amazing gift it had given her. She thought of Jacket, renewing his proposal. That was a good thing, right?

"Do you think all things which come our way serendipitously are good?" he asked.

"Not so much good as necessary, something we must act upon. But they can be very, very good. And it is our responsibility to find out how by working them through to their conclusion."

"My success," he said, "came very serendipitously."

"Oh?"

"Which is not to say I lacked talent, but talent, as you know, is quite different from success."

She did.

"Van Dyck—you know his work, aye?" He continued when she nodded. "I was not his pupil, yet it was impossible not to be influenced by him. He was one of the most famous artists of the time, and I traveled to Antwerp not once, but twice, to see him. He was already quite established as the portraitist to Charles's father here in London."

Cam tried not to move. This was exactly the information she needed.

"He looked at my work—I was exceedingly good—and gave me the usual encouragement. Well, it so happened Elizabeth of Bohemia was at his studio at the time, as were a number of her ladies-in-waiting. There was one—Giselle—" He caught himself. "But perhaps that is a story best left for another time, for it caused Van Dyck trouble he did not fairly deserve. In any case, Elizabeth had the opportunity to admire a painting of mine, and when Van Dyck died, she wrote to her brother recommending my work."

"And her brother was connected with the king?"

He laughed. "Her brother *was* the king. Charles the First. My original patron. The father of my far more troublesome one. But my point is, things came very easily to me—my talent, my position with the court, considerable wealth. I grew accustomed to this success, placing a value on it far beyond its worth and, worse, allowing myself to grow blind to the things I had that really did matter."

He twisted the ring absently, eyes focused on the dark night. He gave her a sidelong smile. "Regrets."

She touched his hand. "One must let failure be enough."

*   *   *

The touch rose up his arm and exploded in his chest, like one of the fiery bursts over the river, only this one seared his heart, like the touch of God upon Adam, and he wanted her. Every particle in his body strained toward her. But she was affianced, or nearly so, and in any case, her body was committed. He had seen it with his own eyes, the way she arched, her lover's hands upon her in her head.

The man, whoever he was, did not deserve her. To have broken her heart and then expect to be welcomed back? Had he been married? Freed now by the death of his wife to offer her his hand? Was he married even now? Did he expect her to take a place as his mistress?

The desire Peter felt for her was no longer healing or instructive. It was like a river closing in over his head. He prayed she would leave, would glance at the clock and make her excuses, saving him from destroying this precious connection. He wanted her for the duration of the portrait, not a stolen hour. He wanted to end their time together with friendship and a hope—faint though it might be— that the future might hold something more for them. Peter was no longer young, but he had the patience of Job, and if Jacob Ryan made the mistake of losing her again, before the Guild selected a new life for him, he would find a way to return to her. If they succumbed now, while she was committed to another, he would never see her again. No woman forgives her tempter.

She removed her hand, and he nearly collapsed, so great was the relief.

She said something about the night air, though he barely heard the words. The scent of her skin was thick in his head. Her hair, collected in its pins, tossed off lambent sparks that put the Guy Fawkes celebration to shame. He strained to concentrate, but the graceful movement of her throat as she spoke captivated him. He wanted to draw his fingers along it, lifting her chin with his thumbs, and bring that mouth to his. In the distance, the boom of fireworks grew more frequent.

He apprehended that she had asked him a question, and his heart hammered, knowing that he'd been caught.

"I-I—"

She laughed, a rush of semiquavers that nearly undid him, and he turned to hide his emotion.

"Oh, Peter," she said as if to an errant child. "There is paint on you." And with a tiny sigh, she lifted her thumb and ran it across his cheek.

It was too much. He caught her hand to stop her, but the softness transfixed him. He held it, unmoving, between his palm and cheek, drinking in the heady warmth and cursing his foolhardy weakness.

"Peter."

Small and pained, the word was like a bruise.

He kept his eyes closed, unwilling to see the look of shocked betrayal.

"Peter."

This time the word was truer, deeper. It demanded his presence. He opened his eyes, and she looked at him, waves crashing in those sea blue eyes.

"I . . . must not," he said, his mouth as dry as untempered pigment. "We cannot, I know."

She pulled her hand free and laid it across his cheek. The last vestige of control left his head and animated his belly. In another instant he would be victim to a mindless, unrelenting urge. She must see the danger. She must.

But she paid no heed to the primitive need she'd aroused, for aroused he was. A primitive, carnal drumbeat pounded in his veins, and his hips ached to possess her.

She brought her face close, brushing a comet of sparks across his lips, and kissed him.

He groaned at the connection, her salty-sweet taste both a balm and a torture.

She was well schooled. Her tongue moved in his mouth like a whip, a plain invitation to the pleasures she offered and a shocking exposé of the pleasures she'd learned to bestow.

He wanted to strip her of those memories. He wanted to own those kisses, master that unapologetic mouth. There were ways to inhabit a woman from toes to forehead, leaving not a whit of space for rivals, to stir her slowly, make her a slave to her changing need, until her cries filled the room. But he also knew the price he would pay.

"Stop," he said. "You do not want this."

But she did. It had been so, so long since she'd felt this, so, so long since she'd felt entirely at ease, the ground was slipping beneath her. She knew she should wait, had told herself as much no more than a moment before, but those lips had melted her resolve. It wasn't a fair fight, though she was certain for Peter it wasn't a fight at all.

His forthrightness, his unremitting honesty stripped her of any ability to object, and any wish to. But with all the power, he must rule gently. He must not try to coax her beyond a few kisses. For if he did, they would both regret it.

A little more, she told herself. A little more. Peter will stop it before we've gone too far.

"Apparently I do want it."

She laughed, a wicked, willing laugh, and Peter felt himself harden. He jerked the gown open, and she gasped. The sweet pink flesh tightened instantly. He drew his palm over its luxuriant stiffness.

"Tell me this pleases you," he whispered.

Her lids came down. "Yes."

He wished he could see her eyes. He wanted what he saw there to guide him. He pulled her close and their mouths locked. Hungrily he supped, his hands in her hair, her arms locked across his back. He could feel her need, more than mere carnality, and the storm of emotion it summoned in him was driving him to the edge of endurance.

"Did he hurt you?" He must know, and the taste of honey on her neck and ear made his need for the knowledge more urgent.

"Yes."

"I hate him for that. Do you understand?"

"Yes."

"Does he love you?"

"Yes."

"Then I will learn to endure it."

He kissed her more and felt her tremble. If was as if she were coming to pieces, and he had to enclose her in his arms to protect her. Beyond them, the sky filled with light. One boom after another. He could feel reverberations deep in his chest and wondered if she could, too. The crowds roared, and their joy floated out into the night.

He rose up and held her. "A night to remember."

"Aye."

He kissed her again, and she kissed back, hard and desirous, shaking him to the marrow. Drunk with an overpowering lust and joy, he brought his mouth lower and traced the edge of her shoulder. He ached to join with her, a soaring pain that ran up his back, squeezed his lungs and bisected his heart. It was nothing but disordered, raw, terrifying need.

Her skin was warm, inebriatingly scented, and in a rush he was at her nipple, tasting at last what had haunted his thoughts this last hour. It hardened further at his touch, and he flicked his tongue roughly over the intricate bas-relief.

Desire screamed in his bones. Blindly he pulled, letting the urge take him, and her earthy, deep rumble frenzied him. The harder he pulled, the louder the sounds grew and the less rational his thoughts became.

His hands knew no master. Her hips ground under his brutish touch, and he desired only to tear them loose of the fabric that covered them. He fastened her hands at her back and bent her to his liking, jerking the bare breast upward. How he longed to plow her.

"Tell me," he said, bringing his lips to her ear. "Tell me you want this."

She did not answer, and he brought the nipple between his fingers and plucked.

She arched, a beautiful, rigid arch, and he plucked again. Her mouth fell open. Oh, how he longed to employ it.

"You have not won me," she whispered, eyes closed. "Not yet."

He laughed and dropped to his knees. "Have I not?"

He rucked the gown to her waist. In the blackness of the night he laid his palms on the amorphous patches of light that must be her thighs and brought his thumbs across the silky tufts to her nexus. Gently he rolled her bud. She gripped the railing, sounding her desire openly.

He would win her. She would rock every rooftop in London with the cries of her pleasure.

He brought his mouth to the bloom and kissed her, a slow, quivering kiss that sent a howl through his brain. She tasted of spiced summer fruit, and he drank deeply, paced by the rhythmic rocking of her hips.

Her fingers threaded his hair, urging him on, but he had better use for them.

He pulled free and waited until she opened her eyes.

"Show me," he demanded.

For an instant she was confused, but when her eyes flashed understanding, he saw the explosion of desire that accompanied it.

"No," she whispered, fearful.

"Aye." He rubbed his chin along her thigh, their gazes still locked. "You showed me in the studio. Show me here."

Two trembling fingers came down. He kissed them as they found their home, and he exalted in her moan. She moved slowly, but the lightest touch of his lips showed him the rhythm—her rhythm—and he supplanted her.

He was hard, harder than he'd ever been. The brush of his linen was like a sword's thrust. He feared for his control and prayed his oblations would not leave him undone before he began.

Quick, hungry noises rose in her throat, and he paled. He must serve her as she deserved to be served. His balls, as tight as stones, pounded between his thighs. He needed to split her wide and plant his seed, perhaps in a single brute movement. It was a battle between his consciousness and his cock, and his cock was winning.

She fretted and cried, tightening around his tongue. He could bear no more.

He stood, jerking her from the balustrade.

He pressed her against the balcony wall, heedless of the hiss she made when her flesh touched the cool brick. He flailed with his buttons. In an instant his breeks and linen were around his ankles.

He opened her skirts and lifted her knee. He knew the angle that would heighten her pleasure and pressed her to it. Her bud throbbed under his thumb, and her eyes were like a wolf's, alight with hunger. He grasped her waist and entered her with a thrust so fevered he swore he felt the brick behind her.

He plowed her hard. Eight, ten, twelve times. By the twentieth he prayed for his soul. It was a shameful, inelegant performance, but in half a dozen more thrusts her cries began to lengthen.

He stepped back, kicked his breeks free and jerked her into his arms.

He could wait no longer.

His chest was hard, and every bone in her body ached. Her legs felt like putty. He carried her to the seducing couch and dropped her roughly. He removed his shoes and stripped off his socks. Then he put one knee on the cushion, took the high-backed frame in his hand and entered her.

With exquisite, hammering blows he filled her.

Her mind left. Only her animal instinct remained, and she anchored her foot wantonly on the arm of the couch, jerking her hips to meet him and letting the fire stoke her already scorched loins. Second peaks were rare, apocalyptical occurrences for Cam. Only twice in her life—never with Jacket—and both times she'd shamed herself with her willingness to abandon propriety for her need.

Her gown, still knotted, revealed both breasts openly. When his eyes came to rest on them, she drew a finger slowly across a nipple, feeling the luscious jolt in her belly. His eyes widened, and the pounding quickened.

"More," he whispered.

She grasped each peak and plucked, and wild desire blossomed on his face.

He reared back, satyrlike, and drew the snowy shirt from his body, still driving himself into her. His chest was broad and taut, and a thick bronze pelt ran down to his thighs. He was more muscular than Jacket and thicker inside her. A Germanic god. And she had no greater wish for this moment than to have him bring her this second, otherworldly gift.

She felt the wave—enthralling and suffocating. Her breath caught, waiting for the world to explode. And just as the cataclysm began, he brought his stroking fingers to her. She launched into nirvana, her limbs searching for purchase. He caught her knees and gave one final, penetrating blow. She could feel him lose himself inside her. Again and again, he shuddered, each movement lengthening her ecstasy.

After a long moment, when the reverberations had slowed, he collapsed beside her, pulling her hips close and cupping her breasts. She was damp, and the cool November air from the open doors blew the faint perfume of their joining from the room.

Victories all around, yes?

She curled the toes still tingling from the action. Yes. Yes?

Yes, dammit. *Yes*. From her tousled hair to the *thump-thump* of her heart to the mind-blowing serenity of her limbs, she had gotten everything she could have possibly wanted out of the exchange.

So why did she feel like crying?

The low table beside them held a drawer. He opened it without looking, pulled out a blanket and with a flip of his arm covered them both. The cashmere was crimson, like the couch, and the silk edge matched the pillow under her head.

Tools of the trade.

She'd offered herself shamelessly, and he'd used her just as she'd offered. There would be no more sittings, no portrait, no patient siege. The castle had been breeched with nothing more than a well-used battering ram. And she herself had hurried to let down the drawbridge.

If she returned, it would not be to be painted or courted. If she came back, they would simply fall into bed, and in a few months the desire, satisfied, would fade. It would be just like the relationship she'd had with every other man in her life.

She was not one to wallow. She'd had her fun. She'd thought Peter would wait. He hadn't, but neither had she. Now it was time to get the information that would help her with her book and get home.

The glow receded, replaced by a familiar emptiness.

21

Part of Peter wanted to laugh or sing or grab her by the shoulders, roll her in the cashmere and tell her how happy she made him. But the other part of him was terrified. He had used her ill. His performance had been loutish at best, brutish at worst. He had taken a gentlewoman, an affianced gentlewoman whose feelings for her husband-to-be had been made clear to him, and lowered her to the level of a courtier or worse. However pleasured she might have been, no woman, in the sober light of day, would thank a man for that.

Unless, of course, her feelings for her husband-to-be were not what he imagined.

He stroked the satin skin of her hip and tried to keep his heart from haring off in three directions at once. Already he was constructing the inducements he might offer the Executive Guild to break a centuries-old ban and let him stay.

But she was so quiet, so still.

Everything depended on the next words from her mouth.

He settled his face into the edges of her hair, trying to lose himself in the gentle, clean smell without disturbing her. He wanted to kiss her, to seek reassurance in her touch, but he was afraid to move.

She sighed and heaved herself from the blanket. He saw her shoulder rising above the gown, straight and unforgiving.

She did not turn.

She stood and drew the flaps of the silk tight around her. He watched, feeling the sudden coolness of the room, as she made her way to the fire. She stooped to pick up her purse and fiddled with it abstractedly.

"It sounded like a most amusing story you were telling earlier," she said. "I'd love to hear the end of it."

"An amusing story?"

"The one about Giselle . . . and Van Dyck."

The hair on Peter's neck bristled. A question about Van Dyck. Surely this was a coincidence. He thought of Mertons's warning.

"It was not amusing at the time," he said slowly. "As I said, it made things difficult between him and me."

"A bit of an intrigue, I suppose." She gave him a sparkling look of encouragement. It was the first time she'd met his eyes since they finished. "It would have to be with a woman named Giselle."

But Mertons had said the writer was a man, a man named Campbell Stratford— His stomach dropped like lead. *Campbell. Cam.* She'd said her name was Cam. He was the one who'd expanded it to Camilla. Camilla, the mortal who ran so fast she could be in two places at once.

He could not have been so stupid. Surely she was the woman she said she was. But Mertons had only read the book. He hadn't met the author. It would be the most natural mistake in the world to assume Campbell was a man.

A thousand thoughts raced through his head, but none of them took him anywhere except right here, to this bed, a witness to the destruction of his dreams.

"Giselle . . ." He shook his head, hoping, praying he was wrong and she'd allow the subject to pass.

"Van Dyck must have been such an interesting character. I'd love to hear a story or two."

He was glad he hadn't eaten, for he thought he might be ill. He rolled onto his back and closed his eyes. He thought of the plan to trick the writer Mertons had constructed. Peter would never have imagined he'd have to implement it with her.

"Would you?" he said. "I've got a few tales that would curl a listener's hair."

She pulled a ringlet from her tousled mass, lifted a brow, and they laughed.

Stephen, who had been sitting at his desk attempting to repair a particularly ill-prepared printing plate, cast an automatic glance down the hall and shifted. He had been made privy to a range of sounds this evening, including some that could only be described, if indeed words could ever be put to them, as indelicate, and he would have just as soon been standing at the riverside next to his fellow revelers with a bottle of ale in his hand, but nothing would have induced him to leave the watching of the stairs to anyone else. Nonetheless, the silence above him seemed ominous, especially given the most particular set of noises that had preceded it.

His experience, while not broad, was consistent, and silence, such utterly perfect silence, did not fit his notion of proper postcoital relations. Which is why when the sudden sound of laughter rattled through the floorboards above, he released a breath he hadn't even been aware he was holding.

Saints be praised. Peter has found his savior.

22

Mertons paced his small room, furious. He'd been banging and shouting for half an hour, but the room was in the lowest floor of the house, and if anyone heard they remained unmoved.

The cunning fox was probably plying Peter with her wares now. If Peter were not smart enough to see a trap when it was laid for him, surely he would not divulge an iota of information on Van Dyck, not when the sole purpose of their trip here had been to save that idiot's reputation.

The locked turned and Mertons started. It was an apprentice from Stephen's troop of apes, though this time, one smaller than a barn, which gave him hope.

"Master wants to see you. Says it's urgent."

"I should think so."

Mertons took the stairs two at a time and pelted down the hall. He listened for the signs that the woman had been subdued but heard nothing. The thought of a gag brought a small smile to his face.

The office was empty, and Mertons was just about to bolt again when the side door banged open and Peter, wearing a rumpled shirt and a stormy, unrested face, flung a canvas so hard into a box for unwanted jetsam that he knocked the box several feet across the room.

"What on earth . . . ?"

Peter silenced him with a molten glare, collapsed into his seat and dropped his head in his hands.

"The deed is done. Take me back."

23

Cam typed quickly, despite occasional breaks to wait out a spell of Jeanne resettling herself with a sleepy sigh on the long office couch or to wipe the lens of wetness from her eyes. She'd been working hard since arriving back in the twenty-first century a few hours earlier, but she wasn't going to stop until she was done—especially because stopping meant she'd have more time to think, and thinking was the last thing she wanted to do after leaving Peter's bed with her tail between her legs.

At least she had gotten a story angle—a great story angle, she might add. Peter had told her about the affair Van Dyck, the old lech, had had with a young girl named Agnes. Giselle, it turned, had been a nonstarter. Nothing but a seventeenth-century stalker. Apparently even painters had those.

Agnes, on the other hand, was a girl who had been identified by Van Dyck early in her young life as a potential wife. Van Dyck had supplied the abbess of the orphanage where Agnes lived with enough money to sponsor the girl's education and to ensure she would never be exposed to anything that might awaken her sexual curiosity. Van Dyck, it seemed, had an unearthly fear of being cuckolded—the hobgoblin of men with small minds and even smaller penises—and wanted his future wife to be entirely devoted to him.

Naturally when she emerged from the orphanage as a young woman Agnes promptly fell in love with a man her own age—Cam had a sneaking suspicion this was Peter, though he referred to the young man as Horace—and Van Dyck laid traps to try to catch them in the act.

It was a fantastic triangle. Plenty of sex. Plenty of behind-the-scenes maneuvering. Now all she had to do was fit it into her biography, send it to her publisher again, and she'd have Ball's gift of the $2.1 million Van Dyck painting as well as a book deal to lay before the museum board. She thought of the scene in *Flashdance,* a scene actually filmed in the Carnegie's great hall, where Jennifer Beals points a victorious finger at every sour-faced judge during her dance audition and wins them over to her obvious suitability.

Yep, she thought as the scene played in her head, that would be her, though there would be no Michael Nouri waiting with a bunch of roses at the end, and there would certainly be no Jake Ryan sitting on top of his Porsche, making sure she celebrated her big day in the best way possible.

Peter had retreated into a polite reserve. He told her the Van Dyck story without emotion, answering whatever questions she asked, before excusing himself, saying he had an appointment he'd forgotten. He had not asked her to stay. He had not asked her to schedule another sitting. He did not mention another Wednesday afternoon. She had simply gathered her purse, stumbled down the stairs with a general murmur about the privy and walked to the models' room. Within a minute she'd called up Amazon on her phone, as Jeanne had suggested, replayed the steps she'd taken before and been deposited with a bang at her desk.

Her only problem was that a biography, at least in theory, was supposed to be based on facts. The Agnes story was a fact, but Cam could hardly footnote it with "From an interview with Van Dyck contemporary Peter Lely, November 5, 1673." She'd need to find some mention of it somewhere in the records.

Jeanne stirred. "*Mmmgph*. Are you still up?"

"Yeah. Thanks for staying."

"You know I like to rack up as much overtime as possible. Besides, the only way I could explain my panic about your absence earlier was saying you'd found a vein of gold, researchwise, and had rushed off to the library without telling anyone."

"I take it you didn't mention the explosion and the orange Crush?"

"Do I look like I want to be carted away by men in white coats? I said I'd heard a noise in your office and that when I went in you were gone."

"You should be a writer."

"Tell me about it. I'm glad the reverse trip worked, though. You didn't come back right away, so I wasn't sure."

Cam thought about how much smarter it would have been if she had. She hadn't told Jeanne anything that had happened after her ill-conceived posing.

"I'm having a problem."

"Hit me." Jeanne sat up and rubbed her eyes.

"This story about the virgin Agnes is great stuff, but I'm supposed to be an academic. What am I going to list as a source on that?"

Jeanne rubbed her chin. "I've got an idea. You know how news used to be objective old men giving us the facts and nothing but the facts?"

"Yeah?"

"But people gave up wanting to hear news? They only wanted to hear fairy tales or WWE smack talk disguised as news?"

"Yeah?"

"Why does your publisher want you to sex up your story? Because it sells better. Which is the same reason those cable news stations have created a new model."

"So are you suggesting I rewrite this so all my characters are either interrupting one another or shouting?"

"No. I'm suggesting you create your own model. Fiction plus biography. Have it be based in fact. Lord knows, you've done the research. But sell it as fiction, or at least a weird hybrid. Campbell Stratford, art world expert, cracks open the world of sex-crazed, egomaniac painters. People will eat it up. Better yet, they'll believe it's true. After all, would a nice girl like you lie?"

Cam leaned back. A fictography. In a flash, she saw the whole book rewrite itself. It was a great idea. And best of all, she wouldn't have to do a stitch more research. Whatever she didn't know, she could make up! It was beautiful!

"Jeanne," she said, "I don't pay you enough."

"Hush." Jeanne punched the cushion and pulled the blanket over her head. "It goes to triple time at twenty-four hours."

Cam's finger went to her lashes. Most of the last twelve hours had been a highly embarrassing mistake. At least she could salvage something.

"Hey," Jeanne said. "I can see that."

Cam put her finger down. "So?"

"So what happened with Lely?"

"Nothing. I found out what I needed to know."

"Uh-oh. That sounds like a scab worth picking."

"Not tonight, huh? I gotta lot of work, okay?"

Jeanne made a considering noise. "All right. For now."

When Jeanne began to snore, Cam turned to her manuscript, inspiration renewed, and began to type.

Her phone buzzed. A text. She picked it up. It was from Jacket.

"CAN'T SLEEP. LOOKING AT THE NIGHT SKY HERE. ARE YOU WORKING? SHOULD I BE WORRIED? MAKE SOME NOISE WHEN YOU COME IN, SO I CAN REST EASY. J"

She smiled. Maybe Porsches come in all shapes and sizes. Maybe one can be parked outside your house all the time, and you just didn't notice.

She thumbed her reply. "WILL DO."

24

Despite three cups of coffee and an inarguable interest in a number of topics on the agenda, Cam found her eyelids slowly closing during the weekly staff meeting until a kick under the table from Jeanne brought her to full attention.

"The status of the Van Dyck donation?" Lamont Packard repeated.

"Er, the paperwork is done," Cam said. "Ball's attorneys have reviewed it. Except for a minor change in the image rights section, they're on board." Cam had been at her desk at home every night since she'd returned, hammering out the pages of *The Girl with a Coral Earring,* then at the museum first thing in the morning to prepare for the exhibit and gala. Everything was going well, but she'd probably need to sleep for a week once the book was turned in.

"Good." Packard tapped his pen. "And the provenance and authenticity?"

Cam swept a deferential hand toward her sister. Even though Cam had been a big fan of seventeenth-century masters since her early teens, when Anastasia finally settled on a college major during Cam's senior year in high school, she'd naturally picked—what else?—art history with a specialty in seventeenth-century masters. The decision hadn't particularly bothered Cam, but a year later, when her parents forbade her to choose the same specialty—"Anastasia's had a hard time of it. Let's give her her own space in which to blossom, okay?"—Cam had breathed a hard sigh, decided to outshine her sister in whatever area she chose and switched to modern art, her second love. Nonetheless, her college thesis was on the influence of Van Dyck on Alfred Sisley and David Hockney, which is why, when it came time to write a biography, she'd returned to the subject with which it had all begun for her.

Anastasia shuffled through files on the table, slipped on a bright red pair of half-moon glasses, gave her sister a look suggesting that despite the amateurishness of Cam's prework, she had been able to create a silk purse out of a sow's canvas and deliver an actual seventeenth-century masterpiece to the collection. "I did manage to get both buttoned down, which was a relief, for there were a number of egregious holes in the history."

Cam rolled her eyes. Anastasia made it sound as if Cam had found it at a garage sale and was trying to sell it herself for beer money. "Yes, I'm certain the Hermitage has a number of performance areas on which they need to be working. I hope the entry in Catherine the Great's diary sufficed."

The side of Packard's mouth rose. "Perfect. Ball wants to sign the papers the night of the gala."

Anastasia refolded her glasses and snapped them into a Chanel case. "If you have anything you'd like for me to tell him, let me know. I'll be seeing him tonight."

Cam made a private growl and was grateful she did not have easy access to a rolled-up broadsheet. One of the downfalls of having every evening full was losing the ability to cultivate your favorite donors.

Packard rose. "Cam, can you hang back for a minute?"

Jeanne gave her a look, pushed the coffee cup in her direction and exited with the rest of the team.

"What's up?" Cam said.

Packard was filing papers into his briefcase. "I just wanted to tell you the board is very pleased. The painting, of course, is a feather in your hat, though to be fair, that is the sort of thing they'd expect any curator to do. But your book is actually of more interest than I would have expected."

"Really?"

"Of course, the academic books will always look good on a C.V. There's no denying that, but there are a few board members who have been talking about the value of the PR, and that's something one doesn't see with an academic book. Will you be able to do the interviews and signings, that kind of thing?"

"Absolutely." In fact, her editor had been very excited and just last week had slipped a story in *Publishers Weekly*—"Art historian Campbell Stratford will turn the art world on its ear with her upcoming 'fictography,' *The Girl with a Coral Earring*"—that mentioned the museum and her position there.

"Good. Keep it up. Keep it positive. Keep getting the

word out about the Carnegie. Can I tell them that's part of your plan?"

"Sure. Definitely."

Packard shut the case and paused. "What about Jacket?"

Cam shuffled a little. Being connected with an artist had always been a tad uncomfortable when it came to museum politics. Jacket had been willing to help whenever he could, but it would be unethical, unfair to him and just plain weird for her to promise that he'd do anything. "What do you mean?"

"He's back, yes?"

"You should know. You invited him."

Packard laughed. "Yes, he was kind enough to do a piece for the show. But I think it would be in your best interest for me to let the board know if Jacket is going to be a permanent addition to Pittsburgh."

Well, the question was about as opaque as he could have made it. Nonetheless Cam felt her cheeks grow warm.

"Yeah, um, we're exploring the topic."

"I apologize. I know the topic's uncomfortable. Hell, it's uncomfortable for me to ask. But if you happen to come to a decision in the two weeks before the next board meeting, please let me know. It'll help."

"Ugh."

"I know, I know. What can I say? That's how the world works. On a personal note, however, may I add that I'd love to see you happy."

"I'm noticing you're not saying, 'I'd love to see you with Jacket.'"

"I'm the father of four daughters. I would never presume."

Now Cam laughed. "Thanks, Lamont." She spotted Jeanne at the door, pointing at her and miming a telephone. "I gotta run. I've got a call."

"Tell Jacket I appreciate the help."

Cam hurried to the hall.

"It's your agent," Jeanne said. "She says it's important."

Cam shook her head and gazed out her office window. This couldn't be happening. "What are you saying, Julie?"

"I'm saying they checked the outline. They can't buy it."

"They already bought it. We signed a contract. It's been announced."

"They want out."

"I ain't gonna let 'em."

"You'll have to."

"Why? What could have happened to an outline they loved so much they asked me to finish it by January fifteenth?"

"It's not your plot."

"If it's not the plot, what is it? The title? For God's sake, they can change it."

"No, I mean, it's not *your* plot. It's the plot of another story."

"*What?*"

"In the executive meeting, a new editor read the outline and said, 'Well, I hope she has Molière listed as a cowriter, because this is the plot of *The School for Wives*.'"

Cam's heart jumped into her throat.

Julie added, "I, of course, pooh-poohed it when the

publisher called, but then she started listing the parallels. Orphanage girl named Agnes. Lecherous old man who waits until she's grown to bed her. Triangle love interest named Horace. Cam, the entire love story is exactly like the play, and some of the phrases you use in the outline . . . my God! They're practically word for word."

Cam felt like she'd been punched. She'd been had. Oh boy, had she been had. Peter fed her a line. He'd fed her more than a line. He'd fed her an entire goddamned play! It couldn't be a coincidence. But why would he do it? Things were starting to add up in an ugly way. Peter had worked his magic to get her to pose, then he'd done his brooding leading-man imitation to get her into bed and then he'd carefully fed her the plot, characters and lines of a play instead of a story about Van Dyck.

She didn't know why or how, but it felt like the most manipulative thing a man had ever done to her. She was breathless with hurt and fury.

"Hang on." She went to Wikipedia, typed in "School for Wives" and hit ENTER.

"Molière's masterpiece, *The School for Wives,* was first staged on December 26, 1662," the entry started. She scanned the plot.

Shit.

"Cam?"

"Yep. Got it. Pull the book. We're sunk."

25

The Afterlife, Artists Section

Mertons waved away the proffered ball politely and shaded his eyes from the sun. He'd never been a fan of bocce. Too much rolling. Not enough cracking. Give him cricket any day. He even liked that odd American version. And though he'd only seen it twice, long ago, the sound of the ball connecting with the hardwood had stayed with him.

"Thank you, no. I'm just here for a few minutes, though the espresso smells delicious. I'd love a cup of that if you have one to spare."

"Certainly," Rembrandt said, lifting the pot. "'Tis excellent today."

"Where's Peter?"

Rembrandt, who was waiting for Velázquez to align his shot, tilted his head toward the rise beyond the end of the path. "At the canvas. Always at the canvas."

Even at this distance, Mertons could see Peter's drawn face. "I take it he's not glad to be back."

"*Glad*?" Rembrandt shrugged. "'Tis not a word we use with Peter."

"I have some news for him."

"He will not be interested," Rembrandt said.

"In this he will." Mertons drew the journal from his suit coat pocket. "It just arrived. I've only scanned the headline myself, but I suspect he'll find it to his liking." He opened it and read. "'*The Girl with a Coral Earring* Stripped to Canvas. Simon & Schuster announced yesterday the much-anticipated novel from Campbell Stratford, *The Girl with a Coral Earring*, a fictography of painter Anthony Van Dyck, has been scrapped due to narrative issues.' Blah, blah, blah. He did it."

Mertons had to smile. Special projects were rare, and not all ended well. They were fraught with complications and a gamble on the best of days. But despite his success in derailing the book, Mertons had been unable to find the hole in the fabric of time Stratford had used. A shame, really, as it would have been quite a feather in his cap. According to Peter, Stratford disappeared after he had adjourned to the scullery to clean his brushes, though the look on Peter's face while he said it had made Mertons wonder.

With a bow, Mertons left the journal on the table, picked up his cup and broke away from the men. He wandered slowly up the fieldstone path cut into the lavender, to the top of the rise.

"How goes it, my friend?"

Peter stiffened, receiving the question almost like a blow. "Another day. They are the same."

Mertons considered the pallid complexion and the eyes, stripped of their usual proud ferocity. "Your new life, the one you will be reborn into, is coming. The Executive Guild is working on it as we speak."

"I— I would be grateful for it."

"There is news that might please you."

The sadness left his face for an instant. "They approved my request to return to 1673?"

"What? Oh, no, Peter. I have told you. It cannot be. Even for a day. I'm sorry. I know now how much it would mean to you to convince Charles to sign that writ."

Peter had confessed his ulterior purpose to Mertons and begged to return for a day or two to convince the king, but the Guild had been adamant. Once the misinformation had been planted with the writer, there was to be no more interaction with the past.

Peter nodded. The sadness returned and he went back to his painting.

"There is something else, though," Mertons said.

"Oh?"

"It was in the news this morning. Miss Stratford's book has been canceled. Seems the narrative took a turn for the worse."

If Mertons had expected a cheer or even a victorious "Aye!" he was disappointed. Peter's only reaction was a brief half smile.

"I am glad for the sake of the Guild." Peter reloaded his brush with paint.

"And the Guild appreciates your time, though, of course, we were not as lucky in discovering the writer's source of travel."

Peter grunted. Mertons knew the man's heart had never been in the assignment.

"I, er, found out a bit more about her motives."

"Did you?"

"It certainly doesn't excuse it, of course, but it seems she is in line for a promotion at her place of business—a museum of art, actually—and publishing a book is apparently an important hurdle in achieving that goal."

"Let us hope she finds contentment elsewhere."

Mertons smiled. Dry wit was an improvement over dour moodiness.

"Uh, she may get the promotion yet."

"How?"

"The variables weren't robust enough for significance, but directionally she appears to be heading for it. It seems she has negotiated the gift of a rather expensive painting to the museum—a Van Dyck, oddly enough, a portrait of the Countess of Moreland—and that may carry the day."

"So, despite everything, our writer profits?"

"But the book is stopped. That is the important thing. As I said, the Guild is quite grateful."

Peter made no reply, and Mertons turned his attention to the portrait. He regarded the flowing, flame-colored hair, sparkling on a gold background, and pale-blue gown. There was a silver hair clip pinned to the top of the easel.

"Is that Ursula?"

Peter daubed speckles of green into the hair. "Sometimes. It is today."

"I must apologize. The Guild gave me no indication of the circumstances regarding her death. If they had, I hope I would have handled the affair with more delicacy. I'm sorry. It must have been very hard for you to go back."

Peter sighed, laid down his brush and extended his hand. "Thank you, Mertons. You are most kind."

Footsteps on the path made them turn. Rembrandt was half running, journal in hand.

Peter held up his palm. "Mertons told me the news. I am glad for Van Dyck's sake.

"No, Peter," Rembrandt said. "There is more. At the bottom." He slipped on his glasses and read, " 'Simon and Schuster will instead publish a different novel from Stratford, *The Artist and the Angel of the Street*, an intimate look into the steamy goings-on in the studio of Peter Lely, bad-boy portraitist to the court of Charles II—where no woman's portrait was complete until she loosened her tongue, her gown and her morals—and the love affair with a prostitute that drove Lely to heartbreak.' "

26

THE AFTERLIFE, VAN DYCK'S HOME

"And that's the whole story?"

"Aye." Peter gazed at the pale-eyed mustached man before him. They had known each other before, but not in this place. It was almost like meeting one's father and discovering he hadn't aged but you had. Peter was older now than Van Dyck, for Van Dyck had died at little more than forty. In the Afterlife, one remained one's dying age until being reborn. He wouldn't have come—it pained him to humble himself here—but he must stop Campbell Stratford, no matter what it took. How dare she meddle in his life, after using him to get to Van Dyck.

"Well, I'm very sorry for your trouble, Peter. Very sorry. Especially after all that you've done for me." Van Dyck pulled at the narrow beard that ran from his lip to his chin. "Is there anything I can do to help?"

"There are two things, actually."

"Name them."

"First, please don't tell the Guild of my visit to you today."

Van Dyck looked at him curiously but nodded. "And the other?"

"I need a letter."

"Peter, I don't have my letters here. You know that. None of us does."

"'Tis a new letter."

"A new letter?"

"Aye. Get a quill."

Peter had constructed his plan carefully, and to have Mertons refuse this simple request was infuriating.

"It's not that simple, Peter."

"The hell it's not." Peter pounded his fist on the long marble worktable in the Executive Guild's Time Lab, and Mertons jumped. "I told you, I need only a few hours."

"Aye, I've been hearing that for two days. But while I'm glad to see you are sensible of the impact such an act could have, it doesn't change the fact that travel into the future is strictly forbidden."

"But not impossible. Mertons, I have done exactly as I've been asked, and at no little cost. The Guild must allow it."

A blue button flashed on the wall next to the door's window. Mertons pressed it and the latch on the door opened. A security guard stuck his head in the door, and Mertons waved him away. Peter eyed the ax, rope and hand and foot cuffs that hung within arm's length of the table. They clearly had a high regard for security in the lab.

"It cannot be done," Mertons said, lowering his voice. "Traveling into one's past is risky enough. Traveling into the future is a recipe for disaster. The models for the future are directional at best. We cannot know what will be affected. Hell, we can barely place someone at the correct destination, let alone ensure that the variables remain stable."

Peter stole a glance at the locked case in the corner. A book, a scope and a box of lenses sat on a counter in front of a stool. The whole thing looked as if it belonged in a tent at some village fair, though he knew from firsthand experience how well it worked. He looked at Mertons and with a loud, resigned sigh lowered himself into a chair.

"You're right," Peter said, nodding. "The risk is too great. In any case, I'm sure it's not as simple as traveling backward. The Guild may have standardized many things, but even they could not have standardized that."

Mertons laughed. "Are you joking? Have you never heard the story? Well, of course, you wouldn't have, but it's a good one. This is, oh, ten, fifteen years ago. A time accountant by the name of Robert DeLaney crashes a party at the university one night and meets the girl of his dreams. She professes a deep love for the work of a poet named John Keats. DeLaney, being a man of limitless determination though not ethics, quickly offers to introduce her. This is before the era of security cards and aura scans, of course. He brings her to the Time Lab and sets her up at *The Book of Years*." Mertons inclined his head toward the book in the locked display. "And just as I did with you, Peter, he opens the book to 1962."

"That magical year that is the focal point of all time travel?"

"Yes. As I said, it is a mystery time scientists may never understand. DeLaney opens the box of spyglasses, and after checking whether she wants the pre- or postconsumptive Keats, begins to fashion the scope into a proper configuration. Being a romantic, she chooses postconsumptive, and DeLaney dutifully selects the '141' lens to get her the hundred and forty-one years she'll need to move from 1962 back to 1821, the year Keats happens to be dying in Rome. Then he sits her in front of the spyglass, turns for a moment to pontificate on the magnificent intricacies of time travel—you know the verbosity of some men when it comes to this topic—and when he turns back, the spyglass is on the chair and she's gone."

"She's left on her own," said Peter, who knew that once you had the right lens it was simply a matter of pointing it at the page in the book.

"Well, that's certainly what he assumes. And being the gentleman he is, he gives her a good thirty minutes to get her fill of Keats's sentimental imagery and wheezy coughing. Then he refocuses the lens to snap her back, and—lo and behold—nothing happens.

"He tries a second time and third time. Still nothing. So he goes back to 1821 himself and takes the glass, for, of course, that's the only way we know of to trigger a return on your own, though it's less dependable, which is why the two-person method, with a traveler on one end and a lensman on the other, is preferred."

Peter gave him a dry smile. "Or perhaps it's preferred because it ensures the person who's traveled stays where they've been sent until the Guild is sure the job has been done."

Mertons cleared his throat. "In any case. DeLaney

finds Keats, plasters on his chest and a flannel around his head, but no sign of the girl. And no matter what he does, he cannot induce Keats to confess any knowledge of having seen her. Stumped, DeLaney decides to wait there to see if she shows.

"But"—Mertons held up a finger—"at the same time, back in the lab, an early-rising colleague arrives, sees the case open and the lenses gone and calls the director. The director rushes over and is just about to rouse the Executive Guild from their beds when DeLaney gives up and returns. Horrified at being caught, he explains the situation as well as his motivation, hoping the confession, delivered in man-to-man tones, will be enough to keep him from losing his job. Well, DeLaney's smart. The director laughs, certain the girl will arrive eventually, and even offers to give DeLaney the morning off in order to capitalize on the opportunity he's set up for himself."

Peter made a fastidious noise. "And?"

"And *nineteen* hours later, after much wringing of hands, examining of equipment and the utter implosion of the Guild, the girl reappears. Except," Mertons said, clapping his hands, "it is the director's *daughter*! DeLaney is fired, the director is suspended, and the Guild takes control of the lab. They restructure the entire security process. Even odder, though, it turns out the girl, who arrives bald and in tears, complaining of being pursued by a band of plethicords—"

"Plethicords?"

Mertons gave him a shrug that suggested he'd asked himself the same question. "It turns out that while De-Laney had his back turned she'd flipped the glass to gaze through the other side, the side without the padded eye-piece, and instead of transporting herself a hundred and forty-one years *before* 1962, she's hurled herself a hundred and forty-one years *beyond* it."

"The future."

"The future." Mertons nodded. "A wild and untamed place. Though who'd have thought it was a simple matter of looking through the other end?"

Peter stroked his chin. It was *quite* an illuminating story—more illuminating than Mertons had probably intended. And since Peter, like Mertons, understood the verbosity of some men when it came to time travel, he said, "I see your point about the risk. Tell me, though, given the outcome, what do you think are the implications for the future of, well, traveling to the future?"

"The implications?" Mertons clasped his hands behind his back and paced slowly along the long row of windows with the air of a philosopher. "There are a number of them to be sure. First, there is a certain amount of ethical debate that will be required before we could reasonably attempt it again, even with trained personnel. Second, the success of the simple reversal of the lens suggests straightforward rearrangements of other time tube paraphernalia may yield similar results. And third . . ." He laughed a private laugh. "A team of time accountants determined nothing significant had been changed, but even now I can tell you that if it were me being sent forward, I'd be prepared for a plethicord wearing a blond wig— What the . . . ?"

Peter snapped one end of the cuff around his ankle and the other around the leg of the granite table.

The color drained from Merton's face. "Oh, Peter, you mustn't."

"I'm sorry. If there was any other way . . ." In three strides Peter was at the case. He lifted his heel and shattered the glass. Instantly an alarm began to ring. He reached in, undid the lock and the door swung open. "I promise to return as soon as I finish."

Mertons essayed a heartfelt speech on the risks and costs, most of which was lost on Peter, who picked through the lens case to find the one that would place him on her doorstep. Someone hammered at the door. Peter figured he had only a moment before a battering ram was contrived. He found the lens, laid it backward in the mount and ran to Mertons.

"Would you care to be punched?"

"I beg your pardon?"

"A plausible defense, Mertons. I'm trying to help you."

Mertons returned to his theme. "The Executive Guild will be furious. They hold all the cards. Peter, think about your future."

The first boom sounded at the door. "Dammit, Mertons, shall I punch you or not?"

"This isn't a joke. You will be brought before the examining board. They'll start by rescinding your—"

Peter threw a reluctant fist into Mertons's nose. Over the outraged rage howl, he yelled, "Crumple," and with the sound of hammering crashes at the door, he returned to the book, put the wrong end of the lens to his eye, focused on the page and disappeared.

27

Jeanne snapped off her desk lamp, slipped off her pumps and dug in the tote for her Sketchers. If I have to listen to one more high-paid business executive complain about how hard it is to be them, she thought, I'm gonna shoot somebody.

Cam was packed off with Mr. Ball, digging into old, rich-guy food somewhere, and Jeanne was looking forward to an easy bus ride home while she finished the sexy romance about the woman who falls into the pages of her favorite book. She actually thought Cam would enjoy it, too, given her amazing adventure, but she'd been so damn moody since the Lely thing started, Jeanne didn't dare risk suggesting it.

She dropped her walking shoes under her desk and was just about to slide a foot in when she noticed a flash of pink on the knuckle of her big toe. Oh, crap. She'd given herself a pedicure this morning—Moorea Dream Mango—and was hoping that wasn't a smear. She leaned into the kneehole to get a better look when the sound of a crash made her jerk upright.

Her head smacked hard into the underside of the desk, and she flung herself back and shot upright.

Trying to catch his balance in front of Cam's laptop was a long-haired man in a ruffled linen shirt, silk stockings and puffy brown pants. *Holy shit. It's Hammer time.*

"Who are you?" he asked, still clinging to the desk for support.

"Jeanne Turner." Dazed, she moved across the floor and bumped the door closed. He looked like something out of Shakespeare, but he had a flesh-and-blood quality no actor could ever convey.

He made a low bow. "I apologize for the interruption. I— What is that?"

"That, my friend, is a laptop."

He tilted his head slowly. "'Tis a lamp of some sort?"

"For some people, yes."

His gaze flicked around the room. The coffeemaker, her dress, the tubes of paint at Cam's little practice easel, the telephone. He took a step backward, alarm on his face, then shook his head and brought his attention back to Jeanne. "I . . . I'm sorry. I'm—"

"Oh, I know exactly who you are."

"You do?"

"Painter by the name of Peter Lely."

His eyes widened. "I'm looking for a woman."

"And I'm pretty sure I know who."

28

"Oh my God. My sister decorates like a fifty-eight-year-old school nurse."

"Hey, me mum's a fifty-eight-year-old school nurse."

"Then she'd love it here. Jesus, sprigged flannel." Anastasia kicked the leg of the bed that had been shoved into the corner of the makeshift studio.

Jacket, who had had no feelings for flannel one way or another, viewed the sheets with little interest.

Anastasia wandered to the window, her long legs disappearing under a tight black leather miniskirt.

"I can't believe she came back here, to Mount Lebanon."

He shrugged. "She always told me she liked being reminded of her childhood. Plus, she can take the bus to the museum. She likes that."

"The bus? Jesus Christ, what next? Twinsets?"

Jacket saw no connection between these items and steered the conversation back on course. "Do you want to see it?"

"The latest Jacket Sprague? I do."

He turned the easel so she could see. She pulled out a pair of glasses and perched them on the end of her nose. Leaving one foot at a right angle to the other, like a ballet dancer, she stepped back. A scent he could only describe as flowers in a harem hung on her shoulders.

"Ballsy," she said at last. "Ironic. Postapocalyptic Duchamp crossed with John Singer Sargent. Congratulations, you've reinvented yourself."

Jacket beamed. That was exactly what he'd wanted to hear. "I told you it was good."

"You were right."

"Did you get a chance to talk to Ball?"

"I did. I don't think this is what he's looking for."

"He hasn't seen this."

"True. Still, the aesthetic is not—"

"It is true what I heard, then—that he's buying big?"

"What you heard, my dear," she said, touching his nose, "is that he's building a new postmodern house in Florida with an entry hall the size of a small Eastern bloc country. He wants a dozen pieces, same artist. He wants to make a statement. He's willing to go as high as twenty-five million."

"Jesus, that's a hell of a statement." He took her arm. "Listen, I want it." Their eyes met, and he felt a tingle of excitement mixed with fear. It was like looking into the eyes of a hungry panther.

"I hope you get what you want, then." She gave him a sly smile and walked past the loft's floor-to-ceiling windows, her stilettos clicking out the ball-tightening code of a streetwalker. "Let me ask you something," she said when she finished a long sweep of the skyline.

"Why is it you're asking me for help with Ball and not Cam?"

He took a breath. He didn't really understand all the rules about women, but he had a sense talking about Cam in this way was crossing the line. "She doesn't like to get involved in that sort of thing."

"For her fiancé?"

"We haven't quite gotten to that stage yet." He shifted from one foot to the other. "We're still in negotiations."

"Jesus. Are you fucking her, or are you actually stuck in the guest room like it looks?"

He rubbed his hands on his jeans. "C'mon, Anastasia."

She dug a cigarette out of her purse and held out a pack of matches. He struck one for her and lit the cigarette. The sound made his heart do a weird sort of jump step, even though he'd never been a smoker.

"What's this?" She looked at the sketchbook on his work desk.

"Oh, that. A detail. For a portrait."

"You're going back to portraits?"

"Well, just one. The last, probably."

"The last portrait of Jacket Sprague," she said with an interested glint. "Now there's something that sounds interesting. Who's your model?"

"Well, I don't usually work with models, but in this case—"

"How about me?"

"What?"

"Me. How about me?" She lifted herself onto the table and crossed her legs. Her hair was as straight and shiny as a slice of onyx.

"I, uh . . ."

His cell phone buzzed. It was Cam. He held up a finger and stepped into the hall. "Where are you, doll?"

"At a restaurant in Regent Square. With Mr. Ball. We just sat down."

"Oh God. Not another fuzzy navel night."

"Don't worry. I'm not driving. What are you doing?"

"You know. Meeting with a potential buyer."

"Cool. See you soon—well, maybe not soon, exactly."

He laughed. "Take your time."

He walked back into the studio. Anastasia was naked, perched effortlessly on heels that seemed to be an extension of her body. The glossy black triangle below her waist looked like a small, hibernating animal. She walked to the bed and lay on her stomach, her lovely tight ass flexing as she crossed her ankles above it. Her breasts, boyish and firm, were visible behind her bent arm.

She looked at him through long, thick lashes. "Perhaps we should start like this."

29

"He's here," Jeanne said over the phone.

"Who's here?" Cam held up a finger to Ball and excused herself from the restaurant's booth.

"Peter Lely."

Her chest made a vigorous thump. "What do you mean 'here'?"

"I mean *here*. In the museum. Whatever you did on your way back from Shakespeare land, you forgot to lock the barn door, and now a very large, very oddly dressed cow is walking around the admin wing."

"Holy cripes! Stop him!" She ran out the door for the privacy of the sidewalk.

"Honey, I'm doing everything I can. He's in the men's room now."

"Hiding?"

"Changing."

Cam's stomach felt like the Boston Marathoners were running through it. "You've got to make him go back."

"Tried it. The man's got no interest in going back. He wants you."

Oh Christ! "I can't."

"According to him, you've got two choices. Either meet with him now or he comes back to the museum tomorrow to talk with 'your master' and goes from there to the 'gentleman who prints your books.'"

When worlds collide. Cam tried to speak but no words came.

"Where's Jacket?" Jeanne demanded.

"Meeting with a potential buyer."

"I'm stowing the guy at your place, then. Get your ass over there."

30

Peter gazed down at the thick boots, the stiff, formfitting brown breeks and the odd tan shirt with half sleeves and its owner's name sewn over the pocket. "Rusty," he said again.

"I told you, he's a maintenance man." Jeanne turned the wheel of the horseless vehicle she called a "car." "He works with the boiler and pipes. That sort of thing."

"In that line of work, such a name does not instill much confidence."

"Look, you're lucky he's always had a thing for me. Otherwise you'd be wearing Linda Armstrong's spare pair of running shorts and a Rage Against the Machine T-shirt."

Nothing after "Armstrong" had made the slightest sense, though it sounded as if the clothes he'd been given were better than what he might have had. He looked at them again. He had always taken great pride in his clothes and frequented the finest tailors in London. But despite the exquisite workmanship of the seams, everything else on the shirt and breeches seemed utilitarian and plain. There were no ribbons, no lace, no dash of color, no delicacy of design. And the sharp, intricate teeth of the device holding his breeks closed were more than a little disconcerting. But he liked the boots. Sturdy and comfortable, they reminded him of his days as a lad in Westphalia, conquering the Soest hills with his friends.

"How much longer?"

Jeanne gave him a look. "It's rush hour."

Peter marveled at the name given the stately pace at which they were proceeding. He could have covered the same ground on a horse in half the time. Nonetheless he took the opportunity to drink in his fill of the new world. Peter had known the future would look different. Everyone in the Afterlife had the sort of general understanding of what existed one acquired from hearing reports by the Guild, but it was quite different to see it all laid out in such a frighteningly crowded and tall landscape. On one side of the river beside which Jeanne drove the houses were small and close, sitting in row upon row along a rising hill, not unlike Cornhill or Hampstead Heath. But on the other side, the structures were almost magical—massive silver and glass things rising hundreds of feet in the air. He spotted a breathtaking building, right out of a storyteller's imagination, all of shining blue glass, with pointed peaks and battlements around its towers. "Is that a castle?"

Jeanne laughed. "Well, it was designed to look that way. It's the PPG Building. A glass company."

The glaziers Peter had known were not so well compensated, though Donovan, the glass merchant he frequented most, had raised his prices sometimes twice a year, so it was not beyond reckoning that by the twenty-first century they would have acquired great wealth.

"What about artists?" he asked. "Where do they live?"

"Depends how well you do. Cam's lives in a row house in Notting Hill."

Cam's artist. His heart sank. Campbell did have an artist fiancé. He had hoped, foolishly, that that part of her deception had been untrue. His hand went to his emerald, and he thought of Ursula. He did not want Ursula to be shamed by Campbell's book. Someday, at the end of Ursula's new life, she would return to the Afterlife, and while he himself had no recollection of the other lives he'd lived on Earth, he had heard of those who did.

His plan was to stop the book and return to 1673. Charles would sign that writ if it was the last thing Peter accomplished. How foolish he'd been not to just hand Campbell over that night. 'Twould have been exactly what the minx deserved.

Oh, Ursula. In whatever life you've been reborn, I hope you are happy.

Jeanne maneuvered the car into place in front of a smaller version of the buildings he had admired in the vicinity of the glass castle. There was a sign on the front that read 650 WASHINGTON ROAD.

She towed him toward the door at a run.

"Why are you hurrying?"

"I'm parked illegally." Through the door they went and on a wall at the end of the low-ceilinged entry hall she pressed a button, which promptly lit up.

Peter gestured toward the entrance. "Look. Someone is admiring your carriage."

She turned and let out a surprisingly vivid oath. "She's not admiring it. She's going to write me a ticket."

The door before them opened. Jeanne pulled him inside the tiny room, inserted a key into a lock at the bottom of a row of numbered buttons and turned it. Then she jumped off, stopping the door, a sort of sideways portcullis, with an arm, while the door registered its unhappiness with loud bells.

"Go up," she instructed. "Her place is at the top. When you get there, remove the key and the door will open. I'll be up as soon as I can."

The doors closed. For an instant he looked for a way to ascend, then the floor jerked upward. His heart jumped to his throat, and he grabbed the narrow railing that ran the circumference of the space.

After a moment that seemed to last a lifetime, the room stopped. He dove for the key and turned it as the woman had said. The portcullis slid back, and the space before him had transformed from a tiny room to a high-ceilinged space lit from floor to ceiling with windows. The sun had set, and the view, past a dining table with high-backed chairs, was of a horizon sparkling with stars. A church sat high on a hill in the distance, and around it dozens and dozens of charming cottages were visible.

He thought of the view from his attic and of the moments he'd shared with Campbell Stratford there. She had captured his heart, joined him in his bed, then varnished it all with a veneer of lies. It had been a cruel punishment for his dormant heart. The nearly spent candle had fluttered weakly to life, then been pinched out and destroyed.

But that wasn't why he was here, he reminded himself. He had been a fool, but men do foolish things. The evening had served as a painful reminder that his place was not in his old life, but in a life that had yet to be chosen for him. He could not rest, however, in any life until he knew that Ursula would be protected.

He took a step. "Miss Stratford?" No answer. He heard music playing in the distance and wondered where the musicians were. It was a plaintive song, and a woman began to sing about how hard she'd try to show a man that he was her only dream. He'd never heard any song that sounded like this. The voice, haunting and low, sent a chill down his back.

The space was open and high, so different than any home in London. It was opulent, but in a spare, unadorned way. The furniture was square and low, bookcases lined the room and an asymmetrical fireplace presided at the room's far end.

He approached the closest bookcase, drawn by an array of portraits—or pictures, as he knew they were called here. There was one of a mother pinning a ribbon on a cherubic child. The child was Campbell Stratford. He would have recognized the red-gold hair anywhere, but the freckles and missing tooth added a young unexpected layer of charm. In the next picture she was an adult in a gallery of some sort with other people her own age. They held pints of ale and were giving the artist exuberant smiles. The last picture was of her from behind, perched over a railing with a man's arm around her, looking at Notre Dame on a sunny summer day.

Peter assessed the man—the position of his hand, the

strength of his profile. He wore no wig and his light hair had been shaved very close, and though Peter could not see the man's eyes well, his affection for Campbell was clear.

This was the last thing he wished to see. He turned, and the work of art on the wall he now faced took his breath away.

It was a woman, half a woman, whose portrait was slashed diagonally through the center, like the shield on a coat of arms. Above the dividing line, the woman was represented by an oil painting. Below the dividing line, clear cubes of varying sizes, holding pieces of fruit and other household objects, represented the rest of her.

Peter stared, amazed. An orange for a breast, a plum for her mons, an ancient lock on the finger of her left hand and a round metal circle with wavy, folded-in edges emblazoned with the words "Budweiser—King of Beers" for a nipple. It was like nothing he'd ever seen before, but the artist's purpose was instantly clear, and he smiled. The artist's mark, in the lower right-hand corner, was the outline of a knife and the letters *JKET.*

Another bell rang, and he jumped. It rang, stopped, rang, stopped. The noise came from a small multibuttoned object on a hallway table. After the third ring, he heard a click and Campbell Stratford's distinctive contralto.

"Jeanne? Jeanne? Are you there? Pick up. Oh, Christ, I'll be there as fast as I can."

The click sounded again, and the noise stopped. It pained him to be reminded that she'd masked her real voice with an English accent to deceive him.

A book called *The Carnegie Museum of Art Collection Highlights* sat on the table in front of a couch, and the cover showed a painting of a woman stepping into a tub. Again he was in awe of the loose technique and the highly unconventional color choice. According to the credit, the artist was one "Hilaire-Germain-Edgar Degas." Despite what Peter's teachers had impressed upon him, it seemed breaking the rules hadn't destroyed the art of painting after all.

Campbell had slipped a piece of paper in to mark a page. He turned to the page and nearly laughed. It was his painting of the Duchess of Portsmouth. She was looking particularly pleased with herself, in red silk, with the sterling and leather appointments of an archer across her lap. But what had made him laugh was the short, blunt mustache Campbell had drawn above her lip.

He was starting to get irritated. The assistant had promised him Campbell would be here. If Campbell didn't arrive, she'd be sorry. He would chance the moving room again, find a place to sleep and return to the museum at first light. He didn't know how her master world would react to finding out she had discovered a time tube hole and used it for personal gain, but he suspected it wouldn't add appreciably to her professional credentials.

Not that he wanted to destroy her career—that is, unless he had to. But the book had to be stopped. He would die before he'd allow the story of him and Ursula to become fodder for the reading public's amusement. And if doing so destroyed what he hoped was at least a mild regard for him—how pathetic it was that he clung to such a hope—he would live with the results of his actions.

He'd wait a few minutes, no more.

Biding his time, he flipped through the Carnegie book, which seemed to hold a surprise on every page. There was a Van Dyck, of course, and a painting of a merchant by his old friend, Frans Hals. He saw the steady progression of techniques as the book covered successive centuries, just as he could trace the changes in style as he walked through the galleries of Hampton Court or Whitehall. But in the latter half of the nineteenth century, everything seemed to change. It was as if a new vision had come into being, and all the old rules had been thrown out the window.

He turned the page and gasped to see a shimmering pond—which a part of his mind recognized immediately, though no sort of close examination of the brushstrokes would have yielded anything like water—upon which gleaming white blossoms floated. "Claude Monet, *Nymphéas* (Water Lilies), c. 1915–1926," the attribution read. Rembrandt had once observed, "There is more to blue than azure and ivory black, my friend." Nothing could have illustrated the point better than Monet's breathtaking work of art.

But it was the paintings noted to be mid- to late-twentieth-century creations that most amazed Peter. The luxurious palette of colors and softly blurred images had been replaced by an urgent and exhilarating clarity of vision, a vision so different from that of the paintings and sculptures and friezes he knew, he hardly knew how to approach them.

There was a painting of numbers—just numbers—by an artist named On Kawara, and a series of painted boxes by Donald Judd and even a painted chain. He found the vivid distillation of a single idea that these pieces seemed to represent startling, and the businessman in him couldn't help but note that the production of such pieces of art, if indeed that's what they were—though they had to be if collected by museums alongside Van Dycks, Lelys and Monets—would be infinitely quicker to produce than his portraits. He himself had made a small fortune selling prints of his paintings, prints that took only a moment or two to produce once the plate had been prepared compared to the twenty to thirty hours it took to complete a canvas. This twentieth-century ease of production was bringing the same notion to a more noble scale. Brilliant ideas coupled with straightforward manufacture. He liked it.

He flipped more pages and saw a nearly white canvas containing a few narrow lines and an absolutely thrilling work of nothing but paint splatters, but paint splatters applied with so much passion he could almost feel the blood pounding in the artist's ears. He had just found a simple line-drawing of a woman or a bull—he wasn't sure which one—done in a wonderfully ironic hand that seemed to dispel everything he had ever learned about portraits, when the music stopped and the muffled voices of two people somewhere else in the apartment made him jump to his feet.

He heard a door bang open, and a man's voice, clearer now, said, "No, you stay there. Let's see . . . she's got a Pinot and a Chardonnay."

"Chardonnay," a sultry-voiced woman said drolly. "For the times when making an impression doesn't matter. Pinot, please. Hold the cherry."

The two laughed, an intimate, shared-story laugh.

Peter had no wish to eavesdrop. "Hello," he called and walked into view.

The man, dressed in a pair of tight, rough-cloth breeks and nothing else, stood alone. He was instantly identifiable as the man in the picture who'd had his arm around Campbell. He was in the middle of a room that bore a vague, otherworldly resemblance to the scullery in Peter's town house, holding open the door of something that looked like a large, lit wardrobe in one hand and a bottle of wine in the other. He stared at Peter in amazement.

"Who are you?"

A Londoner, Peter thought, from the vicinity of Borough Market. So the Irish part of her story was a lie as well. "I'm here for Miss Stratford."

The man's eyes flicked from Peter's breeks to his hair to the name on his pocket. "Are you here for the radiators?"

Peter considered saying "Aye." It would certainly be expedient, so long as it didn't entail actually transacting with the "radiator," whatever that might be. But there was something in the man's demeanor that made him refuse. "No."

The man waited for an explanation of his presence. But Peter had learned long ago that the person who provides the least amount of information in a situation like this usually has the advantage.

Peter inclined his head toward the easel he saw in the next-door room, the room from which the woman's voice had come. "Are you a painter?"

The man swung in the direction Peter was looking. "I am."

"May I look?"

Surprised, the man shrugged. "Sure."

The woman had disappeared, Peter noted as he made his way into the room. The painting was perfectly square, already a discordant note for someone who was used to a more classic ratio of height to width, and the space had been slashed diagonally through the center with a line of brown to separate one working area from another. Below the line, the canvas was blank, though small notes of yellow paper printed with phrases such as "steamed buns—hips," "Rhubarb/barbed wire?" and "meat grinder" hung there. Above the line, though, the man had laid in the rough groundwork of a classic and sensual nude. The woman was exotic and angular, like a crane on a Chinese vase, with her hair cut short like a boy's. She was reclined, not unlike his Nell or Rubens's Angelica, and gazed directly at her painter. Peter felt a knot in his stomach loosen, and he realized he'd been afraid the woman on the canvas would be Campbell Stratford.

"The scale of light in your painting is amazingly well conceived," Peter said. "As is the composition, at least those parts I can see. I did not expect it."

The painter's brows rose. "You didn't?"

"No." Nor had he. The techniques were not far from what he employed himself. His eyes flickered to the unmade bed, and he felt a pang of uneasiness. "Were you guild trained?"

The painter looked at him askance. "Goldsmiths," he said carefully. "University of London."

"Ah. I am not aware of Goldsmiths. What is the purpose of the notes?" Peter pointed to the squares of yellow paper.

"Just some ideas for the reaping."

"Reaping?"

"I translate the part of the figure below the line into everyday objects, which I then enclose in clear acrylic. Look, nothing personal, bloke, but who the hell are you?"

Peter did not need to ask the same question of his host. The moment the man said he enclosed everyday objects, Peter realized with a start this was the same painter who had created the odd amalgam of traditional and naïve in the portrait that hung in the other room. It stung him that the man had earned not only a place in Campbell Stratford's bed, but the place of honor in her drawing room as well.

Nor did Peter need to answer, for a thunderous rush of water sounded from an adjoining room and the painter called, "Yoy! Heads up. We have company."

The door rattled open, and a woman knotting a towel around her chest cried, "Jesus, is it— Oh!"

It was the woman in the painting. There was no question in Peter's mind.

"Hello," she said disinterestedly, then added to the painter, "Jacket, where's the wine?"

When he pointed toward the kitchen, she strode out, and Peter caught the discreet brush she gave the man's hand as she passed. Peter's gaze returned to the bed, and he felt a sickening wave of anger mixed illogically with sorrow, sorrow for Campbell Stratford.

"Jacket?" Peter forced the cold ire under control.

"I'm Jacket Sprague," the man said, and he was clearly

just about to add, "And you are?" when Peter beat him to the punch: "I'm Peter Lely."

Jacket's gaze went to the name over Peter's pocket. "Not Rusty, then. Peter."

"Yes."

"That's the name of a painter, you know."

"I've heard that." Peter tilted his head in the direction of the kitchen, where he could hear the faint pop of a cork. "You work from a model?"

Jacket blinked for a minute, then remembered the painting. "Yeah."

"Usually?" Peter said, then added when Jacket's eyes narrowed, "I only ask because Miss Stratford told me you work from memory."

"Cam told you that?"

"Yes."

"I usually do," Jacket said after a penetrating look in Peter's direction, "but not this time. Look, did she give you a key or something? Is that why you're here?"

"Pardon me for saying so, but I hardly think it's any of your concern."

"Is that so? I'm her fiancé."

The storm in Peter's ears drowned out the music for a moment. Had she actually accepted him? He wasn't sure he could believe it. "Are you indeed?"

"She wears my ring, pal."

"I do not wish to quibble, but I saw her most recently. She wore a ring from her mother, nothing more."

"She wears it on a chain around her neck. Has for a while. Listen, you're starting to annoy me."

Peter knew he was getting dangerously close to getting

tossed out, and now that he'd made it here, he didn't want to go. "For that, I am sorry. Your fiancée and I have friends in common—in London. She gave me her card and told me to stop by the next time I was in town. I arrived at her office, and her assistant, Jeanne, graciously brought me here and let me in." He relaxed his face into something he hoped would pass for a smile. "Jeanne should arrive momentarily."

The ridiculously named Jacket grunted. "Well, Cam's out with a donor. We're not likely to see her for a while."

Convenient for an early evening idyll, Peter thought. It was nothing short of villainous, especially conducted on the lady's own doorstep. He would have scarcely believed it possible, but the mores of the twenty-first century had sunk lower than those of the seventeenth.

"I was told otherwise." Peter held the man's gaze. "Has Miss Stratford seen this portrait? I am of the understanding she has a particular appreciation for painting, and I'm certain this one would interest her."

"No." Jacket shifted uncomfortably. "It was begun this evening."

"Ah."

The dark-haired woman called out, "Can I get a wine for you?"

"A beer, please," Jacket said. "And a second for our friend here."

The woman returned with two bottles and a glass of wine. She handed out the bottles and gave Peter a predatory look. "I'm the model, by the way." She held out her hand.

Peter took it and bowed. "A remarkable kindness. 'Tis not an easy job."

After an uneasy silence, Jacket lifted his bottle. "To Budweiser."

"To Budweiser," Peter repeated. "King of beers."

"*L'chaim,*" the woman said, and they drank.

Jacket wiped his mouth on his sleeve. "I think," he said carefully to the woman, "you had better get dressed. Cam is on her way."

The woman pulled the glass from her lips, coughing. "She is?"

"So it seems. She asked Peter to meet her here. You might want to use the other door."

She scurried into the room she'd come out of, snatching up a pile of clothes from the floor as she went.

When the door closed, Peter said, "I should like to buy it." He pointed to the canvas.

Jacket raised a brow. He drew his eyes over Peter's clothes and returned to his work. "It's not finished," he said dismissively.

"I don't care. Name your price."

"You can't afford it."

"My means are extensive."

"A million," Jacket said, and Peter swayed a little. "A million and four weeks."

"I want it now." Peter pulled off the emerald and thrust out his hand. When Jacket took the ring, Peter felt as if a great weight had been removed.

"How do I know it's real?" Jacket said, examining it closely. "Besides, it's got something engraved on it."

"It's my mark."

Jacket tossed it back. "Nothing personal, man, but I'll stick with cash."

Peter's heart sunk. "I don't have any coins with me," he said, though he knew where he could get them.

"Coins?" Jacket laughed, and Peter's vision darkened. "Come back when ya got 'em, pal."

A voice—Jeanne's voice—called, "Hello? Is anybody here?"

Peter stepped directly into Jacket's line of vision, close enough for him to feel Peter's breath on his face. "Sir, you have misjudged me. Let me make myself plain. I want the painting now, and I will pay you for it." He lowered his voice as the model emerged, hopping in one shoe as she slipped the other onto her foot. "It is as clear to me as it will be to your fiancée what has transpired here. One of us is going to take that painting now, break it in two and destroy it. Which of us shall it be?"

Jacket's eyes flashed, and for a long moment he said nothing.

The model grabbed her coat off the bed. "What are you two whispering about?"

"Nothing," Jacket said without breaking Peter's gaze. "Go."

Jeanne called, "Hello? Hello? I'm sorry it took so long. The meter maid and I were having a little disagreement over how close I was parked to the hydrant."

Anastasia shrugged. "Okay, then. 'Bye." She ducked out of a door in the back.

"It's me," Jeanne called as her footsteps drew closer. "Is anybody here?"

Jacket stepped around Peter, pulled the painting off the easel and snapped it with his foot. He dropped it into a large, barrel-like contrivance and wiped his hands on his breeks. "Fuck you," he said.

Jeanne stuck her head in the door. "Peter? Oh, Christ! Jacket, hi. I, uh, see you've met Peter."

"Oh yes," Jacket said. "We've just been chatting over pints."

"Ah, you Brits," she said, laughing nervously. "It's all *pint* this and *perambulator* that. Peter, can I see you in the other room, please?"

Peter nodded and bowed to Jacket. "Many thanks."

Jeanne pulled him into the main room. "*What* did you say to him?" she demanded. "Please tell me you didn't say anything."

But before Peter had time to answer, the door through which he had entered the apartment opened and Campbell Stratford stepped through.

". . . really isn't necessary," she said to an older man holding the door open. "Really, Mr. Ball, even without a doorman, the building is quite—" She stopped when she saw Peter.

He hadn't seen her for more than a month, and he had never seen her dressed in the clothes of her time. The effect took his breath away. She wore closely tailored men's breeks of a dark, heathered brown that brought her hips and legs into stunning perspective and an equally formfitting shirt. Her hair was loose and fell in streaming ringlets of crimson sunlight over her shoulders. He'd never seen a woman look like this, not even in the salacious tableaux of the king's private parties, and while part of him felt the old wound reopen, another, less estimable part was titillated by the shameless rejection of propriety. Still another, keenly aware of the eyes of the other men upon her—for Jacket had entered the room as well—nearly drove him to madness with the desire to roll up his sleeves and scrap.

"Peter," she said.

His heart soared. Would this woman who had just said his name in that hauntingly sweet voice, who gazed upon him with tremulous uncertainty, destroy everything he loved with a tawdry exposé? They had shared something that night. Surely she had felt it, too.

"Peter," she said softly, "I think we should talk."

Aye, this was a woman who could be reasonable.

31

"*You!*" Cam said, banging open the kitchen's swing door and hoping the return might knock Peter senseless. "You have a goddamned lot of nerve."

She didn't like the way he looked at her, that "been there, had that" gaze that made her want to stick a paintbrush in his eye, and she hated the way her heart had done a high jump when she'd first seen him. It wasn't that he looked so good in the khakis and work shirt, she told herself, though, to be frank, Rusty had never filled out that shirt the way Peter did. It was just that he looked so *different,* so . . . part of her world.

She didn't know how he got here, he had no right to be here and in about three minutes she was going to have to deliver a riveting explanation to a roomful of people who were probably lining up their popcorn and soft drinks right now.

"*I* have a lot of nerve?" Peter rubbed his head. "Is there something you'd like to tell *me,* 'Mrs. Post'?"

She flushed.

"What difference did it make what my name was? You apparently knew it wasn't the truth."

"Aye, the truth was a rather precious commodity that night."

The fire in his eye only fanned her fury. "But you, you're a paragon of honor. *School for Wives*. Hilarious. That was a month of hard work." Her voice choked on the last words, and she had to muster iron determination to banish the memory of nearly destroying her career. "You're a jerk."

He hesitated. "I-I am not proud of that. I was put in a difficult situation by a friend and allowed myself to believe that excused a willful deception. I was wrong, and I apologize."

"Yeah, well, this time I don't need to depend on secondhand sources. This time I know the story perfectly."

"I don't think you do know the story."

"Don't I?"

"I would assert there are pieces of which you are not aware, pieces which might persuade you to abandon your project."

"Such as?"

"There are people who will be hurt."

"Really?" She gave him a look.

"I cannot deny I will be affected, but that is not why I'm asking you to stop."

"Then why are you? Tell me the pieces."

He faltered. She could see the enormous pride in his eyes. "Can you not trust me?"

"Trust? Are you serious? No, I cannot trust you. You nearly destroyed my writing career. "

Their eyes met, and he squared his shoulders. It was eerie the way he projected his position, even in the building engineer's castoffs. She thought of that night at his studio and all the things she had hoped for. She wondered if he had done any of those things he had done that night without an ulterior motive. She wondered if he had done any of those things because he cared for her.

"Since I see you cannot trust me, I will tell you. I should like you to do this for Ursula."

She felt an irrational anger as she watched his fingers seek out the emerald.

"Ursula? The woman of the street raised to pampered society mistress by way of your bed?"

Peter looked as if he had been punched. "How . . . ?"

"We are not entirely without means where I come from." The flip answer did not satisfy as she had expected, and she found her tongue loosening further. "I have seen your models. I have seen your portraits of her. And I have experienced your methods." The past five weeks had given her more than enough time to satisfy her curiosity on the life of Peter Lely, though it had satisfied little else.

"Might I guess which had the most impact on your decision?"

Cam inhaled. "Fuck you."

"I see you and your artist share a deep esteem for poetics."

"What my artist and I share is a deep esteem for the truth."

An odd stiffness came over Peter. He opened his mouth to speak, thought better of his decision and made a deep bow. "I wish you both great joy."

But she didn't want his wishes, and she certainly didn't want his reserve. She wanted his emotion.

"You have much happiness upon you," he said. "Can you not find it in your heart to leave Ursula out of the story?"

How dare he manipulate her to protect a woman who hadn't even bothered to be true to him? "Ursula *is* the story. Rescued from the streets, she abandons her rescuer. It's a classic 'whore with a heart of stone' story."

"It's a lie."

"All art is fiction, mine more than most."

"You're making a mistake. And I hope you see that before it's too late."

"Is that a threat?"

The door swung open slowly and Jeanne's head appeared. "Hey, kids. How's it going?"

"Great," Cam said. "Party in a box. Peter was just going."

"Going . . . ?" Jeanne waited for a location.

"Going?" Ball said, appearing next to her in the doorway.

"Gone." Jacket strode by, tossing a bottle into the recycling bin and reaching for the refrigerator door. "Sounds like a plan to me." He pulled out four beers, handed one each to Jeanne, Ball and Cam, then gave Peter a smile that made Cam wonder exactly what had transpired before she arrived. "Pleasure to meet ya, buddy."

"I'm Woodson Ball," Ball said. "Jeanne tells me you're an artist."

Jacket choked, and Peter accepted Ball's outstretched hand.

"'Tis kind of her," Peter said. "I paint."

"I was just telling Jacket here the stuff he does—oh, it's marvelous, don't get me wrong—just isn't what moves me anymore. It's the new guard pushing the old guard, the Jackets of the world, out of the way. Not that Mr. Sprague here will ever be going hungry, right?" He gave Jacket an affectionate thump on the back, and Jacket grimaced. "I'm looking for something new, something that knocks your loafers off, something that says in the context of everything that's come before me, 'This is where I stand,' you know what I mean? Not an iconoclast for iconoclast's sake. A synthesizer. Someone who stands upon the shoulders of giants and doesn't say . . ."

" 'Fuck you'?" Jacket suggested.

"Well," Ball said, pushing his thick black frames up with a finger, "I think I was going for 'Y'all be damned,' but I suppose 'fuck you' captures the essence as well. Someone who stands on the shoulders of giants and doesn't say 'fuck you,' but says, 'I understand, and I see even more.' Do you see what I mean?"

Jacket tipped the beer and swallowed thoughtfully. "Sounds like an irritating little sod to me."

Peter crossed his arms and slouched against the counter. "You're a patron?" he said to Ball. "A collector?"

Ball beamed. "As if my life depended on it."

"I can see where you find the 'fuck yous' of the world tiresome," Peter said. "They betray a lack of substance. It's all rhetoric. And when the posturing's done, where are you?"

"Exactly," Ball said, and Cam postured a discreet middle finger in Peter's direction.

Ball rubbed his hands. "Well, Cam, I hate to chat and run, but the Gators are on in half an hour."

Cam silenced Jeanne with a sharp look. "No problem, Mr. Ball. I really appreciate the ride." She gestured for Jeanne to follow as she walked Ball to the elevator. When the elevator door closed behind him, Cam whispered, "How did he get here?"

"What do you mean, 'How did he get here?' The same way you did. He landed at your desk."

"Couldn't have. No Amazon in 1673."

"Amazon?"

Peter appeared behind them. He smiled. "Do you mean the river?"

Cam didn't say anything. Jeanne gave her a look and said, "Yes."

"Ah. I'm afraid the river did exist in 1673. And for a good deal before that. I'm certain of it."

"Thank you," Jeanne said.

Cam rolled her eyes and jabbed the DOWN button.

"No, no, no," he said, holding up his palms. "I cannot stay. Thank you for the kind offer, though. I am most sensible of your generous hospitality."

Jeanne giggled, and Cam shot her a glare that would have ignited marble.

Ignoring this, Jeanne said, "Do you need a ride? I'm heading back to the office. I mean, like, what exactly do you do now?" She met Cam's eye in a quick sidelong glance.

"What town do I have the pleasure of visiting?"

"Mount Lebanon," Cam said dryly.

"There is a small public house I spotted across Mount Lebanon's strand. I believe I shall retire there."

"For the night? It doesn't work like that here."

"Don't fret, Miss Turner. I'm very resourceful."

"So, you're not going to go. You'll stay?"

"Jesus, Jeanne." Cam looked to see if Jacket was nearby, but he seemed to have disappeared into the studio. "He can stay or he can go. I don't give a rat's ass."

Peter clapped his hands together. "There you have it. A prettier invitation a man could not desire."

The elevator dinged, and Cam pressed the security button. When the door slid open, she leaned in and pressed 1. "'Bye."

Peter made a courtly bow and stepped through the door.

Jeanne giggled again. "You know who he reminds me of? Cary Grant."

Cam smacked her forehead. "Christ," she muttered, then barked "No!" at Peter when she caught him eyeing the buttons. "Don't touch anything. Just get out when the door opens."

Jeanne squawked, "Oh, wait!" as the doors drifted closed, and lunged to get an arm in but Cam blocked it.

"Now what?" Cam demanded when the DOWN button went dark. "Were you planning to ask him to the prom?"

"Your key," Jeanne said, crossing her arms. "He's got it."

32

Jeanne waved at the Carnegie's night guard and made her way down the long hallway. Eight on a Thursday, and she hadn't even logged on. If she were going to pass Biology and get a degree, she had better stop being the backstop for every weird problem her boss couldn't field, get her ass in that chair and start the virtual frog dissection.

She tugged open the door that led to the administrative wing. When she got to the office door, she stopped. A narrow strip of light was visible along the carpet.

Jeanne hadn't left the lights on, and even if she had left them on, she knew they still should be off. To save energy, the lights worked on movement. When you turned a light on, it stayed on as long as there was movement in the room. After ten minutes of no movement, it went off.

Slowly Jeanne angled herself to look in the door's side window.

A tall, skinny bald man stood, slightly dazed, peering

at Cam's books and rubbing his head, and the fact that he seemed to be nursing a broken nose would have been far more interesting to Jeanne if he hadn't also been wearing puffy wool culottes and the second Adam Ant shirt she'd seen in the last three hours.

"No. Freaking. Way."

33

Peter saw the shadow cross his table and looked up.

" 'Rage Against the Machine'? A bold sentiment, Mertons, for a man clawing his way to the top of the Time-jump Accountants' Guild." He shoved a chair open with his foot and gestured toward it, then, turning to the coffeehouse's publican, called, "Aldo, one of these marvelous coffees for my friend."

"Dammit, Peter, the Guild is going to be furious." Mertons wiped his glasses on his shirt. "You've gone too far."

Peter looked at the sticklike legs extending from the shiny blue drawers his friend was wearing. "Your calves are admirable, to be sure, but next time might I suggest slightly longer hose? Either that or a considerably warmer cloak—especially in this weather." He nodded toward the rain sheeting down beyond the shop window that framed the dark street.

"This is no time for a joke. They have already issued a condemnation."

"I reel from the blow. Speaking of blows, I hope mine

did not importune you too much. It seemed the most expedient path at the time."

Mertons grunted and brushed several drops of water from his brow. Peter hadn't expected him quite so soon, though he had already decided his arrival would not change his plan.

"You have no idea the power they wield," Mertons continued. "Would you care to be reborn as an Assyrian slave? Or perhaps one of the soldiers in the Second Punic War? Or here?" Mertons gave his outfit a look of mild disgust, and when Peter didn't respond he added, "You will never paint again. And they can ensure you remember that you did. Peter, they can ensure you remember everything . . . forever."

Peter felt the budding of a small fear. He did not know the full extent of the Guild's power, though he had heard they had a tendency toward vindictiveness when crossed. While he would sacrifice any happiness his own future might hold, there was one thing he would not risk. "Can they touch Ursula?" he asked hesitantly.

The accountant collapsed into the chair beside him and sighed. For a long moment he said nothing.

"Mertons?"

"I don't know, Peter. I . . . I am not aware of it happening before. Such an act would be quite complicated and is technically beyond the purview of the Guild."

"But?"

"But I did hear a rumor that one of the Guild members suggested it."

"Bloody bastards." A cool, focused anger formed in Peter's gut.

"Peter, you have no idea what you've done. Travel to the future is not like travel to the past. The past is set. It's known. Changing it takes enormous effort. Travel to the future is different. The factors are far more fluid, more susceptible to change, and a very little push can have a very large effect."

"Then it looks as if I'll have to do my pushing with care."

"Dammit, this isn't some prank. You are not a time-jump accountant. You have no training. You haven't run a single simulation for this era. You haven't the faintest idea what the parameters are to which you must adhere."

"What impact is her book going to have? Is the Guild not concerned about that?"

"The new vector she's started down was formed in the past, a place over which we have a modicum of control. I told you, we don't roll dice with the future. The parameters specifically forbid—"

"Stuff the parameters. She's writing about Ursula. I'm going to stop her."

Mertons heaved his chest. "I'm afraid we cannot allow it. And as far as going from here to 1673—and don't look at me like that. I am certainly smart enough to see you are planning to go back to Charles—you may forget it. The Guild has shut down all time tubes indefinitely, except for one, and that one they are monitoring closely."

If Mertons had wanted to return Peter's punch, he couldn't have done better than this. How many times could Peter fail her?

"Furthermore," Mertons said, "they will bring you back, forcibly if necessary."

"Oh, for God's sake, if the Guild had the power to force me to return, you'd be frog-marching me into their council room as we speak."

Silence. Mertons looked at his feet.

Peter lifted his mug. "As I thought."

Mertons dropped his head into his hands, and Peter considered what he could salvage from this adventure. He sensed the small sketchbook in his pocket, and thought of the letter it held, the letter he would use if all else failed. It shamed him even to consider such an unscrupulous act—a letter that would destroy her career—but he consoled himself with the fact that an alternate plan, a plan with which Mertons might help him, should be enough to render the plan involving the letter unnecessary.

"Don't despair, my friend," Peter said after a moment. "I have a deal for you."

"A deal?" Mertons looked up.

"Aye. You help me. I help you."

Mertons covered his nose reflexively. "You're not going to hit me again, are you?"

"No, no. Nothing like it. How would you like to be credited with negotiating my return?"

"Since I'll lose my job if I don't, I can honestly say I would."

"Well, we can't have you losing your job, now can we? 'Twill require only a few essentials. Nothing the Guild can't afford." Peter smiled.

Mertons looked slightly dizzy. "You're going to blackmail the Guild?"

"Blackmail's an ugly word. Think of it as facilitating the most efficient return possible."

"What, pray tell, do you require?"

"You will want to make a list."

As the publican placed a steaming mug on the table, Mertons took the pencil and piece of paper Peter offered him, all the while moving his lips silently, as if in prayer, though his expression was far from ecclesiastical.

"I'm ready."

"Very well," said Peter. "'Tis simple. I want a studio, a dozen bolts of canvas and enough lead white paint to fill the Thames."

34

"There's a man upstairs in the loft for you," Jacket said as he pressed the security button to call the elevator.

"Really?" Cam searched his eyes for a hint but found none.

Jacket had taken to greeting her in the lobby each night when she got off her bus, sometimes even with a much-appreciated glass of wine. The 44U entered Mt. Lebanon where the two big churches sat, at the peak of Washington Road. She had exited there and walked the last quarter mile to her building, past the cemetery where her father was buried, past the hardware store, past the Japanese restaurant, whose sushi she and Jacket loved so much. It was a great way to unwind. The last couple weeks before the opening of an exhibition were always hard, and though everything was coming together, she was glad the long workday was over and all she had to worry about was getting Ursula into the sack, creatively speaking, with Peter. Not that it was all that hard, after all. She knew how persuasive Peter could be when he put his mind to it.

"A man?" she said, juggling the wine and her laptop bag. "Who?"

"Dunno. Didn't give his name. Says he's a friend of yours."

Her heart did a lurch, and then she remembered Jacket and Peter had already met. Whoever the man upstairs was, it wasn't Peter.

When the door opened in the penthouse, Cam saw Peter's nosy apprentice, Mertons, sitting on the edge of her couch. For an instant she didn't know what to say. She knew he'd arrived shortly after Peter, for Jeanne had told her so. She also knew Jeanne had brought him to Aldo's. But that had been a week ago. Where he'd been in the last week, she had no idea. He was dressed in a somber gray suit with a crisp white shirt and a tie so subdued it made regimental stripes look like fluorescent tie-dye. If she didn't know better, she'd swear he was an accountant.

She looked at Jacket, then back at Mertons, waiting for a clue on the backstory Jacket had been handed.

Mertons cleared his throat and stood. "Gregory Mertons. Do you remember our appointment? Sorry to arrive so late. I'm on my way to the airport."

Was he supposed to be a pilot? A chauffeur? The new breed of British middle-class terrorist? She looked at the briefcase at his feet as well as a huge, oversized suitcase next to the fireplace. "Um . . ."

"I'm here to discuss the insurance you asked about. Whole life?" He returned to his seat.

"Riiiiiight." She dropped her laptop bag on the table, hugged the wine a little closer and said to Jacket. "Sorry, I, uh, forgot."

Jacket gave her a questioning look. "Insurance?"

She shrugged. "You're welcome to join us. I'm trying to decide between whole life and term. I want to be covered, you know, with renewable or decreasing term, but I also keep thinking of the cash value. I asked Mr. Mertons to run a few different scenarios for me—"

"Seventeen, actually," Mertons said, patting the briefcase at his feet.

"I might need your advice." She smiled.

Jacket waved away the idea like it was a swarming cloud of locusts and broke into a jog. "Lots of work," he said. "Wine's in the kitchen."

When she heard the studio door shut she turned to demand an explanation, but Mertons had his head buried in the briefcase. Good God, she thought with a start, I'm not actually going to have to hear about insurance, am I?

He pulled out a piece of paper, nearly laid it on the table, then picked it up again. "I need to talk to you about Peter."

She felt a charge of fear. "Is he okay?"

"He's fine." Mertons regarded her closely over the top of his glasses.

"Oh. Good. I guess.

"Have a seat."

She sunk into the couch opposite him and put her wine on the table.

"Is he your boyfriend?"

She flushed. "Look, I don't know what he told you, but sleeping with Peter doesn't exactly make you his girlfriend. If anything, it makes you something a little closer to an idiot."

Mertons examined a nonexistent crease in his tie. "I was talking about Jacket, Miss Stratford."

Great, Cam. Maybe you can post the story on Facebook, too. "Um, yes, I guess you could call him that."

Mertons nodded and balled the paper in his hand. Pressing the bridge of his glasses upward, he said, "You're aware what you've done is illegal."

She felt a different sort of warmth creep across her cheeks, the sort of warmth one feels when called into the principal's office. "I'm not aware of any law I violated."

"Ignorance is a very weak defense."

"Who are you?"

"Gregory Mertons, Guild time-jump accountant." He held out his hand.

"Time-jump accountant?"

"Yes."

"What were you doing in Peter's studio?"

He lowered his hand. "I'm an envoy and an observer. I travel the world to ensure the appropriate rules are being followed. Think of me as a U.N. ambassador, the painting world's version of Angelina Jolie."

She looked at his hangdog eyes and Abraham Lincoln–like lank. "Um . . ."

"The Guild has been watching for you for some time."

"Watching? Spying, do you mean? And what is the Guild?"

Mertons reached into his pocket and retrieved a mechanical pencil. "It's not spying when the use of the time tube is unlicensed."

"Gee, and I swear I sent in my application."

"We don't consider this to be humorous, Miss Stratford. Time travel is exceedingly risky, especially unprecalculated time travel."

"Good news. I aced precalculus in high school. I never travel without my quadratic formula."

"Miss Stratford—"

"Mr. Mertons, why are you here?"

"How shall I put it? Your travel visa has been revoked."

Jacket had won every game of strip blackjack they'd played until he taught her to read the "tell." Mertons clicked his pencil.

"You've shut down the tube?" The laptop with the extra-special version of Amazon was in her bag on the table in the entry hall. She tried to keep her eyes focused on Mertons.

Click click click click. "Yes."

"Gosh, it was my favorite part of the DeLorean."

The pencil stopped. A muscle contracted at the corner of Mertons's eye. She felt like her laptop was practically tapping her on her shoulder, and she cupped a hand around her eye to block her view.

"Yes, well, I'm certain you'll find other uses for it," he said uncertainly.

Well, wherever he'd been in his life, he hadn't been anywhere in the western world in the 1980s. She should have introduced herself as Pat Benatar.

"I also want to talk with you about your book."

"My goodness," she said, "it's just a festival of fun tonight. I think I would have preferred the insurance pitch."

"This is a bit awkward, I know, but I'd like you to consider dropping it."

"Drop my book?"

"Yes."

"Did Peter send you?"

"No. In fact, he would be considerably unhappy to know I was here."

"Well, I'd certainly hate to be the cause of any unhappiness for him."

Mertons paused, clicked his pencil a time or two. His gaze cut to the rolled-up paper, then back to Cam. "May I show you something?"

"Sure." She picked up her wine and tossed back a large gulp. It seemed only a moment ago that the Cabernet had had flavor.

He turned the paper facedown on the table and went over to the suitcase. It was a large beige hard-sided valise with leather straps and buckles, the sort her grandfather might have traveled with. "Gee, where are you heading? Nineteen forty-two?"

He gave a weak laugh, but only enough to remind her that that might be exactly where a time-jump accountant was traveling. She wondered if he used Amazon, too. Jeanne swore the laptop had been turned off the night he and Peter arrived, which had baffled Cam. But he must not know about Amazon's unique "LOOK INSIDE!" feature since he clearly didn't have the faintest idea how she traveled.

He opened the buckles and cracked the top. Using both hands, he pulled a painting out of the case and set it on the table.

It was her. Done by Peter. She wore the olive dressing gown she had worn that night, but it was not quite the pose she remembered. Her hair, which had been pinned up that night in his studio, fell loosely over her shoulder. Instead of frank eroticism, the look in her eyes was one of relaxed delight. And most important, she was clothed. The painting was an imagined moment of quiet joy, one that had not occurred, and she looked at it without knowing quite what to say.

"That's not the painting from that night, is it?"

"No, but it was painted soon after. And many more were painted here."

"*Here?* Peter's still *here?*" She didn't know what she'd assumed, but it wasn't that Peter had remained anywhere in the vicinity of, well, now. "Why?"

"He says his desire is to stop you from writing your book."

The slight emphasis on *says* made her look up. "What's that supposed to mean? You're not going to suggest that that isn't his desire, are you?"

"No. I just wondered if there might be another reason for his single-mindedness as well."

Her gaze went from the painting to the veiled hint in Mertons's eyes. "Look," she said with an iron edge, "the man gave me a bullshit story that nearly ruined me as a writer."

"He did it for a friend. Under duress. I know. I helped make it possible."

"Well, thanks a hell of a lot. You and Peter can take your little two-man Mean Boys act and go back to the seventeenth century."

"Peter can't go back."

"What? Is his foot caught in a time tube? Tell him to hook that DeLorean up to a lightning rod. One point twenty-one jiggowatts of electricity shooting up his ass is just the thing to get him on his way."

"You're thinking of the Peter of 1673. The Peter you and I know lives in another place. The Afterlife. He's dead."

She nearly dropped her wine. "What are you saying?"

Mertons sighed. "The Afterlife is where we go when we die. You, me, Peter, anyone you've ever known. Some stay forever, but only if they've reached the end of all the lives they were meant to live. Most wait for a new life to be assigned. While Peter was waiting for his new-life-to-be, he was asked to return to his former life for a short assignment—stopping you. He had no wish to return and accepted the task with great reluctance."

"He didn't appear very reluctant." She thought of those lips as she and Peter stood on the balcony that night. There wasn't a movement he'd made that had seemed even remotely hesitant.

"Then I would assert you don't know him very well."

She made a peremptory sniff, and her eyes returned to the painting. It certainly seemed to have been drawn with honest regard. She looked at the curls framing her shoulders and felt a shiver as she remembered him removing that hairpin. "And this is what he's been working on?"

Her companion's moral superiority appeared to downshift. She felt the lurch of the Mertons-mobile.

"Peter's been working on a number of projects," he said obscurely.

"So what are you telling me? I should stop the book because Peter found a conscience and now has feelings for me?"

Mertons let out a long sigh. "Yes."

How much of the book is revenge, she asked herself, and how much is a story that should be told? She shifted. "Mertons—"

"Look, I'm not saying you're another Romeo and Juliet—"

"You're aware they ended up dead?"

"Fine, a Scarlett and Rhett—"

"Estranged and unhappy? You're getting warmer."

"What I'm trying to say is, look at the work. You're an art expert. What does that art tell you?"

She allowed herself to remove the lens of anger and hurt that had colored her thoughts about Peter since they'd parted. She was a trained curator, after all. What would she see if she really let herself look?

She closed her eyes and opened them. What she saw made her heart ache, not just because what Peter had seen in his mind's eye when he painted was the sort of moment of comfortable intimacy that makes the best part of a relationship, but because it reflected what she herself had desired for the two of them. If this is what Peter's art said about Peter, she thought, what does my book say about me?

Touching the corner of the canvas with care, as if it might spark under her touch, she said lightly, "It tells me a lot of things, actually."

"You see! I've seen his work! He has not painted something like this ever before, not even of his wife. Don't you see the impact you've had on him?"

Wife? Ursula was his wife? She fought to keep her hand from shaking. "He painted his wife?"

"Oh, any number of times. She was his muse, I am told. But it was never like this."

No, one never paints one's wife the way one does the woman one draws into adultery. She felt ill.

"I think," she said softly, "you had better leave."

Mertons frowned, obviously confused. "But—"

"Go. Please."

"I should like to leave you the painting."

"That's unnecessary. Peter will see it's missing."

"No. No, he—" Mertons came to a dead stop.

"He what?"

Mertons shifted his weight. "He asked me to dispose of it."

"Then I'll ask you to do the same."

"Miss Stratford, all sentiment aside, do you have any idea how much a Peter Lely is worth in today's market?"

"Not enough to tempt me a second time. Take it." Cam made her way to the entry hall, hoping Mertons would take the hint.

His shoulders fell. He slipped on his coat, placed the canvas under his arm and picked up his briefcase and valise. "And the book?"

She pressed the security button to call the elevator. "Tell Peter he's been my muse. Now, if you'll excuse me . . ." Cam made it all the way to her bedroom before she started to cry.

*   *   *

Jacket was sneaking into the kitchen, hoping to grab a beer without being forced into the torturous insurance conversation, when he overheard Cam say, "Go. Please."

He stopped. He'd heard that sound in her voice before. Hell, he'd heard the same words from her before. But why would she be saying them to an insurance agent? He took his hand off the refrigerator door and strained his ear in the direction of the living room.

The next bit was garbled, as the ice maker dropped a fresh batch into the storage compartment, but then, clear as a bell, he heard the insurance guy say, "Miss Stratford, all sentiment aside, do you have any idea how much a Peter Lely is worth in today's market?"

Peter Lely *again*? What the hell was going on? Who was this guy?

He barely had time to process her answer before the sound of approaching steps made him run to the studio, a smart move on his part since she rushed by the door an instant later and went straight into her room.

When he heard the door close, he stuck his head out for a look. The insurance guy stood in front of the elevator with a canvas under his arm. The door opened, and the man hesitated. He held the door with his foot, put his cases on the floor and placed the painting down, front side against the wall. Then he picked up the cases and got in. The door closed.

Jacket ventured from the studio, not sure what to think. He went to the row of windows in the dining room, the ones that faced down onto Washington Road. He saw the man exit the building, cross the street and head into Aldo's coffee shop.

Then Jacket crossed to the elevator and turned the painting. Jesus, it was Cam, and worse, it was good. He wondered if she'd keep it. He wondered if she wanted him even to know about it. He looked to see if Cam's door was open. It wasn't. He pulled his cell phone out and took a snap. There. Clear as day.

35

"Did you ever hear from that weird guy again?" Anastasia asked, tucking the sheet around her. Jacket had been still so long she wondered if his heart had given out. Was it her fault orgasms required somewhere between twenty-four and thirty-eight minutes of hammering friction? She'd done it once in nineteen minutes, but that had been with a vibrator and the sex scene from *Wild Things,* and she could hardly ask Jacket to incorporate anything more into his already overloaded routine.

"Wh-what weird guy?"

Christ, he sounded like her eighty-three-year-old grandpa waking from a nap. "Rusty the repairman-slash-millionaire."

"Ahhhhhh, no. Not really."

"Not really?" Anastasia had wondered about the guy. Despite the lowbrow togs, there had been something in-credibly sexy about him, that capable, workingman sexy, the kind of guy that could pound you over the breakfast counter while he's digging out the nail file that accidentally chewed up your garbage disposal—not that that had happened to Anastasia, of course, except that once, and then the guy had still insisted on being paid, the Neanderthal. She had wondered what Rusty was doing with Cam. Cam was not exactly known for sexy boyfriends, a generalization that firmly included Jacket, whom Anastasia found to be too short to be good for anything except proving she could get whatever her sister had.

"Well, his 'associate' was over the other day talking to Cam."

"An associate? Plumbers have associates now?"

"He's not a plumber. Apparently he's a painter."

"Really?" Not that painters had associates, either, as far as she knew. Nonetheless, this was getting interesting.

"Yeah, come over here and look at this for a minute."

Jacket dragged himself up to sitting with a groan and pulled himself out of bed. She padded over beside him.

He picked his cell phone off the easel and opened the photo album icon.

Jesus, it looked like a Peter Lely!

"It's supposed to be a Peter Lely," Jacket said.

"No shit." But what was infinitely more amazing was that it was a Peter Lely–style portrait of Cam. Or so it seemed to be. Anastasia grabbed the phone and expanded the image with her fingers as much as she could. The artist had captured his sitter in a timeless, ethereal glow and, typical of Lely, who had nothing of the realist about him, her face was idealized, as if the veil of imperfection had been lifted. She could have been Cam, an Irish noblewoman or even Venus.

The woman wore an olive-gold dressing gown that

hung off one shoulder, the folds of the fabric falling gracefully down her arms and across her lap. Her hair was loose, hanging in tousled waves over flawless, pale shoulders and a hint of bosom that disappeared into the gentle curve of the gown's neckline. But it was the expression on her face that set it apart from the usual Lely. The woman's eyes were crinkled in pleasure, as if he'd captured the moment after shared laughter. With its mix of formal and intimate, it was exactly like Lely.

"It looks like him, but I don't know."

"I saw it. Trust me. The overpainting, the glazing could have come straight out of Vermeer. The draping and use of light was remarkable. Hasn't been anything like it in the last century except maybe Hopper."

"Where did she get it?" Anastasia asked, but Jacket did not answer. He was staring at the painting, obviously distressed. "What is it?" she said.

"Look at it. He loves her."

Anastasia looked again. Jacket was right. Taken as a whole, the painting was an ode, a paean, and if the woman did not love the painter in return, then she was on the verge of it. Her eyes glittered, her carriage was loose and open, like that of a woman who is letting herself go for the very first time.

"C'mon," she said. "If it's a Peter Lely, it can't be Cam."

Jacket moved the screen until the woman's hand showed. "The ring," he said. "It's hers."

"How do you know?"

"Because I've seen her wearing it almost every day for the past four years. It was your mother's."

"Nothing personal, but I think you're imagining things. In any case, though, if it is Cam, it's not a Peter Lely." Anastasia frowned. "The technique . . . It just looks so much like a Peter Lely."

Jacket snorted. "Maybe it is, just a different Peter Lely. Did I tell you that this Rusty guy told me his real name was Peter Lely."

"He *did*?"

"Yeah, that day he was here. I didn't tell you?"

"No."

"And what's even weirder is what the guy who brought the painting here said."

"Yeah?"

"Apparently he was trying to give it to Cam, and he said to her, 'Sentiment aside, do you have any idea how much a Lely is worth in today's market?'"

"He said that?"

"Yeah."

"And what did Cam say?"

Jacket sighed. " 'Not enough to tempt me a second time.' She didn't want it. The guy left it next to the front door, which is when I took a snap of it. And it's a good thing I did because it was gone an hour later."

Well, the answer to how much it would be worth, Anastasia knew, was more than a million dollars—that is, if it were a real, undiscovered Lely. The question now was, what the hell was it, and more important, what were Cam and the associate up to?

"So now Peter-slash-Rusty sits over in Aldo's there across the street every afternoon." He jerked his thumb toward Washington Road.

Anastasia peered down into the lighted streetscape. Aldo's coffee shop was directly across from the building. "How do you know?"

"Well, first the associate headed there, so, just to find out, I went down to look. And there they were. That's how I figured out he was working with the guy. Then I started to check. He—Rusty, Peter, whatever his name is—is there every day. Just like clockwork. Jesus, I'd swear to God they were having an affair, but I don't know how since I'm here all day and she's at work."

"Poor Jacket. Infidelity is such a trial."

Jacket didn't reply, and the look in his eyes, still locked on the portrait, suggested he hadn't heard.

" 'Not enough to tempt me a second time,' " he said. "That goddamn well means there was a first."

36

"Wow, you're in early."

Jeanne flipped on the overhead light. Her boss did not usually make it to the museum before nine or nine thirty, but ever since she'd switched the Van Dyck book to a Lely book, it was like she'd been working off some sort of cross-century caffeinated rocket fuel, appearing in the office before the sun rose, shooting off emails in the middle of the night and generally being even more of a pain in the ass than usual. Of course, it didn't help that the gala was tomorrow and the board meeting to decide the new director the day after that. Jeanne prayed Cam would be chosen. That way Jeanne could ramp down to only helping run one of the biggest art museums between New York and Chicago instead of helping run the museum and serving as gopher on all this Lely crap.

Jeanne said, "Are we supposed to be reviewing the interpretive stuff?" One of Cam's jobs for the exhibition was ensuring every piece of art was properly notated and, whenever possible, put into context.

"Done."

"And the insurance riders?"

"Done."

"And the docent guide?"

"Reviewed and approved."

"What about your Van Dyck? No promotion, you know, without that little two-point-one-million-dollar line item on your résumé."

"It's not *my* Van Dyck. And it's in transit as we speak."

Cam had been a powerhouse of efficiency for the last three weeks, clearing away mountains of museum work like a battalion of army tanks in order to preserve as much time as possible for her writing.

"So," Cam said without looking up from the monitor. "Is this all we can find on him?"

Jeanne sighed. By "him," of course, Cam meant "Lely." It had been the only "him" in her life for the past few weeks. It was a wonder Jacket hadn't given up on Cam and gone back to London. She dropped her bag on the floor and hung up her coat.

"Yes, you're now officially the most knowledgeable person on Earth about a subject no one really cares about. I believe there's a special wing of the Star Trek Society that will be honoring you soon."

"No, I mean is this all? Weren't you getting in an article from *Burlington Magazine*?" Cam was at her desk surrounded by a dozen open books. When she was really engrossed in what she was writing, as she was now, the keyboard clicked like a Geiger counter, punctuated by cracks loud enough to make Jeanne jump when she hit ENTER at the end of a paragraph.

"I guess the mimeograph's working kinda slow on their end. The article's from 1932."

"Christ!"

The look on Cam's face reminded Jeanne she needed to pick up some bug spray on her way home. "Maybe you'd like to pull up a chapter on England on your magical little Amazon flying carpet and hop on over there yourself?"

Cam shook her head in disgust and returned to typing.

"You know, you don't actually have to have the book done by the board meeting," Jeanne said. "You only need a contract for it, which you already have."

"This book is practically writing itself." Cam hit the ENTER key so hard Jeanne wondered if the keyboard was going to flip in the air. "I am awash in heavenly inspiration. Meeting Peter Lely was just what I needed."

"*Heavenly* is the word for it, all right. You're like an angel."

"*What*?" Cam grimaced fiercely in her admin's direction.

"Heavenly," Jeanne said louder. "I said you're like one of our Father's celestial seraphim."

Cam grunted. She dug into the stack of books, holding two up with her elbow, and flipped the pages of a particularly large and musty-looking folio while attempting to keep the whole improbable Jenga tower from taking her little easel, the dead Christmas cactus and about sixteen Flair pens over the edge like a biblio-Mount Etna. "Dammit!" she cried. "There's just not enough information on Ursula."

"Information? I thought we decided you were going to make this stuff up."

"I-I—" A warm pink crawled across Cam's cheeks. "I'm not going to make it all up. And there's nothing official anywhere about his marital status. A good author, you know, checks at least some of the facts."

"Yeah, but who cares whether some woman whose last name we don't even know was married or wore a wedding band or liked apples? Apples? I mean, really! Yesterday you had me spend an hour with a magnifying glass trying to tell if her hair was naturally curly or curled with a curling iron."

They both turned to look at the book that held the plate of the demurely capped Ursula, which Cam had placed on an easel on the bookcase, right next to a sketch of the same woman, entitled "Lady Lely." "I mean, c'mon," Jeanne went on, "who's going to care unless you're— Oh my God! You're jealous!"

"I am *not* jealous."

"You told me nothing happened. I fell to my knees, praying something would happen, but you swore to me, nope, nothing happened." Now it all made sense to Jeanne. The book in which the sketch appeared—the sixteenth that had been ordered from various booksellers around the globe—had arrived earlier in the week, and Cam, who flipped through it madly after the package landed on her desk, had sunk slowly into her chair when she'd come to that page and lapsed into a moody silence that lasted for the rest of the day.

It took two more seconds for Jeanne's brain to catch up. "Lady Lely," she said. "It's the title. That's why you're so upset. He didn't tell you he was married."

"I told you, nothing happened."

"Nothing happened? You called me, wearing nothing but a silk sheet and raving so hard about what fun it was to pose naked, I thought my phone was gonna catch fire. If you didn't get laid after that, there's nothing left for you except an IV and bed restraints. No wonder he came barreling back after you. The poor guy's probably got an erection that reaches from here to the Battle of Trafalgar."

"He didn't come back for me. I told you that."

"You have told me exactly nothing since you started revising the Van Dyck biography. You told me nothing when your publisher did an about-face on the book and suddenly it was about Lely instead of Van Dyck. 'I miscalculated,' you said. You told me nothing when I dropped not one but two big-as-life cross-century FedEx packages on your doorstep. You have done nothing but bitch, type, run up a tab at every book store between here and Tokyo and wrinkle your nose like you're smelling donkey poop—yes, just like that—since you got back, and now you're telling me you didn't sleep with him?"

"I did sleep with him," Cam yelled. "The nothing that happened happened *after* we slept together."

"Oh. *Oh.*" Jeanne winced.

"Right. A big, honking awkward mistake. One of those horrible miscalculations where the only upside is the laughs you get when you tell your friends about it two decades later."

"Worse than the photographer you were dating who said you reminded him of an older Lindsay Lohan?"

"Ugh. Yes."

"Worse than the guy from the Planning Commission

who was so thrilled when he realized you and he wore the same size jeans?"

"Oh God! Yes, yes, okay. I make bad decisions when it comes to men. That's why I haven't dated in six months. That's why I've been holding off on giving Jacket an answer. Only this one seemed different. This one seemed . . . Oh, Jeanne, you should have been there. There was this woman whose married lover had broken up with her, and the married lover had told Peter privately he was canceling the painting he'd commissioned of her, but when the woman arrived, Peter carried on as if nothing had changed. He told her that even though she and her paramour had parted ways, the man had said he still wanted to remember her just as she was."

"Wow."

"Exactly. And when he heard that Jacket had never done a portrait of me, he was so careful not to say anything that might make me think that was odd, but I could tell by the look on his face, he was angry with Jacket."

"He's your Jake Ryan."

"Yes! That's what I thought. But I was so wrong. Oh, Jeanne, I was so wrong." Cam collapsed against the back of her chair. "He had to have known I was coming. I don't know how. Mertons—the second cross-century FedEx package—said they'd been watching me. Not that Peter let on, of course. And then he let me . . ." Cam shook her head as if trying to shake the horrible memory out of her brain. "Cripes, you saw how I was dressed. So, the whole time I think I'm pumping him for information—"

"He's actually pumping you."

"Bingo. And it turns out he fed me a load of crap,

which is why the Van Dyck book was withdrawn. And now I find out he's married. And look at this. Came in in my email this morning."

Cam turned her monitor and showed Jeanne a bucolic painting of a man, clearly Lely, surrounded by four women. He had a large cello between his knees and was fingering it.

"Symbolic," Jeanne almost said, but swallowed the jest at the sight of her boss's face. Closer inspection showed the women to be four versions of the same person—a woman with downcast eyes in a simple gown; a woman in a frock almost religious in its plainness whose hair was tucked under a headscarf; a graceful, barebacked model, gazing at the painter from over her shoulder; and a seductress with breasts bared, daring the man to possess her.

"Well."

"Exactly," Cam said.

"They're all, uh . . ."

"Ursula, yes."

"He was apparently quite taken with her."

"Apparently. Look, he even added cherubim, so much the goddess she was."

Jeanne squinted. The image was blurred and only about four inches by four inches on the screen, but there they were, two child angels, one with a flute, keeping time with Lely and his muse. "What's the title?"

"Dunno. It's just a picture from the catalog. That's all the guy was willing to scan. He's overnighting the actual print."

Jeanne rolled her eyes. If Cam's book ever made a profit, she'd be dumbfounded.

"So he's married."

"Yep."

"To Ursula?"

"Lady Lely," Cam said archly.

"That shit." *A lady, huh?* Jeanne remembered all of the princess gear she'd had as a kid. "Just think. You could have been like Lady Diana."

Cam crossed her arms. "You're missing the point here."

"Oh no, I'm getting the point. Your Van Dyck lark has turned into a Lely vendetta."

"Well, I wouldn't say that."

"Then why was I researching premature ejaculation for you?"

Cam took on a prim, magisterial pose. "Characters can't be two-dimensional, you know. They need . . . texture."

"Texture? Premature ejaculation, genital herpes *and* chronic flatulence. That's enough texture to keep Amy Winehouse's hairstylist busy for a year."

"They're not all his." Cam sniffed. "Ursula has the genital herpes."

"Isn't there, like, an ethics code for writers?"

"Writers? Ethics?"

"You know, someday the shoe may be on the other foot."

"That's the beauty of being an author. I don't worry about feet."

"I'm just saying, authors have a responsibility to be fair, especially a biographer."

"*Fict*ographer. You should have seen the way Nell

Gwyn looked at him while he worked. Come to think of it, I've seen pictures of her son, and he bears an uncanny resemblance to Lely." She pulled a pen from behind her ear and dashed off a note.

"I'm not saying he isn't deserving, Cam. But the world has a funny way of balancing things out. You take a couple swings. Maybe he deserves it, maybe he doesn't. But you don't want that swing coming back and knocking your teeth out." She held two fingers over her front teeth and gave her boss a goofy smile.

"Hm."

"You know," Jeanne said, "just because she was married to him doesn't mean she's a bad person."

Cam glanced again at the portrait of the winsome, doe-eyed redhead.

"Maybe," Jeanne said, "she left him because she thought she didn't love him—or because she thought he didn't love her. And maybe, just maybe, he didn't deserve any of it. Or maybe he deserved to be left but didn't deserve any of the other pain she put him through after that."

Cam pursed her lips, still looking at the painting.

"Maybe she's one of those women who isn't quite sure *what* she wants. I've heard they exist." Jeanne saw the gentle jab hit home. "Breaking it off completely can be better than letting him stay and think he has a chance. And maybe he really does love you."

Cam froze and then Jeanne froze. She turned. Jacket stood in the doorway, in a weathered leather coat, holding a to-go bag from Crepes Parisiennes and a large, steaming cup of coffee in his hands.

"Hey." He nodded at Jeanne and gave Cam a warm smile. "I didn't see you this morning."

Jeanne couldn't tell if he'd heard them or not. As usual, his tough-guy eyes were pressed into narrow, constipated slits.

"I brought breakfast," he said.

Jeanne hoped it included fiber. "Oh dear, is that the executive director calling me?" She cupped a hand to her ear. "Better run."

"Wow, this is just what I needed." Cam buried her face in the coffee's rising steam, hoping Jacket would attribute the pink on her cheeks to it.

Jacket twisted the Crepes Parisiennes bag, staring at his boots. It was not like him to display any sort of vulnerability, and Cam felt an inexplicable desire to protect him.

"Christ," he said in that devastating Brixton growl, "I hope you know I love you."

She found herself in his arms, his warm mouth over hers, a waterfall of emotions crashing in her head. She thought of that first night at the gallery, his husky asides in her ear; the time she'd twisted her ankle on the way to the fourth shoe store of the day in New York and how he'd carried her—carried her—all the way to the Lenox Hill emergency room; and the last time they'd been together, before she knew he was sleeping with the jewelry designer, when he'd surprised her with Fourth of July cupcakes from Potomac Bakery decorated with sparklers—"a Brit's attempt to be American."

Oh God, could she trust him again? The lips were easy. The heart was harder.

He fished the coffee out of her hand, placed it and the

bag on her desk and swept her back into his arms. "I've made mistakes, and I've waited and waited. Tell me you'll marry me."

"Jacket . . ." she said into the soft leather. It would be so easy to fall again. He smelled like an Arabian prince and tasted like honey. She made an uncertain noise.

"Tell me at dinner," he said, "after the gala."

They had agreed to celebrate at Eleven, one of their favorite Pittsburgh restaurants, with a late-night dinner after the party ended.

"Yes."

"Yes?" His face broke into a smile so big it made her heart hurt.

"Yes, I'll tell you after the gala," she said, nearly unable to get the clarification out. What chance did she have, looking into eyes like that? She might as well just tell him yes now.

"Brilliant."

He hugged her tightly again. She felt the ring, still on its chain, press into her chest.

37

"Cam."

She jerked, realizing Lamont Packard was speaking to her. "Sorry. Just thinking about the opening."

The senior staff was standing in the north gallery, admiring Packard's arrangement of the exhibition's opening room. The theme was "Behold: Love Through the Eyes of the Artist." What were the odds Packard would have put the Carnegie's most important Lely, *Louise de Penancoet, the Duchess of Portsmouth,* right next to Jacket's *Lornacopia?*

"Do you have a minute?" he asked.

Out of the corner of her eye, Cam caught Anastasia's pinched face. "Sure," she said gleefully.

"Great. Everyone else, off to make our usual Carnegie magic. We've got a little over twenty-four hours before the gala. Let's make everything perfect." He clapped his hands and they dispersed.

Cam's stomach began to churn. The look on Packard's

face did not exactly say promotion. He waited until the last of the staffers had drifted out.

"What's up, boss?"

Packard's brows knitted. Cam felt faint. Almost every dream she'd had about her future included running a museum, this museum. And absolutely no vision of her future had included reporting to her sister.

"You know the nominating committee met on Tuesday—"

"But the Lely book has sold! And the Van Dyck one? A complete misunderstanding. My publisher announced too soon. You know the artistic mind. Things hadn't quite gelled. And don't forget the new gift. Two-point-one million bucks. Right here in our hot little acquiring hands."

"Cam, Cam, Cam." Packard held up his palms. "You're still a candidate. The committee just has a few questions."

"About what?"

Packard sighed. "Look, you know you'd be my choice. But you know Adele Fitcher—"

Cam groaned. Fitcher was a conservative old biddy with a boatload of money—the worst sort of conservative old biddy.

"She doesn't like your book."

"Has she read it?" Cam asked.

"She's read about it."

"Cool. An uninformed backstabber. Hope she posts a review at Amazon, too."

"You know most of the board members don't mind.

In fact, a number think it's just the thing to inject some interest in the masters—sex 'em up a little. Let 'em think it was like backstage at a Mötley Crüe concert. Stretch the truth a little."

Cam coughed. Packard and his similes.

"But Adele doesn't like the sex. She thinks it cheapens our image and is tacky and unnecessary."

"I can see why Mr. Fitcher happily dropped dead at age forty-nine."

"Cam, her opinion carries a lot of weight."

"Let me ask, did she happen to read about the two-point-one-million-dollar Van Dyck in *Meddling Old Crank Quarterly* as well?"

"Of course. The board is thrilled with your work on that."

"But?"

"I'm not going to lie, Cam. There's a chance you're not going to get the job. Fitcher is lobbying hard for Anastasia, whom she calls 'accomplished and smart.'"

"Hey, you know who else was accomplished and smart? Hitler. And he actually read the books before he blacklisted them."

"Cam . . ."

"What do I need to do?"

"Keep a low profile. Don't mention the book when the board interviews you on Saturday. Don't mention the book at all. And if someone asks you about either of them, try to give the impression that this one's been misunderstand, that it's going to be—you know—more turpentine, less diaphragm jelly."

"So lie?"

Packard's face lit up in relief. "Exactly."

"Cripes."

"Cam, all she wants to do is protect the Carnegie. We can't have people thinking our staff members are running around with sex on the brain all day."

Cam looked at the Duchess of Portsmouth's dropping neckline and Lornacopia's Bazooka bubble gum nipples. "Nope, we couldn't have that, sir."

38

Peter took his first sip and let the hard work of the day slide off his shoulders. If the Guild wanted to make the Afterlife feel like a reward, they should forget the bocce ball and start serving up the cappuccino at Aldo's instead. He hadn't expected to like this twenty-first-century world, with its drab clothes, never-ending stream of roaring cars and inhabitants with a prodigious proclivity for talking loudly into their little communication boxes. In fact, given the destruction of his hopes with Cam and his subsequent anger with her over the book, he had fully expected to hate it. But here at Aldo's, amid the smell of roasted beans and cinnamon, the gentle hum of the steam machine and the scene of the high street at twilight framed in the wide front windows, he could almost forget the cares that had brought him low.

Without thinking, he flipped the thin leather-bound sketchbook lying open on the table to the back, gazing at the letter from Van Dyck he had placed there. It would be easy to stop her with this, far easier than this feverish painting that had kept him up night after night. And yet he could not bring himself to use it. Was it the ease with which that disreputable deed would be done or the disreputableness itself that stopped him? Mertons had seen his desperation that day in the time lab, but Mertons did not know Peter had found Van Dyck in the Afterlife earlier that day, before he'd come to the lab, in order to arm himself with the tool he would need in case everything else failed.

A child's laughter made Peter look up. A lad of two or three, clinging to his mother's leg, had reacted to a jumping dog outside the window. Peter looked at the boy's wide blue eyes and blond cowlick and felt the same pang he always did. The boy looked at Peter, and Peter smiled. Immediately the boy stuck a thumb in his mouth and hid his face.

Peter flipped the sketchbook to the page on which he'd been working and looked at his hands. Speckled with white and black paint, the flesh of his knuckles seemed to be growing looser every year. They were the hands of his father. He shook his head, thinking of the man in his army uniform looming over the entry hall in their home. How Peter had enjoyed being lifted in the air and swung in a circle as if he weighed no more than a bag of rags, then being brought tight against his father's chest, feeling that rough wool against his cheek and struggling for breath.

"Bunny."

The boy had appeared at Peter's side and was looking at the latest sketch. Peter had been drawing as he waited for his cappuccino, thinking of the hills of Westphalia.

"A hare, actually," Peter said, smiling, and the boy's eyes went to Peter's head, which had been shorn of its weighty locks at Mertons's insistence, leaving only an inch or two of dark waves. "No, no. Not a hair on your head. A hare is a very large rabbit, with muscles and teeth." He puffed himself up like a Viking about to attack. "Not nearly as nice as a bunny. What's your favorite animal?"

The boy's eyes darted anxiously to his mother, who was talking with an acquaintance in line. He put his finger in his mouth. "Tiger."

"May I draw one for you?"

The boy chewed for a second, then nodded.

Peter bent over his pad. "Do you like them fierce or gentle?"

The lad's eyes lit. "Fierce."

"Ah, a brave one, are we?" Peter quickly sketched a tiger in the middle of a pounce, claws out, teeth bared and body forming a powerful arch.

"Shoes," the boy said.

"On a tiger?"

He nodded, certain. Peter shrugged and added lace-tied shoes like the boy's to the tiger's back feet.

A woman's voice said, "My goodness, you should rent yourself out to parties."

Peter jumped to his feet, fully expecting to greet the lad's mother, but instead found himself eye to eye with the thin, dark-haired woman who had been Jacket's model. He hadn't seen her arrive and wondered how long she'd been in the shop.

"Good afternoon." He bowed.

"Evening, really, at this point." She tilted her head toward the darkening streetscape outside. In her hand was a cup similar to his own, and she sipped it abstractedly, keeping her feline eyes on him. And then it struck him. How could he have missed the resemblance to Cam?

He tore the page out of his book and handed it to the boy, who took it and ran to his mother.

"Peter, right?" the woman said.

He nodded warily. "Yes."

"I don't think we were ever formally introduced. I'm Anastasia." She gave him a smile as breathtaking and elegantly formed as a horse taking a fence on the fields of Hampton.

Peter took her hand and shook it. "How odd. Cam has a sister named Anastasia."

The smile caught like a shoe in a stile and nearly unseated its rider. Mertons had been working his information sources nearly as hard as Peter had been working the canvas this last week.

She dropped onto the chair beside him, curled a leg beneath her and gave him a friendly, self-effacing shrug. "Shit happens."

He sat down. "Indeed."

"I like you better in these clothes," she said. The smile returned.

Peter was wearing what Mertons called dungarees, but Peter had been watching the men each day on his walk between the studio space Mertons had let and Aldo's, or, more specifically, he had been watching the women watching the men, and yesterday he'd had Mertons take him to a place where he'd purchased the silk shirt as well as the tailored aubergine jacket he now wore.

He didn't answer. He doubted sartorial choice was at the bottom of her appearance here. He wondered how she had found him.

"Jacket tells me your name is Lely. Peter Lely."

"Like the painter, yes."

"You know Cam's writing a book about Peter Lely?"

"I've heard that. Do you think it's an allegory of some sort?" He gave her a forced smile.

"Were your parents admirers?"

"Of Peter Lely?"

"Yes."

"I'd like to think so."

Another long silence.

"Are you a painter as well?" She nodded toward the speckles on his hands.

"Aye." He stole a glance over her shoulder, out into the street in which the first snow of the season swirled in the lamplight of the waiting cars. The day had grown colder—unexpectedly colder, according to the proprietor here—and the snow seemed to have taken the town by surprise. Anastasia was here on an expedition of some sort, and he hoped she would get to the point quickly and then be on her way.

"That's, uh, quite a ring."

He had been twisting the emerald without even noticing.

"May I?" She held out a palm.

He pulled off the ring reluctantly and handed it to her. His other choice had been to put his hand in hers, and the notion of touching her did not appeal to him. She was in every way conceivable the opposite of her sister. Cool. Coiled. Deceptively nonchalant. It was like sharing a table with a cobra.

She examined the ring closely. He thought of the Latin words he'd had engraved in the band at Ursula's suggestion—*Per varios usus artem experientia fecit,* which translated roughly as "It takes a long time to bring excellence to maturity"—and shifted. He felt as if Anastasia were perusing his personal diary.

"My Latin's not great," she said with a chuckle.

"Nor mine."

She handed the ring back, letting her fingers brush his palm. "So, you sketch?" She turned the book toward her. Peter wished he had thought to close it.

"I do. A little."

"You're quite good."

He bowed.

Anastasia curled forward and regarded him closely. "Are you and Cam involved?"

At last, the heart of the matter. Or was it? "If you're looking out for Cam's best interests, I might suggest starting your work a little closer to home." As the cars stopped at the red traffic beacon outside, the high street filled with people crossing to the other side. It was the time of day when workers returned from their jobs.

The smile on Anastasia's smile grew tighter. "Touché."

He waited for her to ask him to take Cam off Jacket's hands, for that would mean Jacket's heart was not committed, but Peter doubted Jacket had the capacity to be committed, let alone recognize that he was, and it was clear Anastasia had no more interest in Jacket than she would have in a piece of squab pie. Jacket was a carnal first course, to be consumed and forgotten.

"I notice you're still in Pittsburgh."

Another burst of travelers. He looked at the shop's clock. "I'm finishing a project."

"Is it one Cam is helping you with?"

"I'm afraid I don't know what you mean by that."

"You know, putting it in the hands of the right people, bringing it to the attention of critics?"

"Do you think I would use her in that way?"

She took a long sip. "It's been known to happen."

"Your concern for your sister is admirable."

"Look," she said, "it *is* possible to be concerned about my sister and fucking her boyfriend at the same time. Cam is too nice, too naïve. Men have always used her. It's the reason I've never liked Jacket all that much. I'm just wondering if it's the reason I shouldn't like you."

There she was. In a dark orange shirt that set off her hair and a pair of formfitting breeks that made him ache with the memory of their joining. The wind blew and she clutched her sides. She hadn't dressed warmly enough. He watched her stride across the street, looking up at the sky, then stop when she reached the corner and open her mouth, catching a snowflake on her tongue. Peter's breath caught. The last person he had known to do that was Ursula.

"Happy news." He watched Cam wait for the traffic to clear in order to cross again. "You may choose a different reason for not liking me. That one doesn't apply."

But he realized with a start Anastasia wasn't listening anymore. She had followed his gaze and was watching Cam, too. He felt the heat rise above his collar.

Anastasia wheeled back, mouth agape. "You're in love with her."

He didn't answer, couldn't. His throat had turned to dust. "Pardon me." He stood, eager to remove himself from her gaze. He ventured to the counter and signaled for another cup. When his breathing slowed, he turned back to Anastasia, who was fiddling in her purse. She snapped it closed and gave him a long look. He tried not to let his gaze wander to the orange shirt, still waiting to cross on the far corner.

"You being in love with my sister," Anastasia said when he returned. "That doesn't work for me. Not at all. Jacket is supposed to be taking her to London, leaving me with the museum directorship. For a while there, I wasn't sure, but Jacket's a man, and, well, let's face it: his ethical system is not exactly sophisticated. Cheating he's always been able to justify, but cheating with Cam's sister? That's a trickier proposition. There's only one way to make that go down easier in that little pea-sized thing he calls a conscience, and that's by marrying her."

Peter blanched. Anastasia's machinations sickened him. "And what if I were to let Cam in on your little ruse?"

"Remember what I said about the male ethical system? You may be the opposite of Jacket, but you're still easy to read. You'd cut out your tongue before you'd tell Cam Jacket was sleeping with me. But you're missing my point. You're a diversion I can't afford."

The light turned, and Cam began across the road, this time more quickly. Peter wondered why. In an instant he has his answer. Jacket stood on the corner, holding a long camel coat. She slid into it and turned into his arms, almost the movement of two dancers. Then he clasped her shoulder, and they walked slowly toward the entrance to Cam's building.

Peter said mournfully, "I don't think you're going to have to worry."

39

Cam felt the light on her lids but she pushed herself back into the cocoon of blankets, and specifically into the pair of warm arms that had led her through a slow, heated dream this last hour. She braided her fingers in the fur skimming that taut belly and took in the musky scent laced with turpentine, still tingling from the foggy after-fever of exertion. Deeply, deeply she sunk into those arms, that chest, her leg like an insistent vine, drawing him closer. She could feel the press of that impervious weight and felt the fire rise again, like a wicked, unquenchable flame, between her thighs.

She brought her mouth to his ear. "Again," she whispered. "I want you to—"

"Cam?"

Her eyes snapped open, and a sharp heat filled her cheeks. Jesus, why in God's name was she dreaming of Peter?

Jacket had cracked her door and was looking in. With a groan, she sat up and rubbed her eyes, hoping what had just transpired was not obvious on her face. "What?"

"Call for you, babe. You left your phone in the dining room. It's Ball."

She looked at the clock. Ten thirty! Holy crap! She'd been up until three typing. Somehow the story of Peter Lely just flew off her fingers. And last night had been the seduction scene. Poor Ursula, she thought. Swept off her feet by the sweet-talking artist. Little did she know his ego would eventually muscle her out of his bed.

Not that the scene had had anything to do with Cam's own state of wantonness, she told herself firmly as she scrambled to her feet, wrapping the sheet around her. It was only what came of prolonged deprivation and spicy tuna rolls after ten o'clock.

She could feel Jacket's eyes upon her as she passed.

"I can see sleeping in agrees with you," he said.

She grinned. Ever since he'd kissed her the day before, it was like a whole new Jacket had come to live with her.

"Are we still on for tonight?" he asked.

A late dinner after the gala. Ball and Packard announcing the gift of the Van Dyck. The debut of Jacket's new work. The board to convene the next day to elect the new director. Everything was heady and effervescent, and even if she hadn't gotten that bolt that would tell her this was the right decision, Cam had decided she would give Jacket the answer he wanted to hear. Who gets a bolt in these energy-conscious days anyhow, she thought. All you really need is that steady, consistent hybrid hum to know you're on the right track.

She nodded, and her heart made a wavering skip. He would move from the studio into her room that night.

Cam picked up her phone. "Hey, what's up, Mr. Ball?"

"Cam! You fox! How did you keep this hidden from me?"

"Pardon?"

"Here I thought you'd keep your old friend up-to-date on whatever you found."

"Mr. Ball, I'm not following you."

"Come by, my dear, and we'll celebrate together. Hurry, though. I think my buddy at *Artforum* tipped the press. This is going to be huge—mostly, I suppose, because it *is* huge." He gave a hearty laugh and hung up.

She looked at the phone, confused.

"What's going on?" Jacket asked. "The old guy sounded excited."

"I don't know, but I'm going to find out."

40

Cam pulled into Ball's stately driveway and rolled her Accord to a stop. There were several cars there, none of which appeared likely to belong to Ball, who favored Bentleys and long, low Italian sports cars. A man stood talking on his cell phone in the yard.

Curiosity increasing, Cam jerked her hand brake and opened the door. The man in the yard pulled the phone from his ear as Cam walked by. He was a guy who did stories for *Pop City*, the online city magazine. He'd done an interview with her a while back when the book sold.

"Hey, it's *The Girl with a Coral Earring*," he said amiably. "Oh, wait. It's got a different name now, doesn't it?"

She cringed a little. "Yes. *The Artist and the Angel of the Street*."

"I wish I read historical stuff."

"Hey, I don't need you to read it. I just need you to buy it."

He laughed and pointed toward the former stable. "Everyone's around back."

Everyone?

She nodded her thanks and cut through the English garden Ball and wife had designed to complement the Tudor house and made her way to the massive brick out-building that ran along the north edge of the property. Ball had replaced the wooden carriage doors with a deceptively secure set of sliding ones. Cam pressed the bell and waited while two roving cameras turned their steely eyes in her direction. She smiled, waved, and a moment later, Ball's voice crackled to life on the speaker.

"There you are, my dear. Come in."

The bell box made an unobtrusive *click,* and the door gave way.

She could hear the buzz of voices atop the narrow set of stairs to Ball's office. Rather than interrupt, she stepped around the Klee and the Kelly he had leaning against the wall of the darkened entry hall and walked toward the huge, well-lit gallery-cum-warehouse.

The change in lighting made her gasp unexpectedly, but when her eyes adjusted she saw why. Every wall, every ledge, every nook held a stunning white painted canvas. Not just white. There were occasional undulating waves of black line and flashes of orange, and the white was not just white but a silky, warm, soft white, like gardenia petals, that made her want to leap onto the canvas and roll in it. At first she thought the works were identical in execution, despite the fact some were rectangular, some were square and the sizes ranged from three-by-four or so to well over ten-by-ten. But, no, each painting held a different piece of the puzzle, a different nuance of the artist's message. In some the lines were curved, in others the lines were angular, and in still others there was no line at all. Then there were the intriguing swatches of orange in two or three of the canvases that seemed intended to shock. And the sheer number of canvases! There had to be forty paintings here.

She was dimly aware of the opening of the security door behind her and the *Pop City* guy stepping in. He was still on the phone, and while she was wholly focused on the work in front of her, her mind picked up enough bits and pieces to figure out he was working on a story here.

She took a step back to try to let the sense of the work come to her. She had been taken in by the enormity of the effort, then her observation had cut from detail to detail. She wanted to clear her head to see the collection as a whole.

She closed her eyes and opened them.

This time her gasp reflected a sensibility struck to its core. The paintings weren't simply a collection of variations on an abstract theme. In a gestalt of understanding that nearly knocked her off her feet, she saw the lines transformed into the rise of a hip, the sensual extension of an arm, the peak of a nipple, an eye, the lacing of fingers. It was a woman—or the semblance of one—stretched over many canvases, first in the act of love, a hand over her head, gazing, half lidded, in primal rapture at her lover, then, postcoitus, resting languidly, and finally, locked in her lover's protective arms as she slept, peaceful and secure.

The room grew warm—hot, even—and her breath quickened. She could feel the heat of the desire, the plain, unspoken need, and afterward, the joy in closeness. This artist—clearly a man, but not just any man—knew what it was to possess and to be possessed, by sex, by love and by joy. Cam, who had seen many an untoward canvas, found herself almost uncomfortable to be witness to such unfettered emotion, and especially to be sharing the experience with a reporter she hardly knew. It was like peeking into the bedroom of happily married close friends without their knowing—the image embarrassing, pornographic, yet in some way immeasurably reassuring.

As a work of art, it was amazing—breathtaking in its scale and knee-shaking in the range of emotions it portrayed, from lust and desire to pleasured weariness to deep love. And everything sprang from no more than a few dozen expertly scribed lines. She thought of Wyeth's Helga paintings, the last time she had seen such an affecting opus, and as she did, she heard Ball enter the room, talking. She pushed that aside momentarily, though, too engrossed in the thought of Wyeth's paean to his neighbor, the Scandinavian Helga Testorf, whom he painted scores of times, standing and lying down, dressed and nude, over the course of fifteen years, keeping the paintings secret until he sprang the whole collection on an amazed art world. In fact, it was Helga's Teutonic red hair that—

Cam froze. The flashes of orange were not just an artistic embellishment. They were patches of hair—long waves falling gracefully over shoulders or shorter coarse patches slipping intimately between pale thighs. And in a single heart-stopping instant she realized the patches, all of them, were hers. The slightly lopsided mouth, the upturned nipples, the beauty marks on the neck and cheek. Everything was hers, hers, hers.

". . . amazing, isn't it? Why didn't you tell me, Cam? How long have you known? It's such an eyeful. And from a complete unknown."

Ball was talking to her, though she couldn't begin to summon a response, so horrifying was this assault on her privacy. She wanted to run, but her legs felt like they were made of rubber. She wanted to cry out, but her tongue was paralyzed.

"He won't sign it," Ball went on blithely, "but at least he titled it. It's called *Wednesday Afternoons*."

Suddenly she felt prickles on her neck and knew with complete certainty Peter was behind her, watching her reaction.

"As for more details," Ball said, "I have nothing to contribute. That's just what I was telling this reporter, here. I know he thinks it would be a huge story in the art world, but our friend is quite insistent that the identity of the woman—"

"How *dare* you!" Cam wheeled around and shoved Peter hard.

"—was not to be revealed."

Ball's eyes widened, but not as much as the reporter's. The *Pop City* guy looked at Cam, then said into his phone, "Put me through to Reuters."

41

"What in God's name are you doing?" Cam demanded.

Chaos had exploded in the gallery. The reporter reeled his story into the phone at double speed, like he was afraid it might slip away, while Ball, who knew how much the directorship meant to her and the deleterious effect this story would have on her chances, essayed a series of urgent, low-toned and undoubtedly fruitless pleas as to why the story, or at least the revelation that the subject was Campbell Stratford, should be buried. Three art collector types trooped in on the heels of Ball's wife, who could be heard saying, ". . . It's absolutely the Mount Everest of public fornications." They were followed by a server carrying a tray of coffee and pastries who called, "Careful, Natasha, careful," as she tried not to trip over the family dog, and Natasha herself, who in true Labrador fashion bounded among the humans with a mouth full of plush woodpecker as if she were the only creature on Earth.

"Painting is what I was doing," Peter said irritably. "It is my livelihood, you may recall." He wore a suit the color of midnight, a pale blue shirt open at the neck and a meticulously groomed three-day growth of beard that brought to mind an older Clive Owen. His hair had been cut short, bringing out the curl, and the dog made a beeline for him as if he had a pork chop in his pocket. Dogs, she thought philosophically, should be taught not to reward the wicked.

"*That* is not your livelihood." She pointed to the cyclorama of embarrassment that surrounded them. She began a silent inventory of the people to whom she'd have to explain this that began with her mother and Lamont Packard and ended with Rusty the maintenance man and the nice old lady at the dry cleaners. "Nor, might I add, is it the truth."

"Which part?" Peter crouched to offer a vigorous two-handed scratch to Natasha, who dropped the woodpecker devotedly at his feet.

Cam glanced at each unexpurgated vignette, looking for the one that would prove him a liar, but at each detail a blurred memory of the evening they'd shared sharpened into embarrassing focus, a sort of Polaroid of carnal excess. And yet the details together gave the impression of a much different liaison than had occurred. Why, the title alone suggested secret meetings and a long, clandestine affair—the sort, she thought with a bitter shake of her head, she had actually wanted to share with him once. But there was no one detail to which she could point and say, "That did not occur."

Peter scooped up the bird and offered Natasha the other end. "Aye?"

Then it struck her. She turned, victorious. "I was dressed when we did it!"

The reporter stopped talking, the server sloshed coffee onto the Limoges platter and one of the collectors, a slight man with a Mahatma Gandhi face and Lilly Pulitzer trousers, rubbed his hands together and said, "Now, that is what I call provenance."

Peter looked up from the tug-of-war in which he was engaged and said to Cam under his breath, "I suggest you stop talking about it. You are doing yourself no favors."

"Stop talking about it? Stop talking about it?! I will spend the rest of my life having to talk about this. How could you have done this to me?"

Peter let go of the woodpecker. He took Cam's elbow and guided her into a small alcove off the gallery.

"I didn't do this to you," he whispered fiercely. "If you'll recall, I was chivalrously silent on the matter of my muse. You're the one who revealed yourself. I had no intention—"

"No intention, my *ass*," she said, and caught Mahatma whipping around to see what part of the painting she was referring to now. "Fiction. Those paintings are fiction."

"All art is fiction, someone told me once. Mine more than most."

Cam growled. "If you think for one minute this is going to stop me from writing my book, you're mistaken. It only makes finding the ending a little easier."

"The ending?" Peter's eyes flashed lava sparks. "What ending do you mean?"

Suddenly the room felt far smaller than its eight-by-eight area. She crossed her arms. "I know all about Ursula."

"Do you?"

"Yes," she said quickly, feeling the intensity of his gaze, "I do."

"And?"

"It's not a secret, Peter." She heard the tone of researcher rise defensively in her voice. "There is very little written about your personal life. Because you are a painter of less reputation than Van Dyck or Vermeer, the record you have left behind is almost strictly about your work, a fact I imagine you'll be glad to hear." He hadn't been glad to hear "less reputation," she noted, and made a gratifying wince. "Nonetheless, you left behind several portraits of Ursula, including," she added, hoping her voice did not crack, "one entitled *Lady Lely*."

The muscles in his jaw flexed, and his eyes took on the color of molten iron.

So, it really was true, she thought, feeling the last brutal slap of betrayal. She didn't need a marriage record. The look in his eyes was all the proof she needed. Ursula might have abandoned him, but he had been left not just bitter, but bitter and married, and for whatever sins Cam might have forgiven Peter, she would not forgive him for drawing her into infidelity without her acknowledged consent.

"There is one entitled *Lady Lely*, another *Ursula* and another," she went on, "in which you are so enamored of your wife, you have painted her four times in one painting—the maiden, the Madonna, the muse and the whore."

The last word was a blow, and he seemed to double in bulk.

"And what did you make of this?" His voice was sharp as a blade.

"You mean other than the fact you lied to me?"

"Aye. Other than that."

"What I made of it is a story—and a damned fine one, I might add. I was able to lay out a classic, Peter, a classic. Wealthy painter meets woman of the street. He falls for her face—the Cupid's-bow mouth, the wide, childlike eyes, the porcelain skin—but he falls for her body, too." Cam thought of the slim, high-breasted form, so unlike her own, to which Peter had paid homage on canvas and undoubtedly in his bed, and hated herself for the black jealousy that poured into her heart. "He saves her, he marries her and, in his greatest ode to her, he paints her four times, surrounded by the cherubim of heaven, so great is his love for her."

"They were not cherubim."

She heard a note in his voice that was not there before, but his face was still as cold and hard as steel. She wondered what it would take to break that damnable reserve.

"But his ego is too great. Samuel Pepys, a chronicler of the painter's day, calls him 'a mighty proud man'—"

"Bounding little catchfart."

"—and having won it, the painter tires of his prize and begins to pursue the women of the court, whoever warms his posing chaise, until broken-hearted and cast aside, Ursula, the girl he raised from the streets to the rank of Lady Lely, finds herself falling for—"

"*Stop,*" Peter cried. "She was not my wife."

He said it with such a look of pained sorrow, Cam hesitated.

"I know you're doing this because you are hurt about that night," he said, "and I am sorry. But you must stop. She was not my wife. I never married her."

Cam looked into his haunted eyes and saw the desperation there. "The way I see it," she said slowly, "either you're lying now or you're sacrificing her name to avoid being called a liar. Either way, Ursula would not be proud."

"You're not fit to speak her name." He was white-hot with anger. "And you're certainly not fit to lecture anyone on the truth."

The rebuke was too much. She brought her hand across his cheek, a gratifying *crack* that finally broke his infuriating calm.

Like a tempest unleashed, he took her by the wrists and kissed her, a bruising, searching kiss, and her body betrayed her, telling him her feelings hadn't changed.

When he released her, his salty-sweet taste on her tongue and his crisp scent in her head, she saw him holding up something. It was her ring still on its chain—the ring Jacket had given her—and she realized her shirt was agape.

"Perhaps," he said, still breathing like a runner, "when we write the summary of that fateful night, you'll consider the possibility that not every lie told then was mine."

He opened his hand and the chain fell back against her skin.

The reporter stuck his head around the corner and cleared his throat. "I'd like to ask you a few questions," he said in Peter's direction.

"Nothing," Peter said without turning. "I have nothing to say."

"The reporter looked at Cam. "Would you like to—"

"*No* comment."

"Yep, that's about what I expected."

42

Jake Ryan? Ha! How could she have ever been so blind? Peter's brand of chivalry was far more in the line of, say, Henry VIII than anyone John Hughes had ever dreamed up.

Cam sat at her desk feeling like her world had been turned upside down—upside down, shaken like a maraca and kicked into the end zone of Peter's infuriating game plan. Her face would be splashed across every newspaper in the world, irretrievably linked to a work of art that would excite prurient interest for years to come. She'd be the punch line of a joke. Her relationship with Jacket had set enough tongues wagging. Now she'd be seen as the woman passed around the art world, some paint-and-canvas groupie. She felt powerless. She hated that artists had held all the cards, and she really hated that she'd brought it on herself by shoving Peter in front of the reporter. She might as well have stood next to the painting and had LOOK AT ME, THAT'S MY PUBIC HAIR tattooed across her forehead.

Ball had managed to convince the *Pop City* guy to hold the story until Monday, long enough to allow the board to meet and choose the next executive director. How he'd done it, she didn't know, but she expected it required not only the promise of an exclusive interview, but a big check made out to the reporter's favorite charity as well.

She'd told Ball she thought she should withdraw her name from consideration, but he'd disagreed—vehemently disagreed. "You're the best thing that's ever happened to that place," he'd said. "This *is* the world of art. They should be *thrilled* to find themselves smack dab in the middle of the story. Once I buy the paintings, I'll be taking 'em on tour. I'll start the tour there. That oughta quiet their complaints."

But she noticed Ball's confidence hadn't extended to notifying the board immediately. As certain as he was of her notoriety being seen as a benefit, he didn't think it was a good idea to risk it in advance of the vote.

So Cam was safe for somewhat less than seventy-two hours, assuming no one who'd been in that carriage house talked. Ball had taken care of the reporter. She presumed his wife and friends could be trusted. And when Ball had asked Peter to keep the story under wraps until Monday, Peter had said only, "I have no intention of discussing the paintings ever." But the art world was a small one, even more so in Pittsburgh, and she wondered exactly how long anyone could be counted on to keep what would be such a monumentally satisfying secret to share.

She looked at the clock. The gala started in a few hours. Her outfit was hanging on the back of her door. It was a gorgeous olive angora sweater with pearl buttons

down the front and a shimmering full white organza skirt
that reached to the floor. She knew she should try to look
forward to wearing it. It would probably be the last time
people would remember her wearing clothes at all.

The door banged open and she jumped. It was Anastasia. She was wearing over-the-knee suede boots and what
looked like a jacket of an officer in the Russian Imperial
Guard.

"Nothing like casual Fridays," Cam said.

Anastasia didn't respond. She seemed preoccupied,
which in many ways, Cam thought, was even scarier than
her being mad. Anastasia sank onto the corner of Cam's
desk, tapping a blood-red nail on the stapler.

"I ran into that friend of yours the other day."

Cam girded herself. "Friend?"

"Peter Lely."

Cam nearly slid off her chair. "Peter?"

"That's his name, right?"

"Well, yeah, but— Wait, how did you know he was
my friend?"

"He introduced himself," she said quickly. "He'd heard
me talking about the museum and said he knew someone
who worked there, too. Small world, huh?"

"Yeah."

"We had a very interesting time."

Anastasia's gaze moved slowly from the stapler to
Cam, and Cam immediately felt a disturbing change in
the force. A brisk slide show of potential sister betrayal
flipped through her head. Anastasia slept with him. Anastasia found out about Cam's time travel. Anastasia caught
wind of the *Wednesday Afternoons* horror. Anastasia was

part of the *Wednesday Afternoons* horror. Cam's finger flew to her lashes. "Oh?"

"He's an interesting fellow."

Gulp. "Really? Where, um, was this?"

Anastasia's eyes darted back to the stapler. "Can't remember, actually. A bar downtown, I think."

Cam tried to picture Peter ordering a drink. "Rhenish" would have earned him nothing but confused looks.

"Men seem to have a thing for you."

Cam felt like she was being tested, though for the life of her she had no idea what the answer was. It was like one of those nightmares about the SATs. "I, uh— Pardon?"

"Men. You engender some primitive protectiveness in them."

"Like Jacket?"

"Of course Jacket. Who did you think I meant?"

"Yes, I can see where screwing the woman who designed my engagement ring was the ultimate act of gallantry."

"He loves you. Anyone can see it."

Cam squirmed. It was true. Love and faithfulness occupied quite different galleries in the complicated floor plan of Jacket's head. "I'll admit he's making progress."

"C'mon, Cam. Give him a break. How much does one guy have to suffer in your world?"

A good question. But even if the answer was "a lot," hadn't Jacket satisfied the requirement?

"How's the book going?"

Cam rubbed her neck. It was like watching a Federer–Nadal tennis match, trying to follow the subject line here.

"Good, actually."

"Kinda weird you're writing about Peter Lely, and your friend's named Peter Lely."

"Yeah, well, he kind of inspired it."

"Is he an art collector?

"Mmm. I don't know for sure. Why do you ask?"

"I don't know. I just wondered if he collected paintings or drawings or art-related letters, that sort of thing?"

"It wouldn't surprise me. He's a real art fan."

Anastasia nodded, her bob swinging brusquely. "He looked different when I saw him."

"Different?"

"Sexy."

"Peter?" Cam forced a laugh. It was exactly the same thought she'd had at Ball's, right before her world imploded. He wore the clothes of the twenty-first century as if he belonged here.

"Have you thought about sleeping with him?"

"Jeez, Anastasia, first you're practically shoving me into Jacket's arms, and now you're asking if I've thought about sleeping with Peter?"

"Have you?"

Only every night since Guy Fawkes. "No."

"Good. I know you value fidelity. Once you've entered into a relationship, even at the very, very start, you would never do anything to jeopardize it. You'll laugh, but I admire that about you. You know me. I've always been a bit of a slut."

Like calling K2 a bit of a hill.

"But you . . . You've always honored that connection you have with your partners. You've always been honorable and faithful and true—"

"Yes, yes, yes, we've established I'm the Mother Teresa of the dating world. What is this all about?"

"Nothing." Anastasia stood and brushed off her wide, tasseled sash. She spotted the dry-cleaner's bag hanging on the back of the door, and her eyes popped. "What's this?"

"Evening clothes. I'm sure you've heard of them. They have them in Stalingrad, I believe."

"I don't mean the outfit. I mean the color. I've attended over a dozen museum parties with you, and I've never seen you in anything more daring than black. And now you're wearing olive and white? What gives?"

Cam flushed. "I-I was told I look nice in olive."

"You do. You definitely do." Anastasia walked by the dress, considering. "Now, about tomorrow. The board meets at one. One of us is going to walk out of there the director. I think it's me. Which isn't to say you're not the most qualified candidate—apart from me, of course. But I have a friend who's chummy with three or four of the members. He hears things he passes along to me. The tide has turned in my favor. The selection will be finalized tomorrow."

Cam drew her finger along her lashes with a bold swipe. Anastasia was prone to exaggeration. "They may change their minds when they see the Van Dyck. It's exceptional."

"They may. But they've known about the acquisition for three months now. You've already gotten whatever credit you're going to get out of it. The only thing it could do for you now is lose you points."

"Lose me points? How?"

"I don't know. Not being as good as they expect. You've sold it as a blockbuster, Cam. What if it's not quite everything it's cracked up to be?"

"Yeah, that's right. I forgot how trend intensive seventeenth-century paintings were. Last season it was lace-up Rembrandt still lifes. This season it's plum-colored Vermeer portraits."

"Cam, I'm trying to be a good older sister here. Mom said you're always landing in shit."

"That was the petting zoo when I was five, and you were the one shoving me out of the way to get to the feed dispenser."

"There was a billy goat about to attack."

"There was a guy from *Mt. Lebanon Magazine* with a camera, and you were afraid you weren't going to be the girl in the picture."

"Cam, all I'm saying is it's not going to turn out as you expected. Wouldn't it be better to come up with a graceful bow out?"

Cam gazed into her sister's steely gray eyes. Crap, how was it fair Anastasia got their father's poker face and Cam, her mother's "I even lose at Go Fish" eyes?

"I don't think so. I'm sticking with it to the end."

"You're sure?"

"I guess I'm just going to have to listen to my heart."

Anastasia nodded. At the door, she paused. "Then listen to it, Cam. You know what it's saying."

43

Mertons landed in the small studio and straightened his coat. Peter, he noted, hardly looked up from his painting. It seemed to be all the man ever did.

"The Guild has asked me to make a final plea."

"No."

"Peter—"

"We're not done here."

"We. Ha. Do you ever get tired of having the rest of us focused on your needs?"

"It's not about my needs. It's about Ursula."

"That's a lie. It's about revenge. You're hurt, and you want to hurt her in return."

"No. No. I wanted to stop her. I did not tell the reporter her name. I would never have hurt her willingly."

"Really? Then maybe you'll want to look at this." He dropped a sheaf of papers on the table.

Peter regarded them suspiciously.

"I told you messing about in the future was dangerous. The most recent calculations have come through. You've

changed her future—and I don't mean the stupid canvases. I mean something important."

"What?"

"A child."

Peter stilled.

"That's right. There is supposed to be a marriage and
a child in her future."

"Of course there is. She's a young woman. 'Twould be
natural to expect such things."

"But that marriage is gone now, Peter. Don't you see?
That child is gone. The original calculations on her fu-
ture, the ones I ran after I found you here, showed them."
He tapped the papers. "Today's do not. That's what this
nonsense has gotten you. Is that what you were planning?
To take away her future?"

Peter sunk into his chair. "No."

"You of all people should know what that's like. You
must leave this place. You must leave before you hurt her
more."

44

Cam moved the little name cards around the diagram of tables distractedly. Today had been a Calamity Deathmatch. What was going to bring Cam to her knees first—*Helga: The Swimsuit Issue* or Doctor Zhivago-ess, the Russian tormentor from hell? Cam had a vision of herself as Catwoman, sliding perilously down the side of the crevasse, her nails dug like knives into the edge to keep from falling, with Anastasia, standing over her in a far better Catwoman suit, tapping the toe of her boot on Cam's slipping fingers and shouting for Cam to throw her the keys to the director's office in order to save herself. And somehow Jacket is dangling below her, clutching her foot, trying to save her or pull her down with him, Cam can't tell which.

"Cam?"

She jumped. "What?" Jeanne had arrived unnoticed with an armload of mail.

"Sorry. Didn't mean to scare you."

"No problem." She returned to the seating chart. Micki Catterman regularly got drunk enough to spill full glasses of wine into her purse or fall into her dinner companion's lap. *A little self-control,* Cam lectured silently as she tapped the sticky note that held Catterman's name. *We're talking a museum gala here, not a fraternity rave, okay?* It was probably not a good idea to seat her next to Sister Rose McNair, either. Cam picked up Catterman and let her hover over the empty seat next to Dick Bolton, the insufferable bore who was making her friend Seph's life miserable over at Pilgrim Pharmaceuticals. Poetic justice? A little more of that in this world would certainly be appreciated, Cam considered, thinking for a long moment of the unexpectedly intriguing bristle of Peter's beard and of a dark, stubbled Batman pulling her from the crevasse—

"Who are you moving?" Jeanne dumped the mail on the corner of her desk.

In her mind, Cam flung the keys and caught Batman's gloved hand, all in one graceful movement. "Oh, Catwoman."

"Catwoman?"

Cam frowned, the spell of her daydream broken. "Catwoman? Why did you say that?"

"Because *you* said it."

"I did *not.*"

Jeanne made a deep sigh and rolled her eyes. "Could you please sleep with *one* of them again? I think your brain is turning into mashed potatoes."

"Is that the sort of thing you're learning in that online biology class of yours?"

"Yes, the teacher has asked us all to come to the next webcast dressed as naughty little lab assistants. Do you think that's a problem?"

"I think you're going to have more fun than I am to-night." Cam pressed the Catterman square next to Bolton, then picked up Ball and put him and his wife on either side of Sister Rose. Sister Rose was the city's biggest Pitt Panther fan. She and Ball could talk college football to their hearts' content.

Cam rubbed her eyes and reached for the mail. A large manila envelope slipped off the top of the stack. Probably another book. She grabbed a corner and tore. It was an ancient copy of *The Burlington Magazine,* a much-revered British fine arts monthly. This was the issue from 1932 that had the image of Peter and the four Ursulas. She prayed the picture would be clearer than the tiny blurred scan she'd received. The painting, long held by a wealthy private collector, had not been seen in public in several generations. Cam herself had never seen it, even in print. This would provide her first real look at one of the most revealing of Peter's paintings.

She pushed the table diagrams to one side and slipped a finger under the cover carefully. The yellowed paper crackled. The cover had no picture, only the words "*The Burlington Magazine for Connoisseurs,* Illustrated & Published Monthly" in a turn-of-the-century font and, below that, a table of contents, which she scanned for a reference to Peter.

The author of the article was a viscount, likely the man her research said had owned the painting in the thirties, and the title nearly made Cam fall off her chair: "Lely's Love Story."

Cam flipped to the first page of the article, leaned back in her chair and began to read. By the time she reached the end, everything she thought she knew had changed and the one thing she did know was that she had to find Peter.

45

Peter flung the brush down in disgust. The painting he'd begun the day before, despite its flawlessness from a technical standpoint, lacked the spark that would lift it from the realm of craft to that of beauty. The word his teacher had used was *hout*—"wood" in English. No life. And he knew why. He was wracked with guilt. No matter what Campbell had done or was about to do, she hadn't deserved what he'd just done to her. He hadn't been the one to expose her to the reporter. That was her doing. It was clear her life was something akin to a platter full spinning tops, perennially ready to explode into chaos. But her life was also her own, and if what Mertons said was true, Peter had changed it for the worse.

Was losing a child you had never known the same as losing one you had? Was there a gradient to such a loss? He kicked himself. Who was he to judge?

Peter had told himself he'd come here to protect Ursula, but he had also come to protect his reputation. And he had been willing to go so far as to put a woman's good name at risk for it. He looked at the small sketchbook and the letter it contained. In truth, he had been willing to do more than that. And now, no matter what he had been willing to do or not, he had changed her future. The realization sickened him.

He couldn't change the past, no matter how fervently he might wish to, but he certainly had no business playing God with Campbell's future. He must return to the Afterlife and accept his fate.

But before he left, he had one final deed to perform. He must beg Campbell Stratford's forgiveness. He picked up his coat and scarf, grabbed the sketchbook and left.

46

A block from my building? Cam looked in disbelief at the address on the paper clutched in her hand. Peter's been living a block from my building all these weeks?

She'd driven halfway to Ball's house before she'd been able to raise him on the phone, and only scored Peter's address after reassuring him she was traveling without a weapon. She'd written it down, aghast, at a stoplight, and had driven to Mt. Lebanon in her gala outfit.

She swung the car into the first space open on Alfred Street, hopped out, locked the door and began hurrying back toward Washington Road, holding her long skirt above the sidewalk. She wasn't sure in which direction the number was, so she started south. She made her way past the Anne Gregory For the Bride shop, stopped, then realized this was the address. She almost laughed. He not only was staying a block from her, he was staying in the only building in Mt. Lebanon that was crenelated like a castle.

She doubled back to the residential door to the left of the shop windows, and with a sigh began to scan the names next to the bells. Ball had not given her an apartment number, and, in fact, had only been able to come up with the address by rifling through the papers on his desk to find the delivery slip from the company he'd hired to transport the paintings to his house.

Three bells, three names. "Joshua Smith," "M. Curran" and—*Oh, very funny*—"K.T. Holmes."

Jerk, she thought instantly, then bit her tongue in dismay.

She rang the Holmes bell and waited. No response. She was just about to walk away when the door swung open. Peter was throwing a wool scarf around his neck. He froze when he saw her.

"I need to talk to you," she said.

"That's odd. I was just coming to talk to you." He tucked the scarf in his coat meekly and followed her out onto the sidewalk.

The December wind blew down the street, lifting the curls of hair over his ears. He slipped his hands in his pockets and moved automatically between her and the gusts. "What is it?"

How could she have missed it? That smoky quiver that had always sat in his eyes wasn't laughter or mocking or even desire. It was pain. She should have recognized it. She'd had opportunity enough to examine such a thing, after all.

"I found an article about you."

The quiver disappeared, like the lens of a camera, hidden behind a protective cover.

"Oh?"

She felt her own vulnerability rise, a frightening combination of sorrow and culpability. "Why didn't you tell me?"

It was as if a *whoosh* of vacuum had sucked all the noise and wind and traffic from the street, leaving only a blurred silence and the two of them. The lens lifted briefly, and she saw that he understood. Peter looked down at his shoes. Cam felt her throat cramp, so afraid was she of the next word.

His gaze lifted, and a tear had striped his cheek. "One doesn't easily fit 'My wife died in childbirth' into a conversation."

She flew into his arms. "Oh, Peter. And your son."

"And my son."

She could feel him quake, and she was crying, too, thinking of her brother and the son he'd never see grow up, and for an instant the world seemed filled with such cruelty.

"My brother," she cried into his coat, "lost his wife and son in a car accident. I'm so sorry." And she was—for Peter, for her brother, for anyone who'd ever lost anybody.

Peter hugged her tighter. "You mustn't cry," he said through his own tears. "'Twas many years ago."

She cried harder and felt a fool.

"Come inside," he said. "Let me make you some tea."

"For the longest time," he said, "I didn't know she was with child."

He ran a hand through his hair and spoke distractedly as Cam drank. She held her tongue and let him say what needed to be said.

"I know it seems foolish now. We were, after all"—he flushed—"quite actively in love. But I liked her plump and didn't notice."

The article Cam had read in *The Burlington Magazine* was not about Peter and his painting of the four Ursulas, though that picture had been included, but an analysis of a portrait by Peter of a woman of "haunting beauty" whom the author believed to be Ursula. The woman's head covering, informal pose and domestic negligee suggested to an art expert the author consulted that "the painter was evidently in love with her." The author went on to say that the position of the woman's hands, holding saffron-colored fabric bunched across her lap, suggested she was "enceinte"—pregnant, in the indirect parlance of the day—a fact the author believed was supported by the almost frightened expression in her eyes, which he pointed out was "quite compatible with that condition of expectancy."

Cam had studied that picture for a good ten minutes. The sitter wasn't the seductress of Cam's imagination. She was a woman in her thirties. Beautiful, yes. A goddess, no. And Cam had agreed with the viscount: the drape of fabric and position of the hand were common painterly devices for hiding a pregnancy.

"And when she told me the news . . ." Peter smiled, the faraway look in his eyes suggesting an oft-recalled happiness. "Ah, how we celebrated."

"And you painted her."

"I always painted her, but, aye, then, too. The way her face had changed. It was as if the sun had risen inside her. I couldn't even capture it on canvas. It was remarkable."

Cam watched his thumb and forefinger go to the emerald.

"And the birth . . . It started so easily. I was on top of the world. It was evening. The studio was closed. By morn I would have a son—or a daughter. What did I care? We would have more, as many as she wanted. But not long after the strike of two, she began to bleed. A surgeon was called, but he couldn't stop it. There was nothing to be done. Not, that is"—his voice grew hollow, and Cam bit the inside of her mouth—"until it was over. Then he would bring his awful blade to bear on her and—"

His shoulders hitched, and he lowered his head. Cam returned the cup to the saucer, hand shaking, and the tinkle of china was like the blast of a trumpet in the silent studio.

He brought both hands to his mouth, cupping them as if to catch the outpouring of sorrow. But he could neither catch nor stop it.

"—and he would bring our baby into the world and leave Ursula . . ."

"Oh, Peter, it's all right."

"I held her, until the end, until her hand relaxed and her eyes lost their fear, but I couldn't watch that. I couldn't. I told him I didn't care about the child, that he should save her, but he said he couldn't. He could only save the child, and only if he were very, very lucky."

Cam thought of her brother and how he'd had to tell the story over and over, and how the words had become a potion for him, a way to organize something that couldn't be organized.

"The swaddled child—my son—was placed in my

arms a quarter hour later." Peter wiped the wetness from his cheeks. "I-I wanted to hate him, but I couldn't. He was beautiful. He was her. But he was so small."

And he was named for his father, she thought, for that was what the author's research had uncovered in the records of the Covent Garden church called St. Paul's. Nell had said "Old Pauly" had taken Ursula. Cam assumed "Old Pauly" was a man, but she'd been so wrong.

Cam knew where the story would lead, but she also knew he needed to tell it.

"We did everything. Nursemaids, salves, whatever bolus the doctor could get down his tiny throat. But nothing could save him." Peter made a long, low howl, like a wolf. "Ursula," he said, "was buried on Tuesday and my son, on Saturday. Side by side, forever. And neither have a name to be buried under because I never thought to marry her."

His head dropped into his hand, and Cam slid onto the couch next to him, putting her arms around him.

"Oh, Peter. They didn't need your name. They had you." She knew the churches then had very strict rules about burial. It was entirely possible an unmarried woman and her son would be granted nothing more than their Christian names on the headstones. They were probably lucky to have been buried in consecrated ground at all.

"Campbell," he said, his voice choked with tears, "I have robbed them of the one thing that even the poorest honorable man can give."

"Listen to me. That didn't matter to Ursula. All that mattered to her was that you were there, holding her hand, helping her to the other side. Do you think something as trivial as a name can make a difference to a woman who knows she's loved and protected?"

After a long moment he steadied himself. She let her arm slide down his shoulder and locked her hand into his. He clutched it as if it were a life preserver.

"I lived eight more years, more dead than alive, and I thought dying would free me, but it didn't. By the time death arrived, it was too late. Ursula had been reborn into her new life and so had my son." He caught himself and looked at Cam. "Forgive me. You do not know of what I speak, do you?"

"I know. Mertons came to me. Oh, Peter, I'm so sorry."

"And I, too. I have spent a decade sorry. I do not know what it has won me, though."

She didn't reply, and he just held her hand.

There was something wonderful about the warm ease with which their palms rested together. She gazed at the patternless swirl of bristle across his cheek and the way his earlobe seemed to glide off his jawline like a wing off Mercury's foot, but nothing made her happier than the soft, dry pillow of flesh on which her hand rested.

He lifted her hand and brought it to his mouth. The kiss was neither intrusive nor leading, but Cam felt the breath pressed out of her as if by a cinch around her waist.

"Thank you for listening," he said. "I've never been able to tell it before. Never wanted to."

"Sure."

She could feel his breath on her skin, feel the pulse in his fingers.

"I did a terrible thing," he said, "exposing you in those paintings."

"I did the exposing, and I have a sense that the world was rebalancing things. You can't decide you'll tear the covering off other people's lives without expecting a little defrocking yourself. You know, if I'm so enamored of Jake Ryan, I might try modeling a little Samantha Baker behavior myself."

"Jake Ryan? Samantha Baker?"

"Oh, it's an old movie. Do you know movies?"

"'This could be the start of a beautiful friendship,' aye?" When he saw the look of surprise on her face, he added, "Mertons said it once. I made him explain. From what I could understand, movies are stories told in the form of pictures that move. It sounds interesting, especially this *Casablanca* story, which he went into in some very great detail. Why did Ilsa leave Rick, by the way? Mertons prides himself on being a romantic, but it was very hard to get the nuance from him."

"Hell if I know. Conventional wisdom is she loved Victor Laszlo, and Rick knew it."

Peter nodded. "And Jake?"

"Oh." She chuckled. "Jake. Jake Ryan is the boyfriend every girl dreams about. He's beautiful and wise and popular and rich, and Samantha is turning sixteen and kind of a nerd—" In response to Peter's raised brow, Cam added, "Smart but not standardly beautiful."

His eyes flickered across Cam's face. "I see."

"Samantha is turning sixteen, but because her self-centered older sister is getting married, no one remembers—no one, that is, except Jake, who recognizes her for the worthy woman she is, and the movie ends with them sitting on a table with a cake with sixteen flaming candles between them, and Samantha blows them out and they kiss. It's totally romantic."

"Jake, is it?"

"Yes, Jake. And the really amazing part is the actor who played Jake pretty much disappeared after that movie. Oh, he did a few more—you'd have to understand that being an actor in a movie is considered a really great job, like one of the best in the world—but he decided he didn't want to be an actor anymore, and he gave up all the pinnings of success in order to just live a quiet life with his family."

"It sounds quite wonderful, to be truthful."

For a long moment, Peter was silent, and Cam gazed around the small apartment he occupied. He had already made the space his own. At the front, near the windows that overlooked Washington Road, he had placed his paints and an easel. The couch on which they sat was a wide, rich brocade, the likes of which she had not seen outside of Versailles or *Architectural Digest,* and beside it stood a gleaming mahogany secretary that reached nearly to the ceiling. On the shelves stretching over its intricate warren of cubbies were art books covering topics ranging from Romanticism to Cubism to Op Art. An armchair education, she thought. Then she saw the lone silver hairpin in a low black bowl.

He caught the direction of her gaze and flushed.

"'Tis yours," he admitted.

"It is?"

"I-I have carried it with me since."

She felt her heart skip a beat. It was a stirring tribute, one that she did not take lightly. She didn't know what to say.

"I did not tell Mertons," he said. "It seemed the least of my transgressions."

"Where is Mertons?" she asked.

Peter's thumb, which had been gently brushing her knuckle, stopped.

"Mertons is where I need to be," he answered carefully.

Cam hadn't forgotten what Mertons had said to her— that the Peter here was not the Peter of 1673. The Peter here was a man from the Afterlife who'd been broken by sadness and now awaited release in the form of a new life in which he could forget all that he had once lost. Nonetheless, Peter's words started a quiet thrum of worry in her.

"What do you mean?" she said.

"I mean I shouldn't be here. Apart from the foolish pride which informed this misadventure, my being here is, as Mertons has advised, something akin to yelling 'fire' in a crowded theater. My actions here, in a time that is not my own, will play Old Harry with variables I cannot even begin to understand."

"So what?" Her belligerence surprised her.

"Like a cursed billiard ball, I may force people into directions they shouldn't be moved. I may force you down a road you should not travel. I have already hurt you in a way I could not have foreseen."

"I am entirely capable of making my own bad decisions. Believe me. I don't need you shouldering any of the responsibility for them."

He laughed, but she could see he was unmoved and the thrum rose to a buzz.

"How long can you stay?" The petulance in her voice made her sound like a child.

"In truth, not as long as I could wish."

Their eyes met and he reached for her. The kiss was hungry and sorrowful and told her everything she already knew.

"How long?" she whispered. "How long?"

"Cam, I cannot—"

"I'm leaving the museum."

"Cam!"

"I may have to anyway. You probably don't know this, but I'm in line for the directorship. If I don't get it, I'll leave."

"You'll get it."

"You don't know my competition. Oh, wait, you do." She met his eyes. "Anastasia."

His brow lifted. "She mentioned our meeting?"

His deliberately vague reply made her uneasy. "Yes. She's the other candidate."

"She's also your sister."

"She has excellent credentials."

"Credentials cannot replace rectitude. She is unkind to you. The electors will see that."

Cam flushed at his protectiveness, and he gazed at her, unblinking.

"Unfortunately my extracurricular activities aren't exactly what the electors are looking for—especially the hundred and sixteen acres of activity about to break on Monday—" She caught herself. He felt bad enough about the paintings, and the fault had been hers.

"Nonsense," he said. "Do you think my portrait of the Duchess of Portsmouth made her any less a dynast of society? Do you think the nude of Nell diminished her influence? Self-confidence breeds power, Cam. Frank, unapologetic self-confidence is the ultimate currency."

"Really?"

"Their concerns are beneath you. Show courage in the face of judgment and you will have them in the palm of your hand."

His eyes shone with the same sort of undemanding admiration they'd had when he was painting her. She felt her spine straighten. He was right. What the museum needed was a leader. Leaders rise above distractions. Leaders make things happen.

"Well, I still have that Van Dyck acquisition coming in, you know. Two-point-one million."

"There. You see? Though for the record I must add that two million dollars for a Van Dyck is beyond my understanding." He shook his head in mock disdain. "So, 'tis settled, aye? You will stay and fight." And when Cam threw her chin up then down, he added, "In any case, what would you have done if you had left?"

Had she really thought she would go with Jacket? To London? Away from the town she loved so much? But clearly she had, for why else would she be so sure that leaving was the right thing to do?

Peter saw the calculation in her eyes and must have guessed the reason for it as well.

"What is Jacket to you?" he asked softly. A muscle in his jaw flexed.

"He is nothing."

"Cam."

He lifted her chin, and she hooded her eyes, unwilling to let him see. He brushed the top of her sweater and she flushed. The necklace was gone. She had moved the ring to her finger.

For an instant Peter swayed, but then his hand found the wide band of silver and he found his composure.

"He is a good man, aye? I need to know that much, at least."

"He asked me to marry him," she said.

"There is a certain inarguable goodness in that, I suppose," Peter said, smiling, though the smile died away when he added, "And you will?"

"No," she said. "I want you."

"I am not to be had," he said sadly. "I must return. I have pleased myself here far too long."

"Stay."

"Oh, Campbell."

She leaned forward and brought her mouth to his. She could feel the sense of his body change from sorrow to desire.

"Campbell," he warned when they parted.

She drew her fingers along his jaw and the sleek groove of his ear.

He made a whimpering noise, which Cam heightened with a flick of her tongue. She wanted to chase the sadness from his heart like a wildfire clearing fields, and she would use every tool at her command.

She brought herself against him, feeling the long bones of his legs and girded steel of his hips and letting him feel the press of her breasts.

He stood to free himself. She followed, and he ensnared her in his arms.

"Stop," he begged.

She leaned back, spreading her shoulders across his arms, and he buried himself in the expanse of her collarbone. With the barest twist, she brought the fullness of her bosom to his lips.

He shifted his arm, unbalancing her, and took the jutting peak of cashmere between his teeth.

The plume of fire reached her hips. She tried to shift but only one foot held the floor.

He pulled the nub of flesh slowly, to the furthest reach of pleasure, then let go.

"I want you," she whispered.

"I want you in ways I should not."

Two more tugs, and she made a long, soft cry.

He jerked her to her feet, caught the flap of her sweater and pulled. The pearl buttons opened, except the last, which snapped its thread and skittered across the floor. His eyes glittered. The bra she had put on for Jacket's sake had his full attention. See-through and made of lace the color of flushed skin, its cups were embroidered with seed pearls and the spark of crystal in a scant, twining vine that curved invitingly around her aureoles. The boning held her breasts as high as they had ever reached, and the narrow straps of matching silk that ran from her shoulders around the bottom of her breasts met in a tiny bow over the perilously fastened front clasp. Panties of a similar design stretched hip to hip. It was the sort of lingerie a woman wore for one purpose and one purpose only. For Cam, who faced the prospect of giving Jacket a long-overdue answer to his question, choosing such immodest garments had been a matter of hoping the form of enthusiasm would inspire the substance.

But now, with Peter, they were the most fitting complement to her feelings.

He gazed at her, awestruck. Cam could see his heart beat in the hollow of his throat. He opened his hand as if to ask her permission. She nodded, and his fingertips came to rest on her stomach. Shell-shocked, he stepped around her to take in the view.

"What is this?" he asked in a choked whisper.

"A bra."

"Such fearlessness," he marveled as he paced. "Such damn-it-all harlotry."

Inebriated by the words, she lifted the fabric of her skirt, pooling it over her arm at her waist.

"Holy Mother of God."

"Panties," she said.

Ruffles hung over her ass like a skirt, flutters of translucent fabric weighted by tiny swaying crystals at the hem.

"I think," he said, "I must sit down."

He sunk onto the arm of the couch, elbows on his knees, cupping his hands at his chin. He lifted his gaze to hers. The admiration shone strong, but the desire had been replaced by something more somber.

"All of this," he said, "for Jacket."

She couldn't lie. She let the skirt drop. "It's all I have to give him."

Peter took her hand and pressed it to his mouth. "I do not wish to let you go."

"You won't." She combed a hand through the dark waves of his hair. "We'll hold each other forever."

"Campbell"—his voice lost its certainty—"I-I *must* go."

"No."

"Aye. I can stay for a bit, but not forever."

"How long is 'a bit'?"

"Weeks. A month. No more. Every day is riskier."

"No. Forever. Please."

"I do not choose it, Campbell. My time here is over."

She felt her new happiness slipping away. "Then I'll come with you." She slipped her hand under his jacket, looking for reassurance in the broad, muscular warmth of his chest.

His face turned gray. "You cannot come with me, either."

"Why, Peter? Why?"

"The Guild will not allow it. And in any case, the me you know will be placed in a new life, never to return to these old bones."

She struggled for air. "I-I'll never see you again."

He shook his head sadly.

"No. No! I'll go to them. I'll—"

"No, Campbell, no. You will do exactly this. You will go home to Jacket. It would be best for all of us. You will wear his ring. You will take him to your bed, and you will help him learn to make you happy. That is the gift you can give me."

"Is that what you think?" The blood began to ring in her ears.

"Campbell, you know it to be true. His art is good, that much I can tell you truly, and you saw the goodness in him once. You will see it again. I am the only obstacle."

"You have a damned high opinion of yourself."

"I beg your pardon."

"My heart is the obstacle. I cannot love him. Not now."

"Campbell . . ."

"I choose you, Peter. Now."

Before she could think, his arms were around her, clutching her tightly. The heady scent of his skin—soap and paint—filled her head.

"It is selfish," he said into her hair. "God, help me."

"And me as well."

His grip grew so tight Cam felt her breath gather in her chest. It was as if he were trying to hold the seconds time was tearing from them.

"We cannot stop them," she whispered. "The moments will go. But we can master them. We can hold each in our arms until it surrenders itself to us."

"Surrender to me." He pulled her onto the couch and spread her across his lap. "I want to paint you."

"Here?" She brushed his cheek and saw her hand was trembling.

"No. There isn't time. Later. And often. And forever. But to do that I need to see you, to memorize you, to possess you with every sense."

She squirmed. He was granite beneath her. "How?"

"Your hair," he said. "Let me unpin it."

She bowed her head slightly, and he inhaled. With a gentle tug, the first pin slid free. The curl tumbled down her shoulder, almost to her breast.

"Oh God."

Rocking her gently, he removed the second, third and fourth. Cam felt goose bumps pop as the silky weight tickled her skin.

"Breathtaking," he said. "Rust and paprika and umber and even rich Kentish loam—all filtered through bars of heavenly gold. May I?"

She nodded, and he drew his hands through the waves, scattering them like rays of sunlight.

"Oh Christ, how I have wanted this." He fumbled under her skirt and found his buckle. The *clack-clack* as he loosened it made her belly contract. When he'd lowered his trousers, he lifted her effortlessly, slid her panties aside and entered her.

She came down slowly, savoring the iron press of him. He was bigger even than she'd remembered. The slightest movement brought an exquisite heat that reached almost to her throat. He dandled her slowly, drawing his luminous gaze over her body, and her skirt sizzled as its slippery weight resettled again and again over his hips.

He grazed his palms over her nipples, hardening them into rubies.

Her experience was broad. There wasn't a position or surface she hadn't tried, but to luxuriate here in his adoring gaze, while he rolled the tiny seed pearls of her bra between his thumb and her tender flesh, was beyond any pleasure she had ever known.

His cheeks were flushed, and his eyes held hers, unblinking. She didn't want to think about what would come next. Whatever they could have, she would have here, now.

He found the bow, and in an instant her breasts were loose. She felt him thicken as he brushed the lace and boning away. With a groan, he jerked his hips and the weight of her flesh bounced against her chest. He caught each nipple between knuckles and tortured her, plucking the burning flesh until fire scorched a path between her thighs.

Then his hands left her chest. He brought them to her shoulders and down her arms. He drew his thumbs along her chin and over her cheekbones. She closed her eyes to hold on to the moment, but it was flying too far in front of her to catch.

"No," she whispered, and he stopped.

"No, no," she cried, and began to ply her hips on her own. Each circuit brought the cool metal of his loosened belt under her overheated flesh. He stroked her knees, bringing his hands up her straining thighs until at last he palmed her buttocks. She could feel the panties' crystals as they swayed, and she knew he could feel them, too.

"Harlotry," he said, smiling.

"Yes."

"I shall never forget you."

He sat straighter, pulling her tight against him. They were rocking in tandem now, feverish, slow sways that filled her with a fiery, heartbreaking joy. It was as if he were trying not so much to possess her as disappear into her, and she opened her arms and legs to offer him safe harbor.

He lifted her now to his own purpose, and Cam began to sway dizzily, the overwhelming mixture of fire and sorrow and affection separating her from her senses. She wanted to stop time, to hold him here, safe in her arms forever. She closed her eyes, and he brought her down his length, again and again, in a thumping staccato. When she clasped his shoulders, he kissed the valley between her breasts. He held her there, filling her with his desperate hope, until there was nothing but two hearts, wedded in a fire she could no longer contain.

"Oh, *oh*, " she cried.

His thumb found her bud and he held her at the peak, twitching her higher and higher until her breath stopped and her lungs burned and the conflagration between her legs consumed her.

A long, shuddering moment later, when she realized she hadn't died and that her limbs still functioned, she saw he had not finished. She brought him close, losing herself in the thick brown-black waves of his hair. She moved reverentially, stretching out each moment like taffy. Only when she laid a hand on his cheek did she feel he was crying.

"Oh, Peter. I shall never forget you, either."

He brought himself high into her, pressing her almost to standing with his need, and his groan echoed in her ears.

His body jerked reflexively, once and again, but his shoulders, cool and damp under her touch, did not relax. "Don't move," he said. "Don't move."

She saw their reflection in his mirror, his back as straight as a castle wall, his lips on her glistening breast, and her long white skirt streaming from the couch. It was a wedding night fantasia, and she tried to capture it forever in her mind's eye as a replacement for the wedding night she would never have with him.

With an easy heave, he moved her from his lap to her back on the couch, where he found purchase in the midst of the silk. He laced his fingers in hers, their rings touching, and looked in her eyes.

"Tell Jacket he is to have you, but not until I am done. For now, for today, until I am removed, I will have you for my own."

Her breath caught, and he kissed her.

Peter, now was the only message that registered.

47

She smoothed her skirt and gazed at her reflection. Peter had insisted she wear the sweater without the bra, saying no woman would be tortured by whalebone on his account, but she suspected more than general bonhomie at work as she'd twice caught him stealing sidelong glances at her. With hair streaming in uncombed waves down her shoulders, spots of pink on her cheeks, a button missing from her sweater and a skirt that looked like she'd just crawled through the climbing tower at Burger King, the lack of bra was pretty much in keeping with the theme. She supposed she should just be glad there were no teeth marks on the wool. *Ah, well, self-confidence, right?*

"I won't be too long," she said, giving him a kiss. "Three hours of forced smiles, air kisses and wine spritzers is about all I can take. I don't want to miss a minute with you I don't have to."

Peter's pencil stopped on the words *air kisses*—he had retreated to his desk and was sketching her—but he continued on with a shrug. "You won't miss a minute with me. I am invited. Ball's guest."

"Oh." This threw a slight wrench in the evening because Cam knew she had to talk to Jacket, and Peter's presence would make things more awkward. "I, um—"

"Fear not, fair lady. I shall make myself scarce. You need to focus on filling the room with the confidence of a sultan, er, sultaness, and in any case, I shall not be the cause of any further embarrassment for you and Jacket."

"Thank you, Peter. But after, can we—"

"Aye." He put his arm around her waist and pulled her close. "After. And for as long as we have."

She looked at the clock. Time was her enemy. "Are you ready? My car's around the corner."

He took a glance out the window. "Ball was sending a carriage—I mean, car—for me— Oh, I think it's here. Long and black, aye? I'll tell the driver I don't need him. 'Twould be a pleasure to see you drive."

For an instant she had a vision of Scarlett O'Hara seated high on her carriage, driving her horses around Atlanta, but then the recollection that her eight-year-old Honda hadn't been washed since June cleared her head. "Um, I wouldn't get my hopes up, if I were you."

The corner of his mouth rose. "I shall temper my anticipation."

A particularly loud snippet of "Walking on Sunshine" began to trumpet through the room. It was her ringtone and Cam scurried toward the couch. Her phone was in her purse, but she didn't have the faintest idea where her purse might be.

The noise seemed to be coming from the floor. She

dove to her knees and looked under the coffee table. Nothing. She checked under the couch. No joy.

Peter was looking now, too. He crouched by the desk. "Are we looking for the music?"

"Yes. It's coming out of my purse."

"Ah." He unfolded himself, strode to the credenza and found her clutch on the floor. It must have fallen out of her coat.

She grabbed it and answered just as the music stopped.

"Crap." She looked at the display. "It's my boss." Jabbing the button to call him back, she gave Peter a "no worries" look and said, "I'll just be a minute."

Packard answered on the first ring. "Oh, thank God."

"What is it?" She could hear the concern in his voice.

"Cam, there's a problem with Ball's Van Dyck."

"What do you mean, a problem?" The painting had passed every insurance and curate review and was now sitting on an easel behind a velvet curtain, ready to be revealed at the gala.

"I mean it's not by Van Dyck."

48

Peter buckled the belt across his lap just as Mertons had shown him and watched Cam as she twisted the key and the car roared to life. Even in the shadows of the evening she looked beautiful, and he burned with pride, lust and a terrified gratitude that for however long he could allow himself to stay, she would be with him. As she busied herself with the launching of the vessel, something in the back of the car caught his eye.

A warmth came over him as he realized it was the portrait he'd done of her.

"How . . . ?"

"Mertons," she said inexplicably.

He damned the man silently. He'd asked Mertons to dispose of it and instead he'd given it to her.

"He wanted me to convince you to go back. I was going to return it. Never quite got around to it." She gave him a lopsided smile, but the lights of a passing car showed lines around her eyes that hadn't been there a few minutes earlier.

"What is it?" He laid a tentative hand on her wrist. He knew it was the call. She'd laughed it off, but something in her had changed.

"Nothing, it's . . . I'm sure it's nothing." She pushed the rudder into place, turned the wheel and the car sailed into traffic.

"Tell me."

The beacon turned from yellow to red. The car slowed and stopped. Cam pulled a lever until it squealed and touched her lashes with a finger.

"It's the Van Dyck," she said. "But it just doesn't make any sense."

Peter felt a trace of foreboding. "The painting from Ball?"

"Yes. My boss just called. He says it's not a Van Dyck."

His heart thudded in his chest. "Pull the car off the road. I need to run upstairs."

He flung open the door and hit the switch for the light. In two strides he was at the desk. But his hopes sank before he even flipped to the back of the sketchbook. The letter from Anthony Van Dyck was gone.

49

"I don't know what you mean," Cam said.

He gazed at her in the light of the museum's entryway, looking so beautiful and so worried, "I mean, don't worry."

He kissed her forehead, which felt as soft as a summer breeze, and slipped the coat off her shoulders. "Go talk to your master. The gala doesn't start for half an hour. I'm sure you'll be able to work it out."

"But how . . . ?"

"Have faith."

"Faith, huh?"

"And self-confidence, aye?"

She nodded uncertainly, and he kissed her again, pushing her gently on her way. As he watched her climb the long staircase, he thought that though he'd seen more than one queen crowned in glory at the head of a court, he'd never seen anything to match this Cenerentola with her breathtaking fall of flame-kissed curls, soft olive bodice and skirts trailing behind. If she lost a slipper as she rose higher and higher, he would not have batted an eye.

When she disappeared, he turned to the guard. "Where might I find a woman named Anastasia? I need to speak to her. 'Tis a matter of great import."

50

"This is a disaster, Cam." Lamont Packard stood at the window, gazing out at the rolling hills of Schenley Park, fists stuffed deep in the pockets of his tuxedo.

"But it doesn't make sense. The painting passed every review, including mine."

He turned, sighed and lowered himself onto the edge of his desk. "Experts make mistakes all the time. You know what happened to *Andromeda Chained to a Rock.*"

She did. The painting owned by the Los Angeles County Museum of Art, supposedly by Van Dyck, had been attributed to him and then de-attributed so many times she didn't think anyone believed what the title card read anymore, including the staff.

"But that was different," she said. "That painting had a very sketchy provenance. Ball bought this one from an earl whose family had forgotten it had been stowed in their cellar for the last two hundred years. For God's sake, they still have the bill of sale for eighteen guineas, eight shillings from when the first earl bought it from Van Dyck's agent right after Van Dyck's death. Can you let me see the letter?"

Ball shrugged, reached across his desk and handed her a fragile sheath of vellum.

Her heart sunk. The writing was in Van Dyck's hand. She'd seen it enough times on paintings and letters to recognize his distinctive script anywhere.

"It's Van Dyck's."

Packard nodded. "The paper fits the period as well."

She unfolded the note carefully. It appeared to be a page torn out of a diary.

> *I have made the Decision to close my Studio for a fortnight. Until the Fevre which rages in the city passes, I will take no more commissions. 'Tis a bitter potion, to be Sure, but my Luck this year has been Strong and, with the recent Commissions from His Majesty, I can easilee bere the pause in Income. To pass the Tyme, I have given my Apprentices leave to practice under my Watchful Eye. One, Albertus, a most skylled man of Mantua, has taken the opportunity to attempt a Portrait of his dear wyfe, Sarah. Albertus's lady will be pleased. Albertus's ability to compose a Van Dyck countenance is most pronounced, and the ladye is more comely than even I could render, tho Albertus adds a Lamb and shepherd's hook in a fit of Metaphore that is a distraction to my eye. The ladye beres a Strong resemblance to the new bride of Baron Milton, which*

pleased Albertus when I tolde him, tho why I could
not say. Albertus shall have the painting when—

The entry ended. Cam flipped the page over, but the other side was blank.

Ball tapped his finger. " 'Albertus shall have the painting when . . .' "

" 'I die'?" Cam said, seeing exactly where goddamn Van Dyck was heading.

" '. . . he finishes'?" Ball suggested. "It almost doesn't matter, because instead of Albertus giving it to his lady—"

"He keeps it until Van Dyck can no longer disclaim it and then sells it to Van Dyck's agent as a real Van Dyck."

"Who then turns around and sells it to Baron Milton."

"Crap." Cam felt an iron weight drop in her gut and sunk into a chair. "I guess Albertus wasn't quite the romantic Van Dyck would have liked us to think."

Packard gave her a weak smile. "Perhaps he used the money for a pair of diamond bobs."

Cam tried to summon the painting in her head. Much of her examination technique relied on intuition, intuition based on years of study and admiration. She thought of the ringlets framing the woman's forehead, the sharp, clear expression in her chestnut eyes and the stippled fur tippet that hung over her shoulder. It was a Van Dyck. She had absolutely no doubt—not then, not now. Not that her certainty would carry much weight here, not when her career was the one that would benefit from the decision, which is why she'd taken such care to have others establish its authenticity.

Packard took off his glasses and massaged his temple. "We're in trouble, Cam. Ball's down there waiting to be honored for his generous gift. The museum's already issued the press release. Hell, the gift's going to be the cover story in the paper tomorrow. No matter what we do at this point, it's going to be a huge embarrassment to everyone involved."

Ever the gentleman, Packard made a point not to bring his eyes to rest on her, but Cam realized she was going to be sucked into the quicksand of this debacle as well. In fact, her shoulders were going to be where everyone else would try to find a toehold. She knew what she owed Packard. She knew what she owed the museum.

"I'll tell Ball." She held up a hand to stop Packard's protest. "He's a good guy. He'll be disappointed, but he'll understand. And," she said sadly, "I'll resign."

Packard sighed, and she knew it was over.

"Hate to see it, Cam."

You and me, both, pal. "Best thing, I think." She fought back the wave of disappointment that seemed intent on drowning her tonight. "I'll work the gala—er, unless you'd prefer I didn't."

He clapped her on the shoulder. "I wouldn't have it any other way." He stood to rebutton his jacket and gave her a sly grin. "Too bad, really. I was sort of looking forward to seating an executive director most of the world would have seen nude. Would have knocked the board biddies on their asses."

"*Ack!* You saw the paintings?" She felt her face turn six shades of crimson.

"Of course. Ball called me for advice. Who do you think helped quash the story till Monday?"

"Gosh, thanks." Not that the delay made much difference now.

"Of course, the price was an exclusive. Sam Arnofsky from *Pop City* will be here Monday at nine for an in-depth interview. I left the contact info and a sheaf of photos he dropped off on your desk— Oh, and I also left a note Ball wrote on how he thinks they're going to frame the story. He thought it might help."

"Super. Appreciate it, boss."

"Boss no more. Just an admirer. Tell you what, though. This Peter guy's a hell of a painter. Starkly postmodern, yet this undeniable reference to classical proportion and light. And the scale . . . Jesus, it's like walking into a room and finding yourself face-to-face with the Taj Mahal or the top of the Chrysler Building."

"Or the Jumbotron from Madonna's Truth or Dare Tour."

"Cam, it's a helluva tribute. I don't think the Taj Mahal is too far from the mark. Will I get to meet him?"

"Ah, yes, actually," she said, feeling her heart skip. "He's here tonight."

"Interesting." Packard nodded. "Then you'll be . . . all right?" His country club green eyes had softened to a grassy gray. He meant without her job.

"Yeah," she said quickly. "You know me. Sure. Absolutely."

"That's good. And you've got the book to work on, right?"

"Uh, no, actually."

"What? You've canceled another one?"

"Yeah, um, the Lely thing didn't pan out."

"Are you kidding? What about the muse? The woman

he raised from the streets? C'mon, Cam. Sex, drugs and the King of England?"

"Um, you know me. I like to work with as clean a slate as possible. Turns out there's more known about the woman than I realized. Facts, it seems, only complicate my stories."

"Well, the next one, then?" He gave her an encouraging look.

"You bet."

Cam stood, too, dreading the thought of Ball's face when she told him the news, and handed the page back to Packard. Then it struck her.

"Wait a second. I totally forgot to ask. Where did you get this?"

"It arrived this morning in the mail." Packard pointed to an opened envelope on his desk. "No attached note. No return address. Strangest thing. It was almost as if Van Dyck mailed it in himself."

Mailed it himself? Only one person could make it look like that.

"Cam? What is it?"

She ran for the door. "I need air."

51

With the gala's string quartet warming up as background music, Anastasia found herself nearly skipping down the administrative office hallway, though four-inch heels and her chain-mail tunic made the going a little tricky, even by her standards. By Monday she'd be director and Cam could go to London or not, it really didn't matter anymore. She checked her cell. Fifteen minutes before the first guests arrived. She'd just duck into her office to snag her mink poncho and then—

"Well, howdy, stranger," she said, covering her surprise in the most high-voltage smile she possessed.

Peter Lely sat at her desk, looking straight at her. He wore a charcoal suit in a subtle pattern that spoke of old money and swirled a generous Scotch, which meant he'd helped himself to the bare-bones bar on her coffee table. That was okay. She liked men who helped themselves. In fact, she wondered if this unexpected visit meant he intended to avail himself of some of the office's other charms, like a couch and locking door. She assessed the couch with a quick sideways glance and saw the poncho, which in itself offered some interesting possibilities. She let the door glide close with a quiet *click,* and he stood, though his movement felt more like a first move than a courtesy.

"Mind if I join you?" She tilted her head toward the decanter on the table.

"Suit yourself."

His eyes were so smoky she wondered if they might actually ignite. She made her way to the table and angled herself toward him over the bottle, offering the inquiring eye, should he possess one, a fine view of everything from her neck to her navel. Even with her eyes downcast, she could feel the presence with which he filled the room.

A notebook dropped into view.

She froze. It was his sketchbook, the one he'd had at Aldo's that day. She picked up her glass, settled onto the couch and met his gaze.

"I guess you're wondering about the letter."

He didn't reply, just stared.

She recognized the look in his eye now. It was a look she'd gotten a number of times over the years, mostly from women, rarely from men, and it left her feeling dirty and calculating.

"It's too late," she said. "Packard's read it."

"It's a lie."

"It hardly matters now."

"Why would you do it?"

"Isn't the more important question—and the one Cam will eventually ask: What were you doing with the letter?"

He slammed the glass into her wire wastebasket, where it exploded into a hundred glittering shards. "I expect your position is just as dependent as Cam's on the ability to distinguish the authentic from the false. Know this: there will never be a major acquisition in your tenure that will escape doubt. Your word will be poison—if it isn't already."

Though she had anticipated the brutality of the sentiment, she was surprised to find her eyes welling with wetness. "Who are you?" she demanded.

"Someone who loves your sister, a post you may want to consider at some point. You should be ashamed."

And she was.

52

Cam walked down the hall, stunned. Could Peter have been involved in this? She didn't want to believe it. But he came here to stop her. He'd admitted as much himself. And who was more likely to have had access to an old Van Dyck letter? How would she know? Had everything been a lie?

Calm down. You're blowing this out of proportion.

"Whoa!"

Jacket caught her by the waist in an effort to keep them both from spinning off their feet.

"What's up, babe?"

She turned her face away and burst into tears. "I'm not going to be the director."

"Oh, Cam." He took her in his arms and held her tight. "Who needs that stuffy old job anyway? You're too smart for this place."

"But I wanted it," she cried into his soft lapel, then shuddered under another wave of emotion.

"I know, I know." He patted her head.

"And they're going to give it to Anastasia."

"Jesus, they've lost the plot, then. It's the only way to explain it. You're so much smarter than she is, so much more capable, so much more equipped to lead."

"It's not fair. Nothing is."

"It's not. It's absolutely not. C'mon, let's get you into your office."

He took her by the hand and led her down the hall and through the door.

Cam hurried to the tissues and tried to mop her eyes and cheeks. No job, no book and no more Peter—that is, if she'd ever had him. She knew she'd be okay—she always was—but three blows at once was too much for even her, and a fresh round of tears began to fall.

"The painting," she said, gazing out the window. "It's not a Van Dyck. I mean, I'm sure it is, but Packard has a letter or a page of a diary or something, and it's clearly Van Dyck's handwriting, and it says the painting was done by one of the apprentices in his studio. So now I have to tell Ball, the poor guy, and I have to resign. I have to. It's a huge embarrassment to the museum. And in any case," she said, turning, "if Anastasia is going to be the new director, I don't really want— Oh God."

Jacket had found a seat, and now he stared, dazed, at a dozen photos arranged around her desktop. The photos of the *Wednesday Afternoon* paintings. In his hand were the interview notes from Ball. She recognized his tight block printing.

"Jacket . . ."

If he heard, he didn't acknowledge it. He ran a hand over his forehead, opened his mouth to speak, but whatever it was seemed to catch in his throat. She knew what it must look like.

"Jacket, I'm sorry. I meant to tell you."

" 'The reporter,' " he read from the paper in his hand, " 'will be most interested in the lover angle. The paintings reveal a relationship that goes far beyond the usual rhetoric of artist and subject, seemingly beyond that of artist and lover. Was Stratford Lely's lover or just his muse? Does this relationship have any connection to Stratford's recently announced fictography of Restoration painter Peter Lely? And why is Stratford intent on keeping the paintings a secret?' "

The letter dropped, and he touched the photos hesitantly, only at the edges, as if respecting some imaginary boundary.

"They're good," he said, honestly. "Very good." Then he dropped his head in his hands.

"Jesus, Jacket. I am so sorry. I . . ." She hadn't posed for the paintings, but she had been Peter's lover. "I should have told you. Once you came back in my life, even if we weren't officially a couple, I owed you that much, at least. I know this must hurt. And I know it's going to be embarrassing. I'm sorry."

He leaned back in the chair, rubbing his mouth with a fist, and gave a faint, amused chuckle. "I wish we had the chance to start over. God knows I haven't made it easy for you." He sighed and stood. "You don't owe me an explanation, but I'm grateful for it, anyway. I don't want to lose you from my life, Cam, and I hope someday we can figure out how to make it work for us."

"Yeah," she said. "Me too."

He gazed down at his boots. "*Are* you lovers?"

Her cheeks warmed. "Yes."

"Is he the one? I mean, are you going to move in with him?"

"He lives somewhere else, so no, I guess. This is"—*was*, she thought—"just for now."

He gave her a gentle smile. "I'd better get down there."

"I have this." She pulled the ring out of her pocket and held it out to him. He opened his hand, and she dropped it in, letting the chain fall into a heap beside it. He closed his fingers around hers for an instant, then pulled his arm back and looked. "Keep it. It never belonged to me, not in that way. It's what you designed. I'd like you to have it. Anyhow, it makes my tooth throb whenever it's close."

She laughed.

He handed it back to her, and she unhooked the clasp, slipped the ring off the chain and placed it on her finger. "Thank you, Jacket."

He reached out and pulled her into a tight embrace. "I love you, Cam."

"I love you, too."

With a final squeeze, he shook himself loose. He started for the door, then stopped himself. "Do you need help with Ball?"

She shook her head. "Nah. I'll be fine. What's a couple million between friends, right?"

He smiled. "Right. I'll see you downstairs, then."

"Yep."

When he reached the hall, he turned. "He'd better fucking deserve you."

I hope.

53

Peter stumbled blindly out of Anastasia's office, ashamed of the trouble he'd caused and furious at his impotence to rectify it.

No one—not the lowest brute—deserves what I've wrought.

He'd devised the plan with the sangfroid of a spider, dictating the wording to Van Dyck and placing the letter in his pocket sketchbook before going to Mertons's workshop. That he regretted the plan as blackguardly almost as soon as he'd begun it and changed his mind about going through with it before arriving on Cam's doorstep carried no weight to him in the moral calculation now. If it hadn't been in his sketchbook, Anastasia would not have had the opportunity to steal it that day at the coffee shop. His selfish maneuvering had deprived Cam of a future and her profession. Mertons had been right when he'd said traveling to his future was akin to yelling "fire" in a crowded theater. He'd destroyed her happiness, and she didn't even know the extent or the cause—that is, until he could tell her and beg her forgiveness.

He stopped, surprised in his distracted state to find himself at Cam's door.

His breath caught. Jacket had Cam in his arms. It was not a lover's embrace, but it was filled with an abiding affection, and Peter convinced himself to be glad. This, after all, was the man who would care for her when he was gone.

He pulled himself away from the door. *One thing settled.* But there was more he needed to do for her. He turned and headed for the stairs.

54

Alone, Cam slumped against the desk and stared, unsee-ing, at the small unfinished painting on her desk. The events of the day were threatening to overwhelm her, and the gala hadn't even begun. Saying good-bye to Jacket had felt like a door had closed in her life with an abrupt slam. She felt adrift, rudderless, uncertain of Peter or her fu-ture. More than anything, she longed to see Peter, to find out what he knew about that letter and to be reassured that what she had jettisoned everything for still existed.

She sensed a presence in the doorway and wheeled around expectantly.

But it was Mertons, who regarded her with curiosity.

"Good evening, Miss Stratford. Do you know where I might find Peter?"

There was an undercurrent there she didn't like. Her time with Peter couldn't be over after only a few hours. It would be too cruel. "No," she lied. "I haven't seen him. Why?"

But the effusive, deferential Mertons of a few days ago

was gone. He entered her office as if she were not present and scanned each of her bookshelves in succession. He was a man on a mission, and Cam could guess what it was. She had to work hard not to look at her laptop.

"Something I can do for you?" she asked.

"Miss Stratford, I'm going to be honest with you. We know how you're traveling."

"You do?" She forced her eyes forward.

"Yes. We've fixed the time tube to a book. *Inside the Artist's Studio*."

Cam felt a faint sweat rise on her scalp. "Really?"

"We believe there's a time tube linked to a book in Romania. But we've had that copy under observation for years, so we thought you were relying on some other method, some hole we hadn't yet discovered. However, the most recent calculations show a very similar Brown coefficient. Obviously you have found a way to get a copy."

"Yes, because I like to do all of my reading in Romanian."

"This isn't a laughing matter."

"Do you see me laughing? I would think the Guild has bigger fish to fry."

Mertons frowned.

She said, "It means having more important—"

"I know what it means, Miss Stratford. I was thinking about where else you might keep your books. I've been to your apartment."

"I do a lot of research at Chuck E. Cheese's as well. I find the quiet helps me concentrate."

He narrowed his eyes, obviously sensing a fakeout, but dutifully wrote the name down in his notebook.

"I recommend the pizza," she added. "Close your eyes. You'll swear you're in Naples."

He flipped the pen over, clicked a button and it started to flicker, like a small computer monitor. He ran it across the note he'd just taken. Then he held it up like a thermometer and read, " 'Cheese, Chuck E. Indoor playground-slash-restaurant designed for kid parties. Best known for humanlike rat mascot and terrifying animatronic theater performers. Issues own coinage. Key words: headache, noise, heartburn, juvenile ululation.' " He gave Cam a look.

"I didn't say it was for everyone."

He clicked the pen again and the display went dark. "Miss Stratford, I'm about to lose my patience."

"Hey, it's not my job to assist you every time you decide to go on a fishing expedition. Yes, I know," she said, realizing she was beginning to sound like a one-trick pony as far as metaphors were concerned, "we're big on fish here."

"Would you be interested to know that the Guild has finally decided to invoke the O'Janpa Convention? Yes, Peter is about to be jerked back like a bad dog on a very short leash."

"Even if I knew what the O'Janpa Convention is, which I don't, why would I be interested?" As far as Mertons knew, she was still at odds with Peter.

He waved the pen up and back across the plane in front on her face, then held it up and read. "Stratford, Campbell. Author, curator, art historian, time-tube criminal, subject of a series of paintings entitled *Wednesday Afternoons*. Former life partner: Jacket Sprague. Nurtures a deep and nearly overwhelming love for Restoration-era painter Peter Lely, despite a several-century difference in time spans and her petty jealousy over his long-dead—"

"I am not jealous!" She flushed so hard her ears seemed to crackle with the intensity of deep-fried bologna.

He continued to read. "—a feeling Lely returns."

The bologna reached flashpoint. "I-I— He returns it?"

Mertons lifted a brow and smiled.

"Yes, fine. I have feelings for him. He returns it?"

"Feelings. Feelings one might refer to as love?"

"Yes, love, dammit. *Mertons!*"

He nodded. "He returns it. I believe I practically spelled it out for you when I came to visit."

"Is that pen up-to-date? I mean, like, as of this minute?"

He cleared his throat awkwardly and held up the object in question for her to observe. No lights. He hadn't turned it back on.

"Bastard."

He shrugged. "We can't do mind reading. Not even in the Afterlife." He slipped the pen back in his pocket. "Does this knowledge by any chance change your answer? Do you know where Peter is?"

She shook her head. She never, ever wanted Mertons to find him.

"Whether you tell me or not, the Guild *will* find him, and if I can bring him back before they do, he'll face better odds."

"What's that supposed to mean?"

"It means they are extremely angry, Miss Stratford. No one has ever defied their commands before, so flagrantly and for so long, though I must say, you're getting close.

Look, I don't know how you think you ended up in your current life. But it wasn't a matter of the former you just deciding you were going to be an accomplished art historian in your next reincarnation."

She shifted. She'd never considered her former self.

"It took the generosity of whatever Guild you're covered under," he said, "and years of good behavior. In short, you earned it. Peter, it goes without saying, has squandered every iota of goodwill he possessed chasing you down. He won't be an acclaimed artist in his next life. He won't be a portrait painter. I doubt he'll be a house painter. I don't know what he'll be, but you can be sure it will be monotonously boring, soul grinding and as far removed from a creative life as the Guild can manage."

"No painting?" she said, horrified.

She considered sadly what Peter's existence would become without painting. He'd lost so much already.

"Mertons, you have to intervene. The man has paint in his blood. I've never seen him without a sketch pad within arm's reach. You told me yourself he painted nonstop after he was dead. Oh, Mertons. He won't have Ursula, he won't have me. You can't take painting away. You can't do this to him."

"It's not me. It's the Guild. They've had it up to here. First you and the time tube, then Peter and his damned quest. They're tired of being ignored."

She looked at the laptop and back at Mertons.

"What about a deal?"

"A deal? What deal?"

"Is the Guild as good as its word? If they promise to do something, will they?"

"It is the Afterlife." He gazed at her narrowly.

"The time tube," she said. "I'll give it up. Show you the source. You can dig it up or drop dynamite down it or whatever it is you do to eradicate it."

"And in return?"

"In return, you guarantee Peter the life of a painter."

Mertons stroked his chin. "The life of a painter, eh?"

"Yes."

"I can't guarantee he'll be at the top of his profession. I can't guarantee he'll be rich."

"So long as he can paint, Mertons. He has to be able to paint."

He frowned.

"What?" she asked. "What is the problem?"

"It's not a problem, per se." He gave her a worried look. "I hope, Miss Stratford, you are not thinking he could be reborn here? You have to see that Peter will enter his new life as a babe, not as a man. By the time he is thirty, you would be, well—"

"No, Mertons. I wasn't thinking that." Such a thought had crossed her mind, but now even that possibility had been quashed.

"There is one more thing. You won't be able to use the tube as a way to shortcut your book research anymore."

"I'm not going to write the book. Peter's life will go unrecorded, at least by me."

A flash of something—amusement? understanding?— rose in his eyes. "I see."

"And in any case, when it started I only intended to buy the book, not travel through—" She caught herself. "But that doesn't mean I won't be able to write, especially if we're talking fiction. I'm a researcher, and a novel's like building a campfire. With a few good facts and the right spark, I can make a blaze that'll knock your socks off."

He grinned. "I'll consider my socks forewarned. And that's what you'll do?" he asked carefully.

When Peter is gone, she thought. The part Mertons chose not to utter. God, don't let it be soon. "Yes." She smiled with considerably more optimism than she felt.

"It's damned decent of you to do this for him. I'm pretty sure I can convince the Guild to take the offer."

"Really?"

"I'm afraid you put a scare in them. An unregulated time tube is a very dangerous thing."

"I don't suppose there'll be an artist's life in *my* after-life—or success in any profession, I'm betting."

"No, you'd better grab whatever joy you can now. Though," he added with a grave face, "you never know what can change. That's why life is so interesting. You may do something so good or so helpful that it makes everyone up there forget you were ever a burr in their side."

"Me, the writer of hot fictography, or me, the naked model spread out like some lascivious *Artforum* center-fold?"

He chuckled, and she decided the sight of Mertons laughing was not one to be missed.

"You know," he said, "being entertained brings people immense happiness. Don't underestimate the redemptive power of being able to do that."

She smiled. "Thank you, Mertons. I won't."

"So . . ." He clapped his hands together. "Where is it? Is it in this room? Is the book here?"

She waved a finger back and forth. "Oh, no, no, no. Promise first. Tube later. I've learned how you people work."

He sighed. "I'll head out and be back before you know it."

"Hey, um, take your time? Like, take the long way, maybe with a stopover in the Paleolithic era? I hear they have unbelievable cave art."

Mertons tucked the notebook into his jacket pocket. "I'll do my best, Miss Stratford. I can't put off the Guild forever. Once they agree to this, they'll want him back. The most you can expect is a few days. I think you had better not plan for more than that." He gave her a significant look.

She'd always been the type to appreciate each moment, but even with every intention of savoring, was it possible to make the joy one could squeeze out of a few thousand minutes serve for a lifetime?

She thought of what one could gain and lose in the flash of circumstance. She thought of meeting Peter the first time in that hallway. She thought of her brother. She thought of the single, upending instant Peter's eyes had met hers as she lay on that chaise. She thought of opening that article from *Burlington Magazine,* and she thought of Peter, buoyed at the notion of becoming a father, then losing the wife, the child and any reason to keep on living.

"Mertons, wait."

He turned. "Yes?"

"I want him to be happy."

"Painting, yes."

"No, not just painting. I want him to have a wife—

someone who'll love and understand his work—and a child. At least one. He'd be such a good father. Do you think— I mean, it's not too much to ask the Guild to do that, too, is it?"

Mertons's eyes softened. "It's not too much to ask. Every man deserves it. I will try."

"Thank you."

Cam wished everyone's future could be so easily ordered.

Peter inserted himself into the small group of partygoers surrounding Woodson Ball.

"Howdy, Peter. How goes it?"

"Could I have a word in private? 'Tis a matter of some importance."

Ball eyed him curiously, then put down his glass.

55

Jacket slouched against a wall in the crowded entry gallery of the Carnegie. He decided that gazing dejectedly into his Yuengling and looking like he was passing a kidney stone was more effective than he'd expected at keeping people at bay.

"Jesus, you look like shit."

Well, most people. He turned. It was Anastasia, looking like a cross between a real bad *Idol* contestant and a Knight of the Round Table. Christ Almighty, where did she get this stuff?

"Gee, thanks," he said.

"And don't bother adding I do, too. I already know it."

"What? No," he said. "You look great. Ready for battle."

She blew her nose, hard into a napkin. Her eyes were red.

"Damned allergies," she said. "Have you seen Cam? When is she coming down?"

"Yes, and I don't know. Why?"

"I think you're going to want to stick close to her this weekend. She's going to need a lot of support."

"Really? Why's that?"

"I'm going to be named executive director."

"That's been announced?" *Jesus, what an ego. Missed her calling. Should have been an artist.*

"No. But it will."

He gave her a look. "I wouldn't count my chickens."

"What's that supposed to mean?"

"I dunno. Surprising things happen sometimes. For example, tonight. Cam dumped me." He took a long pull of beer.

"What?"

"For that bloke." He gestured to Peter Lely, who was prowling the opposite corner of the room.

"Shit."

He frowned. "What's it to you?"

"Loyalty, my friend. You know I've always been your number one fan."

He wondered if he'd had too much to drink. He swore he saw fangs when Anastasia smiled. "I'm sure she's better off."

Anastasia snorted. "Is he still passing himself off as Peter Lely?"

"Funny thing about that. It turns out he's a hell of a painter. Could probably pass himself off as anyone if he put his mind to it— *Jesus.*"

"What?"

"Look at her."

Cam was floating down the stairs like a blossom down a lazy stream. His gaze cut to Lely, who was watching her, too. "Belle of the ball."

Anastasia sniffed. "Prosaic."

"Call me crazy. I like that kinda prose."

He turned to see if his rival was equally impressed, but Lely had disappeared.

56

Cam scanned the heads as she descended. Ball should be obvious. Apart from having that rich man's luminescent glow, he was generally a head taller than anyone else in the room.

She noted that the curtained Van Dyck painting had been removed and wondered if Lamont Packard had done the dirty work for her. Then she remembered they'd decided at the last minute to unveil it in the gallery upstairs, not in the space being used for cocktails.

She didn't spot Ball, and, more important, didn't see Peter, either.

Crap.

Anastasia was in a tête-à-tête with Jacket—of course—though when Jacket lifted his eyes and spotted Cam, he gave her a gentle smile.

Wow, this evening's going to be more fun than my prom, when Billy Schuler spilled cherry brandy down the front of my dress, my date left early with Sue Rodriguez, the cheerleader-ho from the theater company, and Anastasia told everyone she could find that she used to think the reason I had decided on Barnard was because I was a closet lesbian, but rejected that theory on the grounds that I really wasn't interesting enough.

She reached the next-to-last stair and sighed. No Ball, no Peter. That could only mean they were upstairs—well, Ball at least—and she reversed direction.

"I don't recall the invitation saying 'bra optional.' Bit of a mustard problem?"

Cam didn't need to turn to recognize Jeanne's voice, or her sense of humor.

"Yes, I've taken to eating in my underwear. Saves on dry-cleaning." She continued up the stairs.

"I'm sure the guy at the café loves it," said Jeanne, who followed, drink in hand. "Remind me to recommend you to my friend at *Hot Dog Quarterly.* They're always looking for the next centerfold. That is, unless you're limiting yourself to art world porn at the moment."

Cam swung around. "You saw the paintings? How?"

"Same way I saw my review, the bill from your mechanic and the present state of your investment portfolio. The notes from Ball were on your desk. By the way, I'd stay away from Pfizer. That pipeline's looking iffy. Did you sleep with him?"

"My mechanic? Nah, it was just a headlight. I wrote him a check."

"Funny," Jeanne said. "You know who I mean. Mr. MC Hammer pants."

"Yes, but not like you probably think."

"You have some pretty funny ideas about how I spend my time."

"I'm not getting the directorship. Did you hear that?"

"Yes, I believe your sister is practically handing out fly-ers. I'm really sorry." She gave Cam a hug. "It sucks."

"Tell me about it."

"Think of the upside. At least you won't be seeing Anastasia every day. I'm going to be reporting to The Devil Wears Chainmail."

They had reached the top of the stairs, and Cam turned right for the first gallery. "It gets worse."

"Worse than Sri Lankan chai with organic lilac honey at precisely nine thirty and bamboo paper notepads with her name in Kanji?"

"Yes."

"Wow. Okay."

"It wasn't that the board didn't pick me. I resigned. Had to. The Van Dyck's a fake."

"What?!"

"And there's more."

"Jesus."

"Peter has to leave."

"So go back to visit him. You know," Jeanne added in a whisper, "Amazon. I mean, it looks like you'll have the time."

"Can't. They're taking my mode of transport away. And anyway, he's going back to a new life. It's a long story, but he was only in 1673 for an assignment. He's really supposed to be in the Afterlife, waiting to be assigned a new life. Oh, Jeanne, I'm afraid I love him."

Jeanne stopped so fast some of her drink sloshed over the rim of the glass. "Love? Oh, Cam. You really love him?"

"I must. Otherwise I'd kill him."

"Have you thought about refusing? Holding him hostage? Packing yourself in his luggage?"

Cam shook her head. "No. He's in the running for a good next life, and if I interfere—" She made a raspberry sound.

"Jeez, this is harder than 'I Survived a Japanese Game Show.' Well, don't give up. There's always a way."

"Not this time." Cam sensed a fat tear quivering in her vision and hurriedly wiped it away. "And now I have to find Ball and tell him his two-point-one-million-dollar gift is worth about as much as a really nice Van Gogh poster."

"Man, this is not your day."

"Have you seen him?" Cam looked past Jeanne's head, down the hall.

"Ball?"

"Either of them. Ball or Peter."

"Peter's *here*?"

Cam nodded. "Guest of Ball's."

"Well, Ball was in the east gallery, like, five minutes ago."

"East gallery, then. Wish me luck."

"Here's my vodka tonic. I think that'll work better."

Cam navigated among the buzzing patrons. Everyone looked so happy and carefree in their evening finery. Ball wasn't in the first gallery or the second. By the third, the crowds had thinned, and at the fourth, the one that held her favorite selections from "Behold: Love Through the

Eyes of the Artist" exhibit, she was one of only three or four people.

Morose, she walked the length of the space, peering into the adjacent rooms, but found herself slowing as the paintings exerted their usual influence over her. Two Alex Katzes, both adoringly painted portraits of his wife, Ada, first as a young mother with striking dark hair and gentle eyes, the view of her mouth, which one imagines to be formed in a maternal kiss, hidden behind the head of her young son; then as a matron, her gray-streaked hair still draped over her shoulders, those arched eyebrows and those gentle dark eyes, now edged with lines. Katz had painted Ada dozens and dozens of times in his career, each time with unmistakable affection.

"Lovely," a voice said.

It was Peter, smiling. He looked magnificent, and Cam wanted to throw her arms around him, but found she was unexpectedly shy and contented herself with catching a corner of his sleeve.

"It's Ada."

"I see that," he said, tilting his head toward the painting's title card. "Is that her as well?"

"Yes, both. The artist, her husband, Alex Katz, painted her over and over."

"One woman, two ages, and he still sees the same thing when he looks at her. The effect upon the viewer is unchanged. That's remarkable."

"We have one of yours, you know."

"Do you?"

She pulled him into the British paintings room, one

gallery over. She knew he would ask her about the Van Dyck shortly, but for one cherished moment she wanted to forget everything.

"You may recognize the woman," she said.

"As one recognizes an oncoming storm at sea." Peter's face lit in a grin. "It's my old friend, the Duchess of Portsmouth. Yet I see no telltale marks of newsprint on her nose."

"Snout, I think you mean. It is not one of your best."

"How you flatter. I don't suppose your opinion is in any way colored by your opinion of the subject?"

"Hello. I'm an art expert. Where my opinions come from is nobody's damn business."

"I see nothing's changed in three hundred years. I want to talk with you about the Van Dyck."

She let go of his sleeve.

"Cam." He pulled her around so she was looking at him. "I'm responsible for the letter your master received."

As a child, she'd once had the wind knocked completely out of her when she fell from a tree. She'd been lucky nothing worse had happened. Nonetheless, she remembered being shocked by the violence of it. Peter's confession gave her the same sense of having been throttled to her core. "I wondered if that's what happened," she said, finding her breath. "And you mailed it to Packard?"

"No. No, no, no. Though I can certainly understand why you would think me capable of it. I had Van Dyck write it and brought it with me to stop you, then realized even I couldn't stoop to such villainy. Oh, Cam, but I was fool enough to carry it in my sketchbook, and it was stolen."

"By whom?"

"I-I don't know."

But he did know. And she knew with whom he'd met and who would be capable of such an act. "My sister."

"Cam . . ."

"It doesn't matter. I'm glad it wasn't you."

"It does matter, Cam, it does," he said. "And I think I can help."

"Peter, there's no help for it." She hated to add to his burden by telling him about her resignation, but she refused to be untruthful. "I'm going to take some time off. I think I'm going to concentrate on my writing. The people here are great, but I need to work on the book—well, whatever the book turns out to be."

Peter raised his brow.

"I'm dropping the Lely book."

"Campbell—"

"Hey, you know how shy I am. I mean, look at *Wednesday Afternoons,* right? There's no way I'm writing any book about a man that would eventually have to get to that scene of me on that chaise."

His mouth rose at her jest, but his eyes remained clouded. "You know as well as I do you can alter any fact you please. Why are you doing this? Please don't say it's for me. I should like to think you could tell the story in such a way that Ursula—"

"Oh, Peter, stop. I am not going to profit from your dead lover. It makes me sick to think I was ever planning to. I'm sorry. The people we lose leave something sacred behind. I see that now. A person shouldn't be allowed to rummage through the past like it's a chest of toys put there for her pleasure."

"Or the future," he said sadly. He took her hand and brought it to his mouth. "Thank you. I think . . . I think I could bear it for me, but not for her."

She squeezed his hand.

"Campbell, I should like to ask you a favor. I told you I did a terrible thing by not marrying her. Would you be willing to go to London, to St. Paul's in Covent Garden, and see to her headstone and that of my son? I don't know if the rules have changed in the last three centuries, but if there's a way you could arrange to have my name put next to theirs, I would appreciate it. I did love her as a husband. It is not the same as marrying, but it would mean so much to me."

"Of course, Peter. I give you my word."

His shoulders relaxed. "Thank you."

"All right, that's just about all the sadness I can take in an evening. I want to get this evening over with and go back to your place. I want you to hold me." She looked at her watch. "Oh, cripes. I have to find Ball—"

"Cam, there you are." Ball bounded up beside her. "C'mon. We're going to unveil the painting now."

"No. Mr. Ball, wait." But he was already dragging her by the hand into the next gallery and through the couples beginning to squeeze into the roped-off area that had been set up for the presentation. At some point, she lost contact with Peter's hand. Ball pulled her through the center, right up to the dais upon which the curtained canvas stood.

Guests were edging their way to the front, some leading with their shoulders, to get a prime viewing spot.

"Mr. Ball, I have to talk to you. Did Lamont find you?"

"Quiet, Cam. This is our moment."

"—to welcome you on this very special evening." Board president Cal Dunevin, great-grandson of an aluminum magnate and unparalleled blowhard, had kicked things off.

"Mr. Ball, please," she whispered. "We have to withdraw the painting. It's not real."

He gave her a sharp look. "That, my dear, is a load of horseshit."

Ball was slightly hard of hearing, a condition made worse in noisy rooms, and his unnecessarily loud "horseshit" rung out just as Dunevin said, ". . . to thank each of you for your generous donation," which sent a ripple of nervous laughter through the room.

"Listen to me," she whispered. "There's a letter from Van Dyck. It destroys any grounds for authenticity."

"Cam, do I know art?" He gazed at her solemnly.

"Yes, sir."

"Do you?"

"Yes." Dunevin was reciting an Emerson poem now, something about a heifer and a sexton, and Cam, who had a dim recollection of this from a college survey class, recalled the thematic construct as something about beauty, but Dunevin was delivering each line with such theatrical lugubriousness she wondered if she was confusing it with one of Emerson's death poems.

"Look me in the eye," Ball said firmly. "Tell me that painting is not a Van Dyck."

"Mr. Ball. Please. It doesn't matter what I believe." She searched the room for Packard or even Anastasia, someone—anyone—who could help her convince Ball to bring this to a halt.

Ball shook his head as if disappointed with a young child. "Aren't you an art expert?"

"Yes, but—"

" 'Yes, but' nothing. Where's your confidence, my girl?"

Where indeed?

With a tentative stretch, she pushed her shoulders back. It did make her feel fractionally better, but it didn't seem to improve the odds anyone would believe the painting was a Van Dyck.

"We'll nail their asses to the wall." Ball winked at her.

"Whose asses, sir?" *Oh boy.* Dunevin was trudging through alder boughs and sparrow nests now.

"Nonbelievers!"

She put a hand on each of his shoulders. "Mr. Ball, listen. This is going to be a huge embarrassment to you. We have to stop this. Now. Wave Dunevin out of his alder tree and tell him you've changed your mind."

"Embarrassment? Really?" Ball pulled off his glasses and rubbed them with his hanky, considering. "Well, I suppose. But it's not like finding myself spread across sixty feet of canvas wearing nothing more than two moles and what we in Flow-da like to call a genuine look of surprise."

"Mr. Ball!"

"Woodson Ball!" Cal Dunevin boomed. "C'mon up, and let's get a look at this thing!"

Ball pulled himself out of Cam's grip and hopped up on the stage.

"I'm happy to be here," Ball drawled. "I'm happy to be giving this to the Carnegie. I think I know a little bit about art—"

The room tittered.

Oh, Mr. Ball. Oh, Mr. Ball. Cam closed her eyes.

"And I think this is one of the prettiest darn paintings ever. And I want to thank Cam Stratford especially for helping me see that I really did want to part with two-point-one million dollars."

More laughter.

"She's a very persuasive lady. The Carnegie's damned lucky to have her. Oops. Can I say *damned*, Lamont?"

Cam's head whipped around. Packard was in the back—smiling!

"You can say anything you damned well please," Packard called. "Just keep those paintings coming."

The room filled with applause.

"Well, now," Ball said. "I guess there's no delaying it. That two-point-one's gotta go at some point."

He grabbed the silk cord. Cam closed her eyes.

There was a hush in the room. The hush of awe and something more. Surprise? Then a gasp. Cam slitted an eye.

"Now, I know you were expecting a Van Dyck." Ball stood not in front of the disputed Van Dyck, but the painting of Cam Mertons had brought to her loft. "I started thinking 'bout it, though, and I thought, *pfft*, Van Dycks are a dime a dozen. They're yesterday's news. What this museum needs is a painting a damned sight prettier—there, I said it again—than the one old Anthony did. This one's a Peter Lely, folks, the royal portraitist to Charles the Second, and see if you don't think the same thing I do: He musta known one of Campbell Stratford's distant relatives."

The room was stone silent. Cam was terrified. It was so apparently not a Lely, well, not a seventeenth-century Lely, not with her on the front of it. Then, in a random spot in the room, a person started clapping. Then half a dozen other guests began clapping as well, and then the room filled with thunderous applause.

A pair of strong arms slid around her waist, and Peter whispered into her ear, "I thought this might help."

She turned and flung her arms around him. "Thank you."

Packard strode up to shake Ball's hand. He hopped on the stage.

"This museum has always been able to count on Woodson Ball," Packard said. "And today is no exception. Woodson has informed me that in addition to this gorgeous Lely, he will also be putting a fantastic new work on view here soon. Massive in scope, revolutionary in vision, this is a piece you'll be hearing more about in the news on Monday. It's exciting. It's never been seen by the viewing public. It represents a stunning new discovery by the art world. And you, ladies and gentlemen—and board members," he added significantly, "will be the first people to experience *Wednesday Afternoons*."

Cam looked at Peter.

"Er, a bit of a negotiation to make the Van Dyck switch possible," Peter whispered. "Hope you don't mind. At least your debut will be on home ground."

The guests were still applauding. Packard had the room in the palm of his hand.

"But for now, enjoy the Lely," he said, "and before I send you back to your browsing, I want to say thank you once again to an arts patron who knows how to make a difference. Woodson Ball, everyone."

The room exploded in a roof-lifting cheer.

57

A throng of guests surrounded Cam to congratulate her, and when she finally broke loose, Peter was gone. She followed the happy crowd down the hall, trying to spot him, but no matter how she strained her head, she couldn't see him.

She felt a tug at her sleeve. "Peter," she said and turned.

"Not Peter."

It was Anastasia. She looked like she'd been crying. Cam put a hand on her instinctively. "What is it?"

"Nothing." She shook her head. "Nothing. Listen, do you have a minute?"

Cam nodded and led her to a quiet hall next to the freight elevator. "What's up?"

"I need to talk to you about the Peter Lely painting. I know it's not real."

Cam felt her stomach tighten. The game was over. If Anastasia, the museum's European art curator, was going to challenge it, the painting wouldn't stand.

"I know it's not real," she said, "but I'm not going to say anything."

Cam didn't know what to say. She could hardly believe what she was hearing. "But . . . ?"

"I know all about it. I know how you got it, and I know who did it."

She couldn't mean she knew about Peter and the After-life. "What do you mean?"

"I mean, I know Peter or Rusty or whatever your friend's name is painted it."

Cam breathed a sigh of relief. "Then why are you going to keep quiet?"

"I know you don't think I have the best interests of this museum in mind most days, but I'd like to think that I'm a little better than that. If Ball wants to give the painting, and Packard wants to accept it, that's good for the museum. You heard the people out there. They love it."

Cam blinked. What had come over her sister?

"And they should love it," she went on. "It's a damned fine painting. Exceptional, really. Any museum in the world would accept it as a Lely. Hell, any museum in the world would accept it even though it's not a Lely. The only trouble is, I know the sitter's you."

"Me?" The freight elevator *ding*-ed and both women moved a step farther away.

"It's pretty obvious, Cam. Jacket saw it. I did, too. And that's the real reason I'm going to keep quiet. You just don't get that sort of feeling from an artist with any sitter. He loves you, Cam. You have a way with men I'll never have. Even Jacket loves you, and you just dumped him. That painting's a good, pure thing, and Peter's love is a good pure thing. I won't be a part of ruining either one."

"Thank you, Stacy."

Anastasia threw her arms around her. "Which isn't to say I'm not going to get the directorship, you know."

Cam laughed and hugged tighter. "I know. Game on."

Anastasia pulled away. "There. Now it doesn't matter that the paint looks too new. It doesn't matter that the canvas has been stretched too carefully, or that the style is not quite right. No one will ever know the painting is a fake."

Cam froze. Mrs. Fitcher, the old biddy from the board, gazed at them, mouth agape, from the elevator.

58

Thirty minutes later, Cam slammed the door of Packard's office, leaving Packard, Anastasia, Dunevin, Ball and Mrs. Fitcher behind her.

Jeanne stopped the game she was playing on her phone and jumped to her feet. "What can I do to help?"

"It depends. Do you still have that business card for the 'We Hit Old Biddies' firm?"

Jeanne nodded toward the door. "What happened in there?"

"Oh, the usual. Even though there's no signature and no record of it in Lely's documents—er, the real Lely, I mean, the Lely who painted in 1673—the composition, theme and color choice point to authenticity. In that case, especially with a situation as sensitive as this, experts usually take a generally positive-but-not-yet-definitive point of view. However, Mrs. Fitcher happened to overhear the museum's leading expert of Restoration-era art say it's a fake. Since then, Anastasia's done everything she can to backpedal, and when Mrs. Fitcher has pushed her, she went mum—"

"*Anastasia?*"

"She's really trying to cover for me, bless her heart. It's hard for me to believe it myself."

"Hard for you to believe? Traveling through time? That's hard to believe. Anastasia being kind? That's impossible."

"Yeah, so Anastasia's stayed mum and Ball won't let anyone, including Packard, who's getting really nervous, look at it."

"Now what?"

"Who knows? Either way, I'm still going to be out of a job tomorrow."

"You're not going to leave me with the chain-mail Czarina, are you?"

"She'll change. You'll see."

"You're scaring me."

"Where's Peter?"

"In your office. At least he was fifteen minutes age."

Cam flew to her office. The disputed Lely painting was tucked behind her door, but Peter was nowhere to be seen. She trotted down the hall.

"Are you looking for the hottie with Johnny Depp eyes?" a college student on the catering crew asked.

"I, um . . . maybe."

"Old?" she said, and realized her mistake and flushed. "Older than you, I mean."

"That's the one."

"He told me to tell you he's with Ada."

Cam laughed. "Thanks."

When she stepped into the gallery, Peter was not, in fact, with Ada. He was eyeing a small painting in the corner, next to a couple both looking at their BlackBerrys.

Cam watched him for a moment, the line of his back, the tilt of his head as he considered the work before him, the luxurious gleam of light on his hair. Could she re-member all that? Could she lock it up in a place where the memory would sit, unmuddied by events, longing or grief, for her to unwrap like a cherished holiday ornament to fill her heart when it was empty?

As if he felt her presence, his shoulders relaxed and he turned. He beamed as she approached, and the other couple drifted off absently, still working their keyboards.

"Ah, true love," she said as Peter watched their egress.

"I have observed practices which have raised a consid-erable number of questions for me."

"You and me both. It's a religious thing."

"In truth?"

"Cult of the Self-absorbed. Every member's a one-person church. So, what are you looking at?"

He stepped aside to let her see.

"Ah, the Bonnard." It was one of the many paintings Pierre Bonnard had done of his wife. In a bathroom as luminescent and richly colored as a Matisse, Pierre's wife, Marte, lay peacefully still in her shimmering bath. "He painted her always at the same age, no matter how old she'd gotten. It was as if he wanted her frozen in time." She thought of the gorgeous portrait Peter had done of her, just a few rooms away, and put her hand on his cheek and kissed him. "I thank you for my painting."

"Which part?" he asked, smiling. "Painting it or giving it away?"

"Both. How did you think to go to Ball?"

"It wasn't difficult. Collectors place an enormous

amount of importance on what others think of their paintings. I suspected he'd be open to a timely trade. And he was. He's a decent cove. A damned fine eye as well. The only problem was your car. I'm afraid the window is, well, shall we say, a trifle out of sorts—which will, perhaps, be more of a problem than I'd originally anticipated, given the incipient snow."

Cam glanced out the window and saw the steady downfall of white. "Oh, fuck— Oops." She clapped a hand over her mouth. "Sorry."

"But on that topic, here is a question. Could it possibly be considered within the bounds of acceptable behavior here to describe oneself as a fornicator?"

She frowned for a moment, and then it hit her. Ball. She threw her head back and laughed. "Well, only if your parents were as well, I suppose."

"Ball did mention something to that effect. I could barely summon a reply. When it comes down to it, I suppose all of our parents were, but to state it so unashamedly . . . 'Tis quite shocking, and yet he seemed to be so proud."

"It is a mark of distinction—especially where he comes from."

"I am amazed."

"Oh, Peter, the painting you did is beautiful. I could see that, even while I was telling Mertons to shove it up his, er, storage facility. Is that really how you see me?"

He tucked a rogue curl behind her ear. "Aye."

"Do you think you'll have time to paint one of you? I should like to have something to remember you by."

The pained look in his eyes sent an ache through her heart.

"I have never been much of a self-portraitist," he said, "but for you, milady, aye."

"Thank you."

He brought her close and kissed her forehead. She loved the clean smell of his skin.

"It stands, I hope," he said. "The painting, I mean." She stiffened automatically and he stepped back and looked in her eyes. "What?"

"I don't know yet. They haven't decided. It's sitting in my office."

"Haven't decided?" His face darkened. "Do they doubt my word? I am portraitist to the *king*, you know."

"Credentials that sadly must remain unspoken—much as the carnal status of Ball and his parents should be."

"What is the objection?" he demanded. "'Tis an exquisite piece."

"It is. But the odds of finding an undiscovered Lely after more than three hundred years are practically nil, and there's not enough yet to tip the balance in the favor of authenticity. Besides, Ball's so mad he hasn't let anyone look at it."

He harrumphed. "Philistines."

"But the good news is, Anastasia is doing everything she can to help. Between you and me, she told me she knows the painting's not real." Then, in answer to the look of insult in his eye, she added, "It's not old and real. But she said because you did it for me, she won't say anything. Oh, Peter, this is going to sound silly, but in some ways, that's the best part of all."

Peter squeezed her waist. "I'm glad."

Forlorn, Cam gazed down at the ballet flat peeking

out from her skirt. Her friend, Seph, told her pink shoes always lighten one's spirit, but Cam did not feel uplifted. "Peter, what do you know of the O'Janpa Convention?"

His arm fell away. "Where did you hear that?"

"Mertons."

"Hell."

"Can they really take you away?"

"Aye—well, no. It would be a battle." The lines around his eyes deepened. "I'd prefer to go on my own."

"And you have to go?"

"What I do here impacts you."

"Of course it impacts me."

"No, Cam. I-I—" He cast his eyes downward. "I have already hurt you. You may have lost your job because of me, and . . . and there may be even more I've cost you that you don't see."

"No, Peter, no. Listen to me. When two people love one another, every choice they make affects what comes next. But that doesn't mean the choices shouldn't be made. That's life. If your being here, in the future, means my life has to change, that's a change I choose freely."

"Cam—"

"Peter, no—"

"Cam, listen to me. I have cost you a marriage . . . and a child."

"A *child*?" She frowned. "What do you mean?"

"You and Jacket were to have a child. That child is gone. Simply by the fact of my being here. Mertons showed me the calculations. It's true. And I—I with a wife and child who cannot even have the comfort of a name in their final resting place—I have no right to interfere. Cam, I knew what perfect happiness was once. I won't take it from you."

"You fool." She wanted to shove him and hug him at the same time. "That mythical future baby is gone because that baby wasn't meant to be. Was it because of you? Yes. Was it because of me? Yes. Was it because of Jacket? Yes. Don't you see? Everything we do in this crazy beaker of ooze sends ripples in every direction—left, right, forward, backward. So what if your being here took away a child? Did you happen to ask if staying would bring me another one?"

"Cam . . ."

"Fight them. We'll do it together."

She heard an odd rushing noise and wheeled around. Mertons was brushing snow off his coat, a sort of telescope in hand, looking momentarily confused. "Ah," he said, spotting them. "There you are at last."

Mertons wore an odd, unreadable look, and she dreaded what he was going to say. Peter shifted, growing taller and broader. She couldn't help but notice Mertons avoided her eyes.

"My negotiations have been successful."

"What negotiations?" Peter asked.

"You didn't tell him?" Mertons said to Cam.

Peter's gaze cut to her. "Didn't tell me what?"

Mertons made a show of placing the scope in his pocket.

She swallowed. "I wanted you to have a painter's life."

The look of confusion on Peter's face grew. He looked to Mertons and back. "What, Cam? What did you do?"

"I promised to show them how I travel."

"So they can shut it down?"

"Yes."

"And in return," Mertons said to Peter, "you will be given a painter's life. Money, time, recognition. You'll have it all."

Cam looked at Peter. She could see the effect this offer had on him.

"No," Peter said. "I'd rather stay. Even if it's only for a short time."

Merton's face purpled. "Are you insane? Do you know what you'd be giving up?"

"Aye, I think I do." Peter caught Cam's hand and squeezed.

"No, Peter," Mertons said. "You don't. I haven't just negotiated any painter's life. I've negotiated *your* painter's life. You will be allowed to return to Ursula."

Peter gasped. After a moment that seemed like forever to Cam he said, "I have no wish to return to her knowing what will happen. You might as well tie me to a rock and let an eagle feast on my entrails."

"You won't know."

"What?"

"I said, you won't know. The Guild has agreed to let you return to your former life insentient of your future or hers. Peter, think of it. You will fall in love with her again. You will paint her again. You'll have more than a decade to live over."

Peter's posture changed. The lines around his eyes grew softer. "And she will die, still the same?"

"We cannot change that," Mertons said sadly. "You know the limitations. But, Peter, listen. I have gotten special permission for a variance. It wasn't easy, and I had the team triangulating the calculations for the last hour to support it. I have gotten permission to allow you to marry her."

"Oh." It came out like a faint puff of wind, and Cam felt her world break in two.

"Your name," Mertons said. "She'll have your name. And so will your son."

Peter blinked, dizzy with the wealth that had just been laid at his feet. "I-I—"

"But you must come tonight."

"Tonight!" Cam cried. She felt as if she'd spent the evening having chunks of her happiness hacked away with a butcher knife. "No, please."

Mertons looked down, ashamed. "I'm sorry, Miss Stratford. The Guild insists. The whole affair's been an embarrassment to them. They want it to end. Peter, you'll be back in your studio by morning."

Peter was lost in a world he'd let slip through his fingers. Cam watched him work the emerald signet ring, savoring his first taste of a life free from guilt and pain, a parched man handed water.

"I-I don't know."

"Peter, you must," she said.

He licked his lips, staring far into the snowy night. She touched his hand. He looked surprised, and she directed him to open it. When he did, she pulled a hairpin from her hair and placed it there. "Just think of me every once in a while. That will be all I need."

"Campbell, I . . ."

"You know what you must choose. For her. For your son."

Cam heard a clatter behind her and turned. It was Jeanne, running toward them, looking panicked. "You look different in men's clothes," she said to Mertons, and to Cam: "C'mon, Packard wants to see you."

"Not now."

"It's important."

Peter caught Cam's hand and squeezed it. "Self-confidence, remember. Go. I will wait."

Cam could barely breathe. "You will?"

"Yes." His dark eyes affirmed the promise. "I swear it."

"Peter," Mertons warned.

But Cam didn't have to run. Packard strode in, mouth tight. "I need you to convince Ball to let us look at it."

"Sure," Cam said. "Where is he?"

"The boardroom."

"I'm sorry, Peter," Packard said. "Our curator was overheard saying it was a fake and that you did it. I don't believe you did it, but I'm in a tough spot, with my key expert having once disputed it."

Peter made a low growl. "I think you will find proof enough when you examine it."

Mertons looked at his watch. "We cannot stay long. A quarter hour at most."

Peter, awash in a raging sea of emotion, said, "We'll stay." He gazed at the Bonnard. He knew exactly why Bonnard had done it. He thought of Ursula and his son and what it means to love someone. He thought of that ring, back on Cam's finger after she'd removed it this afternoon and placed it in her pocket. He thought of his own ring and the many years it had represented a burden he could not unshoulder. He even thought of Rick and Ilsa. How long he stood there he did not know. He knew what he had to do.

"Where did they say they were?"

Mertons looked at his watch. "Peter, you don't have time."

"To hell with you and your requirements. I'm saying good-bye." Peter ran.

59

Ball gazed at his hands on the boardroom table and sighed. Cam said a silent prayer.

"Fine," he said. "Let's get it over with."

"Thank you, Mr. Ball."

Packard gave Cam a grateful look. "Excellent. Should we head down to Cam's office?"

She glanced at the clock. Her only thoughts were with Peter. How long would he stay? Could she say good-bye?

The group exited Packard's office single file, Cam last. Anastasia stood with a drink, halfway down the hall. She gave Cam a sorrowful look. Cam thumped her on the back.

"Anastasia," Packard said. "Let's go."

Then Cam saw Peter, and her heart sunk. He stood in an archway, nearly out of sight, with the grave look of a man facing down his fate. He motioned her toward him, and the movement was so poignant, her eyes began to fill.

"Cam," Packard said. "Are you coming?"

"What? No." Her lip started to tremble and a tear ran down her cheek. "I have to do something. You go without me."

"Cam—"

"Let her go," said Ball, who was looking down the same archway.

She ran to Peter and threw her arms around him. He hugged her back, hard. The tears ran freely now, and she didn't care. For one last time she could dry them against Peter's broad chest and take comfort in the iron circle of his arms.

"I want to say good-bye."

Her shoulders heaved as a new round of tears overtook her. "I know. I know." She laced her fingers at his back, trying to keep time from moving.

"I want you to wear this." He pulled away and opened her hand. Without ceremony, he dropped the emerald ring onto her palm. Shaking and uncertain until she looked into his eyes, she slipped the ring on her middle finger, where it towered, enormous, over her knuckle.

"Careful," he said, "there may be paint on it."

She wiped her eyes, confused.

"I want to say good-bye, Cam, but not to you. To Ursula. Mertons warned me once that if I put my mark on any piece of art outside my true place in time, I would be captive there forever. Cam, I know Ursula wouldn't have wanted me to live our life over—to hold it in some bell jar, like a Bartholomew Day's Fair curiosity, to gawk at, mesmerized, as Bonnard did. Our life had life, a life of its own that can never be again, though I loved it—loved it—when I lived it."

"Oh, Peter." She could barely breathe.

"I want to be with you. I want to paint you. I want to be your Alex Katz."

She hugged him. "I'll be your Ada."

Mertons appeared, scanning the air with his computer pen. "Peter," he said, "something just happened. The variables went haywire."

"I struck it," Peter said. "The painting. I have struck my mark upon it." He held up Cam's hand and pointed to the ring. Instantly the sound of Ball's triumphant hoot reached their ears from the direction of Cam's office followed by Anastasia's happy *"I told you. Curators make mistakes all the time. Look, that's Lely's mark. I'd recognize it anywhere."*

"You have no idea what you've done," Mertons cried.

"I don't," Peter said. "But I'm willing to find out."

60

"'Tis good of you to do this." Peter laid in some vermillion and watched it spark in the light. The early morning sun flooding in from Washington Road cast a beautiful pink-gold gleam on his canvas.

Cam shifted on Peter's long brocade couch, still giddy from the night before, tilting her head toward the window as Peter had directed, but also to see the fat, gleaming emerald on her finger. "Well, when Mertons agreed to sneak the painting of Nell out of your Covent Garden studio for a night, impact on the tangent arcs aside, I could hardly say no."

"That was a brilliant idea. With the painting in hand, Charles will sign the edict and Ursula will get my name. I can't tell you how much that means to me."

"I'm glad you told me. I wish I had known before."

"I just hope Stephen doesn't notice the painting's absence. Mertons says he'll have it back to London tomorrow and on its way to Charles the next."

"That Mertons . . . He's an enigma."

"I think I've decided he's a romantic at heart. Besides, he told me the Guild was in such disarray when he broke the news last night—had to roust the chairman out of his bed at midnight—he probably could have reversed the outcome of the Thirty Years' War and no one would have noticed."

"Do you think Nell will mind?"

"I doubt it. Her nakedness has been well admired over the years, and there have been, shall we say, countless monuments erected to it. One naked painting more or less will not be missed by our Miss Gwyn."

Cam laughed and then shivered, remembering the monument that had been erected to her last night in Peter's warm, dark bed. She still didn't know if Anastasia was going to get the executive directorship, and it didn't matter. She'd told Packard last night her resignation stood, and Ball immediately offered her twice the salary to curate his stuff. "My own museum," he'd said to her dreamily. "I'm seeing 'The Ball Collection' in big lights. Tasteful, but big."

"Can I get a peek?" she said, and Peter obliged by turning the easel. What had been Barbara Villiers and then Nell was now Cam, the reddish brunette waves interwoven with orange and gold, the nose made just a touch more retroussé, and the gray eyes streaked with blue. It was amazing what could be altered with a few masterful touches of paint.

"But if you're only changing the face," she said, "I don't understand why you needed me naked under here." She gazed down at the black dressing gown she held tightly around her.

Spots of color appeared on his cheeks. "*Hmm,* aye, that's a fair question. Well, when Charles asked for a painting of you in a, um, mythological setting in exchange for signing the marriage edict, he was quite clear he wanted everything to be as accurate as possible."

"Everything?" Cam repeated, confused.

"Everything." Peter's eyes trailed down the gown, and a small, shameless curve appeared on his mouth.

"Ah. I see." She felt her heart start to thrum. "I should think at this point you could do it from memory."

"One might think that, that is, if one didn't recall that you were clothed from the waist down the first two times we made love and bathed in darkness the third. I beg you not to consider this a complaint," he added quickly. "But there is a certain question," he said, looking at his palette, "with women of your coloring as to what, er, shade would be appropriate."

"Is there?" she said drolly.

"Oh, indeed there is. There is cinnabar, red ochre, raw umber and even ivory black—any or all could be required. That is the question men—I mean artists—grapple with. All of this you shall learn when we begin your lessons."

"My lessons? I wasn't aware I needed any lessons."

"In certain areas, no. In fact, in certain areas I would almost defer to your expertise."

"Almost?" She smiled.

"But in painting, aye. Your work shows good promise, and I will teach you to be great. Peaches, plums and oranges to the end of your day, milady. We shall be overrun with still lifes."

She grinned. The Ball Collection with Jeanne as her

assistant and painting lessons with Peter. Could life be more perfect?

"But for now . . ." He tilted his head toward the gown.

Cam flushed to her toes. She took a deep breath, stood and turned away. She fumbled with the belt. She could feel his gaze on her and the fire that always comes from sporting at the edge of danger. The belt fell loose, and she brushed the flaps open. Screwing up her courage, she lowered her shoulders and let the gown slip.

"*Ah.*"

She caught the silk on her wrists before it fell completely, and looked over her shoulder at him. "What?"

His eyes danced over the view this movement had bestowed upon him. "The blackness of the gown will turn you gray. Toss it over there, please."

The basket where he pointed seemed a long way away. Nonetheless, she tossed the gown and turned.

And with a deeply contented smile that made her smile as well, Peter reached for the cinnabar.

AUTHOR'S NOTE

On May 2, 2007, the *London Times* reported that research undertaken by well-known fine art auction house, Christie's, suggests that the sitter in a Peter Lely masterpiece may not be Nell Gwyn, perhaps the most famous mistress of Charles II, as long believed. An in-depth analysis of the painting, a reclining nude, led Christie's to conclude that the sitter is actually another of Charles's mistresses.

Experts, however, continue to disagree. The painting was originally discovered behind a secret sliding panel in Charles's bedroom, three years after his death.

—G.C.

Turn the page for a sneak peek at
Gwyn Cready's
next romantic time-travel romp,

Aching for Always

Coming soon from Pocket Books

I

Boardroom, Brand O'Malley Map Company, Pittsburgh

"What *do* men see in maps?" Joss O'Malley asked fondly as she watched her friend's four-year-old son, Peter, staring intently at a framed antique map from his not-quite-steady perch on top of a lateral file cabinet.

"Key to the past?" suggested Peter's mom, Diane Daltrey, the former chief financial officer of Brand O'Malley Maps, lifting her eyes for a moment from the quarterly cash flow statement over which she was poring.

"Hints of the unknown?" Joss offered, thinking of her own fascination.

"Does this have a Skull Island?" Peter said enthusiastically, waving his beloved light saber. "I'll kill Hook if he finds the treasure first."

"Or perhaps it's something slightly less poetic. Speaking of which"—Diane let her fingers come to rest on the calculator—"things aren't looking so good here."

"I know we're a little strapped for cash," Joss said, biting a fingernail, "but that's not so bad, right?"

"Right," Di said drily. "I mean, how important is money?"

"I'm heading up to see Rogan. I need a number," Joss said.

"*Another* loan?"

"It's not a loan exactly."

"Honey," Di said, "when a man's already agreed to the price for a company and you're going back to ask for more, that's either a loan or insanity. Peter, please take the highlighter out of your mouth."

Peter, who had jumped off the lateral file, sighed and, with a Day-Glo green pout, handed the marker to Joss.

Joss frowned. "Should we—"

"Not poisonous," Diane said without looking up. "Well, not too poisonous."

Peter tugged the arm of Joss's blouse. "Did you know that if you suck enough highlighter, your pee turns green?"

"Actually, I didn't know that."

"It's true. Green works best."

"I'll keep that in mind."

Diane flipped the page of the report, and Joss, who had long ago decided that running a barely surviving company was nothing compared to raising a four-year-old boy, said, "I really appreciate you coming in."

"Oh, please. If I didn't get out of the house sometimes, I'd go nuts."

Joss looked at Peter, slashing his saber like a miniature Zorro. "Yeah, I can see where a trip like this would be pretty relaxing."

Rogan's admin stuck her head in the doorway. "Mr. Reynolds will be ready for you in five minutes."

If only I'll be ready for him, Joss thought. She gave Di a look.

"I'm close. I'll have the number by the time we're up there."

Di tucked the report under her arm and stood, her fingers still running furiously over the calculator. Peter trailed behind, protecting the rear from pirates and Sith lords. If Joss couldn't make payroll, she'd have to lay people off. Di had been the first to go six months earlier, raising her hand to save the jobs of others. Now Joss used her only when she could afford to.

They reached the elevator, and Joss pointed to the UP button so Peter would know which one to press.

Joss prayed Rogan would be amenable. He'd been looking only to buy her father's company, Brand Industries, and the name of her mother's—Brand O'Malley, the most famous name in maps—for use on his GPS devices, but he was a good guy and he'd understood Joss's desire to keep her thirty-two-person business, her only inheritance from her mother, afloat and under her control.

Since her mother's death not long after Joss's eighth birthday, Joss felt like her life had been laid out strictly to ensure that she'd be able to assume control of the firm when she turned eighteen. She'd interned here every summer in high school. Then, despite having been interested in literature, she'd pursued a dual major in business and geography in college while she worked full time, learning the ropes from the very able managers. At age twenty, even before she'd graduated, she'd accepted in practice what she'd already had in theory—the top executive role, and for the past three years, as the sales of paper maps dropped, she's been doing everything she could to keep these fine, hardworking people—and herself—employed.

The elevator arrived and they got on. Joss lifted Peter to the rows of buttons. "Eighteen," she said, and pointed to the correct one. Peter poked it and then leaped to the floor in front of the mirrored walls, pointing the saber at his image with a sneer. His mother, lost in her calculations, pressed her clipboard against Joss's back to make a notation.

"So, how are you going to effect this miraculous largesse?" Di asked.

"The loan, you mean?"

"Yes."

"Rogan owes me a favor."

"A fifty-thousand-dollar favor?" Di said.

"The number's *fifty* thousand?"

"The number's at least fifty thousand. I'm still checking."

"Crap."

"Crap," Peter repeated happily.

"Oops." Joss shot Di an apologetic look.

Ann, the institutional sales manager, got on on fifteen. She looked a little pale, not a surprise, Joss thought, given that her six-year-old son had just been put on dialysis. Ann waved and said to Joss, "Say, I understand congratulations are in order. The wedding's next week, isn't it?"

Joss gazed down at the diamond sparkling languidly on her finger, so large as to almost be worthy of being a pirate's treasure itself. "Yep. No point in waiting. When it's right, it's right."

"Yes, and you'll need to hurry with your office," Di said. "The caterer needs time to set up the tables."

Ann's brows shot up, and Joss waved away her worry. "I'm not having my reception in your office. Di thinks that just because I'm getting married in the Founders' Room upstairs, it's an all-business wedding."

"It's the conference room for the Sales department," Di said curtly.

"It's a gorgeous space."

"Well, in any case, I'm sure it will be beautiful," Ann said as she exited on sixteen. "Congratulations."

"Now, should we all wear business suits to the ceremony," Di asked, "or is that just you?"

Joss sighed. "It's not a business suit. It's a skirt."

Di gave her a look.

"Okay, a business skirt—but it's Chanel!"

Di just didn't understand. Simple and straightforward was how Joss wanted things. Businesslike.

Peter asked Joss, "Will I get to see your wedding? Mommy says I can only come if I dress like the mail-delivery guy."

"Your mommy's hilarious. And, yes, you know I couldn't get married without you, pal. I'm counting on you to give me away." She returned her thoughts to the problem at hand. Fifty big ones. At *least* fifty big ones. "I think," she said to Di, "I'm going to have to resort to something more than a favor for fifty thousand." Joss gazed at herself in the mirror, then unbuttoned the top button of her blouse. "I'm going to have to try a little more—"

She found herself looking straight into Peter's curious eyes.

"A little more what, Aunt Joss?"

Di gave her a "try to get yourself out of this one" look.

"A little more hard work, Peter. That's what being a grown-up is all about." She returned Di's look with a tiny tongue stick-out.

"Exactly how *hard* is this work going to be?" Di asked.

"Jeez Louise, I'm hardly going to—" Peter's eyes shot right to her face. *What is it with kids these days?* "I'm not going to work so hard that I'll regret it."

"Good to hear," Di said. "Girls who work that hard can get a reputation."

Peter's gaze narrowed and moved between his mother's face and Joss's.

"But let's face it," Joss said, "I'm gonna do what it takes." She thought of Ann and her other thirty-one employees, their spouses, children and health care plans.

The jesting smile left Di's face, replaced with a raised brow. "Really?"

"Really. It's not like I haven't gotten hints he'd be amenable."

"I know, but . . . really?"

"It seems a small price, if you know what I mean."

"You're not going to . . . you know?" Di gave her a look to fill in the missing idea.

"*No.* Absolutely not." Even bald-faced manipulation had its limits.

The door opened on eighteen, and they trooped out and into Rogan's empty office. He strode in a moment later, an impossibly handsome man with soft blond curls and clear blue eyes that cut to the bones of any business deal.

"Hey," he said affably to Peter and nodded at Di. "Good to see you. Are we—?"

"Nope." Di grabbed Peter's hand. "We're on our way out." She handed the cash flow report to Joss. "Don't work too hard, eh?

Joss glanced down at the paper. *This may be the time to go all the way,* Di's scribbled note read. *The number is $63K.*

Oh, crap.

"Hey," Rogan said with a cheery grin. "What's up?"

"I'm here with a request."

"Oh." He nodded, replacing the smile with a more impassive look, and made his way to the desk.

"I need another loan."

"Oh, Joss." The words bloomed with disappointment, and he sat. "How much?"

"Sixty-three thousand."

He leaned forward, elbows perched on the desk, and ran his thumbs back and forth across his lips, considering. "I wonder," he said gently, "if you should think about closing."

"No," she said. "We'll be fine once this quarter is over."

He shook his head. "The board won't go for it. They barely went for the last one."

She felt a spark of panic. "They will if you endorse it. Rogan, c'mon. You know I'm good for it. " She'd made it a point this morning to put on her sexiest bra. It was a demi in pink that lifted her breasts up like two scoops of French vanilla ice cream. Rogan was a decent fellow—the big surprise when she'd first met him. A little flash of ice cream. Perhaps a peek at some unskirted thigh. He'd do it. He had to.

That was about the one advantage women had in the business world. Men didn't always think with their frontal lobes, and anyone who'd ever dated a man knew it. And when the thought process did its little dance out of the frontal lobes and over to the basal ganglia, it left a trail of mush in its wake.

She put the cash flow report on the chair beside her, stood up and leaned over—way over—to reach for his desk clock. It was an ugly, ornate thing he said his old girlfriend had given him. It managed to be both gaudy and tethered by a power cord—the worst of both worlds. Her disdain kept her from breaking into a total sweat.

She had never done this before. It wasn't her operating style. But if this was all it took to keep the company afloat, in the scheme of things, it wasn't too much to ask. Business was business. Some people had the marbles. Some people wanted the marbles. Unless you could think of a way to sneak some marbles for yourself, you wouldn't get to play.

She could hear the *tick tick tick,* and even though she wasn't looking, she could feel his gaze. The tenor of the room changed, as did the cadence of his breathing.

"I think," she said, "you can convince them."

He had the good sense to flush. Rather a charming thing, if you thought about it. The little spots of color on his cheeks were the first step in the mush process.

He adjusted his position and with a crooked smile said, "Are you trying to seduce me?"

"No, actually. I'm trying to meet payroll."

"It's a damned effective strategy."

"I would think so. C'mon. I swear I'll pay it back at the end of the quarter—with ten percent interest."

"It seems to me," he said, leaning forward in earnest, "that for sixty-three thousand dollars I could expect a little more."

She breathed a sigh of relief. "Sure. Whatever. Twelve percent?"

"Not interest. Skin."

He said it in the same tone that he might say, "Hand me the stapler," or "Let's go over the Ryneman numbers." Joss had to re-review it in her head to ensure she'd heard it right.

"I . . . I . . ."

"I'd be risking my reputation. Why shouldn't you risk yours?" he said.

"How much?" she asked, shocked. This peek of paradise was supposed to be enough. Jeez, what was happening to business ethics?

He gestured toward everything north of her belt. "All of it."

Risk and reward. The seesaw of business. She could barely think over the pounding in her ears. The diamond on her finger glinted and she nearly said no, but then she thought of her mother. Was her mother's dream for this company going to die with Joss? Was Ann's son going to go without dialysis? No effing way. Time to put her business acumen to work.

She lifted her shaking hand and loosened the buttons.

"And open, please," he said.

"Your admin is sitting outside."

He pressed a button on his phone. "Pat?"

"Yes, Mr. Reynolds?"

"Close the door, will you? I don't want to be disturbed."

Joss sat frozen while Pat stepped into the rear of the office, no doubt thinking the meeting would continue to be about negotiations and outcomes, which, come to think of it, wasn't far from the truth. Pat closed the door. Rogan leaned back in his chair.

Joss had at least imagined this possibility. It would have been foolish to entertain this strategy without having done so. But she'd been so certain Rogan would stop at a certain, albeit, not purely innocent, level of flirtation.

She spread the silk.

His irises widened. It was a biological effect he couldn't hide no matter how skilled he was—or perhaps she should say one of the effects. The trick was going to be teasing that effect as far as it would go under her control without starting a biological apocalypse. She was reminded of the men who in 1945 were about to set off the first experimental atomic explosion and were "pretty certain" it wouldn't destroy the Earth's atmosphere. She hoped pretty certain was enough. She also hoped no one in the building across the street had binoculars.

Her cell vibrated. The sound of a text. She cut her gaze to the display. It was from Di. "R u doing it?" Joss clapped her hand over the screen.

Rogan pointed to the clasp between her breasts from which a tiny pearl dangled. "Does that little thing there open it?"

"It does." God, she needed to get on top of this situation.

"Would you mind . . . ?"

"I wouldn't," she said, leaning slightly forward, "but it

seems to me that's something you might rather do your-self."

He made a dry, choking noise. *Ha! Mush prevails!*

"And all it takes is a quick call to Charlie." Charlie was the president of the Brand Industries board. "Just to let him know the plan."

This was it. If he talked to Charlie, he'd be committed. Rogan licked his lips.

"May I?" He gestured to the clasp with an earnest look in his eye. "Just a touch?"

Bless his mother; he'd been raised to be polite. She nodded.

He brought his hand to the metalwork, slipping his forefinger under the clasp and letting his thumb brush the swaying pearl. He tugged slightly, measuring the tension.

"Oh Lord," he whispered.

The electricity from his touch surprised her, as did the smell of sandalwood on his skin.

"Charlie," she reminded carefully.

"Right." He picked up his cell and pressed a couple buttons. Then his eyebrows went up and he hit the keyboard quickly. "Oops. Misdialed." He made a nervous laugh.

Joss was glad to see he was nervous, too. This wasn't exactly a stroll through the Nordstrom handbag department for her.

He tried the call again and held up a finger. "Ringing." She nodded and he leaned forward. "Charlie— Oh." He put his hand over the receiver. "Voicemail," he whispered then said, "Charlie, it's Rogan. I, ah, need to run a quick Brand O'Malley situation by you. I know the acquisition price has been agreed, but there's a request on the table for sixty-three more in the form of a thirty-day loan. Give me your thoughts." He hit the END button and smiled.

She crossed her arms, drawing in the flaps of her blouse closed. "We've got a problem."

"What? I did it."

The first hint of desperation had broken in his voice. Now she had him. "You forgot something. Your support." Without Rogan's enthusiastic endorsement of the plan, all Charlie had to do was say no. She began to button her blouse.

"Wait."

She stopped and lifted her brow.

"The thing is," he said, "it's hard to be a cheerleader for something I don't fully support."

"Oh, dear. I wouldn't want anything to be hard for you."

She came around the table, seated herself on the desk, and leaned back on her palms. The flaps slipped open wider and wider.

He inhaled and closed his eyes. "Does this plan include touch?"

She knew he didn't mean the acquisition. "Um . . ." She swallowed. This was certainly way more than she'd bargained for. "Can you be more specific?"

He pursed his lips, considering. "Palms, fingers, knuckles, cheeks and lips."

Oh. My. God.

"Palms, yes," she said at last. "The rest, no."

His cell started to vibrate, and he opened his eyes. "It's Charlie. I have to tell you, I'm not feeling very enthusiastic."

The phone buzzed, paused and buzzed again. He lifted his shoulders in a question.

"Palms and cheek," she offered.

The third buzz, and then the fourth.

"Fine," she said. "Palms, cheeks and a single kiss."

"Nip," he corrected, and picked up the phone. "Charlie, hi. You got my message?" He gestured for her to open her blouse even more. "It might inspire me," he whispered. "Yeah. It's a short-term thing. Thirty days, paid in full. How do I feel?" He lifted a brow in Joss's direction and waited for her to remove more silk. "Well, sales are improving. There've been a couple very nice peaks today." He gave her a broad smile. "And there's a big order coming in—a very big one, in fact. So, overall, I'm feeling pretty good about it."

Bingo.

"All right. I'll give them the good word." Rogan laid down his cell.

"Nice work," Joss said. "But there's no big order, my friend. Except in your head."

"That's not where it is, but I take your point." He unfolded himself from the chair.

She braced herself.

He drew a finger from her belly to her sternum and flicked the pearl.

She gasped. It was as if all the current in the room was being driven through that single digit.

He slipped the silk off her shoulders. It slid like a breath of air down her bare skin. He brought his hands to the clasp and released it, letting the fabric spread slowly, then traced the soft rise that began on each side of her collarbone.

She inhaled sharply.

"Nice," he said.

"You bet your—"

He brushed the wire and lace aside, and Joss's ability to speak vanished.

Dialysis, she reminded herself.

"Your breasts," he said, "are magnificent."

"Thank you."

He stood up, spread apart her knees and inserted himself carefully between them. His suit was the finest Italian wool, but even Armani couldn't have planned for the particular tailoring challenge Rogan was facing.

Slowly, he placed his palms over the tip of her nipples, and moved them back and forth. Just the barest touch. Heat rose between her legs. *Dialysis,* she reminded herself. *Dialysis.*

He brought her hands behind her again, palms on the desk. Her breasts poked skyward. He lowered his face to them and rubbed his bristled cheek across one nipple, then brushed the other. *This,* she thought nervously, *is how you lose the Earth's atmosphere.*

He took the first gently in his teeth, and she arched against him involuntarily. If she wasn't careful, that big order would be coming in just as he described.

"I want more," he said.

"I'm getting that impression. There's only one problem." She unwrapped her leg from behind him and returned it to a locked position across its mate. "We've finished the deal. Which isn't to say we might not play again sometime." Though she sincerely hoped not. Not this game, at least. She reached for her bra and allowed herself a huge internal exhale of relief.

"Hold on. Let's think this through."

Think? She almost laughed. "Deal's done, Rogan."

"Please. Listen. You're spread out on my desk like this and still out of reach?" He lowered his voice. "I'm going to die if I don't have you. Right here. Right now."

"This is business, Rogan. Stick to the deal."

"Deal. Right." With obvious effort, he lowered himself into his chair.

She picked herself up and re-clasped the bra, then hopped onto the floor. "I'm off."

He stood up. "Oh. One thing."

"What?"

"I'm assuming the odds are pretty high you'll be able to pay back the loan, right?"

"Well . . . sure. I mean, what are you asking?" She wished she could put off thinking about next month's problems, especially after what she'd just done to resolve this month's.

"What are the odds—I mean, realistically—that you will, a) have the money to pay this back, and b) not need more?"

"High." The business world ran on lies, right? Ask anyone on Wall Street.

Rogan slouched against the desk, hands in his pockets, and gave her a gentle smile. "That's good. Because next month, the deal won't be quite the same."

"Meaning?"

"Meaning that if you come to me next month and for any reason can't pay back that sixty-three grand, the terms are going to become significantly less attractive."

He leaned forward and whispered the revisions to the

terms in her ear. Two items involved his Maserati. One, a speakerphone. And a fourth, an act so technically challenging as to be impossible without guide wires and a spotter, Joss thought, wide-eyed.

"But," he said cordially, "I'd be willing to forgive the loan right now—for a little consideration."

Joss knew exactly what sort of consideration he was talking about. She took a deep breath, and considered her options.